WESTWAYS

Books by
Dr. S. Weir Mitchell.

❦

Fiction.

HUGH WYNNE.
CONSTANCE TRESCOT.
THE YOUTH OF WASHINGTON.
CIRCUMSTANCE.
THE ADVENTURES OF FRANÇOIS.
THE AUTOBIOGRAPHY OF A QUACK.
DR. NORTH AND HIS FRIENDS.
IN WAR TIME.
ROLAND BLAKE.
FAR IN THE FOREST.
CHARACTERISTICS.
WHEN ALL THE WOODS ARE GREEN.
A MADEIRA PARTY.
THE RED CITY.
HEPHZIBAH GUINNESS.
A COMEDY OF CONSCIENCE.
A DIPLOMATIC ADVENTURE.
THE GUILLOTINE CLUB.
JOHN SHERWOOD, IRONMASTER.
WESTWAYS.

Essays.

DOCTOR AND PATIENT.
WEAR AND TEAR—HINTS FOR THE
OVERWORKED.

Poems.

COLLECTED POEMS.
THE WAGER, AND OTHER POEMS.
THE COMFORT OF THE HILLS.

WESTWAYS
A VILLAGE CHRONICLE

BY

S. WEIR MITCHELL, M.D., LL.D.
Author of "Hugh Wynne," "The Adventures of François,"
"Constance Trescot," etc., etc.

NEW YORK
THE CENTURY CO.
1913

I DEDICATE THIS BOOK
WHICH RECALLS CERTAIN SCENES OF THE CIVIL WAR
TO THE MEMORY OF MY THREE BROTHERS

R. W. M.

N. C. M.

E. K. M.

ALL OF WHOM SERVED IN THE ARMIES
OF THEIR COUNTRY

PREFACE

There will be many people in this book; some will be important, others will come on the scene for a time and return no more. The life-lines of these persons will cross and recross, to meet once or twice and not again, like the ruts in a much used road. To-day the stage may be crowded, to-morrow empty. The corner novels where only a half dozen people are concerned give no impression of the multitudinous contacts which affect human lives. Even of the limited life of a village this is true. It was more true of the time of my story, which lacking plot must rely for interest on the influential relations of social groups, then more defined in small communities than they are to-day.

Long before the Civil War there were in the middle states, near to or remote from great centres, villages where the social division of classes was tacitly accepted. In or near these towns one or more families were continuously important on account of wealth or because of historic position, generations of social training, and constant relation to the larger world. They came by degrees to constitute what I may describe as an indistinct caste, for a long time accepted as such by their less fortune-favoured neighbours. They were, in fact, for many years almost as much a class by themselves as are the long-seated county families of England and like these were looked to for helpful aid in sickness and in other of the calamities of life. The democrat time, increasing ease of travel and the growth of large industries, gradually altered the relation between these small communities, and the families who in the smaller matters of life long remained singularly familiar with their poorer neighbours and in the way of closer social intimacies far apart.

It seemed to me worth while to use the life of one of these groups of people as the background of a story which also deals with the influence of politics and war on all classes.

WESTWAYS

WESTWAYS

CHAPTER I

THE first Penhallow crossed the Alleghanies long before the War for Independence and on the frontier of civilisation took up land where the axe was needed for the forest and the rifle for the Indian. He made a clearing and lived a hard life of peril, wearily waiting for the charred stumps to rot away.

The younger men of the name in Colonial days and later left the place early, and for the most part took to the sea or to the army, if there were activity in the way of war. In later years, others drifted westward on the tide of border migration, where adventure was always to be had. This stir of enterprise in a breed tends to extinction in the male lines. Men are thinned out in their wooing of danger — the *belle dame sans merci*. Thus there were but few Penhallows alive at any one time, and yet for many years they bred in old-fashioned numbers.

As time ran on, a Penhallow prospered in the cities, and clinging to the land added fresh acres as new ambitions developed qualities which are not infrequently found in descendants of long-seated American families. It was not then, nor is it now, rare in American life to find fortune-favoured men returning in later days to the homes of their youth to become useful in many ways to the communities they loved. One of these, James Penhallow,— and there was always a James,— after greatly prospering in the ventures of the China trade, was of the many who about 1800 bought great tracts of land on the farther slope of

3

the Pennsylvania Alleghanies. His own purchases lay near and around the few hundred acres his ancestor took up and where an aged cousin was left in charge of the farm-house. When this tenant died, the house decayed, and the next Penhallow weary of being taxed for unproductive land spent a summer on the property, and with the aid of engineers found iron in plenty and soft coal. He began about 1830 to develop the property, and built a large house which he never occupied and which was long known in the county as " Penhallow's Folly." It was considered the more notably foolish because of being set, in un-American fashion, deep in the woods, and remote from the highway. What was believed to be the oldest pine-tree in the county gave to the place the popular name of " Grey Pine " and being accepted by the family when they came there to live, " Penhallow's Folly " ceased to be considered descriptive.

The able and enterprising discoverer of mines had two sons. One of them, the youngest, married late in life, and dying soon after left a widow and a posthumous son John, of whom more hereafter. The elder brother was graduated from West Point, served some years with distinction, and marrying found himself obliged to resign his captaincy on his father's death to take charge of the iron-mills and mines, which had become far more important to the family than their extensive forest-holdings on the foot-hills of the western watershed of the Alleghanies.

The country had long been well settled. The farmers thrived as the mills and mines needed increasing supplies of food and the railway gave access to market. The small village of Westways was less fortunate than the county. Strung along the side of the road opposite to Penhallow's woods, it had lost the bustling prosperity of a day when the Conestoga wagons stopped over-night at the " General Wayne Inn " and when as yet no one dreamed that the new railroad would ruin the taverns set at intervals along the highway to Pittsburgh. Now that Westways Crossing, two miles away, had been made the nearest station,

Westways was left to live on the mill-wages and such profits as farming furnished.

When Captain James Penhallow repaired the neglected house and kept the town busy with demands for workmen, the village woke up for a whole summer. In the autumn he brought to Grey Pine his wife, Ann Grey, of the well-known Greys of the eastern shore of Maryland. A year or two of discomfort at Western army-posts and a busy-minded, energetic personality, made welcome to this little lady a position which provided unaccustomed luxuries and a limitless range of duties, such as were to her what mere social enjoyments are to many women. Grey Pine — the house, the flower and kitchen-gardens, the church to be built — and the schools at the mills, all were as she liked it, having been bred up amid the kindly despotism of a great plantation with its many dependent slaves.

When Ann Penhallow put Grey Pine and the Penhallow crest on her notepaper, her husband said laughing that women had no rights to crests, and that although the arms were surely his by right of good Cornish descent, he thought their use in America a folly. This disturbed Ann Penhallow very little, but when they first came to Grey Pine the headings of her notepaper were matters of considerable curiosity to the straggling village of Westways, where she soon became liked, respected, and moderately feared. A busy-minded woman, few things in the life of the people about her escaped her notice, and she distributed uninvited counsel or well-considered charity and did her best to restrain the more lavish, periodical assistance when harvests were now and then bad — which made James Penhallow a favourite in the county.

Late in the summer of 1855, John Penhallow's widow, long a wandering resident in Europe, acquired the first serious illness of a self-manufactured life of invalidism and promptly died at Vevey. Her only child, John, was at once ordered home by his uncle and guardian, James Penhallow, and after some delay crossed the sea in charge of his tutor. The dependent little fellow hid under a natural reserve what grief he felt, and accustomed to being sent here and there by an absent mother, silently submissive, was turned over by the tutor to James Penhallow's agent in Philadelphia. On the next day, early in November, he was put in charge of a conductor to be left at Westways Crossing, where he was told that some one would meet him.

The day was warm when in the morning he took his seat in the train, but before noon it became clouded, and an early snow-storm with sudden fall of temperature made the boy sensible that he was ill-clothed to encounter the change of weather. He had been unfortunate in the fact that his mother had for years used the vigilant tyranny of feebleness to enforce upon the boy her own sanitary views. Children are easily made hypochondriac, and under her system of government he became self-attentive, careful of what he ate and extremely timid. There had been many tutors and only twice long residence at schools in Vevey and for a winter in Budapest. The health she too sedulously watched she was fast destroying, and her son was at the time of her death a thin, pallid, undersized boy, who disliked even the mild sports of French lads, and had been flattered and considered until he had acquired the conviction that he was an important member of an important family. His other mother — nature — had given him, happily, better traits. He was an observer, a born lover of books, intelligent, truthful, and trained in the gentle, somewhat formal, manners of an older person. Now for the first time in his guarded life he was alone on a railway journey in charge of the conductor. A more unhappy, frightened little fellow could hardly have been found.

The train paused at many stations; men and women got on or got out of the cars, very common-looking people, surely, he concluded. The day ran by to afternoon. The train had stopped at a station for lunch, but John, although hungry, was

afraid of being left and kept the seat which he presumed to be
his own property until a stout man took half of it. A little
later, a lean old woman said, " Move up, sonny," and sat down.
When she asked his name and where he lived, he replied in the
coldly civil manner with which he had heard his mother repress
the good-natured advances of her wandering countrymen.
When again the seat was free, he fell to thinking of the unknown
home, Grey Pine, which he had heard his mother talk of to English friends as " our ancestral home," and of the great forests,
the mines and the iron-works. Her son would, of course, inherit
it, as Captain Penhallow had no child. " Really a great estate,
my dear," his mother had said. It loomed large in his young
imagination. Who would meet him? Probably a carriage with
the liveried driver and the groom immaculate in white-topped
boots, a fur cover on his arm. It would, of course, be Captain
Penhallow who would make him welcome. Then the cold, which
is hostile to imagination, made him shiver as he drew his thin
cloak about him and watched the snow squadrons wind-driven
and the big flakes blurring his view as they melted on the panes.
By and by, two giggling young women near by made comments
on his looks and dress. Fragments of their talk he overheard.
It was not quite pleasant. " Law! ain't he got curly hair, and
ain't he just like a girl doll," and so on in the lawless freedom
of democratic feminine speech. The flat Morocco cap and large
visor of the French schoolboy and the dark blue cloak with the
silver clasp were subjects of comment. One of them offered
peanuts or sugar-plums, which he declined with " Much obliged,
but I never take them." Now and then he consulted his watch
or felt in his pocket to be certain that his baggage-check was secure, or looked to see if the little bag of toilet articles at his feet
was safe. The kindly attentions of those who noticed his evident discomfort were neither mannerless nor, as he thought, impertinent. A woman said to him that he seemed cold, would n't
he put around him a shawl she laid on his knees. He declined

it civilly with thanks. In fact, he was thinly and quite too lightly clad, and he not only felt the cold, but was unhappy and utterly unprepared by any previous experience for the mode of travel, the crowded car and the rough kindness of the people, who liking his curly hair and refined young childlike face would have been of service if he had accepted their advances with any pleasure. Presently, after four in the afternoon, the brakeman called " All out for Westways Crossing."

John seized his bag and was at the exit-door before the train came to a stand. The conductor bade him be careful, as the steps were slippery. As the engine snorted and the train moved away, the conductor cried out, " Forgot your cane, sonny," and threw the light gold-mounted bamboo from the car. He had a new sense of loneliness as he stood on the roofless platform, half a foot deep in gathering snow, which driven by a pitiless gale from the north blew his cloak about as he looked to see that his trunk had been delivered. A man shifted a switch and coming back said, " Gi'me your check." John decided that this was not safe, and to the man's amusement said that he would wait until the carriage of Captain Penhallow arrived. The man went away. John remained angrily expectant looking up the road. Presently he heard the gay jingle of bells and around a turn of the road came a one-horse sleigh. It stopped beside him. He first saw only the odd face of the driver in a fur cap and earlets. Then, tossing off the bear skins, bounded on to the platform a young girl and shook herself snow-free as she threw back a wild mane of dark red hair.

" Halloa! John Penhallow," she cried, " I 'm Leila Grey. I 'm sent for you. I 'm late too. Uncle James has gone to the mills and Aunt Ann is busy. Been here long? "

" Not very," said John, his teeth chattering with cold.

" Gracious! you 'll freeze. Sorry I was late." She saw at a glance the low shoes, the blue cloak, the kid gloves, the boy's look of suffering, and at once took possession of him.

"Get into the sleigh. Oh! leave your check on the trunk or
give it to me." She was off and away to the trunk as he climbed
in, helpless. She undid the counter check, ran across to the
guard's house, was back in a moment and tumbled in beside him.

"But, is it safe? My trunk, I mean," said John.

"Safe. No one will steal it. Pat will come for it. There
he is now. Tuck in the rugs. Put this shawl around you and
over your head." She pinned it with ready fingers.

"Now, you'll be real comfy." The chilled boy puzzled and
amused her.

As he became warm, John felt better in the hands of this
easy despot, but was somewhat indignant. "To send a chit of
a girl for him — John Penhallow!"

"Now," she cried to the driver, "be careful. Why did they
send *you?*"

Billy, a middle-aged man, short-legged and long of body,
turned a big-featured head as he replied in an odd boyish
voice, "The man was busy giving a ball in the stable."

"A ball"— said John —"in the stable?"

"Oh! that is funny," said the girl. "A ball's a big pill for
Lucy, my mare. She's sick."

"Oh! I see." And they were off and away through the wind-
driven snow.

The girl, instinctively aware of the shyness and discomfort
of her companion, set herself to put him at ease. The lessening
snow still fell, but now a brilliant sun lighted the white radiance
of field and forest. He was warmer, and the disconnected chat
of childhood began.

"The snow is early. Don't you love it?" said the small maid
bent on making herself agreeable.

"No, I do not."

"But, oh! — see — the sun is out. Now you will like it. I
suppose you don't know how to walk in snow-shoes, or it would
be lovely to go right home across country."

"I never used them. Once I read about them in a book."

"Oh! you 'll learn. I 'll teach you."

John, used to being considered and flattered, as he became more comfortable began to resent the way in which the girl proposed to instruct him. He was silent for a time.

"Tuck in that robe," she said. "How old are you?"

"This last September, fifteen. How old are you?"

"Guess."

"About ten, I think." Now this was malicious.

"Ten, indeed! I 'm thirteen and ten months and — and three days," she returned, with the accuracy of childhood about age. "Were you at school in Europe?"

"Yes, in France and Hungary."

"That 's queer. In Hungary and France — Oh! then you can speak French."

"Of course," he replied. "Can't you?"

"A little, but Aunt Ann says I have a good accent when I read to her — we often do."

"You should say 'without accent,'" he felt better after this assertion of superior knowledge. She thought his manners bad, but, though more amused than annoyed, felt herself snubbed and was silent for a time. He was quick to perceive that he had better have held his critical tongue, and said pleasantly, "But really it don't matter — only I was told that in France."

She was as quick to reply, "You should n't say 'don't matter.' I say that sometimes, and then Uncle James comes down on me."

"Why? I am really at a loss —"

"Oh! you must say 'does n't'— not 'don't.'" She shook her great mass of hair and cried merrily, "I guess we are about even now, John Penhallow."

Then they laughed gaily, as the boy said, "I was n't very — very courteous."

"Now that 's pretty, John. Good gracious, Billy!" she cried, punching the broad back of the driver. "Are you asleep? You are all over the road."

"Oh! I was thinkin' how Pole, the butcher, sold the Squire a horse that's spavined — got it sent back — funny, was n't it?"

"Look out," said Leila, "you will upset us."

John looked the uneasiness he felt, as he said, "Do you think it is safe?"

"No, I don't. Drive on, Billy, but do be careful."

They came to the little village of Westways. At intervals Billy communicated bits of village gossip. "Susan McKnight, she's going to marry Finney —"

"Bother Susan," cried Leila. "Be careful."

John alarmed held on to his seat as the sleigh rocked about, while Billy whipped up the mare.

"This is Westways, our village. It is just a row of houses. Uncle James won't sell land on our side. Look out, Billy! Our rector lives in that small house by the church. His name is Mark Rivers. You'll like him. That's Mr. Grace, the Baptist preacher." She bade him good-day. "Stop, Billy!"

He pulled up at the sidewalk. "Good afternoon, Mrs. Crocker," she said, as the postmistress came out to the sleigh. "Please mail this. Any letters for us?"

"No, Leila." She glanced at the curly locks above the thin face and the wrapped up form in the shawl. "Got a nice little girl with you, Leila."

John indignant said nothing. "This is a boy — my cousin, John Penhallow," returned Leila.

"Law! is that so?"

"Get on," cried Leila. "Stop at Josiah's."

Here a tall, strongly built, very black negro came out. "Fine frosty day, missy."

"Come up to the house to-night, Uncle Jim wants you."

"I'll come — sure."

"Now, get along, Billy."

The black was strange to the boy. He thought the lower orders here disrespectful.

"Josiah's our barber," said Leila. "He saved me once from a dreadful accident. You 'll like him."

"Will I?" thought John, but merely remarked, "They all seem rather intimate."

"Why not?" said the young Republican. "Ah! here's the gate. I 'll get out and open it. It's the best gate to swing on in the whole place."

As she tossed the furs aside, John gasped, "To swing on —"

"Oh, yes. Aunt Ann says I am too old to swing on gates, but I do. It shuts with a bang. I 'll show you some day."

"What is swinging on a gate?" said John, as she jumped out and stood in the snow laughing. Surely this was an amazing kind of boy. "Why, did you never hear the rhyme about it?"

"No," said John, "I never did."

"Well, you just get on the gate when it's wide open and give a push, and you sing —

> If I was the President of these United States,
> I 'd suck molasses candy and swing upon the gates.

There! Then it shuts — bang!" With this bit of child folk-lore she scampered away through the snow and stood holding the gate open while Billy drove through. She reflected mischievously that it must have been three years since she had swung on a gate.

John feeling warm and for the first time looking about him with interest began to notice the grandeur of the rigid snow-laden pines of an untouched forest which stood in what was now brilliant sunshine.

As Leila got into the sleigh, she said, "Now, Billy, go slowly when you make the short turn at the house. If you upset us, I — I 'll kill you."

"Yes, miss. Guess I'll drive all right." But the ways of drivers are everywhere the same, and to come to the end of a drive swiftly with crack of whip was an unresisted temptation.

"*Sang de Dieu!*" cried John, "we will be upset."

"We are," shouted Leila. The horse was down, the sleigh on its side, and the cousins disappeared in a huge drift piled high when the road was cleared.

CHAPTER II

JOHN was the first to return to the outer world. He stood still, seeing the horse on its legs, Billy unharnessing, Leila for an instant lost to sight. The boy was scared. In his ordered life it was an unequalled experience. Then he saw a merry face above the drift and lying around it a wide-spread glory of red hair on the white snow. In after years he would recall the beauty of the laughing young face in its setting of dark gold and sunlit silver snow.

"Oh, my!" she cried. "That Billy! Don't stand there, John; pull me out, I'm stuck."

He gave her a hand and she bounded forth out of the drift, shaking off the dry snow as a wet dog shakes off water. "What's the matter, John?"

He was trying to empty neck, pocket and shoes of snow, and was past the limits of what small endurance he had been taught. "I shall catch my death of cold. It's down my back — it's everywhere, and I — shall get — laryngitis."

The brave blue eyes of the girl stared at his dejected figure. She was at heart a gentle, little woman-child, endowed by nature with so much of tom-boy barbarism as was good for her. Just now a feeling of contemptuous surprise overcame her kindliness and her aunt's training. "There's your bag on the snow, and Billy will find your cap. What does a boy want with a bag? A boy — and afraid of snow!" she cried. "Help him with that harness."

He made no reply, but looked about for his lost cane. Then the young despot turned upon the driver. "Wait till Uncle James hears; he'll come down on you."

14

"My lands!" said Billy, unbuckling a trace, "I'll just say, I'm sorry; and the Squire he'll say, don't let it happen again; and I'll say, yes, sir."

"Yes, until Aunt Ann hears," said Leila, and turned to John. His attitude of utter helplessness touched her. "Come into the house; you must be cold." She was of a sudden all tenderness.

Through an outside winter doorway-shelter they entered a hall unusually large for an American's house and warmed by two great blazing hickory wood-fires. "Come in," she cried, "you'll be all right. Sit down by the fire; I'll be down in a minute, I want to see where Aunt Ann has put you."

"I am much obliged," said John shivering. He was alone, but wet as he was the place captured an ever active imagination. He looked about him as he stood before the roaring fire. To the right was an open library, to the left a drawing-room rarely used, the hall being by choice the favoured sitting-room. The dining-room was built out from the back of the hall, whence up a broad stairway Leila had gone. The walls were hung with Indian painted robes, Sioux and Arapahoe weapons, old colonial rifles, and among them portraits of three generations of Penhallows. Many older people had found interesting the strange adornment of the walls, where amid antlered trophies of game, buffalo heads and war-worn Indian relics, could be read something of the owner's tastes and history. John stood by the fire fascinated. Like many timid boys, he liked books of adventure and to imagine himself heroic in situations of peril.

"It's all right. Come up," cried Leila from the stair. "Your trunk's there now. There's a fine fire."

Forgetful of the cold ride and of the snow down his back, he was standing before the feathered head-dress of a Sioux Chief and touching the tomahawk below it. He turned as she spoke. "Those must be scalp-locks — three." He saw the prairie, the wild pursuit — saw them as she could not. He went after her upstairs, the girl talking, the boy rapt, lost in far-away battles on the plains.

"This is your room. See what a nice fire. You can dry yourself. Your trunk is here already." She lighted two candles. "We dine at half-past six."

"Thank you; I am very much obliged," he said, thinking what a mannerless girl.

Leila closed the door and stood still a moment. Then she exclaimed, "Well, I never! What will Uncle Jim say?" She listened a moment. No one was in the hall. Then she laughed, and getting astride of the banister-rail made a wild, swift and perilous descent, alighting at the foot in the hall, and readjusting her short skirts as she heard her aunt and uncle on the porch. "I was just in time," she exclaimed. "Wouldn't I have caught it!"

The Squire, as the village called him, would have applauded this form of coasting, but Aunt Ann had other views. "Well!" he said as they came in, "what have you done with your young man?"

Now he was for Leila anything but a man or manly, but she was a loyal little lady and unwilling to expose the guest to Uncle Jim's laughter. "He's all right," she said, "but Billy upset the sleigh." She was longing to tell about that ball in the stable, but refrained.

"So Billy upset you; and John, where is he?"

"He's upstairs getting dried."

"It is rather a rough welcome," remarked her aunt.

"He lost his cap and his cane," said Leila.

"His cane!" exclaimed her uncle, "his cane!"

"I must see him," said his wife.

"Better let him alone, Ann." But as usual she took her own way and went upstairs. She came down in a few minutes, finding her husband standing before the fire — an erect, soldierly figure close to forty years of age.

"Well, Ann?" he queried.

"A very nice lad, with such good manners, James."

"Billy found his cap," said Leila, "but he could n't get the sleigh set up until the stable men came."

"And that cane," laughed Penhallow. "Was the boy amused or — or scared?"

"I don't know," which was hardly true, but the chivalry of childhood forbade tale-telling and he learned very little. "He was rather tired and cold, so I made him go to his room and rest."

"Poor child!" said Aunt Ann.

James Penhallow looked at Leila. Some manner of signals were interchanged. "I saw Billy digging in the big drift," he said. "I trust he found the young gentleman's cane." Some pitying, dim comprehension of the delicately nurtured lad had brought to the social surface the kindliness of the girl and she said no more.

"It is time to dress for dinner," said Ann. Away from the usages of the city she had wisely insisted on keeping up the social forms which the Squire would at times have been glad to disregard. For a moment Ann Penhallow lingered. "We must try to make him feel at home, James."

"Of course, my dear. I can imagine how Susan Penhallow would have educated a boy, and now I know quite too well what we shall have to undo — and — do."

"You won't, oh! you will not be too hard on him."

"I — no, my dear — but — I suspect his American education has begun already."

"What do you mean?"

"Ask Leila — and Billy. But that can wait." They separated.

While his elders were thus briefly discussing this new addition to the responsibilities of their busy lives, the subject of their talk had been warmed into comfortable repossession of his self-esteem. He set in order his elaborate silver toilet things marked with the Penhallow crest, saw in the glass that his dress and unboylike length of curly hair were as he had been taught they should be; then he looked at his watch and went slowly downstairs.

"Halloa! John," he heard as he reached the last turn of the stairs. "Most glad to see you. You are very welcome to your new home." The man who hailed him was six feet two inches, deep-chested, erect — the West Point figure; the face cleanshaven, ruddy, hazel-eyed, was radiant with the honest feeling of desire to put this childlike boy at ease.

The little gentleman needed no aid and replied, "My dear uncle, I cannot sufficiently thank you." A little bow went with his words, and he placidly accepted his aunt's embrace, while the hearty Miss Leila looked on in silence. The boy's black suit, the short jacket, the neat black tie, made the paleness of his thin large-featured face too obvious. Then Leila took note of the court shoes and silk socks, and looked at Uncle Jim to see what he thought. The Squire reserved what criticism he may have had and asked cheerfully about the journey, Aunt Ann aiding him with eager will to make the boy feel at home. He was quite enough at home. It was all agreeable, these handsome relations and the other Penhallows on the walls. He had been taught that which is good or ill as men use it, pride of race, and in his capacity to be impressed by his surroundings was years older than Leila. He felt sure that he would like it here at Grey Pine, but was surprised to see no butler and to be waited on at dinner by two neat little maids.

When Ann Penhallow asked him about his schools and his life in Europe, he became critical, and conversed about picture-galleries and foreign life with no lack of accuracy, while the Squire listened smiling and Leila sat dumb with astonishment as the dinner went on. He ate little and kept in mind the endless lessons in regard to what he should or should not eat.

Meanwhile, he silently approved of the old silver and these well-bred kinsfolk, with a reserve of doubt concerning his silent cousin.

His uncle had at last his one glass of Madeira, and as they rose his aunt said, " You may be tired, John; you ought to go to bed early."

" It is not yet time," he said. " I always retire at ten o'clock."

" He ' retires,' " murmured his uncle. " Come, Ann, we will leave Leila to make friends with the new cousin. Try John at checkers, Leila. She defeats me easily."

" I — never saw any one could beat me at *jeu des dames*," said John. It was a fine chance to get even with Leila for the humiliating adventures of a not very flattering day.

" Well, take care," said the Squire, not altogether amused. " Come, Ann." Entering the large library room he closed the door, drew over it a curtain, filled his pipe but did not light it, and sat down at the fire beside his wife.

" Well, James," she said, " did you ever see a better mannered lad, and so intelligent? "

" Never — nor any lad who has as good an opinion of his small self. He is too young for his years, and in some ways too old. I looked him over a bit. He is a mere scaffolding, a sickly-looking chap. He eats too little. I heard him remark to you that potatoes disagreed with him and that he never ate apples."

" But, James, what shall we do with him? It is a new and a difficult responsibility."

" Do with him? Oh! make a man of him. Give him and Leila a week's holiday. Turn him loose with that fine tom-boy. Then he must go to school to Mark Rivers with Leila and those two young village imps, the doctor's boy and Grace's, that precious young Baptist. They will do him good. When Mark reports, we shall see further. That is all my present wisdom, Ann. Has the *Tribune* come? Oh! I see — it is on the table."

Ann was still in some doubt and returned to the boy. "And where do I come in?"

"Feed the young animal and get the tailor in the village to make him some warm rough clothes, and get him boots for the snow — and thick gloves — and a warm ready-made overcoat."

"I will. But, James, Leila will half kill him. He is so thin and pale. He looks hardly older than she does." Then Ann rose, saying, "Well, we shall see, I suppose you are right," and after some talk about the iron-works left him to his pipe.

When she returned to the hall, the two children were talking of Europe — or rather Leila was listening. "Well," said the little lady, Ann Penhallow, "how did the game go, John?"

"I am rather out of practice," said John. Leila said nothing. He had been shamefully worsted. "I think I shall go to bed," he remarked, looking at his watch.

"I would," she said. "There are the candles. There is a bathroom next to you."

He was tired and disgusted, but slept soundly. When at breakfast he said that he was not allowed tea or coffee, he was fed with milk, to which with hot bread and new acquaintance with griddle cakes he took kindly. After breakfast he was driven to the village with his aunt and equipped with a rough ready-made overcoat and high boots. He found the dress comfortable, but not to his taste.

When he came back, the Squire and Leila had disappeared and he was left to his own devices. He was advised by his aunt to walk about and see the stables and the horses. That any boy should not want to see the horses was inconceivable in this household. He did go out and walk on the porch, but soon went in chilled and sat down to lose himself in a book of polar travel. He liked history, travel and biographies of soldiers, fearfully desiring to have his own courage tested — a more common boy-wish than might be supposed. He thought of it as he laid down the book and began to inspect again the painted buffalo skins on the wall, letting his imagination wander when once more he touched a Sioux tomahawk with its grim adornment of scalp-locks. He was far away when he heard his aunt say, " You were not out long, John. Did they show you the horses? "

Shy and reserved in novel surroundings, he was rather too much at his ease amid socially familiar things, and now said lightly that he had not seen the stables. " Really, Aunt Ann, I prefer to read or to look at these interesting Indian relics."

" Ask your uncle about them," she said, " but you will find out that horses are important in this household." She left him with the conviction that James Penhallow was, on the whole, right as to the educational needs of this lad.

After lunch his uncle said, " Leila will show you about the place. You will want to see the horses, of course, and the dogs."

" And my guinea pigs," added Leila.

He took no interest in either, and the dogs somewhat alarmed him. His cousin, a little discouraged, led him away into the woods where the ancient pines stood snow laden far apart with no intrusion between them of low shrubbery. Leila was silent, half aware that he was hard to entertain, and then mischievously wilful to give this indifferent cousin a lesson. Presently he stood still, looking up at the towering cones of the motionless pines.

" How stately they are — how like old Vikings! " he said. His imagination was the oldest mental characteristic of this over-guarded, repressed boyhood.

Leila turned, surprised. This was beyond her appreciative capacity. " Once I heard Uncle Jim say something like that. He 's queer about trees. He talks to them sometimes just like that. There 's the biggest pine over there — I 'll show it to you. Why! he will stop and pat it and say, ' How are you? ' — Is n't it funny? "

"No, it is n't funny at all. It 's — it 's beautiful!"

"You must be like him, John."

"I — like him! Do you think so?" He was pleased. The Indian horseman of the plains who could talk to the big tree began to be felt by the boy as somehow nearer.

"Let 's play Indian," said Leila. "I 'll show you." She was merry, intent on mischief.

"Oh! whatever you like." He was uninterested.

Leila said, "You stand behind this tree, I will stand behind that one." She took for herself the larger shelter. "Then you, each of us, get ready this way a pile of snowballs. I say, Make ready! Fire! and we snowball one another like everything. The first Indian that 's hit, he falls down dead. Then the other rushes at him and scalps him."

"But," said John, "how can he?"

"Oh! he just gives your hair a pull and makes believe."

"I see."

"Then we play it five times, and each scalp counts one. Now, is n't that real jolly?"

John had his doubts as to this, but he took his place and made some snowballs clumsily.

"Make ready! Fire!" cried Leila. The snowballs flew. At last, the girl seeing how wildly he threw exposed herself. A better shot took her full in the face. Laughing gaily, she dropped, "I 'm dead."

The game pleased him with its unlooked-for good luck. "Now don't stand there like a ninny — scalp me," she cried.

He ran to her side and knelt down. The widespread hair affected him curiously. He touched it daintily, let it fall, and rose. "To pull at a girl's hair! I could n't do it."

Leila laughed. "A good pull, that 's how to scalp."

"I could n't," said John.

"Well, you are a queer sort of Indian!" She was less merci-ful, but in the end, to her surprise, he had three scalps. "Uncle

Jim will laugh when I tell him," she said. "Shall we go home?"

"No, I want to see Uncle Jim's big tree."

"Oh! he's only Uncle Jim to me. Aunt don't like it. He will tell you some day to call him Uncle Jim. He says I got that as brevet rank the day my mare refused the barnyard fence and pitched me off. I just got on again and made her take it! That's why he's Uncle Jim."

John became thoughtful about that brevet privilege of a remote future. He had, however, persistent ways. "I want to see the big pine, Leila."

"Oh! come on then. It's a long way. We must cut across." He followed her remorselessly swift feet through the leafless bushes and drifts until they came upon a giant pine in a wide space cleared to give the veteran royal solitude. "That's him," cried Leila, and carelessly cast herself down on the snow.

The boy stood still in wonder. Something about the tree disturbed him emotionally. With hands clasped behind his back, he stared up at its towering heights. He was silent.

"What's the matter? What do you see?" She was never long silent. He was searching for a word.

"It's solemn. I like it." He moved forward and patted the huge bole with a feeling of reverence and affection. "I wish he could speak to us. How are you, old fellow?"

Leila watched him. As yet she had no least comprehension of this sense of being kindred to nature. It is rare in youth. As he spoke, a little breeze stirred the old fellow's topmost crest and a light downfall of snow fell on the pair. Leila laughed, but the boy cried, "There! he has answered. We are friends."

"Now, if that isn't Uncle Jim all over. He just does make me laugh."

John shook off the snow. "Let's go home," he said. He was warm and red with the exercise, and in high good-humour

over his success. "Did you never read a poem called 'The
Talking Oak'? I had a tutor used to read it to me."

"Now, the idea of a tree talking!" she said. "No, I never
heard of it. Come along, we'll be late. That's funny about
a tree talking. Can you run?"

They ran, but not far, because deep snow makes running hard.
It was after dark when they tramped on to the back porch.
John's experience taught him to expect blame for being out late.
No one asked a question or made a remark. He was ignored,
to his amazement. Whether, as he soon learned, he was in or
out, wet or dry, seemed to be of no moment to any one, provided
he was punctual at meal-times. It was at first hard to realize
the reasonable freedom suddenly in his possession. The appearance of complete want of interest in his health and what he
did was as useful a moral tonic as was for the body the educational out-of-doors' society of the fearless girl, his aunt's niece
whom he was told to consider as his cousin. To his surprise,
he was free to come and go, and what he or Leila did in the woods
or in the stables no one inquired. Aunt Ann uneasy would
have known all about them, but the Squire urged, that for a
time, "let alone" was the better policy. This freedom was so
unusual, so unreservedly complete, as to rejoice Leila, who was
very ready to use the liberty it gave. In a week the rector's
school would shut them up for half of the day of sunlit snow.
Meanwhile, John wondered with interest every morning where
next those thin active young legs would lead him.

The dogs he soon took to, when Leila's whistle called them,—
a wild troop, never allowed beyond the porch or in the house.
For some occult reason Mrs. Ann disliked dogs and liked cats,
which roamed the house at will and were at deadly feud with
the stable canines. No rough weather ever disturbed Leila's
out-of-door habits, but when for two days a lazy rain fell and
froze on the snow, John declared that he could not venture to

get wet with his tendency to tonsilitis. As Leila refused in-door society and he did not like to be left alone, he missed the gay and gallant little lady, and still no one questioned him. On the third day at breakfast Leila was wildly excited. The smooth ice-mailed snow shone brilliant in the sunshine.

" Coasting weather, Uncle Jim," Leila said.

" First class," said her uncle. " Get off before the sun melts the crust."

" Do be careful, dear," said Ann Penhallow, " and do not try the farm hill."

" Yes, aunt." The Squire exchanged signal glances with Leila over the teacup he was lifting. " Come, John," she said. " No dogs to-day. It's just perfect. Here's your sled."

John had seen coasting in Germany and had been strictly forbidden so perilous an amusement. As they walked over the crackling ice-cover of the snow, he said, " Why do you want to sled, Leila? I consider it extremely dangerous. I saw two persons hurt when we were in Switzerland." His imagination was predicting all manner of disaster, but he had the moral courage which makes hypocrisy impossible. From the hill crest John looked down the long silvery slope and did not like it. " It's just a foolish risk. Do you mean to slide down to that brook? "

" Slide! We coast, we don't slide. I think you had better go back and tell Uncle Jim you were afraid."

He was furious. " I tell you this, Miss Grey — I am afraid — I have been told — well, never mind — that — well — I won't say I'm not afraid — but I'm more afraid of Uncle James than — than — of death."

She stood still a moment as she faced him, the two pair of blue eyes meeting. He was very youthful for his years and was near the possibility of the tears of anger, and, too, the virile qualities of his race were protesting forces in the background of undeveloped character. The sweet girl face grew red and kinder. "I was mean, John Penhallow. I am sorry I was rude."

"No — no," he exclaimed, "it was I who was — was — ill-mannered. I — mean to coast if I die."

"Die," she laughed gaily. "Let me go first."

"Go ahead then." She was astride of the sled and away down the long descent, while he watched her swift flight. He set his teeth and was off after her. A thrill of pleasure possessed him, the joy of swift movement. Near the foot was an abrupt fall to a frozen brook and then a sharp ascent. He rolled over at Leila's feet seeing a firmament of stars and rose bewildered.

"Busted?" cried Leila, who picked up the slang of the village boys to her aunt's disgust.

"I am not what you call busted," said John, "but I consider it most disagreeable." Without a word more he left her, set out up the hill and coasted again. He upset half-way down, rolled over, and got on again laughing. This time somehow he got over the brook and turned crossly on Leila with, "I hope now you are satisfied, Miss Grey."

"You'll do, I guess," said she. "I just wondered if you would back out, John. Let's try the other hills." He went after her vexed at her way of ordering him about, and not displeased with John Penhallow and his new experience in snatching from danger a fearful joy.

CHAPTER III

THE difficult lessons on the use of snow-shoes took up day after day, until weary but at last eager he followed her tireless little figure far into the more remote woods. "What's that?" he said.

"I wanted you to see it, John." It was an old log cabin. "That's where the first James Penhallow lived. Uncle Jim keeps it from tumbling to pieces, but it's no use to anybody."

"The first Penhallow," said John. "It must be very old."

"Oh! I suppose so — I don't know — ask Uncle Jim. They say the Indians attacked it once — that first James Penhallow and his wife fought them till help came. I thought you would like to see it."

He went in, kicking off his snow-shoes. She was getting used to his silences, and now with some surprise at his evident interest followed him. He walked about making brief remarks or eagerly asking questions.

"They must have had loop-holes to shoot. Did they kill any Indians?"

"Yes, five. They are buried behind the cabin. Uncle Jim set a stone to mark the place."

He made no reply. His thoughts were far away in time, realizing the beleaguered cabin, the night of fear, the flashing rifles of his ancestors. The fear — would he have been afraid?

"When I was little, I was afraid to come here alone," said the girl.

"I should like to come here at night," he returned.

"Why? I wouldn't. Oh! not at night. I don't see what fun there would be in that."

27

" Then I would know —"

" Know what, John? What would you know? "

" Oh! no matter." He had a deep desire to learn if he would be afraid. " Some day," he added, " I will tell you. Let 's go home."

" Are you tired? "

" I 'm half dead," he laughed as he slipped on his snow-shoes.

A long and heavy rain cleared away the snow, and the more usual softness of the end of November set in. Their holiday sports were over for a time, to John's relief. On a Monday he went through the woods with Leila to the rectory. Mark Rivers, who had only seen John twice, made him welcome. The tall, thin, pale man, with the quiet smile and attentive grey eyes, made a ready capture of the boy. There were only two other scholars, the sons of the doctor and the Baptist preacher, lads of sixteen, not very mannerly, rather rough country boys, who nudged one another and regarded John with amused inter-est. In two or three days John knew that he was in the care of an unusually scholarly man, who became at once his friend and treated the lazy village boys and him with considerate kindliness. John liked it. To his surprise, no questions were asked at home about the school, and the afternoons were often free for lonely walks, when Leila went away on her mare and John was at liberty to read or to do as best pleased him. At times Leila bored him, and although with his well-taught cour-teous ways he was careful not to show impatience, he had the imaginative boy's capacity to enjoy being alone and a long re-pressed curiosity which now found indulgence among people who liked to answer questions and were pleased when he asked them. Very often, as he came into easier relations with his aunt, he was told to take some query she could not answer to Uncle James or the rector. A rather sensitive lad, he soon be-came aware that his uncle appeared to take no great interest in him, and, too, the boy's long cultivated though lessening reserve kept them apart. Meanwhile, Ann watched with pleasure his gain in independence, in looks and in appetite. While James Penhallow after his game of whist at night growled in his den over the bitter politics of the day, North and South, his wife read aloud to the children by the fireside in her own small sitting-room or answered as best she could John's questions, confessing ignorance at times or turning to books of reference. It was not always easy to satisfy this restless young mind in a fast developing body. " Were guinea pigs really pigs? What was the hematite iron-ore his uncle used at the works?" Once he was surprised. He asked one evening, " What was the Missouri Compromise?" He had read so much about it in the papers. " Hasn't it something to do with slavery? Aunt Ann, it must seem strange to own a man." His eager young ears had heard rather ignorant talk of it from his mother's English friends.

His aunt said quietly, " My people in Maryland own slaves, John. It is not a matter for a child to discuss. The abolitionists at the North are making trouble. It is a subject — we — I do not care to talk about."

" But what is an abolitionist, aunt? " he urged.

She laughed and said gaily, " I will answer no more conundrums; ask your uncle."

Leila who took no interest in politics fidgeted until she got her chance when Mrs. Ann would not answer John. " I want to hear about that talking oak, John."

She was quicker than he to observe her aunt's annoyance, and Ann, glad to be let off easily, found the needed book, and for a time they fell under the charm of Tennyson, and then earlier than usual were sent to bed.

The days ran on into weeks of school, and now there were snow-shoe tramps or sleigh rides to see some big piece of casting at the forge, where persistently-curious John did learn from some

one what hematite was. The life became to him steadily more
and more pleasant as he shed with ease the habits of an over-
regulated life, and living wholesome days prospered in body and
mind.

Christmas was a disappointment to Leila and to him. There
was an outbreak of measles at Westways and there would be no
carols, nor children gathered at Grey Pine. Ann's usual bounty
of toys was sent to the village. John's present from his uncle
was a pair of skates, and then Leila saw a delightful chance to
add another branch of education. Next morning, for this was
holiday-week, she asked if he would like to learn to skate. They
had gone early to the cabin and were lazily enjoying a rest after
a snow-shoe tramp. He replied, in an absent way, " I suppose I
may as well learn. How many Indians were there?"

"I don't know. Who cares now?"

"I do."

"I never saw such a boy. You can't ride and you can't
skate. You are just good for nothing. You're just fit to be
sold at a rummage-sale."

He was less easily vexed than made curious. "What's a
rummage-sale?"

"Oh! we had one two years ago. Once in a while Aunt Ann
says there must be one, so she gathers up all the trash and
Uncle Jim's old clothes (he hates that), and the village people
they buy things. And Mr. Rivers sells the things at auction,
you know — and oh, my! he was funny."

"So they sell what no one wants. Then why does any one
buy?"

"I'm sure, I don't know."

"I wonder what I would fetch, Leila?"

"Not much," she said.

"Maybe you're right." He had one of the brief boy-moods
of self-abasement.

Leila changed quickly. "I'll bid for you," she said coyly.

He laughed and looked up, surprised at this earliest indication of the feminine. " What would you give? " he asked.

" Well, about twenty-five cents."

He laughed. " I may improve, Leila, and the price go up. " Let us go and learn to skate — you must teach me."

" Of course," said Leila, " but you will soon learn. It's hard at first."

At lunch, on Christmas day, John had thanked his uncle for the skates in the formal way which Ann liked and James Penhallow did not. He said, " I am very greatly obliged for the skates. They appear to me excellent."

" What a confoundedly civil young gentleman," thought Penhallow. " I have been thinking you must learn to skate. The pond has been swept clear of snow."

" Thank you," returned the boy, with a grin which his uncle thought odd.

" Leila will teach you."

John was silent, regarding his uncle with never dying interest, the soldier of Indian battles, the perfect rider and good shot, adored in the stables and loved, as John was learning, in all the country side. John was in the grip of a boy's admiration for a realized ideal — the worship, by the timid, of courage. Of the few things he did well, he thought little; and an invalid's fears had discouraged rough games until he had become like a timorous girl. He had much dread of horses, and was alarmingly sure that he would some day be made to ride. Once in Paris he had tried, had had a harmless accident and, willingly yielding to his mother's fears, had tried no more.

Late in the afternoon, Leila, with her long wake of flying hair, burst into the Squire's den. " What the deuce is the matter? " asked Penhallow.

" Oh! Uncle Jim, he can skate like — like a witch. I couldn't keep near him. He skated an ' L ' for my name. Uncle Jim, he's a fraud."

Penhallow knew now why the boy had grinned at him. "I think, Leila, he will do. Where did he learn to skate?"

"At Vevey, he says, on the Lake."

"Yes, of Geneva."

"Tom McGregor was there and Bob Grace. We played tag. John knows a way to play tag on skates. You must chalk your right hand and you must mark with it the other fellow's right shoulder. It must be jolly. We had no chalk, but we are to play it to-morrow. Is n't it interesting, Uncle John?"

Penhallow laughed. "Interesting, my dear? Oh! your aunt will be after you with a stick."

"Aunt Ann's — stick!" laughed Leila.

"My dear Leila," he said gravely, "this boy has had all the manliness coddled out of him, but he looks like his father. I have my own ideas of how to deal with him. I suppose he will brag a bit at dinner."

"He will not, Uncle Jim."

"Bet you a pound of bonbons, Leila."

"From town?"

"Yes."

"All right."

"Can he coast? I did not ask you."

"Well! pretty well," said Leila. For some unknown reason she was unwilling to say more.

"Does n't the rector dine here, to-day, Leila?"

"Yes, but — oh! Uncle Jim, we found a big hornets' nest yesterday on the log cabin. They seemed all asleep. I told John we would fight them in the spring."

"And what did he say?"

"He said: 'Did they sting?'— I said: 'That was the fun of it!'"

"Better not tell your aunt."

"No, sir. I 'm an obedient little girl."

" You little scamp! You were meant to be a boy. Is there anything you are afraid of? "

" Yes, algebra."

" Oh! get out," and she fled.

At dinner John said no word of the skating, to the satisfaction of Leila who conveyed to her uncle a gratified sense of victory by some of the signs which were their private property.

Leaving the cousins to their game of chess, Penhallow followed his wife and Mark Rivers into his library. " Well, Mark," he said, " you have had this boy long enough to judge; it is time I heard what you think of him. You asked me to wait. The youngster is rather reticent, and Leila is about the only person in the house who really knows much about him. He talks like a man of thirty."

" I do not find him reticent," remarked Mrs. Ann, " and his manners are charming — I wish Leila's were half as good."

" Well, let's hear about him."

" May I smoke? " asked the rector.

" Anywhere but in my drawing-room. I believe James would like to smoke in church."

" It might have its consolations," returned Penhallow.

" Thanks," said Rivers smiling. Neither man took advantage of her unusual permission. " But you, Squire, have been closer than I to this interesting boy. What do you make of him? "

" He can't ride — he hardly knows a horse from a mule."

" That's not his fault," said Mrs. Penhallow, " he's afraid of horses."

" Afraid! " said her husband. " By George! afraid of horses."

" He speaks French perfectly," said Mark Rivers.

" He can't swim. I got that out of Leila. I understand he tried it once and gave it up."

" But his mother made him, James. You know Susan. She

was as timid as a house-fly for herself, and I suppose for him."

"I asked him," said Rivers, "if he knew any Latin. He answered me in Latin and told me that at Budapest where he was long at school the boys had to speak Latin."

"And the rest, Rivers. Is he well up in mathematics?"

"No, he finds that difficult. But, upon my word, Squire, he is the most doggedly persistent fellow I have ever had to teach and I handled many boys when I was younger. I can take care of my side of the boy."

"He can skate, James," said Mrs. Ann.

"Yes, so I hear. I suppose that under Leila's care and a good out-of-door life he will drop his girl-ways — but —"

"But what, James?"

"Oh! he has been taught that there is no shame in failure, no disgrace in being afraid."

"How do you know he is afraid, my dear James?"

"Oh! I know." Leila's unwillingness to talk had given him some suspicion of the truth. "Well, we shall see. He needs some rough boy-company. I don't like to have the village boys alone with Leila, but when she has John with her it may be as well to ask Dr. McGregor's son Tom to coast and play with them."

"He has no manners," said Mrs. Penhallow.

"Then he may get some from John. He never will from Leila. I will take care of the rest, Rivers. He has got to learn to ride."

"You won't be too hard on him, James?" said his wife.

"Not unless he needs it. Let us drop him."

"Have you seen yesterday's papers?" asked Rivers. "Our politics, North and South, look to me stormy."

Penhallow shook his head at the tall rector. The angry strife of sections and parties was the one matter he never discussed with Ann Penhallow. The rector recalled it as he saw Mrs. Ann sit up and drop on her lap the garment upon which her ever industrious hands were busy. Accepting Penhallow's hint, Rivers said quickly, " But really there is nothing new," and then, " Tom McGregor will certainly be the better for our little gentleman's good manners, and he too has something to learn of Tom."

" I should say he has," said Penhallow.

" A little dose of West Point, I suppose," laughed Mrs. Ann. " It is my husband's one ideal of education."

" It must once, I fancy, have satisfied Ann Grey," retorted the Squire smiling.

" I reserve any later opinion of James Penhallow," she said laughing, and gathering up her sewing bag left them, declaring that now they might smoke. The two men rose, and when alone began at once to talk of the coming election in the fall of 1856 and the endless troubles arising out of the Fugitive Slave Act.

The boy who had been the subject of their conversation was slowly becoming used to novel surroundings and the influence they exerted. Ann talked to him at times of his mother, but he had the disinclination to speak of the dead which most children have, and had in some ways been kept so much of a child as to astonish his aunt. Neither Leila nor any one could have failed to like him and his gentle ways, and as between him and the village boys she knew Leila preferred this clever, if too timid, cousin. So far they had had no serious quarrels. When she rode with the Squire, John wandered in the woods, enjoying solitude, and having some appreciative relation to nature, the great pine woods, the strange noises of the breaking ice in the river, the sunset skies.

Among the village boys with whom at the rector's small school and in the village John was thrown, he liked least the lad McGregor, who had now been invited to coast or skate with the Grey Pine cousins. Tom had the democratic boy-belief that very refined manners imply lack of some other far more practical qualities, and thus to him and the Westways boys John Penhallow was simply an absurd Miss Nancy kind of lad, and it was long after the elders of the little town admired and liked him that the boys learned to respect him. It was easy to see why the generous, good-tempered and pleasant lad failed to satisfy the town boys. John had been sedulously educated into the belief that he was of a class to which these fellows did not belong, and of this the Squire had soon some suspicion when, obedient as always, John accepted his uncle's choice of his friend the doctor's son as a playmate.

He was having his hair cut when Tom McGregor came into the shop of Josiah, the barber. "Wait a minute," said John. "Are you through, Mr. Josiah?"

Tom grinned, "Got a handle to your name?"

"Yes, because Master John is a gentleman."

"Then I'll call you Mister too."

"It won't ever make you Mister," said the barber, "that kind's born so."

John disliked this outspoken expression of an opinion he shared. "Nonsense," he said. "Come up, Tom, this afternoon. Don't forget the muskrat traps, Mr. Josiah."

"No, sir. Too early yet."

"All right," returned Tom. "I'll come."

March had come and the last snow still lay on the land when thus invited Tom joined John and Leila in the stable-yard. "Let's play tag," cried Leila. Tom was ready.

"Here's a stick." They took hold of it in turn. Tom's hand came out on top. "I'm tagger. Look out!" he cried.

They played the game. At last he caught Leila, and crying out, "You're tagged," seized her boy-cap and threw it up on to the steep slope of the stable roof.

"Oh! that's not fair," cried the girl. "You are a rude boy. Now you've got to get it."

"No, indeed. Get the stable-man to get it."

She turned to John, " Please to get it."

" How can I ? " he said.

" Go up inside — there 's a trap door. You can slide down the snow and get it."

" But I might fall."

" There 's your chance," said Tom grinning. John stood, still irresolute. Leila walked away into the stable.

" She 'll get a man," said Tom a little regretful of his rudeness, as she disappeared.

In a moment Leila was up in the hayloft and out on the roof. Spreading out arms and thin legs she carefully let herself slide down the soft snow until, seizing her cap, she set her feet on the roof gutter, crying out, " Get a ladder quick." Alarmed at her perilous position, they ran and called out a groom, a ladder was brought, and in a moment she was on the ground.

Leila turned on the two lads. " You are a coward, Tom McGregor, and you too, John Penhallow. I never — never will play with you again."

" It was just fun," said Tom; " any of the men could have poked it down."

" Cowards," said the girl, tossing back her dark mass of hair and moving away without a look at the discomfited pair.

" I suppose now you will go and tell the Squire," said Tom. He was alarmed.

She turned, " I — a tell-tale ! " Her child-code of conduct was imperative. " I am neither a tell-tale nor a coward. ' Telltale pick a nail and hang him to a cow's tail ! ' " and with this well-known declaration of her creed of playground honour, she walked away.

" She 'll tell," said Tom.

" She won't," said John.

" Guess I 'll go home," said Tom, and left John to his reflections. They were most disagreeable.

John went into the woods and sat down on a log. " So,"

he said aloud, " she called me a coward — and I am — I was —
I can't bear it. What would my uncle say?" His eyes filled.
He brushed away the tears with his sleeve. A sudden remembrance of how good she had been to him, how loyally silent,
added to his distress. He longed for a chance to prove that
he was not that — that — Eager and yet distrustful, he got
up and walked through the melting snow to the cabin, where
he lay on the floor thinking, a prey to that fiend imagination,
of which he had a larger share than is always pleasant when
excuses are needed.

Leila was coldly civil and held her tongue, but for a few
days would not go into the woods with him and rode alone or
with her uncle. Tom came no more for a week, until self-as-
sured that the Squire had not heard of his behaviour, as he
met him on the road with his usual hearty greeting. Ann
Penhallow saw that the boy was less happy than usual and suspected some mild difficulty with Leila, but in her wise way
said nothing and began to use him for some of her many
errands of helpfulness in the village and on the farms, where
always he made friends. Seeing at last that the boy was too
silent and to her eye unhappy, she talked of it to Mark Rivers.
The next day, after school, he said to John, " I want to see
that old cabin in the woods. Long as I have lived here I have
never been that far. Come and show me the way. I tried
once to find it and got lost. We can have a jolly good talk,
you and I."

The word of kindly approach was timely. John felt the invitation as a compliment, and was singularly open to the approval his lessons won from this gentle dark-eyed man. "Oh!"
he said, " I should like that."

After lunch, Leila, a little penitent, said with unwonted shyness, " The woods are very nice to-day, and I found the first
arbutus under the snow."

When John did not respond, she made a further propitiatory

advance, "It will soon be time for that hornets' nest, we must go and see."

"What are you about?" said Mrs. Ann; "you will get stung."

"Pursuit of natural history," said Penhallow smiling.

"You are as bad as Leila, James."

"Won't you come?" asked the girl at last.

"Thank you. I regret that I have an engagement with Mr. Rivers," said John, with the prim manner he was fast losing.

"By George!" murmured Penhallow as he rose.

John looked up puzzled, and his uncle, much amused, went to get his boots and riding-dress. "Wait till I get you on a horse, my Lord Chesterfield," he muttered. "He and Leila must have had a row. What about, I wonder." He asked no questions.

With a renewal of contentment and well-pleased, John called for the rector. They went away into the forest to the cabin.

"And so," said Rivers, "this is where the first Penhallow had his Indian fight. I must ask the Squire."

"I know about it," said John. "Leila told me, and"— he paused, "I saw it."

"Oh! did you? Let's hear." They lay down, and the rector lazily smoked. "Well, go ahead, Jack, I like stories." He had early rechristened him Jack, and the boy liked it.

"Well, sir, they saw them coming near to dusk and ran. You see, it was a clearing then; the trees have grown here since. That was at dusk. They barred the door and cut loop-holes between the logs. Next morning the Indians came on. She fired first, and she cried out, 'Oh! James, I've killed a man.'"

"She said that?" asked Rivers.

"Yes, and she wouldn't shoot again until her man was wounded, then she was like a raging lioness."

"A lioness!" echoed Rivers.

"By evening, help came."

"How did you know all this?"

"Oh! Leila told me some — and the rest — well, sir, I saw it. I've been here often."

The rector studied the excited young face. "Would you like to have been there, Jack?"

"No."

"Why not?"

"I should have been afraid, and —" Then quickly, "I suppose he was; she was; any one would have been."

"Like as not. He for her, most of all. But there are many kinds of fear, Jack."

John was silent, and the rector waited. Then the boy broke out, "Leila told me last week I was a coward."

"Indeed! Leila told you that! That was n't like her, Jack. Why did she say it?"

This was a friendly hearer, whose question John had invited. To-day the human relief of confession was great to the boy. He told the story, in bits, carefully, as if to have it exact were essential. Mark Rivers watched him through his pipe smoke, trying to think of what he could or should say to this small soul in trouble. The boy was lying on the floor looking up, his hands clasped behind his head. "That's all, sir. It's dreadful."

The young rector's directness of character set him on the right path. "I don't know just what to say to you, Jack. You see, you have been taught to be afraid of horses and dogs, of exposure to rain, and generally of being hurt, until — Well, Jack, if your mother had not been an invalid, she would not have educated you to fear, to have no joy in risks. Now you are in more wholesome surroundings — and — in a little while you will forget this small trouble."

The young clergyman felt that in his puzzle he had been rather vague, and added pleasantly, "You have the courage of truth. That's moral courage. Tom would have explained

or denied, or done anything to get out of the scrape, if the
Squire had come down on him. You would not."

"Oh! thank you," said John. "I'm sorry I troubled you."

"You did in a way; but you did not when you trusted a
man who is your friend. Let us drop it. Where are those
Indian graves?"

They went out and wandered in the woods, until John said,
"Oh! this must be that arbutus Leila talks about, just peep-
ing out from under the snow." They gathered a large bunch.

"It is the first breath of the fragrance of spring," said
Rivers.

"Oh! yes, sir. How sweet it is! It does not grow in
Europe."

"No, we own it with many other good and pleasant things."

When they came to the house, Leila was dismounting after
her ride. John said, "Here Leila, I gathered these for you."

When she said, "Thank you, John," he knew by her smiling
face that he was forgiven, and without a word followed her
into the hall, still pursued by the thought; but I was afraid.
He put aside this trouble for a time, and the wood sports with
Leila were once more resumed. What thought of his failure
the girl still kept in mind, if she thought of it at all, he never
knew, or not for many days. He had no wish to talk of it,
but fearfully desired to set himself right with her and with
John Penhallow.

One day in early April she asked him to go to the stable
and order her horse. He did so, and alone with an unpleasant
memory, in the stable-yard he stood still a moment, and then
with a sudden impulse threw his cap up on to the roof. He
took a moment to regret it, and then saying, "I've got to do
it!" he went into the stable and out of the hay-loft on to the
sloping roof. He did not dare to wait, but let himself slide
down the frozen snow, seized his cap, and knew of a sudden
that the smooth ice-coating was an unsuspected peril. He

rolled over on his face, straightened himself, and slid to the edge. He clutched the gutter, hung a moment, and dropped some fifteen feet upon the hard pavement. For a moment the shock stunned him. Then, as he lay, he was aware of Billy, who cried. "He's dead! he's dead!" and ran to the house, where he met Mrs. Ann and Leila on the porch. "He's killed — he's dead!"

"Who? Who?" they cried.

"Mr. John, he's dead!"

As Billy ran, the dead got his wits about him, sat up, and, hearing Billy howling, got on his feet. His hands were torn and bleeding, but he was not otherwise damaged. He ran after Billy, and was but a moment behind him.

Mrs. Ann was shaking the simple fellow, vainly trying to learn what had happened. Leila white to the lips was leaning against a pillar. John called out, "I'm all right, aunt. I had a fall — and Billy, do hold your tongue."

Billy cried, "He's not dead!" and fled as he had come.

"My poor boy," said Mrs. Ann, "sit down." He gladly obeyed.

At this moment James Penhallow came downstairs. "What's all this row about, Ann? I heard Billy — Oh, so you're the dead man, John. How did you happen to die?"

"I fell off the stable roof, sir."

"Well, you got off easily." He asked no other questions, to John's relief, but said, "Your hands look as if you had fought our big tom-cat."

John had risen on his uncle's approach. Now Penhallow said, "Sit down. Put some court-plaster on those scratches, Ann, or a postage stamp — or — so — Come, Leila, the horses are here. Run upstairs and get my riding-whip. That fool brought me down in a hurry. When the chimney took fire last year he ran through the village yelling that the house was burned down. Don't let your aunt coddle you, John."

"Do let the boy alone, James."

"Come, Leila," he said.

"I think I won't ride to-day, Uncle Jim."

A faint signal from his wife sent him on his way alone with, "All right, Leila. Any errands, my dear?"

"No — but please call at the grocer's and ask him why he has sent no sugar — and tell Mrs. Saul I want her. If Pole is in, you might mention that when I order beef I do not want veal."

While John was being plastered and in dread of the further questions which were not asked, Leila went upstairs, and the Squire rode away to the iron-works smiling and pleased. "He'll do," he murmured, "but what the deuce was my young dandy doing on the roof?" The Captain had learned in the army the wisdom of asking no needless questions. "Leila must have been a pretty lively instructor in mischief. By and by, Ann will have it out of the boy, and — I must stop that. Now she will be too full of surgery. She is sure to think Leila had something to do with it." He saw of late that Ann was resolute as to what to him would be a sad loss. Leila was to be sent to school before long — accomplishments! "Damn accomplishments! I have tried to make a boy out of her — now the inevitable feminine appears — she was scared white — and the boy was pretty shaky. I am sure Leila will know all about it." That school business had already been discussed with his wife, and then, he thought, "There is to come a winter in the city, society, and — some nice young man, and so good-bye, my dear comrade. Get up, Brutus." He dismissed his cares as the big bay stretched out in a gallop.

After some surgical care, John was told to go to his room and lie down. He protested that he was in no need of rest, but Ann Penhallow, positive in small ways with every one, including her husband, sent John away with an imperative order, nor on the whole was he sorry to be alone. No one had been too curious. He recognized this as a reasonable habit of the family. And Leila? He was of no mind to be frank with her; and this he had done was a debt paid to John Penhallow! He may not have so put it, but he would not admit to himself that Leila's contemptuous epithet had had any influence on his action. The outcome was a keen sense of happy self-approval. When he had dressed for dinner, feeling pretty sore all over, he found Leila waiting at the head of the stairs.

"John Penhallow, you threw your cap on the roof and went up to get it, you did."

"I did, Leila, but how did you know?"

She smiled and replied, "I — I don't know, John. I am sorry for what I said, and oh! John, Uncle Jim, he was pleased!"

"Do you think so?"

"Yes." She caught his hand and at the last landing let it fall. At dinner, the Squire asked kindly: "Are you all right, my boy?"

"Yes, sir," and that was all.

Mark Rivers, who had heard of this incident from Mrs. Penhallow, and at last from Leila, was alone in a position to comprehend the motives which combined to bring about an act of rashness. The rector had some sympathy with the boy and liked him for choosing a time when no one was present to witness his trial of himself. He too had the good sense like the Squire to ask no questions.

Meanwhile, Tom McGregor came no more, feeling the wound to his pride, but without the urgent need felt by John to set himself in a better position with himself. He would have thought nothing of accepting Leila's challenge, but very much wanted to see the polite girl-boy brought to shame. In fact, even the straightforward Squire, with all his ready cordiality, at times found John's extreme politeness ridiculous at his age, but knew it to be the result of absurd training and the absence of natural association with other and manly boys. To Tom it was unexplained and caused that very common feeling of vague suspicion of some claim to superiority which refined manners imply to those who lack manners altogether.

CHAPTER IV

APRIL passed, the arbutus fragrance was gone, while the maples were putting forth ruddy buds which looked like a prophecy of the distant autumn and made gay with colour the young greenery of spring. Meanwhile, school went on, and John grew stronger and broader in this altogether wholesome atmosphere of outdoor activity and indoor life of kindness and apparently inattentive indifference on the part of his busy uncle.

On an evening late in May, 1856 (John long remembered it), the Squire as usual left their little circle and retired to the library, where he busied himself over matters involving business letters, and then fell to reading in the *Tribune* the bitter politics of Fremont's contest with Buchanan and the still angry talk over Brooks's assault on Senator Sumner. He foresaw defeat and was with cool judgment aware of what the formation of the Republican Party indicated in the way of trouble to come. The repeal of the Missouri Compromise had years before disturbed his party allegiance, and now no longer had he been able to see the grave question of slavery as Ann his wife saw it. He threw aside the papers, set his table in order, and opening the door called John to come in and pay him a visit. The boy rose surprised. Never once had this over-occupied man talked to him at length and he had never been set free to wander in the tempting wilderness of books, which now and then when James Penhallow was absent were remorselessly dusted by Mrs. Ann and the maid, with dislocating consequences over which James Penhallow growled in belated protest.

John went in, glanced up at the Captain's sword over the

mantelpiece, and sat down as desired by the still-needed fire.

"John," said his uncle in his usual direct way, "have you ever been on the back of a horse?"

"Yes, sir, once — in Paris at a riding-school."

"Once! You said ' once '— well?"

"I fell off — mother was with me."

"And you got on again?"

"No, sir."

"Why not?"

John flushed and hesitated, watched by the dark-eyed Squire. "I was afraid!" He would not say that his mother forbade it.

"What is your name?"

"John, sir," he returned astonished.

"And the rest — the rest, sir," added his uncle abruptly.

John troubled by the soldier's impatient tones said: "Penhallow, sir." He was near to a too emotional display.

"And you, John Penhallow, my brother's son, were afraid?"

"I was." It was only in part true. His mother had forbidden the master to remount him.

"By George!" said Penhallow angrily, "I don't believe you. I can't!"

John rose, "I may be a coward, Uncle James, but I never lie."

Penhallow stood up, "I beg your pardon, John."

"Oh! no, Uncle James. I — please not." He felt as if the tall soldier was humiliating himself, but could not have put it in words.

"I was hasty, my boy. You must, of course, learn to ride. By the way, do you ever read the papers?"

"Not often, sir — hardly ever. They are kept in your library or Aunt Ann's."

"Well, it is time you did read them. Come in here when you want to be alone — or any time. You won't bother me.

Take what books you want, and ask me about the politics of
the day. The country is going to the devil, but don't discuss
this election with your aunt."

"No, sir." He had gathered from the rector enough to
make him understand the warning.

John went out with the idea that this business of learning
to ride was somewhere in the future. He was a little disturbed
when the next day after breakfast his uncle said, "Come, John,
the horses are in the training-ring."

Mrs. Ann said, "James, if you are going to apply West
Point riding-school methods to John, I protest."

"Then protest, my dear," he said.

"You will kill him," she returned.

"My dear Ann, I am not going to kill him, I am going to
teach him to live. Come, John. I am going to teach him to
ride." Raising horses was one of the Squire's amusements,
and the training-course where young horses were broken usually
got an hour of his busy day.

"May I come?" asked Leila.

"Please, not," said John, anticipating disaster and desiring
no amused spectators.

"In a week or so, yes, Leila," said Penhallow, "not now."

There were two stable-boys waiting and a pony long retired
on grassy pension. "Now," said Penhallow, "put a foot on
my knee and up you go."

"But, there's no saddle."

"There are two. The Lord of horses put one on the back
of a horse and another under a man. Up! sir." John got on.
"Grip him with your legs, hold on to the mane if you like, but
not by the reins." The pony feeling no urgency to move stood
still and nibbled the young grass. A smart tap of the Squire's
whip started him, and John rolled off.

"Come, sir, get on." The boys from the stable grinned.
John set his teeth. "Don't stiffen yourself. That's better."

He fell once again, and at the close of an hour his uncle said, "There that will do for to-day, and not so bad either."

"I 'd like to try it again, sir," gasped John.

"You young humbug," laughed Penhallow. "Go and console your distracted aunt. I am off to the mills."

The ex-captain was merciless enough, and day after day John was so stiff that, as he confessed to Leila, a jointed doll was a trifle to his condition. She laughed, "I went through it once, but one day it came."

"What came, Leila?"

"Oh! the joy of the horse!"

"I shall never get to that." But he did, for the hard riding-master scolded, smiled, praised, and when at last John sat in the saddle the bareback lessons gave him a certain confidence. The training went on day after day, under the rule of patient but relentless efficiency. It was far into June when, having backed without serious misadventures two or three well-broken horses, Penhallow mounted him on Leila's mare, Lucy, and set out to ride with him.

"Let us ride to the mills, John." The mare was perfectly gaited and easy. They rode on, talking horses.

"You will have to manage the mills some day," said Penhallow. "You own quite a fifth of them. Now I have three partners, but some day you and I will run them." The boy had been there before with Rivers, but now the Squire presented him to the foreman and as they moved about explained the machinery. It was altogether delightful, and this was a newly discovered uncle. On the way home the Squire talked of the momentous November elections and of his dread of the future with Buchanan in power, while he led the way through lanes and woods until they came to the farm.

"We will cross the fields," he said, and dismounting took down the upper bars of a fence. Then he rode back a little, and returning took the low fence, crying, "Now, John, sit like a sack — loosely. The mare jumps like a frog; go back a bit. Now, then, give her her head!" For a moment he was in the air as his uncle cried, "You lost a stirrup. Try it again. Oh! that was better. Now, once more, come," and he was over at Penhallow's side. He had found the joy of the horse! "A bit more confidence and practice and you will do. I want you to ride Venus. She shies at a shadow — at anything black. Don't forget that."

"Oh, thank you, Uncle James!"

"It is Uncle Jim now, my boy. I knew from the first you would come out all right. I believe in blood — horses and men. I believe in blood." This was James Penhallow all over. A reticent man, almost as tenderly trustful as a woman, of those who came up to his standards of honour, truth and the courage which rightly seemed to him the backbone of all the virtues.

What John thought may be readily imagined. Accustomed to be considered and flattered, his uncle's quiet reserve had seemed to him disappointing, and now of late this abrupt praise and accepting comradeship left the sensitive lad too grateful for words. The man at his side was wise enough to say no more, and they rode home and dismounted without further speech.

After dinner John sought a corner with Leila, where he could share with her his new-born enthusiasm about horses. The Squire called to the rector and Mrs. Ann to come into his library. "Sit down, Mark," he said, "I am rash to invite you; both you and Ann bore me to death with your Sunday schools and the mill men who won't come to church. I don't hear our Baptist friend complain."

"But he does," said Rivers.

"I do not wonder," said Ann, "that they will not attend the chapel."

"If," said Penhallow, "you were to swap pulpits, Mark, it would draw. There are many ways — oh, I am quite in ear-

nest, Ann. Don't put on one of your excommunicating looks.
I remember once in Idaho at dusk, I had two guides. They
were positive, each of them, that certain trails would lead to
the top. I tossed up which to go with. It was pretty serious —
Indians and so on — I'll tell you about it some time, rector.
Well, we met at dawn on the summit. How about the moral,
Ann?"

Ann Penhallow laughed. In politics, morals and religion,
she held unchanging sentiments. " My dear James, people who
make fables supply the morals. I decline."

" Very good, but you see mine."

" I never see what I do not want to see," which was pretty
close to the truth.

" The fact is," said Rivers, " I have preaccepted the Squire's
hint. Grace is sick again. I tell him it is that last immer-
sion business. I have promised to preach for him next Sunday, as your young curate at the mills wants to air his
eloquence here."

" Not really!" said Mrs. Ann, " at his chapel?"

" Yes, and I mean to use a part of our service."

" If the Bishop knew it."

" If! he would possibly forbid it, or be glad I did it."

Mrs. Ann totally disapproved. She took up her knitting
and said no more, while Rivers and Penhallow talked of a disturbance at the works of no great moment. The rector noticed Mrs. Penhallow's sudden loss of interest in their talk and
her failure to comment on his statement, an unusual thing
with this woman, who, busy-minded as the bee, gathered honey
of interest from most of the affairs of life. In a pause of the
talk he turned to her, " I am sorry to have annoyed you," he
said —" I mean about preaching for Grace."

" But why do you do it?"

" Because," he returned, " my Master bids me. Over and
over one finds in His Word that he foreknew how men would

differ and come to worship Him and use His revelations in ways which would depend on diversity of temperaments, or under the leadership of individual minds of great force. It may be that it was meant that we should disagree, and yet — I — yet as to essentials we are one. That I never can forget."

"Then," she said quickly, "you are of many creeds."

"No and yes," he returned smiling. "In essentials yes, in ceremonial usage no; in some other morsels of belief held by others charitably dubious — I dislike argument about religion in the brief inadequateness of talk — especially with you from whom I am apt to differ and to whom I owe so much — so very much."

She took up her knitting again as she said, "I am afraid the balance of debt is on our side."

"Then," said Penhallow, who, too, disliked argument on religion, "if you have got through with additions to the useless squabbles of centuries, which hurt and never help, I —"

"But," broke in his wife, "I have had no answer."

"Oh, but you have, Ann; for me, Rivers is right."

"Then I am in a minority of one," she returned, "but I have not had my say."

"Well, dear, keep it for next time. Now I want, as I said, a little counsel about John."

"And about Leila, James. Something has got to be done."

The Squire said ruefully, "Yes, I suppose so. I do not know that anything needs to be done. You saw John's condition before dinner. He had a swollen nose and fair promise of a black eye. I asked you to take no notice of it. I wanted first to hear what had happened. I got Leila on the porch and extracted it by bits. It seems that Tom was rude to Leila."

"I never liked your allowing him to play with the children, James."

"But the boy needs boy-company."

"And what of Leila? She needs girl-company."

" I fear," said Rivers, " that may be the case."

" It is so," said Mrs. Ann decisively, pleased with his support. " What happened, James? "

" I did not push Leila about what Tom did. John slapped his face and got knocked down. He got up and went at Tom like a wildcat. Tom knocked him down again and held him. He said that John must say he had had enough."

" He did n't," said Rivers, " I am sure he did n't."

" No, Mark, he said he would die first, which was what he should have said. Then Billy had the sense to pull the big boy off, and as Leila was near tears I asked no more questions. It was really most satisfactory."

" How can you say that? " said his wife. " It was brutal."

" You do not often misunderstand me, Ann. I mean, of course, that our boy did the right thing. How does it strike you, Mark? "

He had a distinct intention to get the rector into trouble. " Not this time, Squire," and he laughed. " The boy did what his nature bade him. Of course, being a nice little boy, he should have remonstrated. There are several ways —"

" Thanks," said Penhallow. " Of course, Ann, the playing with Tom will end. I fancy there is no need to interfere."

" He should be punished for rudeness to Leila," said Mrs. Penhallow.

" Oh, well, he 's a rough lad and like enough sorry. How can I punish him without making too much of a row."

" You are quite right, as I see it," said Rivers. " Let it drop; but, indeed, it is true that Leila should have other than rough lads as school-companions."

" Oh, Lord! Rivers."

" I am glad to agree with you at least about one thing," said Mrs. Penhallow. " In September John will be sixteen, and Leila a year or so younger. She is now simply a big, daring, strong boy."

"If you think that, Ann, you are oddly mistaken."

"I am," she said; "I was. It was only one end of my reasons why she must go to school. Before John came and when we had cousins here — girls, she simply despised them or led them into dreadful scrapes."

"Well, Ann, we will talk it over another time."

Rivers smiled and Ann Penhallow went out, longing to attend to the swollen face now bent low over a book. The two men she left smoked in such silence as is one of the privileges of friendship. At last Penhallow said, "Of course, Mark, my wife is right, but I shall miss the girl. My wife cannot ride with me, and now I am to lose Leila. After school come young men. Confound it, rector, I wish the girl had less promise of beauty — of — well, all the Greys have it — attractiveness for our sex. Some of them are fools, but they have it all the same, and they keep it to the end. What is most queer about it is that they are not easily won. The men who trouble hearts for a game do not win these women."

"Some one will suffer," said Rivers reflectively. He wondered if the wooing of Ann Grey by this masterful man had been a long one. A moment he gave to remembrance of his own long and tender care of the very young wife he had won easily and seen fade with terrible slowness as her life let fall its joys as it were leaf by leaf, with bitter sense of losing the fair heritage of youth. Now he said, "Were all these women, Squire, who had the gift of bewitchment, good?"

"No, now and then hurtful, or honest gentlewomen, or like Ann Grey too entirely good for this wicked world —"

"As Westways knows," said Rivers, thinking how the serene beauty of a life of noble ways had contributed spiritual charm to whatever Ann Penhallow had of attractiveness. "But," he went on, "Leila cannot go until the fall, and you will still have the boy. I had my doubts of your method of education, but it has worked well. He has a good mind and is so far ahead of his years in education that he will be ready for college too early."

"Well, I hate to think of these changes. He must learn to box."

"Another physical virtue to be added," laughed Rivers.

"Yes, he must learn to face these young country fellows." After a brief pause he added, "I am looking forward to Buchanan's nomination and election, Mark, with anxiety. Both North and South are losing temper."

"Yes, but shall you vote for him? I presume you have always been a Democrat, more or less — less of late."

"I shall vote for Fremont if he is nominated; not wholly a wise choice. I am tired of what seems like an endless effort North and South, to add more exasperations. It will go on and on. Each section seems to want to make the other angry."

"It is not Mrs. Penhallow's opinion, I fear. The wrongdoing is all on our side."

Said the Squire gravely, "That is a matter, Mark, we never now discuss — the one matter. Her brothers in Maryland, are at odds. One at least is bitter, as I gather from their letters."

"Well, after the election things will quiet down, as usual."

"They will not, Mark. I know the South. Unhappily they think we live by the creed of day-book and ledger. We as surely misunderstand them, and God alone knows what the future holds for us."

This was unusual talk for Penhallow. He thought much, but talked little, and his wife's resolute attitude of opinions held from youth was the one trouble of an unusually happy life.

"We can only hope for the best," said Rivers. "Time is a great peacemaker."

"Or not," returned his host as Rivers rose. "Just a word, Mark, before you go. I am desirous that you should not misunderstand me in regard to my politics. I see that slavery is to be more and more in question. My own creed is, ' let it alone, obey the laws, return the runaways,— oh! whether you like it or not,— but no more slave territory.' And for me, my friend, the States are one country and above all else, above slave questions, is that of an unbroken union. I shall vote for Fremont. I cannot go to party meetings and speak for him because, Mark, I am in doubt about the man, and because — oh! you know."

Yes, he knew more or less, but knowing did not quite approve. The Squire of Grey Pine rarely spoke at length, but now he longed, as he gave some further clue to his reticence, to make public a political creed which was not yet so fortified by the logic of events as to be fully capable of defence.

" The humorous side of it," he said, " is that my very good wife has been doing some pretty ardent electioneering while I am sitting still, because to throw my weight into the local contest would oblige me to speak out and declare my whole political religion of which I am not quite secure enough to talk freely."

The young rector looked at his older friend, who was uneasy between his uncertain sense of duty and his desire not to go among people at the mills and in the town and struggle with his wife for votes.

" I may, Mark, I may do no more than let it be known how I shall vote. That is all. It will be of use. I could wish to do more. I think that here and at the mills the feeling is rather strong for Buchanan, but why I cannot see."

Mrs. Ann had been really active, and her constant kindness at the mills and in the little town gave to her wishes a certain influential force among these isolated groups of people who in their remoteness had not been disturbed by the aggressive policy of the South.

" Of course, Mark, my change of opinion will excite remark. Whoever wins, I shall be uneasy about the future. Must you go? Good-night."

He went to the hall door with the rector, and then back to his pipe, dismissing the subject for the time. On his return, he found John in the library looking at the sword hanging over the mantelpiece. "Well, Jack," he said, "a penny for your thoughts."

"Oh, I was thinking what the sword had seen."

"I hope it will see no more, but it may — it may. Now I want to say a word to you. You had a fight with Tom McGregor and got the worst of it."

"I did."

"I do not ask why. You seem to have shown some pluck."

"I don't know, uncle. I was angry, and I just slapped his face. He deserved it."

"Very well, but never slap. I suppose that is the French schoolboy way of fighting. Hit hard — get in the first blow."

"Yes, sir. I had n't a chance."

"You must take my old cadet boxing-gloves from under the sword. I have spoken to Sam, the groom. I saw him last year in a bout with the butcher's boy. After he has knocked you about for a month, you will be better able to take care of the Penhallow nose."

"I shall like that."

"You won't, but it will help to fill out your chest." Then he laughed, "Did you ever get that cane?"

"No, sir. Billy found it. Leila gave him twenty-five cents for it, and now she won't give it to me."

"Well, well, is that so? The ways of women are strange."

"I don't see why she keeps it, uncle."

"Nor I. Now go to bed, it is late. She is a bit of a tease, John. Mark Rivers says she is now just one half of the riddle called woman."

John understood well enough that he was some day expected by his uncle to have it out with Tom. He got two other bits of advice on this matter. The rector detained him after school, a few days later. "How goes the swimming, John?" he asked.

The Squire early in the summer had taken this matter in hand, and as Ann Penhallow said, with the West Point methods of kill or cure. John replied to the rector that he was now given leave to swim with the Westways boys. The pool was an old river-channel, now closed above, and making a quiet deep pool such as in England is called a "backwater" and in Canada a "bogan." The only access was through the Penhallow grounds, but this was never denied.

"Does Tom McGregor swim there?" asked Rivers.

"Yes, and the other boys. It is great fun now; it was not at first."

"About Tom, John. I hope you have made friends with him."

Said John, with something of his former grown-up manner, "It appears to me that we never were friends. I regret, sir, that it seems to you desirable."

"But, John, it is. For two Christian lads like you to keep up a quarrel —"

"He's a heathen, sir. I told him yesterday that he ought to apologize to Leila."

"And what did he say?"

"He said, he guessed I wanted another licking. That's the kind of Christian he is."

"I must speak to him."

"Oh, please not to do that! He will think I am afraid." Here were the Squire and Rivers on two sides of this question.

"Are you afraid, John? You were once frank with me about it."

"I do not think, Mr. Rivers, you ought to ask me that." He drew up his figure as he spoke.

The rector would have liked to have whistled — a rare habit with him when alone and not in one of his moods of depression. He said, "I beg your pardon, John," and felt that he had not only done no good, but had made a mistake.

John said, "I am greatly obliged, sir." When half-way home he went back and met Rivers at his gate.

"Well," said the rector, "left anything?"

"No, sir," said the boy, his young figure stiffening, his head up. "I wasn't honest, sir." And again with his old half-lost formal way, "I — I — you might have thought — I wasn't — quite honourable. I mean — I'll never be able to forgive that blackguard until I can — can get even with him. You see, sir?"

"Yes, I see," said Rivers, who did not see, or know for a moment what to say. "Well, think it over, John. He is more a rough cub than a blackguard. Think it over."

"Yes, sir," and John walked away.

The rector looked after the boy thinking — he's the Squire all over, with more imagination, a gentleman to the core. But how wonderfully changed, and in only eight months.

John was now, this July, allowed to ride with Leila when his uncle was otherwise occupied. He had been mounted on a safe old horse and was not spared advice from Leila, who enjoyed a little the position of mistress of equestrianism. She was slyly conscious of her comrade's mildly resentful state of mind.

"Don't pull on him so hard, John. The great thing is to get intimate with a horse's mouth. He's pretty rough, but if you wouldn't keep so stiff, you wouldn't feel it."

John began to be a little impatient. "Let us talk of something else than horses. I got a good dose of advice yesterday from Uncle Jim. I am afraid that you will be sent to school in the fall. I hate schools. You'll have no riding and snow-balling, and I shall miss you. You see, I was never friends with a girl before."

"Uncle Jim would never let me go."

"But Aunt Ann?" he queried. "I heard her tell Mr. Rivers that you must go. She said that you were too old, or would be, for snowballing and rough games and needed the society of young ladies."

"Young ladies!" said Leila scornfully. "We had two from Baltimore year before last. I happened to hit one of them in the eye with a snowball, and she howled worse than Billy when he plays bear."

"Oh, you'll like it after a while," he said, with anticipative wisdom, "but I shall be left to play with Tom. I want you to miss me. It is too horrid."

"I shall miss you; indeed, I shall. I suppose I am only a girl, but I won't forget what you did when that boy was rude. I used to think once you were like a girl and just afraid. I never yet thanked you," and she leaned over and laid a hand for a moment on his. "I believe you would n't be afraid now to do what I dared you to do."

He laughed. There had been many such dares. "Which dare was it, Leila?"

"Oh, to go at night — at night to the Indian graves. I tried it once and got half way —"

"And was scalped all the way back, I suppose."

"I was, John. Try it yourself."

"I did, a month after I came."

"Oh! and you never told me."

"No, why should I?"

It had not had for him the quality of bodily peril. It was somehow far less alarming. He had started with fear, but was of no mind to confess. They rode on in silence, until at last she said. "I hope you won't fight that boy again."

"Oh," he said, "I did n't mind it so very much."

She was hinting that he would again be beaten. "But I minded, John. I hated it."

He would say no more. He had now had, as concerned Tom,

three advisers. He kept his own counsel, with the not unusual
reticence of a boy. He did not wish to be pitied on account
of what he did not consider defeat, and wanted no one to discuss it. He was better pleased when a week later the English
groom talked to him after the boxing-lesson. "That fellow,
Tom, told me about your slapping him. He said that he did n't
want to lick you if you had n't hit him."

"It's not a thing I want to talk about, Sam. I had to hit
him and I did n't know how; that's all. Put on the gloves
again."

"There, that 'll do, sir. You 're light on your pins, and he 's
sort of slow. If you ever have to fight him, just remember that
and keep cool and keep moving."

The young boxing-tutor was silently of opinion that John
Penhallow would not be satisfied until he had faced Tom again.
John made believe, as we say, that he had no such desire. He
had, however, long been caressed and flattered into the belief
that he was important, and was, in his uncle's army phrase, to
be obeyed and respected accordingly by inferiors. His whole
life now for many months had, however, contributed experiences
contradictory to his tacitly accepted boy-views. Sometimes in
youth the mental development and conceptions of what seem
desirable in life appear to make abrupt advances without apparent bodily changes. More wholesomely and more rarely at
the plastic age characteristics strengthen and mind and body
both gather virile capacity. When John Penhallow met his
cousin on his first arrival, he was in enterprise, vigour, general
good sense and normal relation to life, really far younger than
Leila. In knowledge, mind and imagination, he was far
in advance. In these months he had passed her in the race of
life. He felt it, but in many ways was also dimly aware that
Leila was less expressively free in word and action, sometimes
to his surprise liking to be alone at the age when rare moods of
mild melancholy trouble the time of rapid female florescence.

There was still between them acceptance of equality, with on his part a certain growth of respectful consideration, on hers a gentle perception of his gain in manliness and of deference to his experience of a world of which she knew as yet nothing, but with some occasional resentment when the dominating man in the boy came to the surface. When his aunt praised his manners, Leila said, " He is n't always so very gentle." When his uncle laughed at his awkward horsemanship, she defended him, reminding her uncle, to his amusement, of her own early mishaps.

CHAPTER V

JOHN'S intimacy with the Squire prospered. Leila had been a gay comrade, but not as yet so interested as to tempt him to discussion of the confusing politics of the day. "She has not as yet a seeking mind," said the rector, who in the confessional of the evening pipe saw more and more plainly that this was a divided house. The Squire could not talk politics with Ann, his wife. She held a changeless belief in regard to slavery, a conviction of its value to owner and owned too positive to be tempted into discussing it with people who knew so little of it and did not agree with her. James Penhallow, like thousands in that day of grim self-questioning, had been forced to reconsider opinions long held, and was reaching conclusions which he learned by degrees made argument with the simplicity of his wife's political creed more and more undesirable. Leila was too young to be interested. The rector was intensely anti-slavery and saw but one side of the ominous questions which were bewildering the largest minds. The increasing interest in his nephew was, therefore, a source of real relief to the uncle. Meanwhile, the financial difficulties of the period demanded constant thought of the affairs of the mills and took him away at times to Philadelphia or Pittsburgh. Thus the summer ran on to an end. Buchanan and Breckenridge had been nominated and the Republicans had accepted Fremont and Dayton.

Birthdays were always pleasantly remembered at Grey Pine, and on September 20th, when John, aged sixteen, came down to breakfast, as he took his seat Ann came behind him and said as she kissed him, "You are sixteen to-day; here is my present."

The boy flushed with pleasure as he received a pair of silver spurs. " Oh! thank you, Aunt Ann," he cried as he rose.

" And here is mine," said Leila, and laughing asked with both hands behind her back, " Which hand, John? "

" Oh! both — both."

" No."

" Then the one nearest the heart." Some quick reflection passed through Ann Penhallow's mind of this being like an older man's humour.

Leila gave him a riding-whip. He had a moment's return of the grown-up courtesies he had been taught, and bowed as he thanked her, saying, " Now, I suppose, I am your knight, Aunt Ann."

" And mine," said Leila.

" I do not divide with any one," said Mrs. Ann. " Where is your present, James? "

He had kept his secret. " Come and see," he cried. He led them to the porch. " That is mine, John." A thorough-bred horse stood at the door, saddled and bridled. Ann thought the gift extravagant, but held her tongue.

" Oh, Uncle Jim," said John. His heart was too full for the words he wanted to say. " For me — for me." He knew what the gift meant.

" You must name him," said Leila. " I rode him once, John. He has no name. Uncle Jim said he should have no name until he had an owner. Now I know."

John stood patting the horse's neck. " Wasn't his mother a Virginia mare, James? " said Ann.

" Yes."

" Oh, then call him Dixy."

For a moment the Squire was of a mind to object, but said gaily, " By all means, Ann, call him Dixy if you like, and now breakfast, please." Here they heard Dixy's pedigree at length.

" Above all, Jack, remember that Dixy is of gentle birth;

make friends with him. He may misbehave; never, sir, lose your temper with him. Be wary of use of whip or spur."

There was more of it, until Mrs. Ann said, "Your coffee will be cold. It is one of your uncle's horse-sermons."

John laughed. How delightful it all was! "May I ride to-day with you, uncle?"

"Yes, I want to introduce you to — Dixy — yes —"

"And may I ride with you?" asked Leila.

"No, my dear," said the aunt, "I want you at home. There is the raspberry jam and currant jelly and tomato figs."

"Gracious, Leila, we shall not have a ride for a week."

"Oh, not that bad, John," said Mrs. Ann, "only two days and — and Sunday. After that you may have her, and I shall be glad to be rid of her. She eats as much as she preserves."

"Oh! Aunt Ann."

A few days went by, and as it rained in the afternoon there was no riding, but there was the swimming-pool, and for rain John now cared very little. On his way he met a half dozen village lads. They swam, and hatched (it was John's device) a bit of mischief involving Billy, who was fond of watching their sports when he was tired of doing chores about the stable. John heard of it later. The likelihood of unpleasant results from their mischief was discussed as they walked homeward. There were in all five boys from the village, with whom by this time John had formed democratic intimacies and moderate likings which would have shocked his mother. He had had no quarrels since long ago he had resented Tom McGregor's rudeness to Leila and had suffered the humiliation of defeat in his brief battle with the bigger boy. The easy victor, Tom, had half forgotten or ignored it, as boys do. Now as they considered an unpleasant situation, Joe Grace, the son of the Baptist preacher, broke the silence. He announced what was the general conclusion, halting for emphasis as he spoke.

"I say, fellows, there will be an awful row."

"That's so," said William, the butcher's son.

"Anyhow," remarked Ashton, whose father was a foreman at the mills, "it was great fun; did n't think Billy could run like that."

It will be observed that the young gentleman of ten months ago had become comfortably democratic in his associations and had shed much of his too-fine manners as the herding instincts of the boy made the society of comrades desirable when Leila's company was not attainable.

"Oh!" he said, "Billy can run, but I had none of the fun." Then he asked anxiously, "Did Billy get as far as the house?"

"You bet," said Baynton, the son of the carpenter, "I saw him, heard him shout to the Squire. Guess it's all over town by this time."

"Anyhow it was you, John, set it up," said a timid little boy, the child of the blacksmith.

"That's so," said Grace, "guess you'll catch it hot."

John considered the last spokesman with scorn as Tom, his former foe, said, "Shut up, Joe Grace, you were quick enough to go into it — and me too."

"Thanks," said John, reluctantly acknowledging the confession of partnership in the mischief, "I am glad one of you has a little — well, honour."

They went on their way in silence and left him alone. Nothing was said of the matter at the dinner-table, where to John's relief Mr. Rivers was a guest. John observed, however, that Mrs. Ann had less of her usual gaiety, and he was not much surprised when his uncle leaving the table said, "Come into the library, John." The Captain lighted his pipe and sat down.

"Now, sir," he said, "Billy is a poor witness. I desire to hear what happened."

The stiffened hardness of the speaker in a measure affected the boy. He stood for a moment silent. The Captain, impatient, exclaimed, " Now, I want the simple truth and nothing else."

The boy felt himself flush. " I do not lie, sir. I always tell the truth."

" Of course — of course," returned Penhallow. " This thing has annoyed me. Sit down and tell me all about it."

Rather more at his ease John said, " I went to swim with some of the village boys, sir. We played tag in the water —"

The Squire had at once a divergent interest, " Tag — tag — swimming? Who invented that game? Good idea — how do you play it? "

John a little relieved continued, " You see, uncle, you can dive to escape or come up under a fellow to tag him. It 's just splendid! " he concluded with enthusiasm.

Then the Captain remembered that this was a domestic court-martial, and self-reminded said, " The tag has nothing to do with the matter in question; go on."

" We got tired and sat on the bank. Billy was wandering about. He never can keep still. I proposed that I should hide in the bushes and the boys should tell Billy I was drowned."

" Indeed! "

" We went into the water; I hid in the bushes and the boys called out I was drowned. When Billy heard it, he gathered up all my clothes and my shoes, and before I could get out he just yelled, ' John 's drowned, I must take his clothes home to his poor aunt.' Then he ran. The last I heard was, ' He 's drowned, he 's drowned! ' "

" And then? "

" Well, the other fellows put on something and went after him; they caught him in the cornfield and took away my clothes. Then Billy ran to the house. That is all I know."

The Squire was suppressing his mirth. " Are n't you ashamed? "

" No, sir, but I am sorry."

" I don't like practical jokes. Billy kept on lamenting your fate. He might have told Leila or your aunt. Luckily I received his news, and no one else. You will go to Westways and say there is to be no swimming for a week in my pool."

" Yes, sir."

" You are not to ride Dixy or any other horse for ten days." This was terrible. " Now, be off with you, and tell Mr. Rivers to come in."

" Yes, sir."

When Rivers sat down, the Squire suppressing his laughter related the story. " The boy's coming on, Mark. He's Penhallow all over."

" But, Squire, by the boy's looks I infer you did not tell him that."

" Oh, hardly. I hate practical jokes, and I have stopped his riding for ten days."

" I suppose you are right," and they fell to talking politics and of the confusion of parties with three candidates in the field.

Mrs. Ann who suspected what had been the result of this court-martial was disposed towards pity, but John retired to a corner and a book and slipped away to bed early. Penalties he had suffered at school, but this was a terrible experience, and now he was to let the other boys know that the swimming-pool was closed for a week. At breakfast he made believe to be contented in mind, and asked in his best manner if his uncle had any errands for him in Westways or at the mills. When the Captain said no and remarked further that if he wished to walk, he would find the wood-roads cooler than the highway John expressed himself grateful for his advice with such a complete return of his formal manner as came near to unmasking the inner amusement which the Squire was getting from the evident annoyance he was giving Mrs. Ann, who thought that he was needlessly irritating a boy who to her mind was hurt and sore.

"Come, Leila," she said rising. "We may meet you in the village, John; and do get your hair cut, and see Mr. Spooner and tell him — no, I will write it."

John was pleased to feel that he had other reasons for visiting Westways than his uncle's order. He went down the avenue whistling, and in no hurry.

Leila had some dim comprehension of John's state of mind. Of Billy and of the Squire's court-martial she had heard from Mrs. Ann, and although that lady said little, the girl very well knew that her aunt thought her husband had been too severe. She stood on the porch, vaguely troubled for this comrade, and watched him as he passed from view, taking a short cut through the trees. The girl checked something like a sob as she went into the house.

It was the opinion of the county that Mrs. Penhallow was a right good woman and masterful; but of Leila the judgment of the village was that she was just sweet through and through. The rector said she radiated the good-nature of perfect health. What more there was time would show. Westways knew well these two young people, and Leila was simply Leila to nearly every one. "Quite time," reflected Mrs. Ann, "that she was Miss Leila." As she went with her through the town there were pleasant greetings, until at last they came to the butcher's. Mr. Pole, large after the way of his craft, appeared in a white apron. "Well, now, how you do grow, Leila."

"Not enough yet," said Leila.

"Fine day, Mrs. Penhallow." He was a little uneasy, divining her errand.

"Now, Pole, before I make a permanent change to the butcher at the mills, I wish to say that it is because a pound of beef weighs less at Grey Pine than in your shop."

At this time John was added to the hearers, being in search of William Pole with the Squire's order about the swimming. He waited until his aunt should be through. He was a little amused, which on the whole was, just then, good for him.

"Now ma'am, after all these years you won't drop me like that."

"Short weights are reason enough."

Leila listened, sorry for Pole, who reddened and replied, "Fact is, ma'am, I don't always do the weighing myself, and the boys they are real careless. What with Hannah's asthma keeping me awake and a lot of fools loafing around and talking politics, I do wonder I ever get things right. It's Fremont and it's Buchanan — a man can't tell what to do."

Mrs. Penhallow was not usually to be turned aside, and meant now to deal out even justice. But if the butcher knew it or not, she was offered what she liked and at home could not have. "I hope, Pole, you are not going to vote for Fremont."

"Well, ma'am, it ain't easy to decide. I've always followed the Squire." Ann Penhallow knew, alas! what this would mean.

"I've been thinking I'll stand to vote for Buchanan. Was you wanting a saddle of lamb to-day? I have one here, and a finer I never saw."

"Well, Pole, keep your politics and your weights in order. Send me the lamb."

The butcher smiled as Mrs. Ann turned away. Whether the lady of Grey Pine was conscious of having bought a vote or not, it was pretty clear to her nephew that Peter Pole's weights would not be further questioned as long as his politics were Democratic.

When his aunt had gone, John called Bill Pole out of the shop and said, "There's to be no swimming for a week, for any of us. Where are the other fellows?"

"Guessed we would catch it. They're playing ball back of the church. I'll go along with you."

He was pleased to see how the others would take their deprivation of a swim in the September heat. They came on the other culprits, who called to John to come and play. He was not so minded and was in haste to get through with a disagreeable errand. As he hesitated, Pole eager to distribute the unpleasant news cried out, " The Squire says that we can't swim in the pool for a week — none of us. How do you fellows like that ? "

" It 's mighty mean of him."

" What 's that ? " said John. " He was right and you know it. I don't like it any better than you do — but —"

Bill Baynton, the youngest boy, broke in, " Who told the Squire what fellows was in it ? "

" It was n't Billy," said another lad; " he just kept on yelling you was dead."

" Look here," said Tom McGregor turning to John, " did you tell the Squire we fellows set it up ? "

John was insulted. He knew well the playground code of honour, but remembered in time his boxing-master's advice, the more mad you are the cooler you keep yourself. He replied in his old formal way, " The question is one you have no right to ask; it is an insult."

To the boys the failure to say " no " meant evasion. " Then, of course, you told," returned the older lad. " If I was n't afraid you 'd run home and complain, I 'd spank you."

It had been impossible for John to be angry with his uncle, although the punishment and the shame of carrying the news to the other boys he felt to be a too severe penalty. But here was cause for letting loose righteous anger. He had meant to wait, having been wisely counselled by his boxing-master to be in no haste to challenge his enemy, until further practice had made success possible; but now his rising wrath overcame his prudence, " Well, try it," he said. " You beat me once. If you think I 'll tell if I am licked, I assure you, you are safe. I took the whole blame about Billy and I was asked no names."

Tom hesitated and said, " I never heard that."

" I will accept an apology," said John in his most dignified way. The boys laughed. John flushed a little, and as Tom remained silent added, " If you won't, then lick me if you can."

As he spoke, he slipped off his coat and rolled up his sleeves. The long lessons in self-defence had given him some confidence and, what was as useful, had developed chest and arms.

" Hit him, Tom," said the small boy. In a moment the fight was on, the non-combatants delighted.

To Tom's surprise his wild blows somehow failed to get home. It was characteristic of John then as in later days that he became cool as he realized his danger, while Tom quite lost his head as the success of the defence disappointed his attack. To hit hard, to rush in and throw his enemy, was all he had of the tactics of offence. The younger lad, untouched, light on his feet, was continually shifting his ground; then at last he struck right and left. He had not weight enough to knock down his foe, but as Tom staggered, John leaped aside and felt the joy of battle as he got in a blow under the ear and Tom fell.

" Get on him — hit him," cried the boys. " By George, if he ain't licked ! "

John stood still. Tom rose, and as he made a furious rush at the victor, a loud voice called out, " Halloa ! quit that."

Both boys stood still as Mark Rivers climbed over the fence and stood between them. John was not sorry for the interruption. He was well aware that in the rough and tumble of a close he had not weight enough to encounter what would have lost him the fight he had so far won. He stood still panting, smiling, and happy.

" Had n't you boys better shake hands ? " said the rector. Tom, furious, was collecting blood from his nose on his handkerchief. Neither boy spoke. " Well, John," said Rivers waiting.

" I 'll shake hands, sir, when Tom apologizes."

The rector smiled. Apologies were hardly understood as endings to village fights. " He won't do it," said John with a glance at the swollen face ; " another time I 'll make him."

"Will you!" exclaimed Tom.

The rector felt that on the whole it might have been better had they fought it out. Now the peacemaking business was clearly not blessed. "You are a nice pair of young Christians," he said. "At all events, you shall not fight any more to-day. Come, John."

The boy put on his jacket and went away with Rivers, who asked presently what was this about. "Mr. Rivers, soon after I came that fellow was rough to Leila; I hit him, and he beat me like — like a dog."

"And you let all these suns go down upon your wrath?"

"There wasn't any wrath, sir. He wouldn't apologize to Leila; he wouldn't do it."

"Oh! indeed."

"Then he said something to-day about Uncle Jim."

"Anything else?"

"Yes, he made it pretty clear that he thought me a liar."

"Well, but you knew you were not."

"Yes, sir, but he didn't appear to know."

"Do you think you convinced him?"

"No, sir, but I feel better."

"Ah! is that so? Morally better, John?" and he laughed as he bade him good-bye.

The lad who left him was tired, but entirely satisfied with John Penhallow. He went to the stable and had a technical talk with the English groom, who deeply regretted not to have seen the fight.

There being no riding or swimming to fill the time, he took a net, some tackle and a bucket, and went down to the river and netted a "hellbender." He put him in a bucket of water and carried him to the stable, where he was visited by Leila and Rivers, and later departed this life, much lamented. In the afternoon, being in a happy mood, John easily persuaded Leila to abandon her ride, and walk with him.

When they sat down beside the Indian graves, to his surprise she suddenly shifted the talk and said, " John, who would you vote for? I asked Aunt Ann, and she said, ' Buchanan, of course '; and when I asked Uncle Jim, he said, ' Fremont '; but I want to understand. I saw in the paper that it was wicked to keep slaves, but my cousins in Maryland have slaves; it can't be wicked."

" Would you like to be bought and sold? " he said.

" But, I am not black, John."

" I believe old Josiah was a slave."

" Every one knows that. Why did he run away, John? "

" Because he wanted to be free, I suppose, and not have to work without pay."

" And don't they pay slaves? " asked Leila.

" No, they don't." John felt unable to make clear to her why the two people they respected and loved never discussed what the village talked about so freely. These intelligent children were in the toils of a question which was disturbing the consciences and the interests of a continent. The simpler side was clear to both of them. The idea of selling the industrious old barber was as yet enough to settle their politics.

" Aunt Ann must have good reasons," said John. " Mr. Rivers says she is the most just woman he ever knew." It puzzled him. " I suppose we are too young to understand."

" Aunt Ann will never talk about slaves. I asked her last week."

" But Uncle Jim will talk, and he likes to be asked when we are alone. I don't believe in slavery."

" It seems so queer, John, to own a man."

John grinned, " Or a girl, Leila."

" Well, no one owns me, I tell you; they 'd have a hard time."

She shook what Rivers called her free-flowing cascade of hair in the pride of conscious freedom. The talk ran on. At last she said, " I 'll tell you a queer thing. I heard Mr. Rivers say to uncle — I heard him say, we were all slaves. He said that no one owns himself. I think that's silly," said the young philosopher, "don't you, John?"

"I don't know," returned John; "I think it's a big puzzle. Let's go."

No word reached the Squire of the battle behind the church until four days later, when Rivers came in after dinner and found Penhallow in his library deep in thought.

"Worried, Squire?" he asked.

"Yes, affairs are in a bad way and will be until the election is over. It always disturbs commerce. The town will go Democratic, I suppose."

"Yes, as I told you, unless you take a hand and are in earnest and outspoken."

"I could be, but it has not yet the force of imperative duty, and it would hurt Ann more than I feel willing to do. Talk of something else. She would cease her mild canvass if she thought it annoyed me."

"I see — sir. I think I ought to tell you that John has had another battle with Tom McGregor."

"Indeed?" The Squire sat up, all attention. "He does not show any marks of it."

"No, but Tom does."

"Indeed! What happened?"

"Well, I believe, Tom thought John told you what boys were in that joke on Billy. I fancy something was said about you — something personal, which John resented."

"That is of no moment. What else? I ought to be clear about it."

"Well, Squire, Tom was badly mauled and John was tired when I arrived as peacemaker. I stopped the battle, but he was not at all disposed to talk about it. I am sure of one thing — he has had a grudge against Tom — since he was rude to Leila."

The Squire rose and walked about the room. "H'm! very

strange that — what a mere child he was when he got licked — boys don't remember injuries that way." Then seeming to become conscious of Rivers' presence, he stopped beside him and added, "What with my education and Leila's, he has grown amazingly. He was as timid as a foal."

"He is not now, Squire, and John has been as useful mentally to Leila. She is learning to think."

"Sorry for it, Mark, women ought not to think. Now if my good Ann would n't think, I should be the happier."

"My dear Squire," said Rivers, setting an affectionate hand on his arm, "my dear Mrs. Penhallow does n't think, except about the every-day things of life. Her politics and religion are sacred beliefs not to be rudely jostled by the disturbance of thinking. If there is illness, debt or trouble, at the mills or in Westways, she becomes seraphic and intelligent enough."

"Yes, Rivers, and if I put before her, as I sometimes do, a perplexing business matter, I am surprised at her competence. Of course, she is as able as you or I to reason, but on one subject she does not reason or believe that it admits of discussion; and by Heaven! my friend, I am sometimes ashamed to keep out of this business. So far as this State is concerned, it is hopeless. You know, dear friend, what you have been to us, and that to no other man on earth could I speak as I have done to you; but Mark, if things get worse — and they will — what then? John asked me what we should do if the Southern States did really secede. Things seem to stick in his mind like burrs — he was at it again next day."

Rivers smiled. "Like me, I suppose."

"Yes, Mark. He is persistent about everything — lessons, sports, oh! everything; an uncomfortably curious lad, too. These Southern opinions about reclaiming a man's slaves bother the boy. He reads my papers, and how can I stop him? I don't want to. There! we are at it again."

"Yes, there is no escape from these questions."

" And he has even got Leila excited and she wants to know —
I told her to ask Ann Penhallow — I have not heard of the result. Well, you are going. Good-night."

The Squire sat still in the not very agreeable company of his thoughts. Leila was to go to school this September, Buchanan's election in November was sure, and John — He had come to love the lad, and perhaps he had been too severe. Then he thought of the boy's fight and smiled. The rector and he had disagreed. Was it better for boys to abuse one another or to settle things by a fight? The rector had urged that his argument for the ordeal of battle would apply with equal force to the duel of men. He had said, " No, boys do not kill; and after all even the duel has its values." Then the rector said he was past praying for and had better read the Decalogue.

When next day Mark Rivers was being shaved by the skilled hand of Josiah, he heard the voice of his friend and fishing-companion, the Rev. Isaac Grace, " What about the trout-brook this afternoon? "

" Of course," said Mark, moveless under the razor. " Call for me at five."

" Seen yesterday's *Press?* "

" No. I can't talk, Grace."

" This town's all for Buchanan and Breckenridge. How will the Squire vote? "

" Ask him. Take care, Josiah."

" If the Squire isn't taking any active part, Mrs. Penhallow is. She is taking a good deal of interest in the roof of my chapel and — and — other things."

The rector did not like it. " I can't talk, Grace."

" But I can."—" Well," thought the rector, " for an intelligent man you are slow at taking hints." The good-natured rotund preacher went on, amazing his helpless friend, " I wonder if the Squire would like her canvassing —"

" Ask him."

"Guess not. She's a good woman, but not just after the fashion of St. Paul's women."

"She hasn't done no talking to me," said Josiah, chuckling. "There, sir, I'm through."

Then the released rector said, "If you talk politics again to me for the next two months, Grace, I will never tie for you another trout-fly. Your turn," and he left the chair to Grace, who sat down saying with the persistency of the good-humoured and tactless, "If I want a roof to my chapel, I've got to keep out of talking Republican politics, that's clear —"

"And several other things," returned Mark sharply.

"Such as," said Grace, but the rector had gone and Josiah was lathering the big red face.

"Got to make believe sometimes, sir," said Josiah. "She's an uncommon kind lady, and the pumpkins she gives me are fine. A fellow's got time to think between this and November. Pumpkins and leaky roofs do make a man kind of thoughtful." He grinned approval of his own wisdom. "Now don't talk, sir. Might chance to cut you."

This sly unmasking of motives, his own and those of others, was disagreeable to the good little man who was eager to get his chapel roofed and no more willing than Mrs. Penhallow to admit that how he would vote had anything to do with the much needed repairs. His people were poor and the leaks were becoming worse and worse. He kept his peace, and the barber smiling plied the razor.

Now the Squire paused at the open door, where he met his nephew. "Come to get those scalp-locks trimmed, John? They are perilously long. If you were to get into a fight and a fellow got hold of them, you would have a bad time." Then as his uncle went away laughing, John knew that the Squire must have heard of his battle from Mark Rivers. He did not like it. Why he did not know or ask himself, being as yet too immature for such self-analysis.

Mr. Grace got up clean-shaven, adjusted a soiled paper-collar, and said, "Good-morning, John. I am sorry to hear that a Christian lad like you should be fighting. I am sure that neither Mr. Rivers nor your aunt would approve of it. My son told me about it, and I think it my duty —"

John broke in, "Then your son is a tell-tale, Mr. Grace, and allow me to say that this is none of his business. When I am insulted, I resent it." To be chaffed by his own uncle when under sentence of a court-martial had not been agreeable, but this admonition was unendurable. He entered the shop.

"Well, I never," exclaimed the preacher, as John went by him.

The barber was laughing. "Set down, Mr. John."

"I suppose the whole of Westways knows it, Mr. Josiah?"

"They do, sir. Wish I 'd seen it."

"Damn!" exclaimed John, swearing for the first time in his life. "Cut my hair short, please, and don't talk."

"No, sir. You ain't even got a scratch."

"Oh, do shut up," said John. There was a long silence while the curly locks fell.

"You gave it to the Baptist man hot. I don't like him. He calls me Joe. It is n't respectable. My name 's Josiah."

"Have n't you any other name?" said John, having recovered his good-humour.

"Yes, sir, but I keeps that to myself."

"But why?" urged John.

Josiah hesitated. "Well, Mr. John, I ran away, and — so it was best to get a new name."

"Indeed! Of course, every one knows you must have run away — but no one cares."

"Might say I was run away with — can't always hold a horse," he laughed aloud in a leisurely way. "When he took me over the State-line, I did n't go back."

"I see," said John laughing, as he rose and paid the barber. The cracked mirror satisfied him that he was well shorn.

"You looks a heap older now you're shorn. Makes old fellows look younger — ever notice that?"

"No."

Then Josiah, of a sudden wisely cautious, said, "You won't tell Mrs. Penhallow, nor no one, about me, what I said?"

"Of course not; but why my aunt, Mr. Josiah? She, like my uncle, must know you ran away."

When John first arrived the black barber's appearance so impressed the lad that he spoke to him as Mr. Josiah, and seeing later how much this pleased him continued in his quite courteous way to address him now and then as Mr. Josiah. The barber liked it. He hesitated a moment before answering.

"You needn't talk about it if you don't want to," said John.

"Guess whole truth's better than half truth — nothin' makes folk curious like knowin' half. When I first came here, I guessed I'd best change my name, so I said I was Josiah. Fact is, Mr. John, I didn't know Mrs. Penhallow came from Maryland till I had been here quite a while and got to like the folks and the Captain."

John's experience was enlarging. He could hardly have realized the strange comfort the black felt in his confession. What it all summed up for Josiah in the way of possible peril of loss of liberty John presently had made plain to him. He was increasingly urgent in his demand for answers to the many questions life was bringing. The papers he read had been sharp schoolmasters, and of slave life he knew nothing except from his aunt's pleasant memories of plantation life when a girl on a great Maryland manor. That she could betray to servitude the years of grey-haired freedom seemed to John incredible of the angel of kindly helpfulness. He stood still in thought, troubled by his boy-share of puzzle over a too mighty problem.

Josiah, a little uneasy, said, "What was you thinkin', Mr. John?"

The young fellow replied smiling, "Do you think Aunt Ann would hurt anybody? Do you think she would send word to some one — to take you back? Anyhow she can't know who was your master."

The old black nodded slowly, "Mr. John, she born mistress and I born slave; she can't help it — and they was good people too — all the people that owned me. They liked me too. I did n't have to work except holdin' horses and trainin' colts — and housework. They was always kind to me."

"But why did you run away?"

"Well, Mr. John, it was sort of sudden. You see ever since I could remember there was some one to say, Cæsar you do this, or you go there. One day when I was breakin' a colt, Mr. Woodburn says to me — I was leanin' against a stump — how will that colt turn out? I said, I don't know, but I did. It was n't any good. My mind was took up watchin' a hawk goin' here and there over head like he was enjoyin' hisself. Then — then it come over me — that he 'd got no boss but God. It got a grip on me like —" The lad listened intently.

"You wanted to be free like the hawk."

"I don't quite know — never thought of it before — might have seen lots of hawks. I ain't never told any one."

"Are you glad to be free?"

"Ah, kind of half glad, sir. I ain't altogether broke in to it. You see I 'm old for change."

As he ended, James Penhallow reappeared. "Got through, John? You look years older. Your aunt will miss those curly locks." He went into the shop as John walked away, leaving Josiah who would have liked to add a word more of caution and who nevertheless felt somehow a sense of relief in having made a confession the motive force of which he would have found it impossible to explain.

John asked himself no such question as he wandered deep in boy-thought along the broken line of the village houses. Josiah's confidence troubled and yet flattered him. His imagination was captured by the suggested idea of the wild freedom of the hawk. He resolved to be careful, and felt more and more that he had been trusted with a secret involving danger.

While John wandered away, the barber cut the Squire's hair, and to his surprise Josiah did not as usual pour out his supply of village gossip.

CHAPTER VI

I T was now four days since John's sentence had been pronounced, and not to be allowed to swim in the heat of a hot
September added to the severity of the penalty. The heat as
usual made tempers hot and circumstances variously disturbed
the household of Grey Pine. Politics vexed and business
troubled the master. Of the one he could not talk to his wife —
of the other he would not at present, hoping for better business
conditions, and feeling that politics and business were now too
nearly related to keep them apart. Ann, his wife, thought him
depressed — a rare mood for him. Perhaps it was the unusual
moist heat. He said, " Yes, yes, dear, one does feel it." She
did not guess that the obvious unhappiness of the lad who had
won the soldier's heart was being felt by Penhallow without his
seeing how he could end it and yet not lessen the value of a just
verdict.

Of all those concerned Leila was the one most troubled. On
this hot afternoon she saw John disappear into the forest.
When Mrs. Ann came out on the porch where she had for a minute left the girl, she saw her sewing-bag on a chair and caught
sight of the flowing hair and agile young figure as she set a hand
on the low stone wall of the garden and was over and lost among
the trees. " Leila, Leila," cried Mrs. Ann, " I told you to
finish —" It was useless. " Everything goes wrong to-day,"
she murmured. " Well, school will civilize that young barbarian, and she must have longer skirts." This was a sore subject and Leila had been vainly rebellious.

Meanwhile the flying girl overtook John, who had things to
think about and wished to be alone. " Well," he said, with some
impatience, " what is it?"

"Oh, I just wanted a walk, and don't be cross, John."

He looked at her, and perhaps for the first time had the male perception of the beauty of the disordered hair, the pleading look of the blue eyes, and the brilliant colour of the eager flushed face. It was the hair — the wonderful hair. She threw it back as she stood. No one could long be cross to Leila. Even her resolute aunt was sometimes defeated by her unconquerable sweetness.

"I am so sorry for you, John," she said.

"Well, I am not, Leila, if you mean that Uncle Jim was hard on me."

"Yes, he was, and I mean to tell him — I do."

"Please not." She said nothing in the way of reply, but only, "Let us go and see the spring."

"Well, come along."

They wandered far into the untouched forest. "Ah! here it is," she cried. A spring of water ran out from among the anchoring roots of a huge black spruce. He stood gazing down at it.

"Oh, Leila, isn't it wonderful?"

"Were you never here before, John?"

"No, never. It seems as if it was born out of the tree. No wonder this spruce grew so tall and strong. How cold it must keep the old fellow's toes."

"What queer ideas you have, John." She had not yet the gift of fancy, long denied to some in the emergent years of approaching womanhood. "I am tired, John," she said, as she dropped with hands clasped behind her head and hidden in the glorious abundance of darkening red hair, which lay around her on the brown pine-needles like the disordered aureole of some careless-minded saint.

John said, "It is this terrible heat. I never before heard you complain of being tired."

"Oh, it's just nice tired." She lay still, comfortable, with open eyes staring up at the intense blue of the September sky seen through the wide-cast limbs of pine and spruce. The little rill, scarce a finger thickness of water, crawled out lazily between the roots and trickled away. The girl was in empty-minded enjoyment of the luxury of complete relaxation of every muscle of her strong young body. The spring was noiseless, no leaf was astir in all the forest around them. The girl lay still, a part of the vast quietness.

John Penhallow stood a moment, and then said, " Good gracious! Leila, your eyes are blue." It was true. When big eyes are wide open staring up at the comrade blue of the deep blue sky, they win a certain beauty of added colour like little quiet lakelets under the azure sky when no wind disturbs their power of reflecting capture.

" Oh, John, and didn't you know my eyes were blue? " She spoke with languid interest in the fact he announced.

" But," he said, looking down at her as he stood, " they're so — so very blue."

" Oh, all the Greys have blue eyes."

He laughed gentle laughter and dropped on the pine-needles of the forest floor. The spring lay between them. He felt, as she did not, the charm of the stillness. He wanted to find words in which to put his desire for expression. She broke into his mood of imaginative seekings.

" How cold it is," she said, gathering the water in the cup of her hand, and then with both hands did better and got a refreshing drink.

" That makes a better cup," he said. " Let us follow the water to the river."

" It never gets there. It runs into Lonesome Man's swamp, and that's the end of him."

" Who, Lonesome Man or the spring? And who was Lonesome Man? "

"Nobody knows. What does it matter?"

He watched her toy with the new-born rill, a mere thread of water, build a Lilliputian dam, and muddle the clear outflow as it broke, and then build again. He had the thought that she had suddenly become younger, more like a child, and he himself older.

"Why don't you talk, John?" she said.

"I can't. I am wondering about that Lonesome Man and what the trees are thinking. Don't you feel how still it is? It's disrespectful to gabble before your betters." He felt it and said it without affectation, but as usual his mood of wandering thought failed to interest Leila.

"I hate it when it's quiet! I like to hear the wind howl in the pines —"

He expressed his annoyance. "You never want to talk anything but horses and swimming. Wait till you come back next spring with long skirts — such a nice well-behaved Miss Grey." He was, in familiar phrase, out of sorts, with a bit of will to annoy a disappointing companion. His mild effort had no success.

"Oh, John, it's awful! You ought to be sorry for me. The more you grow up the more your skirts grow down. Bother their manners! Who cares! Let's go home. It feels just as if it was Sunday."

"It is, in the woods. Well, come along." He walked on in the silence, she thinking of that alarming prospect of school, and he of the escaped slave's secret and, what struck the boy most — the hawk. Never before had he been told anything which was to be sacredly guarded from others. It gave him now a pleasant feeling of having been trusted. Suppose Leila had been told such a thing, how would she feel, and Aunt Ann? He was like a man who has too large a deposit in a doubtful bank. He was vaguely uneasy lest he might tell or in some way betray his sense of possessing a person's confidence.

As they came near the house, Leila said, " Catch me, I 'll run you home."

" Tag," he cried.

As they came to the side porch, Ann Penhallow said, " Finish that handkerchief — now, at once. It is time you were taught other than tom-boy ways."

John went by into the house. After dinner the Squire had his usual game of whist, always to the dissatisfaction of Leila, whose thoughts wandered like birds on the wing, from twig to twig. John usually played far better, but just now worse than his cousin, and forgot or revoked, to his uncle's disgust. A man of rather settled habits, now as usual Penhallow went to his library for the company of the pipe, which Ann disliked, and the *Tribune,* which she regarded as the organ of Satanic politics. Seeing both John and her aunt absorbed in their books, Leila passed quickly back of them, opened the library door, and said softly, " May I come in, Uncle Jim ? "

During the last few days he had missed, and he well knew why, John's visits and intelligent questions. Leila was welcome. " Why, of course, pussy cat. Come in. Shut the door ; your aunt dislikes the pipe smoke. Sit down." For some reason she desired to stand. " Don't stand," he said, " sit down on my knee." She obeyed. " There," he said, " that 's comfy. How heavy you are. Good gracious, child ! what am I to do without you ? "

" Is n't it awful, Uncle Jim."

" It is — it is. What do you want, my dear ? Anything wrong with the horses ? "

" No, sir. It 's — John —"

" Oh ! it 's John. Well, what is it ? "

" It is n't John — it 's John and the horses — I mean John and Dixy. Patrick rides Dixy for exercise every day."

" Well, what 's the matter ? First it 's John, then Dixy, then John and Dixy, and then John and Dixy and Pat."

The girl saw through the amusement he had in teasing her and said with gravity, "I wish you would be serious, Uncle Jim. I want five minutes of uninterrupted attention."

The Squire exploded, "Good gracious! that is Ann Grey all over. You must have heard her say it."

"I did, and you listen, too. Sometimes you don't, Uncle Jim. I guess you were n't well broke when you were young."

"Great Scott! you minx! Some day a girl I know will have to stand at attention. Go ahead."

"Pat's ruining Dixy's mouth. You ought to see him sawing at the curb. You always rode him on the snaffle."

"That boy Pat needs a good licking, Leila."

"But Dixy don't. The fact is, Uncle Jim, you 're neglecting the stables for politics."

"Is that your own wisdom, Miss Grey? What with the weight of wisdom and years, you 're getting heavy. Try a chair."

"No, I 'm quite comfy. It was Josiah who told me. He often comes up to look over the colts, of a Sunday —"

"Nice work for Sunday, Miss Grey."

She made no direct reply. "He told me that horse ought to be ridden by — by John or you, and no one else. He says the way to ruin a horse is to have a lot of people ride him like Pat — they 're just spoiling Dixy —"

"What! in four days? Nonsense."

"But," said the counsel in the case, "it 's to be ten. It is n't about John, it 's Dixy's mouth, uncle."

"Oh, you darling little liar!" Here she kissed him and was silent. "It won't do," he said. "There 's no logic in a kiss. Miss Grey. First comes Ann Grey and says, too much army discipline; and then you tell me what that gossiping old darkey says, and then you try the final argument — a kiss. Can't do it. There will be an end of all discipline. I hate practical jokes. There!"

If he thought to finish the matter thus, he much undervalued the ingenuity and persistency of the young Portia who was now conducting the case.

"Suppose you take a chair, Miss Grey. It is rather warm to provide permanent human seats for stout young women —"

"I'm not stout," said Leila with emphasis, accepting the hint by dropping with coiled legs upon a cushion at his feet. "I'm not stout. I weigh one hundred and thirty and a half pounds. And oh! is n't it hot. I have n't had a swim for — oh, at least five days counting Sunday." The pool was kept free until noon for Leila and her aunt.

"Why did n't you swim?" he asked lightly, being too intellectually busy clearing his pipe to see where the leading counsel was conducting him.

"Why, Uncle Jim, I would n't swim if John was n't allowed too; I just could n't. I'm going to bed — but, please, don't let Pat ride Dixy."

"I can attend to my stables, Miss Grey. John won't die of heat for want of a swim. You don't seem to concern yourself with those equally overbaked young scamps in Westways."

"Uncle Jim, you're just real mean to-night. Josiah told me yesterday that my cousin beat Tom McGregor because he said it was mean of you to stop the swimming. John said it was just, and Tom said he was a liar, and — oh, my! John licked him — wish I'd seen it."

This was news quite to his liking. He made no reply, lost in wonder over the ways of the mind male and female.

"You ought to be ashamed, you a girl, to want to see a fight. It's time you went to school. Is n't the rector on the porch? I thought I heard him."

Now, of late Leila had got to that stage of the game of thought-interchange when the young proudly use newly acquired word-counters. "I think, Uncle Jim, you're — you're irreverent."

The Squire shut the door on all outward show of mirth, and

said gravely, "Isn't it pronounced irrelevant, my dear Miss Malaprop?"

"Yes — yes," said Leila. "That's a word John uses. It's just short for 'flying the track'!"

"Any other stable slang, Leila?"

He was by habit averse to changing his decisions, and outside of Ann Penhallow's range of authority the Squire's discipline was undisputed and his decrees obeyed. He had been pleased and gaily amused for this half hour, but was of a mind to leave unchanged the penalties he had inflicted.

"Are you through with this nonsense, Leila?" he said as he rose. "Is this an ingenious little game set up between you and John?" To his utter amazement she began to cry.

"By George!" he said, "don't cry," which is what a kind man always says when presented with the riddle of tears.

She drew a brown fist across her wet cheeks and said indignantly, "My cousin is a gentleman."

She turned to go by him. "No, dear, wait a moment." He held her arm.

"Please, let me go. When John first came, you said he was a prig — and if he would just do some boy-mischief and kick up his heels like a two-year-old with some fun in him — you said he was a sort of girl-boy —" There were for punctuation sobs and silences.

"And where did you get all this about a prig?" he broke in, amazed.

"Oh, I heard you tell Aunt Ann. And now," said Portia, "the first time he does a real nice jolly piece of mischief you come down on him like — like a thousand of bricks." Her slang was reserved for the Squire, as he well knew.

The blue eyes shining with tears looked up from under the glorious disorder of the mass of hair. It was too much for the man.

"How darned logical you are!" He acknowledged some consciousness of having been inconsistent. He had said one thing and done another. "You are worse than your aunt." Then Leila knew that Ann Penhallow had talked to the Squire. "Well," he said, "what's your opinion, Miss Grey?"

"I think you're distanced."

"What — what! Wait a little. You may tell that young man to ride when he pleases and to swim, and to tell those scamps it's too hot to deprive them of the use of the pool. There, now get out!"

"But — Uncle Jim — I — can't. Oh, I really can't. You've got to do it yourself." This he much disliked to do.

"I hear your aunt calling. Mr. Rivers is going."

She kissed him. "Now, don't wait, Uncle Jim, and don't scold John. He's been no use for these four days. Good-night," and she left him.

"Well, well," he said, "I suppose I've got to do it."

He found Ann alone.

"About John! I can't stand up against you two. He is to be let off about the riding and swimming. I think you may find it pleasant to tell him, my dear."

She said gravely, "It will come with more propriety from you; but I do think you are right." Then he knew that he had to do it himself.

"Very well, dear," he said. "How that girl is developing. It is time she had other company than John, but Lord! how I shall miss her —"

"And I, James."

He went out for the walk he generally took before bed-time. She lingered, putting things in order on her work-table, wondering what Leila could have said to thus influence a man the village described as "set in his ways." She was curious to know, but not of a mind to question Leila. Before going to bed, she went to her own sitting-room on the left of the hall. It was sacred to domestic and church business. It held a few books and was secured by long custom from men's tobacco smoke. She sat down and wrote to her cousin, George Grey.

"DEAR GEORGE: If politics do not keep you, we shall look for you this month. There are colts to criticize and talk over, Leila is eager to see her unknown cousin before she goes to school near Baltimore this September.

"I believe this town will go for Buchanan, but I am not sure. James and I, as you know, never talk politics. I am distressed to believe as I do that he will vote for Fremont; that 'the great, the appalling issue,' as Mr. Buchanan says, 'is union or disunion' does not seem to affect him. I read Forney's paper, and James reads that wild abolition *Tribune*. It is very dreadful, and I am without any one I can talk to. My much loved rector is an extreme antislavery man.

"Yours always,

"ANN PENHALLOW.

"I am not at all sure of you. Be certain to let us know when to expect you. You know you are — well, I leave your social conscience to say what.

"Yours sincerely,

"ANN PENHALLOW."

At breakfast Ann Penhallow sat down to the coffee-urn distributing cheerful good-mornings. The Squire murmured absently over his napkin, "May the Lord make us thankful for this and all the blessings of life." He occasionally varied his grace, and sometimes to Ann's amazement. Why should he ask to be made thankful, she reflected. These occasional slips and variations on the simple phrase of gratitude she had come to recognize as signs of preoccupation, and now glanced at her husband, anxious always when he was concerned. Then, as he turned to John, she understood that between his trained belief in the usefulness of inexorable discipline and an almost womanly

tenderness of affection the heart had somehow won. She knew
him well and at times read with ease the signs of distress and
annoyance or resolute decision. Usually he was gay and merry
at breakfast, chaffing the children and eating with the appetite
of a man who was using and renewing his tissues in a wholesome way. Now he was silent, absent, and ate little. He was
the victim of a combination of annoyances. Had he been wise
to commit himself to a reversal of his sentence? Other and
more important matters troubled him, but as usual where bothers
come in battalions it is the lesser skirmishers who are felt for
the moment.

"I see in the hall, Ann," he said, "a letter for George Grey
— I will mail it. When does he come?"

"I do not know."

"John," he said, "you will oblige me by riding to the mill
and asking Dr. McGregor to come to Westways and see old
Josiah. Of course, he will charge it to me." The Squire was
a little ashamed of this indirect confession of retreat.

John looked up, hesitated a moment, and said, "What horse,
sir?"

"Dixy, of course."

"Another cup, James," said Mrs. Ann tranquilly amused.

John rose, went around the table to his uncle, and said in
his finest manner, "I am greatly obliged, sir."

"Oh, nonsense! He's rather fresh, take care."

Then Leila said, "It's very hot, Uncle Jim."

"You small fiend," said Penhallow. "Hot! On your way.
John, tell those rascals at Westways they may use the pond."
The faint smile on Ann Penhallow's face somehow set the whole
business in an agreeably humorous light. The Squire broke
into the relief of laughter and rose saying, "Get out of this,
all of you, if you want to keep your scalps."

John went to the stable not quite pleased. He had felt that
his punishment for a boy-frolic and the unexpected results of

Billy's alarm had been pretty large. His aunt had not said so to him, but had made it clear to her husband that the penalty was quite disproportioned to the size of the offence; a remark which had made him the more resolute not to disturb the course of justice; and now this chit of a girl had made him seem like an irresolute fool, and he would have to explain to Rivers, who would laugh. As he went out of the hall-door, he felt a pretty rough little paw in his hand and heard a whisper. "You're just the dearest thing ever was."

Concerning John Penhallow, it is to be said that he did not understand why he was let off so easily. He had a suspicion that Leila was somehow concerned, and also the feeling that he would rather have suffered to the end. However, it would be rather good fun to announce this swimming-permit to the boys.

Seeing from his shop door John riding down the avenue, Josiah came limping across the road. He leaned on the gate facing the boy and looking over the horse and rider with the pleasure of one who, as the Squire liked to say, knew when horse-flesh and man-flesh were suitably matched.

"Girth's a bit slack, Master John. Always look it over, sir, before you mount."

"Thanks, Josiah. Open the gate, please. How lame you are. I am to send the doctor to look after you and Peter Lamb."

The big black man opened the gate and adjusted the girth. "That's right now. I've got the worst rheumatics I ever did have. Peter Lamb's sick too. That's apple-whisky. The Squire's mighty patient with that man, because his mother nursed the Squire when he was a baby. They're near of an age, but you would n't think it to look at Peter and the Captain; whisky does hurry up Old Time a lot." And so John got the town gossip. "I ain't no faith in doctorin' rheumatics; would n't have him now if I had n't lost my old buck-eye. My rabbit-foot's turned grey this week. That's a sign of trouble."

John laughed and rode from the gate on which Leila had invited him to indulge in the luxury of swinging. It seemed years ago since she had sung to his astonishment the lyric of the gate. She appeared to him now not much older. And how completely he felt at home. He rode along the old pike through Westways, nodding to Mrs. Lamb, the mother of the scamp whom the Squire was every now and then saving from the consequences of the combination of a revengeful nature and bad whisky. Then Billy hailed John with malicious simplicity.

"Halloa! — John — can't swim — can't swim — ho, ho!"

The butcher's small boy was loading meat on a cart. John stayed to say a word to him, pleased to have the chance, as the boy grinned at Billy's mocking malice. "Halloa! Pole," he called. "My uncle says we fellows may swim. Tell the other fellows."

"Gosh! but that's good — John. I'll tell 'em."

John rode on and fell to thinking of Leila, with some humiliating suspicion in regard to her share in the Squire's change of mind; or was it Aunt Ann's influence? And why did he himself not altogether like it? Why should his aunt and Leila interfere? He wished they had let the matter alone. What had a girl to do with it? He was again conscious that he felt of a sudden older than Leila, and did not fully realize that in the race of life he had gone swiftly past her during these few months, and that in the next year she in turn would sweep past him in the developmental changes of life. Now she seemed to him more timid, more childlike than usual; but long thinkings are not of the psychic habits of normal youth, and Dixy recovered his attention.

He satisfied the well-bred horse, who of late had been losing his temper in the society of a rough groom, ignorant of the necessity for good manners with horses. Neither strange noises nor machines disturbed Dixy as John rode through the busy iron-mills to the door of a small brick house, so well known that no sign announced it as the home of the only medical man available at the mills or in Westways. John tied Dixy to the hitching-post, gnawed by the doctor's horse during long hours of waiting on an unpunctual man.

The doors were open, and as John entered he was aware of an odour of drugs and saw Dr. McGregor sound asleep in an armchair, a red silk handkerchief over his bald head, and a swarm of disappointed flies hovering above him. In the back room the clink and rattle of a pestle and mortar ceased as Tom appeared.

John, in high good-humour, said, "Good afternoon, Tom. My uncle has let up on the swimming. He asked me to let you fellows know."

"It's about time," said Tom crossly. "After all it was your fault and we had to pay for it."

"Now, Tom, you made me pretty angry when you talked to me the other day, and if you want to get me into another row, I won't object; but I was not asked for any names, and I did not put the blame on any one. Can't you believe a fellow?"

"No, I can't. If that parson hadn't come, I'd have licked you."

"Perhaps," said John.

"Isn't any perhaps about it. You look out, that's all."

John laughed. He was just now what the Squire described as horse-happy and indisposed to quarrel. "Suppose you wake up the old gentleman. He *can* snore."

Tom shook the doctor's shoulder, "Wake up, Dad. Here's John Penhallow."

The Doctor sat up and pulled off his handkerchief. The flies fell upon his bald pate. "Darn the flies," he said. "What is it, John?"

"My uncle wants you to come to Westways to-morrow and doctor old Josiah's rheumatism."

"I'll come."

"He wants you to look after Peter Lamb. He's been drinking again."

"What! that whisky-rotted scamp. It's pure waste of time. How the same milk came to feed the Squire and that beast the Lord knows. He has no more morals than a tom-cat. I'll come, but it's waste of good doctoring." Here he turned his rising temper on Tom. "You and my boy have been having a fight. You licked him and saved me the trouble. I heard from Mr. Rivers what Tom said."

"It was no one's business but Tom's and mine," returned John much amused to know that the peaceful rector must have watched the fight and overheard what caused it. Tom scowled, and the peacemaking old doctor got up, adding, "Be more gentle with Tom next time."

Tom knew better than to reply and went back to pill-making furious and humiliated.

"Good-bye, John," said the Doctor. "I'll see the Squire after I have doctored that whisky sponge." Then John rode home on Dixy.

CHAPTER VII

BEFORE the period of which I write, the county and town had unfailingly voted the Democratic ticket. But for half a decade the unrest of the cities reflected in the journals had been disturbing the minds of country communities in the Middle States. In the rural districts of Pennsylvania there had been very little actively hostile sentiment about slavery, but the never ending disputes over Kansas had at last begun to weaken party ties, and more and more to direct opinion on to the originating cause of trouble.

The small voting population of Westways had begun to suspect of late that James Penhallow's unwillingness to discuss politics meant some change in his fidelity to the party of which Buchanan was the candidate. What Mrs. Ann felt she had rather freely allowed to be known. The little groups which were apt to gather about the grocer's barrels at evening discussed the grave question of the day with an interest no previous presidential canvass had caused, and this side eddy of quiet village life was now agreeably disturbed by the great currents of national politics. Westways began to take itself seriously, as little towns will at times, and to ask how this man or that would vote at the coming election in November. The old farmers who from his youth still called the Squire "James" were Democrats. Swallow, the only lawyer the town possessed, was silent, which was felt as remarkable in a man who usually talked much more than occasion demanded and wore a habit-mask of good-fellowship, which had served to deceive many a blunt old farmer, but not James Penhallow.

At Grey Pine there was a sense of tension. Penhallow was

a man slow in thinking out conclusions, but in times demanding action swiftly decisive. He had at last settled in his mind
that he must leave his party and follow a leader he had known
in the army and never entirely trusted. Whether he should take
an active share in the politics of the county troubled him, as
he had told Rivers. He must, of course, tell his wife how he
had resolved to vote. To speak here and there at meetings, to
throw himself into the contest, was quite another matter. His
wife would feel deeply grieved. Between the two influential feelings the resolution of forces, as he put it to himself with a sad
smile, decided him to hold his tongue so far as the outer
world was concerned, to vote for the principles unfortunately
represented by Fremont, but to have one frank talk with Ann
Penhallow. There was no need to do this as yet, and he smiled
again at the thought that Mrs. Ann was, as he pretty well knew,
playing the game of politics at Westways. He might stop her.
He could ask her to hold her hand, but to let her continue on
her way and to openly make war against her, that he could not
do. It did not matter much as the State in any case would
go for Buchanan. He hesitated, and had better have been plain
with her. She knew that he had been long in doubt, but did
not as yet suspect how complete was his desertion of opinions
she held to as she did to her religious creed. He found relief
in his decision, and too in freedom of talk with Rivers, who
looked upon slavery as simply wicked and had no charity for
the section so little responsible for an inherited curse they were
now driven by opponent criticism to consider a blessing for all
concerned.

John too was asking questions and beginning now and then
to wonder more and more that what Westways discussed should
never be mentioned at Grey Pine. He rode Dixy early in the
mornings with Leila at his side, fished or swam in the afternoons, and so the days ran on. On September 30th, Ann was to
take Leila to the school in Maryland. Three days before this

terrible exile was to begin, as they turned in at the gate of the stable-yard, Leila said, " I have only three days. I want to go and see the Indian graves and the spring, and all the dear places I feel as if I shall never see again."

" What nonsense, Leila. What do you mean ? "

" Oh, Aunt Ann says I will be so changed in a year, I won't know myself."

" You mean, you won't see things then as they are seen now."

" Yes, that 's what I wanted to say, but you always know how to find the right words."

" Perhaps," he said. " Things never look just the same tomorrow, but they may look — well, nicer — or — I can't always find the right word. Suppose we walk to the graves after lunch and have a good talk." It was so agreed.

They were never quite free from the chance of being sent on errands, and as Aunt Ann showed signs they well knew, they slipped away quietly and were gone before the ever-busy lady had ready a basket of contributions to the comfort of a sick woman in the village. They crossed the garden and were lost to view in the woods before Leila spoke. " We just did it. Billy will have to go." They laughed merrily at their escape.

" Just think, John, how long it is since you came. It seems years. Oh, you *were* a queer boy ! I just hated you."

" I do suppose, Leila, I must have looked odd with that funny cap and the cane —"

" And the way you looked when I told you about swinging on the gate. I had n't done that for — oh, two years. What did you think of me ? "

" I thought you were very rude, and then — oh, Leila ! when you came up out of the drift —" He hesitated.

" Oh, go on; I don't mind — not now."

" I thought you beautiful with all that splendid hair on the snow."

" Oh, John ! How silly ! " Whether or not she was unusually

good to look at had hardly ever before occurred to her. She flushed slightly, pleased and wondering, with a new seed of gentle vanity planted in her simple nature, a child on the threshold of the womanly inheritance of maidenhood.

Then he said gravely, "It is wonderful to me how we have changed. I shall miss you. To think you are the only girl I ever played with, and now when you come back at Christmas —"

"I am not to come back then, John. I am to stay with my uncles in Baltimore and not come home until next June."

"You will be a young lady in long skirts and your hair tucked up. It's dreadful."

"Can't be helped, John. You will look after Lucy, and write to me."

"And you will write to me, Leila?"

"If I may. Aunt says they are very strict. But I shall write to Aunt Ann, of course."

"That won't be the same."

"No."

They walked on in silence for a little while, the girl gazing idly at the tall trees, the lad feeling strangely aware, freshly aware, as they moved, of the great blue eyes and of the sun-shafts falling on the abundant hair she swept back from time to time with a careless hand. Presently she stood still, and sat down without a word on the moss-cushioned trunk of a great spruce, fallen perhaps a century ago. She was passing through momentary moods of depression or of pleasure as she thought of change and travel, or nourishing little jealous desires that her serious-minded cousin should miss her.

The cousin turned back. "You might have invited me to sit down, Miss Grey." He laughed, and then as he fell on the brown pine-needles at her feet and looked up, he saw that her usual quick response to his challenge of mirth was wanting.

"What are you thinking about?" he asked.

"Oh, about Aunt Ann and Uncle Jim, and — and — Lucy, and who will ride her —"

"You can trust Uncle Jim about Lucy."

"I suppose so," said the girl rather dolefully and too near to the tears she had been sternly taught to suppress.

"Is n't it queer," he said, "how people think about the same things? I was just going to speak of Aunt Ann and Uncle Jim. Uncle Jim often talks to me and to Mr. Rivers about the election, but if I say a word or ask a question at table, Aunt Ann says, 'we don't talk politics.'"

"But once, John, I heard Mr. Rivers say that slavery 'was a curse and wicked. Uncle Jim, he said Aunt Ann's people held slaves, and he did n't want to talk about it. I could n't hear the rest. I told you once about this."

"How you hear things, Leila. Prince Fine Ear was a trifle to you."

"Who was Prince Fine Ear?" she asked.

"Oh, he was the fairy prince who could hear the grass grow and the roses talk. It 's a pretty French fairy tale."

"What a gabble there must be in the garden, John."

"It does n't need Prince Fine Ear to hear. Don't these big pines talk to you sometimes, and the wind in the pines — the winds —?"

"No, they don't, but Lucy does."

Something like a feeling of disappointment faintly disturbed the play of his fancies. "Let us go to the graves."

"Yes, all right, come."

They got no further than the cabin and again sat down near by, Leila carelessly gathering the early golden-rod in her lap as they sat leaning against the cabin logs.

"This is our last walk," she said, arranging the golden plumes. "There is a white golden-rod; find me another, John."

He went away to the back of the cabin and returning threw in her lap a half dozen. "Old Josiah says the blacks in the

South think it is good luck to find the first white golden-rod. Then, he says, you must have a luck-wish. What shall it be? Come — quick now."

"Oh, I — don't know. Yes, I wish to have Lucy at that terrible boarding-school."

John laughed. "Oh, Leila, is that the best you can do?"

"Yes, wish a wish for me, if mine does n't suit."

Then he said, "I wish the school had small-pox and you had to stay at Grey Pine."

"I did n't think you 'd care as much as that. Are n't these flowers beautiful? Wish me a real wish."

"Then, I wish that when we grow up you would marry me."

"Well, John, you are a silly." She took on an air of authoritative reprimand. "Why, John, you are only a boy, but you ought to know better than to talk such nonsense."

"And you," he said, "are just a little girl."

"Oh, I 'm not so very little," returned Miss Grey.

"When I 'm older, I shall ask you again; and if you say no, I 'll ask again — and — until —"

"What nonsense, John. Let 's go home."

He rose flushed and troubled, and said, "Are you vexed, Leila?"

"No, of course not; but it was foolish of you."

He made no reply, in fact hardly heard her. He was for the moment older in some ways than his years. What had strangely moved him disturbed Leila not at all. She talked on lightly, laughing at times, and was answered briefly; for although he had no desire to speak, the unfailing courteous ways of his foreign education forced him to disregard his desire to say, "Oh, do let me alone; you don't understand." He hardly understood himself or the impulsive stir of emotion — a signal of coming manhood. Annoyed by his unwillingness to talk, she too fell to silence, and they walked homeward.

During the time left to them there was much to do in the way of visits to the older village people and some of the farmer families who had been here on the soil nearly as long as the Penhallows. There were no other neighbours near enough for country intercourse, and the life at Grey Pine offered few attractions to friends or relatives from the cities unless they liked to tramp with the Squire in search of game. The life was, therefore, lonely and would for some women have been unendurable; but as the Baptist preacher said to Rivers, "Duties are enough to satisfy Mrs. Penhallow, and I do guess she enjoys her own goodness like the angels must do."

Mark Rivers answered, "That is pretty nearly true, but I wish she would not invent duties which don't belong to women."

"About the election, you mean?"

"Yes. It troubles me, and I am sure it troubles the Squire. What about yourself, Grace?" and a singularly sad smile went with the query and a side glance at his friend's face. He had been uneasy about him since Grace had bent a little in the House of Rimmon.

"Oh, Rivers, the roof has got to leak. I have kept away from Mrs. Penhallow. I can't accept her help and then preach against her party, and — I mean to do it. I've wrestled with this little sin and — I don't say I wasn't tempted — I was. Now I am clear. We Baptists can stand what water leaks down on us from Heaven."

"You mean to preach politics, Grace?"

"Yes, that's what I mean to do. Oh! here comes Mrs. Penhallow."

They had met in front of Josiah's shop. As Mrs. Penhallow approached, Mr. Grace discovering a suddenly remembered engagement hurried away, and Rivers went with her along the rough sidewalk of Westways.

"I go away to-morrow with Leila," she said, "and Mr. Penhallow goes to Pittsburgh. We shall leave John to you for at least a week. He will give you no trouble. He has quite lost his foreign boyish ways, and don't you think he is like my husband?"

" He is in some ways very like the Squire."

" Yes, in some things — I so rarely leave home that this journey to Baltimore with Leila seems to me like foreign travel."

" Does Leila like it?"

" No, but it is time she was thrown among girls. She is less than she was a mere wild boy. It is strange, Mark, that ever since John came she has been less of a hoyden — and more of a simple girl."

" It is," he said, " a fine young nature in a strong body. She has the promise of beauty — whatever that may be worth."

"Worth! It is worth a great deal," said Mrs. Ann. " It helps. The moral value of beauty! Ah, Mark Rivers, I should like to discuss that with you. She is at the ugly duck age. Now I must go home. I want you to look after some things while I am away, and Mr. Penhallow is troubled about his pet scamp, Lamb."

She went on with her details of what he was to do, until he said laughing, " Please to put it on paper."

" I will. Not to leave John quite alone, I have arranged for you to dine with him, and I suppose he will go to you in the mornings for his lessons as usual."

" Oh, yes, of course. I enjoy these fellows, but the able ones are John and Tom McGregor. Tom is in the rough as yet, but he will come out all right. I shall lose him in a year. He is over seventeen and is to study medicine. But what about Lamb?"

" I am wicked enough to wish he were really ill. It is only the usual drunken bout, but he is a sort of Frankenstein to the Squire because of that absurd foster-brother feeling. He is still in bed, I presume."

" As you ask it," said Rivers, " I will see him, but if he belongs to any flock, he is a black sheep of Grace's fold. Anything else, Mrs. Penhallow?" he asked smiling —"but don't trust my memory."

"If I think of anything more, I shall make a note of it and, of course, you will see us at the station — the ten o'clock train — and give me a list of the books you wanted. I may find them in Philadelphia."

"Thank you."

"Oh," she said, turning back, "I forgot. My cousin, George Grey, is coming, but he is so uncertain that he may come as he advises me in ten days, or as is quite possible to-morrow, or not at all."

"Very good. If he comes, we will try to make Grey Pine agreeable."

"That is really all, Mark, I think," and the little lady went away, with a pleasant word for the long familiar people as she went by.

In the afternoon Leila saw the Squire ride to the mills with John, and went herself to the stable for a last mournful interview with Lucy. It was as well that her aunt with unconscious good sense kept her busy until dinner-time. The girl was near to accepting the relieving bribe of unrestrained tears, being sad and at the age of those internal conflicts which at the time of incomplete formation of character are apt to trouble the more sensitive sex. A good hard gallop would have cured her anticipative homesickness, for it must be a very black care indeed that keeps its seat behind the rider.

The next morning the rector and John were at the station of Westways Crossroads when the Grey Pine carriage drove up. Mrs. Ann and Leila were a half hour too early, as was Mrs. Penhallow's habit. Billy was on the cart with the baggage, grinning as usual and full of self-importance.

"Well, Billy," said Leila, talking to every one to conceal her child-grief at this parting with the joyous activities of her energetic young life. "Well, Billy, it's good-bye for a year."

"Won't have no more fun, Miss Leila — and nobody to snowball Billy, this winter."

"No, not this winter."

"Found another ground-hog yesterday. I'll let her alone till you come back."

John laughed. "Miss Leila will have long skirts and — hoops, Billy. There will be no more coasting and no more snowballing or digging up ground-hogs."

"Hoops — what for?" said Billy. John laughed.

"Please don't, John," she said, "it's too dreadful. Oh! I hear the whistle."

"Mark," said Mrs. Ann, "if George Grey comes — James, did you leave the wine-closet key?"

"Yes, my dear."

He turned to Leila, and kissing her said, "A year is soon over. Be a good girl, my child. It is about as bad for me as for you. God bless you. There, get on, Ann. Yes, the trunks are all right. Good-bye."

He stood a moment with John looking after the vanishing train. Then, he said, "No need to stay here with me, Mark," and the rector understanding him left him waiting for the westbound train and walked home across the fields with John Penhallow.

John was long silent, but at last said, "It will be pretty lonesome without Leila."

"Nice word, lonesome, John. Old English, I believe — has had its adventures like some other words. Lonely does n't express as well the idea of being alone and sorrowful. We must do our best for your uncle and aunt. Your turn to leave us will come, and then Leila will be lonesome."

"I don't think she will care as much."

Rivers glanced at the strong young face. " Why do you say that? "

" I don't know, Mr. Rivers. I — she is more of a child than I am."

" That hardly answers my question. But I must leave you. I am going to see that scamp misnamed Lamb. See you at dinner. Don't cultivate lonesomeness, John. No one is ever really alone."

Leaving his pupil to consider what John thought rather too much of an enigma, the young clergyman took to the dusty highway which led to Westways. John watched the tall figure awkwardly climbing a snake fence, and keeping in mind for explanation the clergyman's last remark he went away through the woods.

CHAPTER VIII

PENHALLOW had gravely told John that in his absence he must look after the stables and the farm, so that now he had for the first time in his life responsibilities. The horses and the stables were to be looked over every day. Of course, too, he must ride to the Squire's farm, which was two miles away, and which was considered a model of all that a farm should be. The crop yield to the acre was most satisfactory, but when some one of the old Quaker farmers, whose apple-orchards the Squire had plundered when young, walked over it and asked, "Well, James, how much did thee clear this last year?" the owner would honestly confess that Mrs. Ann's kitchen-garden paid better; but then she gave away what the house did not use.

Very many years before slavery had become by tacit consent avoided as a subject for discussion, Mrs. Ann critical of what his farm cost, being herself country-bred, had said that if it were worked with Maryland blacks it would pay and pay well.

"You mean, dear, that if I owned the labour, it would pay."

"Yes," she returned gaily, "and with me for your farmeress."

"You are, you are!" he laughed, "and you have cultivated me. I am well broken to your satisfaction, I trust; but to me, Ann, the unpaid labour of the slave seems impossible."

"Oh, James, it is not only possible, but right for us who know what for all concerned is best."

"Well, well," he laughed, "the vegetable garden seems to be run at a profit without them — ah! Ann, how about that?"

The talk was, as they both knew, more serious than it would have seemed to any one who might have chanced to be present.

The tact born of perfect love has the certainty of instinct, and to be sensitive even to tenderness in regard to the prejudices or the fixed opinions of another does much to insure happiness both in friendship and in love. Here with these two people was a radical difference of belief concerning what was to be more and more a hard subject as the differences of sentiment North and South became sharply defined. Westways and the mills understood her, and what were her political beliefs, but not the laughingly guarded silence of the much loved and usually outspoken Squire, who now and then relieved his mind by talking political history to John or Rivers.

The stables and farm were seriously inspected and opinions expressed concerning colts and horses to the amusement of the grooms. He presided in Penhallow's place at table with some sense of newly acquired importance, and on the fourth day of his uncle's absence, at Mark Rivers's request, asked Mr. Grace to join them. The good Baptist was the more pleased to come in the absence of Mrs. Penhallow, who liking neither his creed nor his manners, respected the goodness of a life of self-denial, which, as his friend Rivers knew, really left him with hardly enough to keep his preaching soul alive.

"Grace is late, as usual," said Rivers to John. "He has, I believe, no acquaintance with minutes and no more conception of time than the angels. Ah! I see him. His table-manners really distress your aunt; but manners are — well, we will leave that to another time. Good evening, Grace."

"Glad to see you, sir," said John.

On a word from Rivers, the guest offered thanks, which somewhat amazed John by its elaborate repetitions.

The stout little preacher, carefully tucking his napkin between his paper shirt-collar and his neck, addressed himself to material illustration of his thankfulness, while the rector observed with a pitiful interest the obvious animal satisfaction of the man. John with more amusement saw the silver fork used for a time and at last abandoned for use of the knife. Unconsciously happier for an unusually good dinner, Grace accepted a tumbler of the Penhallow cider, remarking, "I never take spirits, Rivers, but I suppose cider to be a quite innocent beverage."

Rivers smiled. "It will do you no harm."

"It occurs to me, Rivers," said Grace, "that although wine is mentioned in the Bible, cider is not. There is no warning against its use."

It also occurred to Rivers that there was none against apple-jack. "Quite right," he said. "You make me think of that scamp, Lamb. McGregor tells me that he is very ill."

"A pity he would n't die," remarked the young host, who had indiscreetly taken two full tumblers of old hard cider before Rivers had noticed his unaccustomed use of this rather potent drink.

"You should not desire the death of any man, John," said Grace, "least of all the death of a sinner like Lamb."

"Really," said John with the dignity of just a trifle too much cider, "my phrase did not admit of your construction."

"No," laughed Rivers, seeing it well to intervene, "and yet to say it is a pity may be a kindly wish and leaves it open to charitable interpretation."

"He is quite unprepared to die," insisted Grace, with the clerical intonation which Rivers disliked.

"How do you know that?" asked Rivers.

"I know," said John confidently. "He told me he was a born thief and loved to lie. He was pretty drunk at the time."

"That is too nearly true to be pleasant," remarked Rivers, "'in vino veritas.' The man is a very strange nature. I think he never forgives a benefit. I sometimes think he has no sense of the difference between right and wrong — an unmoral nature, beyond your preaching or mine, Grace, even if he ever gave us a chance."

"I think he is a cruel beast," said John. "I saw him once —"

Rivers interrupted him saying, as he rose, "Suppose we smoke."

With unconscious imitation of the courteous Squire he represented, John said, "We will smoke in the library if you have had enough wine."

Rivers said, "Certainly, Squire," not altogether amused as John, a little embarrassed, said quickly, "I should have said cider."

"Of course, we have had no wine, quite a natural mistake," remarked Grace, which the representative squire felt to be a very disagreeable comment.

"You will find cigars and pipes on the table," said the rector, "and I will join you in a moment." So saying he detained John by a hand on his arm and led him aside as they crossed the hall.

"You are feeling that old hard cider, my boy. You had better go to bed. I should have warned you."

"Yes, sir — I — did not — I mean — I —"

"*C'est une diablesse* — a little devil. There are others, and worse ones, John. Good-night."

On the stairs the young fellow felt a deepening sense of humiliation and surprise as he became aware of the value of the banister-rail.

Rivers went into the library blaming his want of care, and a little sorry for the lad's evident distress. "What, not smoking, Grace?"

"No, I have given it up."

"But, why?"

"Well, I can't smoke cheap strong tobacco, and I can't afford better stuff."

"Then, be at ease, my friend. The Squire has sent me a large supply. I am to divide with you," which was as near to a fib as the young clergyman ever got in his blameless life.

"I shall thank him," returned Grace simply, "and return to my pipe, but I do sometimes think it is too weak an indulgence of a slavish habit."

"Hardly worth while to thank Penhallow; he will have forgotten all about it."

"But I shall not."

They smoked and talked politics, and the village and their work, until at last, after one of the pipe-filling pauses, Grace said, "I ought not to have taken that cider, but it singularly refreshed me. You did not partake."

"No, it disagrees with me."

"I feel it, Brother Rivers. I feel it slightly, and — I — a man who preaches temperance, total abstinence —"

"My dear Grace, that is not temperance. There may be intemperance in the way a man puts his opinions before others — a man may hurt his own cause —"

Grace returned quickly, "You were in our church Wednesday night — I saw you. You think I was intemperate?"

"Frankly, yes. You were abusive. You are too well self-governed to understand the working-man's temptations. You preached from the heart as you felt, without the charity of the head."

"Perhaps — perhaps," he returned humbly; and then with a quite gentle retort, "Don't you sometimes preach too much from the head, Brother Rivers?"

"Yes, that may be the case. I am conscious sometimes that I lack your power of direct appeal — your personal application of the truth. I ought to preach the first half of the sermon — the appeal to the reason, the head part — and ask you to conclude with the heart share — the personal application of my cold logic."

"Let us try it," said Grace rising and much amused; "cold, Rivers! your cold logic! There is nothing cold in all your nature. Let us go home; we have had a good talk."

As they walked down the avenue Grace said, " What are you doing about Lamb? Is it really wise to talk to him? "

" Just now," said the rector, " he has acquired a temporary conscience in the shape of a congested stomach. I talked to him a little. He is penitent, or says he is, and as his mother is sometimes absent, I have set Billy to care for him; some one must. I have found that to keep Billy on a job you must give him a daily allowance of chewing tobacco; that answers."

" Bad company, Brother Rivers."

" Oh, there is no guile in Billy."

They parted at the Grey Pine gate. Rivers had innocently prepared remote mischief, which by no possible human foresight could he have anticipated. When, walking in the quiet of a lonely wood, a man sets his foot on a dead branch, the far end stirs another, and the motion so transmitted agitates a half dozen feet away the leaves of a group of ferns. The man stops and suspects some little woodland citizen as the cause of the unexplained movement; thus it is in the affairs of life. We do some innocent thing and are puzzled to explain how it brings about remote mischief.

Meanwhile an unendurable craving for drink beset the man Lamb, who was the prey of slowly lessening delusions. Guardian Billy chewed his daily supply of tobacco and sat at the window in the hot second-storey room feeding Lamb with brief phrases concerning what he saw on the street.

" Oh! there go Squire's horses for exercise; Joe's on Lucy."

" Damn Lucy! Do you go to mother's room —"

" What for? "

" Oh, she keeps her money in it, and Mrs. Penhallow paid her in advance the day she left."

" Can't do it," said Billy, who had strict orders not to leave Lamb alone.

" Oh, just look in the top drawer. She keeps a bit of money

rolled up in one of her stockings. That will get me a little whisky and you lots of tobacco."

"Can't do it," said Billy. "Want me to steal? Won't do it."

"Then I'll get even with you some day."

Billy laughed. "Why I could lick you — like Mr. John licked the doctor's son. Gosh! there goes Pole's wagon."

Lamb fell to thought of how to get that whisky. The ingenuity of the man who craves alcohol or morphia is sometimes surprising even to the most experienced doctor. The immorality of the means of attainment is never considered. If, as with Lamb, a lie or worse be needed, there is a certain satisfaction in having outwitted nurse and doctor.

On the day after the two clergymen had heard John's final opinion of Lamb, the bed-fast man received his daily visit from his spiritual physician, and the clergyman met at the house door the doctor of the body. "I suppose," said McGregor, "that you and I as concerns this infernal rascal are under orders from Penhallow and his wife. I at least have the satisfaction of being paid —"

"Oh, I am paid, Doctor," the clergyman smiled.

"Of course, any one and every one who serves that very efficient and positive saint, Mrs. Penhallow, is paid. She's too terrifyingly good. It must be — well, inconvenient at times. Now she wants this animal looked after because of Mrs. Lamb; and the squire has some sort of absurd belief that because the same breasts that nursed him nursed our patient, he must befriend the fellow — and he does. Truth is, Rivers, that man's father was a sodden drunkard but, I am told, not otherwise bad. It's a pretty sure doom for the child. This man's body has damned his soul, and now the soul is paying it back in kind."

"The damnation will be settled elsewhere," said Rivers gravely. "You are pleading for him when you say he had a father who drank."

"Well, yes, yes. That is true, but I do confoundedly mistrust him. He never remembers a kindness and never forgets the smallest injury. But when Mrs. Penhallow puts a hand on your arm and you look at her, you just go and do what she wants done. Oh, me too! Let's get out of this unreasonable sun and see this fellow."

Billy was chasing blue-bottle flies on the window panes, and the patient in bed was lying still, flushed, with red eyes. He was slowly recovering from an attack of delirium tremens and reassembling his scattered wits.

"Well," said McGregor, "better, I see. Bugs gone?"

"Yes, sir; but if I had a little, just a nip of whisky to taper off on, I'd be all right."

"Not a drop, Peter."

"I'll die if I don't get it."

"Then die sober."

Peter made no reply. McGregor felt his pulse, made his usual careful examination, and said at last, "Now keep quiet, and in a few days you'll be well."

"For God's sake, give me whisky — a little. I'm so weak I can't stand up."

"No," said McGregor, "it will pass. Now I must go. A word with you, Mr. Rivers." When outside of the room he said, "We must trust Billy, I suppose?"

"Yes, there is no one else."

"That man is giving his whole mind to thinking how he can get whisky. He will lie, cheat, steal, do anything to get it."

"How can he? Neither Billy nor his old mother will help him. He will get well, Doctor, I suppose?"

"Yes, I told him he would. More's the pity. He is a permanent nuisance, up to any wickedness, a hopelessly ruined wild beast."

"Perhaps," said Rivers; "perhaps. Who can be sure of that?" He despaired of no one.

The sadly experienced doctor shook his head. "He will live to do much mischief. The good die young; you may be sure the wicked do not. In some ways the man's case has its droll side. Queer case! in some ways interesting."

"How is it interesting?" said Rivers.

"Oh, what he saw — his delusions when he was at his worst."

"What did he see?"

"Oh, bugs — snakes — the common symptoms, and at last the 'Wilmot Proviso.' Imagine it. He knew no more of that than of the physiology of the man in the moon. He described it as a 'plucked chicken.'"

"I suppose that was a wild contribution from the endless political talk of the town."

"Well, a 'plucked chicken' was not so bad. He saw also 'Bleeding Kansas.' A 'stuck pig' that was; and more — more, but I must go."

Rivers went back to the room. "Here is your tobacco, Billy, and wait downstairs; don't go away."

The big man turned over in bed as the clergyman entered. "Mr. Rivers. I'm bad. I might have died. Won't you pray for me?"

Rivers hesitated, and then fell on his knees at the bedside, his face in his hands. Peter lay still smiling, grimly attentive. As Rivers rose to his feet, Lamb said, "Could n't I have just a little whisky? Doctors don't always know. I've been in this scrape before, and just a little liquor does help and it don't do any harm. I can't think, I'm so harried inside. I can't even pray, and I want to pray. Now, you will, sir, won't you?"

This mingling of low cunning, of childlike appeal and of hypocrisy, obviously suggested anything but the Christian charity of reply; what should he say? Putting aside angry comment, he fell back upon his one constant resource, What would Christ have said to this sinful man? He stood so long silent by the bed, which creaked as Lamb sat up, that the man's agony of morbid thirst caught from his silence a little hope, and he said, "Now you will, I know."

Rivers made no direct answer. Was it hopeless? He tried to read the face — the too thin straight nose, white between dusky red cheeks, the projecting lower lip, and the lip above it long, the eyes small, red, and eagerly attentive. This was not the time for reason. He said, "I should be your worst enemy, Peter. Every one has been good to you; over and over the Squire has saved you from jail. Mrs. Penhallow asked me to help you. Try to bear what your sin has brought on you, oh! do try. Pray God for help to bear it patiently."

"I'm in hell. What's the use of praying in hell? Get me whisky and I'll pray."

Rivers felt himself to be at the end of his resources, and that the enfeebled mind was incapable of response to any appeal to head or heart. "I will come again," he said. "Good-bye."

"Oh, damn everybody," muttered Peter.

Rivers went out and sent Billy up to take charge. Lamb was still sitting up in bed when Billy returned. The simple fellow poured out in brief sentences small bits of what he had seen at the street door.

"Oh, shut up," said Peter. "The doctor says I'll feel better if I'm shaved — ain't been shaved these three weeks. Doctor wants you to go and get Josiah to come and fix me up to-night. You tell him it's the doctor's orders. Don't you be gone long. I'm kind of lonely."

"All right," said Billy, in the cheerful way which made him a favourite despite his disinclination for steady work.

"Now, don't be gone long. I need a good shave, Billy."

"Guess you do — way you look you wouldn't fetch five cents at one of them rummage-sales. Ain't had but one in four years."

"Oh, get out, Billy." Once rid of his guard he tried in vain to stand up and fell back cursing.

The order from the doctor was to be obeyed. "Guess he's too shaky to shave himself," said Josiah. "I'll come about half-past eight."

As Josiah walked to the far end of the village, he thought in his simple way of his last three years. After much wandering and fear of being traced, he had been used at the stables by Penhallow. That he had been a slave was suspected, but that troubled no one in Westways. He had long felt at ease and safe. He lived alone, a man of some forty years, cooked for himself, and had in the county bank a small amount of carefully saved earnings. He had his likes and dislikes, but he had the prudently guarded tongue of servitude. Long before John Penhallow had understood better the tall black man's position and won the confidence of a friendly hour, he saw with his well-bred courtesy how pleased was the man to be called Mr. Josiah. It sounded queer, as Pole remarked, to call a runaway darkey Mister, but this in no way disturbed John. The friendly feeling for the black grew as they fished together in the summer afternoons, or trapped muskrats, or dug up hellbenders. The barber had one half-concealed dislike. The man he was now to shave he both feared and hated. "Could n't tell you why, Master John. It's like the way Crocker's wife's 'feared of cats. They ain't never hurt her none."

"Well," he said, "here I am," and in unusual silence set about his work by dim candlelight. The patient was as silent. When Josiah had finished, he said no word of his fee, knowing it to be a hopeless debt.

"Guess you do look the better for a shave," he remarked, as he was about to leave. "I'll send up Billy." The uneasy guardian had seized on the chance to get a little relief.

"No, don't go," said Lamb. "I'm in a hell of thirst. I want you to get me some whisky. I'll pay you when I get work."

Josiah was prudent and had no will to oblige the drunkard

nor any belief in future repayment. " Could n't do that — doctor would n't like it."

" What, you won't do it? "

" No, I can't do it."

" If you don't, I 'll tell what I know about you."

" What do you know? " The long lost terror returned — but what could he know?

" Oh, you ran away — I know all about it. You help me now and I 'll keep quiet — you 'd better."

A fierce desire rose in the mind of Josiah to kill the rascal, and then, by long habit prudent, he said, " I 'll have to think about it." But what could this man know?

" Best to think damn quick, or you 'll have your old master down on you. I give you till to-morrow morning early. Do you hear? It 's just a nip of whisky I want."

" Yes, I hear — got to think about it." He went out into the night, a soul in fear. No one knew his former master's name. Then his very good intelligence resumed control. No one really knew — only John — and he very little. He put it aside, confident in the young fellow's discretion. Of course, the town suspected that he was a fugitive slave, but nobody cared or seemed to care. And yet, at times in his altogether prosperous happy years of freedom, when he read of the fugitive-slave act, and he read much, he had disturbing hours. He stood still a moment and crossed the road. The Episcopal church, which he punctually attended, was on Penhallow's land, and near by was the rectory where Mark lived with an old woman cook and some help from Mrs. Lamb. The night was warm, the windows were open, and the clergyman was seen writing. Josiah at the window spoke.

" Excuse me, sir, could I talk to you? I am in a heap of trouble."

" In trouble, Josiah? Come in, the front door is open."

As he entered the rector's study, Rivers said, " Sit down."

Something in the look of the man made him think of hunted animals. "No one else is in the house. What is it?" The black poured out his story.

"So then," said Rivers, "he lied to you about the doctor and threatened you with a lie. Why, Josiah, if he had known who was your master, he would have told you, and whether or not you ran away from slavery is none of his business. Mr. Penhallow believes you did, others suspect it, but no one cares. You are liked and you have the respect of the town. There would be trouble if any man tried to claim you."

"I'd like to tell you all about it, sir."

"No — no — on no account. Tell no one. Now go home. I will settle with that drunken liar."

"Thank you. May God bless — and thank you."

The clergyman sat in thought a while, and the more he considered the matter which he had made light of to the scared black, the less he liked it. He dismissed it for a time as a lie told to secure whisky, but the fear Josiah showed was something pitiful in this strong black giant. He knew Lamb well enough to feel sure that Josiah would now have in him an enemy who was sure in some way to get what he called " even " with the barber, and was a man known and spoken of in Westways as " real spiteful."

When next day Rivers entered the room where Lamb lay abed, he saw at once that he was better. He meant to make plain to a revengeful man that Josiah had friends and that the attempt to blackmail him would be dangerous. Lamb was sitting up in bed apparently relieved, and was reading a newspaper. The moment he spoke Rivers knew that he was a far more intelligent person than the man of yesterday.

Lamb said, " Billy, set a chair for Mr. Rivers. The heat's awful for October." Billy obeyed and stepped out glad to escape.

Rivers said, " No, I won't sit down. I have something to

say to you, and I advise you to listen. You lied to Billy about the doctor yesterday, and you tried to frighten Josiah into getting you whisky — you lied to him."

Josiah had not returned, and now it was plain that he had told the clergyman of the threat. Lamb was quick to understand the situation, and the cleverness of his defence interested and for a moment half deceived the rector.

"Who says I lied? Maybe I did. I don't remember. It's just like a dream — I don't feel nowise accountable. If — I — abused Josiah, I'm sorry. He did shave me. Let me think — what was it scared Josiah?" He had the slight frown of a man pursuing a lost memory.

"It is hardly worth while, Peter, to go into the matter if you don't recall what you said." He realized that the defence was perfect. Its too ready arguments added to his disbelief in its truth.

Lamb was now enjoying the game. "Was Josiah really here, sir? But, of course, he was, for he shaved me. I do remember that. Won't you sit down, sir?"

"No, I must go. I am pleased to find you so much better."

"Thank you, sir. I don't want whisky now. I'll be fit for work in a week or so. I wonder what I did say to Josiah?"

This was a little too much for Rivers's patience. "Whatever you said had better never be said again or you will find yourself in very serious trouble with Mr. Penhallow."

"Why, Mr. Rivers, I know I drink, and then I'm not responsible, but how could I say to that poor old darkey what I don't mind I said yesterday?"

"Well, you may chance to remember," said Rivers; "at least I have done my duty in warning you."

"I'd like, sir," returned Lamb, leaning forward with his head bent and uplift of lids over watchful eyes —"Oh, I want you to know how much I thank you, sir, for all your kindness."

" You may credit the Squire for that.   Good-bye," and he went out.

Neither man had been in the least deceived, but the honours of the game were with the big man in the bed, which creaked under his weight as he fell back grinning in pleased self-approval. " Damn that black cuss," he muttered, " and the preacher too. I 'll make them sorry."

At the outer doorstep Mark Rivers stood still and wiped the sweat from his forehead.   There must be minutes in the life of the most spirtually minded clergyman when to bow a little in the Rimmon House of the gods of profane language would be a relief.   He may have had the thought, for he smiled self-amused and remembered his friend Grace.   Then he took himself to task, reflecting that he should have been more gently kind, and was there not some better mode of approaching this man?   Was he not a spirit in prison, as St. Peter said?   What right had he with his beliefs to despair of any human soul?   Then he dismissed the matter and went home to his uncompleted sermon. He would have to tell the Squire; yes, that would be advisable.

The days at Grey Pine ran on in the routine of lessons, riding, and the pleasure for John of representing his uncle in the oversight of the young thoroughbred colts and the stables.   Brief talks with Rivers of books and politics filled the after-dinner hour, and when he left John fell with eagerness on the newspapers of the day.   His uncle's mail he forwarded to Pittsburgh, and heard from him that he would not return until mid-October.   His aunt would be at home about the 8th, and Leila was now at her school.   The boy felt the unaccustomed loneliness, and most of all the absence of Leila.   One letter for his aunt lay on the hall table.   It came too late to be sent on its way, nor had she asked to have letters forwarded.

Two days before her return was to be expected, when John came down dressed for dinner, he found Mr. Rivers standing with his back to a fire, which the evening coolness of October in the hills made desirable. The rector was smiling.

"Mr. George Grey came just after you went upstairs. It seems that he wrote to your aunt the letter on the table in the hall. As no one met him at Westways Crossing, he was caught in a shower and pretty well soaked before he got some one to bring him to Grey Pine. I think he feels rather neglected."

"Has he never been here before?" asked John, curious in regard to the guest who he thought, from hearing his aunt speak of him, must be a person of importance.

"No, not for a long while. He is only a second cousin of Mrs. Penhallow; but as all Greys are for her — well, *the* Greys — we must do our best to make it pleasant for him until your aunt and uncle return."

"Of course," said John, with some faint feeling that it was needless to remind him, his uncle's representative, of his duties as the host. Rivers said, smiling, "It may not be easy to amuse Mr. Grey. I did not tell you that your aunt wrote me, she will not be here until the afternoon train on the 9th. Ah! here is Mr. Grey."

John was aware of a neatly built, slight man in middle life, clad in a suit of dark grey. He came down the stairs in a leisurely way. "Not much of a Grey!" thought Rivers, as he observed the clean-shaven face, which was sallow, or what the English once described as olivaster, the eyes small and dark, the hair black and so long as to darkly frame the thin-featured, clean-shaven refinement of a pleasant and now smiling face.

John went across the hall to receive him, saying, "I am John Penhallow, sir. I am sorry we did not know you were to be here to-day."

"It is all right — all right. Rather chilly ride. Less moisture outside and more inside would have been agreeable; in fact, would be at present, if I may take the liberty."

Seeing that the host did not understand him, Rivers said

promptly, " I think, John, Mr. Grey is pleasantly reminding us that we should offer him some of your uncle's rye."

" Of course," said John, who had not had the dimmest idea what the Maryland gentleman meant.

Mr. Grey took the whisky slowly, remarking that he knew the brand, " Peach-flavoured, sir. Very good, does credit to Penhallow's taste. As Mr. Clay once remarked, the mellowing years, sir, have refined it."

" Dinner is ready," said John.

There was no necessity to entertain Mr. Grey. He talked at length, what James Penhallow later described as " grown-up prattle." Horses, the crops, and at length the proper methods of fining wine — a word of encouragement from Rivers set him off again. Meanwhile the dinner grew cold on his plate. At last, abruptly conscious of the lingering meal, Mr. Grey said, " This comes, sir, of being in too interesting society."

Was this mere quaint humour, thought Rivers; but when Grey added, " I should have said, sir, too interested company," he began to wonder at the self-absorption of what was evidently a provincial gentleman. At last, with " Your very good health ! " he took freely of the captain's Madeira.

Rivers, who sipped a single glass slowly, was about to rise when to his amusement, using his uncle's phrase, John said, " My uncle thinks that Madeira and tobacco do not go well together; you may like to smoke in the library."

Grey remarked, " Quite right, as Henry Clay once said, ' There is nothing as melancholy as the old age of a dinner; who, sir, shall pronounce its epitaph ? ' That, sir, I call eloquence. No more wine, thank you." As he spoke, he drew a large Cabana from his waistcoat pocket and lighted it from one of the candles on the table.

Rivers remarked, " We will find it warmer in the library."

When the two men settled down to pipe or cigar at the library fire, John, who had felt the rôle of host rather difficult, was eager to get a look at the *Tribune* which lay invitingly on the table, and presently caught the eye of Mr. Grey.

"I see you have the *Tribune*," he said. "A mischief-making paper — devilish. I presume Penhallow takes it to see what the other side has to say. Very wise, sir, that."

Rivers, unwilling to announce his friend's political opinions, said, smiling, "I must leave Mr. Penhallow to account for that wicked journal."

Grey sat up with something like the alert look of a suddenly awakened terrier on his thin face. "I presume the captain (he spoke of him usually as the captain) must be able to control a good many votes in the village and at the iron-works."

"I rather fancy," said Rivers, "that he has taken no active part in the coming election."

"Unnecessary, perhaps. It is, I suppose, like my own county. We have n't a dozen free-soil voters. 'Bleeding Kansas' is a dead issue with us. It is bled to death, politically dead, sir, and buried."

"Not here," said John imprudently. "Uncle James says Buchanan will carry the State by a small majority, but he may not carry this county."

"Then he should see to it," said Grey. "Elect Fremont, my boy, and the Union will go to pieces. Does the North suppose we will endure a sectional President? No, sir, it would mean secession — the death-knell of the Union. Sir, we may be driven to more practical arguments by the scurrilous speeches of the abolitionists. It is an attack on property, on the ownership of the inferior race by the supremely superior. That is the vital question."

He spoke with excitement and gesticulated as if at a political meeting. Mark Rivers, annoyed, felt a strong inclination to box John's ears. He took advantage of the pause to say, "Would you like a little more rye, Mr. Grey?"

"Why, yes, sir. I confess to being a trifle dry. But to resume our discussion —"

"Pardon me. John, ask for the whisky."

To John this was interesting and astonishing. He had never heard talk as wild. The annoyance on Rivers's face was such as to be easily read by the least observant. Elsewhere Mr. Rivers would have had a ready answer, but as Grey sat still a little while enjoying his own eloquence, the fire and the whisky, Rivers's slight negative hint informed John that he was to hold his tongue.

As the clergyman turned to speak to Grey, the latter said, " I wish to add a word more, sir. You will find that the men at the South cling to State rights; if these do not preserve for me and others my property and the right, sir, to take my body-servant to Boston or Kansas, sure that he will be as secure as my — my — shirt-studs, State rights are of no practical use."

"You make it very plain," said Rivers, feeling at last that he must defend his own opinions. " I have myself a few words to say — but, is that all? "

"Not quite — not quite. I am of the belief that the wants of the Southern States should be considered, and the demand for their only possible labour considered. I would re-open the slave-trade. I may shock you, reverend sir, but that is my opinion."

"And, as I observe," said Rivers, " that also of some governors of States." He disliked being addressed as " reverend," and knew how Penhallow would smile when captained.

There was a brief silence, what Rivers used to call the punctuation value of the pipe. The Maryland gentleman was honestly clear in the statement of his political creed, and Rivers felt some need to be amiable and watchful of his own words in what he was longing to say. John listened, amazed. He had had his lesson in our history from two competent masters and was

now intensely interested as he listened to the ultimate creed of
the owner of men.

Grey had at last given up the cigar he had lighted over and
over and let go out as often. He set down his empty glass, and
said with perfect courtesy, "I may have been excessive in statement. I beg pardon for having spoken of, or rather hinted at,
the need for a resort to arms. That is never a pleasant hint
among gentlemen. I should like to hear how this awful problem presents itself to you, a clergyman of, sir, I am glad to
know, my own church."

"Yes, that is always pleasant to hear," said Rivers. "There
at least we are on common ground. I dislike these discussions,
Mr. Grey, but I cannot leave you without a reply, although in
this house (and he meant the hint to have its future usefulness) politics are rarely discussed."

"Indeed!" exclaimed Grey. "At home we talk little else. I
do believe the watermelons and the pumpkins talk politics."

Rivers smiled. "I shall reply to you, of course. It will not
be a full answer. I want to say that this present trouble is
not a quarrel born within the memory of any living man. The
colonial life began with colonial differences and aversions due to
religion — Puritan, Quaker and Church of England, interco-
lonial tariffs and what not. For the planter-class we were mere
traders; they for us were men too lightly presumed to live an
idle life of gambling, sport and hard drinking — a life foreign
to ours. The colonies were to one another like foreign coun-
tries. In the Revolution you may read clearly the effect of
these opinions, when Washington expressed the wish that his officers would forget that they came from Connecticut or Virginia, and remember only they were Americans."

Grey said, "We did our share, sir."

"Yes, but all Washington's important generals were Northern
men; but that is not to the point. Washington put down the
whisky-tax revolt with small regard for State rights. The Con-

stitution unhappily left those State rights in a condition to keep up old differences. That is clear, I regret to say. Then came the tariff and a new seed of dissension. Slavery and its grow· ing claims added later mischief, but it was not the only cause of our troubles, nor is it to-day with us, although it is with you, the largest. We have tried compromises. They are of the history of our own time, familiar to all of us. Well, Mr. Grey, the question is shall we submit to the threat of division, a broken land and its consequences? — one moment and I have done. I am filled with gloom when I look forward. When nations differ, treaties or time, or what not, may settle disputes; too often war. But, Mr. Grey, never are radical, civil or religious differences settled without the sword, if I have read history aright. "You see," and he smiled, "I could not let pass your hint without a word."

"If it comes to that — to war," said Grey, "we would win. In that belief lies the certainty I dread."

"Ah! sir, in that Southern belief lies the certainty I too dread. You think we live merely lives of commerce. You do not realise that there is with us a profound sentiment of affection for the Union. No people worth anything ever lived without the very human desire of national self-preservation. It has the force of a man's personal desire for self-preservation. Pardon me, I suppose that I have the habit of the sermon."

Grey replied, "You are very interesting, but I am tired. A little more rye, John. I must adjourn this discussion — we will talk again."

"Not if I can help it," laughed Rivers. "I ought to say that I shall vote the Republican ticket."

"I regret it — I deeply regret it. Oh! thanks, John." He drank the whisky and went upstairs to bed.

Rivers sat down. "This man is what I call a stateriot. I am or try to be that larger thing, a patriot. I did not say all, it was useless. Your uncle cares little — oh, too little — about slavery, and generally the North cares as little; but the anti-slavery men are active and say, as did Washington, that the Union of the States was or will be insecure until slavery comes to an end. It may be so, John; it is the constant seed of discord. I would say, let them go in peace, but that would be only to postpone war to a future day. I rarely talk about this matter. What made you start him? You ought to have held your tongue."

The young fellow smiled. "Yes, sir, I suppose so."

"However, we won't have it again if I can help it."

"It was very interesting."

"Quite too interesting, but will he try it on the Squire and your aunt? Now I am going home. I hate these talks. Don't sit up and read the *Tribune*."

"No, sir, and I will take Mr. Grey to ride to-morrow."

"Do, and send him home too tired to talk politics."

"I think if I put him on uncle's big John it will answer."

CHAPTER IX

WHILE the two maids from Westways waited on the family at breakfast, the guest was pleased to express himself favourably in regard to the coffee and the corn bread. John being left alone in care of the guest after the meal proposed a visit to the stables. Mr. Grey preferred for a time the fire, and later would like to walk to the village. Somewhat relieved, John found for him the Baltimore paper, which Mrs. Penhallow read daily. Mr. Grey would not smoke, but before John went away remarked, "I perceive, my boy, no spittoon." He was chewing tobacco vigorously and using the fireplace for his frequent expectoration. John, a little embarrassed, thought of his Aunt Ann. The habit of chewing was strange to the boy's home experience. Certainly, Billy chewed, and others in the town, nor was it at that time uncommon at the North. He confided his difficulty to the groom, his boxing-master, who having in his room the needed utensil placed it beside the hall-fire, to Mr. Grey's satisfaction — a square tray of wood filled with sawdust.

"Not ornamental, but useful, John, in fact essential," said Mr. Grey, as John excused himself with the statement that he had to go to school. When he returned through the woods, about noon, to his relief he saw far down the avenue Mr. Grey and the gold-headed, tasselled cane he carried.

A little later Mr. Grey in the sun of a cool day early in October was walking along the village street in keen search of news of politics. He talked first to Pole, the butcher, who hearing that he was a cousin of Mrs. Penhallow assured him that the town would go solid for Buchanan. Then he met

131

Billy, who was going a-fishing, having refused a wood-cutting job the rector offered.

"A nice fishing-rod that," said Grey.

Billy who was bird-witted and short of memory replied, "Mrs. Penhallow she gave me a dollar to pay pole-tax if I vote for — I guess it was Buchanan. I bought a nice fishing-pole."

Grey was much amused and agreeably instructed in regard to Mrs. Ann's sentiments, as he realized the simple fellow's mental condition. "A fishing-pole-tax — well — well —" and would tell John of his joke. "Any barber in this town?" he asked.

"Yes, there's Josiah," and Billy was no longer to be detained.

Mr. Grey mailed a letter, but the post-mistress would not talk politics and was busy. At last, wandering eastward, he came upon the only unoccupied person in Westways. Peter Lamb, slowly recovering strength, was seated on his mother's doorstep. His search for money had been defeated by the widow's caution, and the whisky craving was being felt anew.

"Good morning," said Grey. "You seem to be the only man here with nothing to do."

"Yes, sir. I've been sick, and am not quite fit to work. Sickness is hard on a working man, sir."

Grey, a kindly person, put his hand in his pocket, "Quite right, it is hard. How are the people here going to vote? I hope the good old ticket."

"Oh! Buchanan and Breckenridge, sir, except one or two and the darkey barber. He's a runaway — I guess. Been here these three or four years. Squire likes him because he's clever about breaking colts."

"Indeed!"

"He's a lazy nigger, sir; ought to be sent back where he belongs."

"What is his name? I suppose he can shave me."

"Calls himself Josiah," said Peter. "Mighty poor barber — cut my face last time he shaved me. You see, he's lost two fingers — makes him awkwarder."

"What! what!" said Grey, of a sudden reflecting, "two fingers —"

"Know him?" said Lamb quickly.

"I — no — Do you suppose I know every runaway nigger?"

"Oh, of course not. Might I ask your name, sir?"

"I am a cousin of Mrs. Penhallow. My name is Grey." Peter became cautious and silent. "Here is a little help, my man, until you get work. Stick to the good old Party." He left two dollars in Lamb's eager hands.

Surprised at this unusual bounty, Peter said, "Thank you, sir. God bless you. It'll be a great help." It meant for the hapless drinker whisky, and he was quick to note the way in which Grey became interested in the man who had lost fingers.

Grey lingered. "I must risk your barber's awkwardness," he said.

"Oh, he can shave pretty well when he's sober. He's our only darkey, sir. You can't miss him. I might show you his shop." This Grey declined.

"I suppose, sir," said Peter, curious, "all darkies look so much alike that it is hard to tell them apart."

"Oh, not for us — not for us."

Then Peter was still more sure that the gentleman with the gold-headed cane was from the South. As Grey lingered thoughtful, Lamb was maliciously inspired by the size of Grey's donation and the prospect it offered. He studied the face of the Southern gentleman and ventured to say, "Excuse me, sir, but if you want to get that man back —"

"I want him! Good gracious! I did not own him. My inquiries were, I might say, casual, purely casual."

Lamb, thanks to the Penhallows, had had some education at

the school for the mill children, but what was meant by "purely casual" he did not know. If it implied lack of interest, that was not the case, or why the questions and this gift, large for Westways. But if the gentleman did not own Josiah's years of lost labour, some one else did, and who was it?

As Grey turned away, he said, "I may see you again. I am with my cousin at Grey Pine. By the bye, how will the county vote?"

Peter assured him that the Democratic Party would carry the county. "I am glad," said Grey, "that the people, the real backbone of the country, desire to do justice to the South." He felt himself on the way to another exposition of constitutional rights, but realising that it was unwise checked the outflow of eloquence. He could not, however, refrain from adding, "Your people then are a law-abiding community."

"Yes, sir," said the lover of law, "we are just that, and good sound Democrats."

Grey, curious and mildly interested, determined to be reassured in regard to this black barber's former status. He walked slowly by Josiah's shop followed at a distance by Peter. The barber was shaving Mr. Pole, and intent on his task. Grey caught sight of the black's face. One look was enough — it was familiar — unmistakable. In place of going in to be shaved he turned away and quickened his steps. Peter grinned and went home. "The darn nigger horse-thief," murmured Grey. "I'll write to Woodburn." Then he concluded that first it would be well without committing himself to know more surely how far this Democratic community would go in support of the fugitive-slave law. He applauded his cautiousness.

A moment later Pole, well shaven, overtook him. Grey stopped him, chatted as they went on, and at last asked if there was in Westways a good Democratic lawyer. Pole was confident that Mr. Swallow would be all that he could desire, and pointed out his house.

Meanwhile Peter Lamb began to suspect that there was mischief brewing for the man who had brought down on him the anger of Mark Rivers, and like enough worse things as soon as Penhallow came home.

As Pole turned into his shop-door, Mr. Grey went westward in deep thought. He was sure of the barber's identity. If Josiah had been his own property, he would with no hesitation have taken the steps needful to reclaim the fugitive, but it was Mr. Woodburn who had lost Josiah's years of service and it was desirable not hastily to commit his friend. He knew with what trouble the fugitive-slave law had been obeyed or not obeyed at the North. He was not aware that men who cared little about slavery were indignant at a law which set aside every safeguard with which the growth of civilization had surrounded the trial of even the worst criminal. As he considered the situation, he walked more and more slowly until he paused in front of Swallow's house. Every one had assured him that since General Jackson's time the town and county had changelessly voted the good old Democratic ticket. Here at least the rights of property would be respected, and there would be no lawless city mobs to make the restoration of a slave difficult. The brick house and ill-kept garden before which he paused looked unattractive. Beside the house a one-storey wooden office bore the name "Henry W. Swallow, Attorney-at-law." There was neither bell nor knocker. Mr. Grey rapped on the office door with his cane, and after waiting a moment without hearing any one, he entered a front room and looked about him.

Swallow was a personage whose like was found too often in the small Pennsylvania villages. The only child of a close-fisted, saving farmer, he found himself on his father's death more than sufficiently well-off to go to college and later to study law. He was careful and penurious, but failing of success in Philadelphia returned to Westways when about thirty years old, bought a piece of land in the town, built a house, married a pretty, commonplace young woman, and began to look for business. There was little to be had. The Squire drew his own leases and sold lands to farmers unaided. Then Swallow began to take interest in politics and to lend money to the small farmers, taking mortgages at carefully guarded, usurious interest. Merciless foreclosures resulted, and as by degrees his operations enlarged, he grew richer and became feared and important in a county community where money was scarce. Some of his victims went in despair to the much loved Squire for help, and got, over and over, relief, which disappointed Swallow who disliked him as he did no other man in the county. The Squire returned his enmity with contemptuous bitterness and entire distrust of the man and all his ways.

Mr. Grey saw in the further room the back of a thin figure in a white jacket seated at a desk. The man thus occupied on hearing his entrance said, without looking back, " Sit down, and in a moment I 'll attend to you."

Grey replied, " In a moment you won't see me ; " and, his voice rising, " I am accustomed to be treated with civility."

Swallow rose at once, and seeing a well-dressed stranger said, " Excuse me, I was drawing a mortgage for a farmer I expected. Take a seat. I am at your service."

Somewhat mollified, Grey sat down. As he took his seat he was not at all sure of what he was really willing to say or do. He was not an indecisive person at home, but here in a Northern State, on what might be hostile ground, he was in doubt concerning that which he felt he honourably owed as a duty to his neighbour. The word had for him limiting definitions, as indeed it has for most of us. Resolving to be cautious, he said with deliberate emphasis, " I should like what I have to say to be considered, sir, as George Washington used to remark, as ' under the rose '— a strictly professional confidence."

" Of course," said Swallow.

"My name is George Grey. I am at Grey Pine on a visit to my cousin, Mrs. Penhallow."

"A most admirable lady," said the lawyer; "absent just now, I hear." He too determined on caution.

"I have been wandering about your quiet little town this morning and made some odd acquaintances. One Billy, he called himself, most amusing — most amusing. It seems that my cousin gave him money to pay his poll-tax. The poor simple fellow bought a fishing-pole and line. He was, I fancy, to vote for Buchanan. My cousin, I infer, must be like all our people a sound Democrat."

"I have heard as much," returned Swallow. "I am doing what I can for the party, but the people here are sadly misled and our own party is slowly losing ground."

"Indeed! I talked a little with a poor fellow named Lamb, out-of-work and sick. He assured me that the town was solid for Buchanan, and also the county."

Swallow laughed heartily. "What! Peter Lamb. He is our prize drunkard, sir, and would have been in jail long ago but for Penhallow. They are foster-brothers."

"Indeed!" Mr. Grey felt that his knowledge of character had been sadly at fault and that he had been wise in not having said more to the man out-of-work.

"Do you think, Mr. Swallow, that if a master reclaimed a slave in this county that there would be any trouble in carrying out the law?"

"No, sir," said Swallow. "The county authorities are all Democrats and would obey the law. Suppose, sir, that you were frankly to put before me the whole case, relying on my secrecy. Where is the man?"

"Let me then tell you my story. As a sound Democrat it will at least have your sympathy."

"Certainly, I am all attention."

"About the tenth of June over four years ago I rode with

my friend Woodburn into our county-town. At the bank we left our horses with his groom Cæsar, an excellent servant, much trusted; used to ride quarter races for my father when a boy. When we came out, Woodburn's horse was hitched to a post and mine was gone, and that infernal nigger on him. He was traced to the border, but my mare had no match in the county."

"So he stole the horse; that makes it an easy case."

"No, sir. To be precise, he left the horse at a tavern in this State, with my name and address. Some Quakers helped him on his way."

"And he is in this county?" asked Swallow.

"Yes, sir. His name here is Josiah — seems to be known by that name alone."

"Josiah!" gasped Swallow. "A special favourite of Penhallow. A case to be gravely considered — most gravely. The Squire —"

"But surely he will obey the law."

"Yes — probably — but who can say? He was at one time a Democrat, but now is, I hear, likely to vote for Fremont."

"That seems incredible."

"And yet true. I should like, sir, to think the matter over for a day or two. Did the man see you — I mean, recognize you?"

"No, but as I went by his shop, I at once recognized him; and he has lost two fingers. Oh! I know the fellow. I can swear to him, and it is easy to bring his master Woodburn here."

"I see. Well, let me think it over for a day or two."

"Very good," returned Grey, "and pray consider yourself as in my debt for your services."

"All right, Mr. Grey."

With this Mr. Grey went away a thoughtful man. He attracted some attention as he moved along the fronts of the houses. Strangers were rare. Being careful not to go near

Josiah's little shop, he crossed the road and climbing the fence went through the wood, reflecting that until this matter was settled he would feel that his movements must be unpleasantly governed by the need to avoid Josiah. He felt this to be humiliating. Other considerations presented themselves in turn. This ungrateful black had run away with his, George Grey's, horse — a personal wrong. His duty to Woodburn was plain. Then, if this black fellow was as Swallow said, a favourite of Captain Penhallow, to plan his capture while himself a guest in Penhallow's house was rather an awkward business. However, he felt that he must inform his friend Woodburn, after which he would turn him over to Swallow and not appear in the business at all. It did not, however, present itself to the Maryland gentleman as a nice situation. If his cousin Ann were, as he easily learned, a strong Democrat, it might be well to sound her on the general situation. She had lived half her life among slaves and those who owned them. She would know how far Penhallow was to be considered as a law-abiding citizen, or whether he might be offended, for after all, as George Grey knew, his own share in the matter would be certain to become known. " A damned unpleasant affair," he said aloud as he walked up the avenue, " but we as Southern gentlemen have got to stand by one another. I must let Woodburn know, and decide for himself."

Neither was the lawyer Swallow altogether easy about the matter on which he had desired time for thought. It would be the first case in the county under the fugitive-slave act. If the man were reclaimed, he, Swallow, would be heard of all through the State; but would that help him before the people in a canvass for the House? He could not answer, for the old political parties were going to pieces and new ones were forming. Moreover, Josiah was much liked and much respected. Then, too, there was the fee. He walked about the room singularly disturbed. Some prenatal fate had decreed that he should be old-aged at forty. He had begun to be aware that his legs were aging faster than his mind. Except the pleasure of accumulating money, which brought no enjoyment, he had thus far no games in life which interested him; but now the shifting politics of the time had tempted him, and possibly this case might be used to his advantage. The black eyebrows under fast whitening hair grew together in a frown, while below slowly gathered the long smile of satisfaction. "How Penhallow will hate it." This thought was for him what the stolen mare was for George Grey. He must look up the law.

Meanwhile George Grey, under the necessity of avoiding the village for a time, was rather bored. He had criticized the stables and the horses, and had been told that the Squire relied with good reason on the judgment of Josiah in regard to the promise of good qualities in colts. Then, used to easy roadsters, he had been put on the Squire's rough trotter and led by the tireless lad had come back weary from long rides across rough country fields and over fences. The clergyman would talk no more politics, John pleaded lessons, and it was on the whole dull, so that Mr. Grey was pleased to hear of the early return of his cousin. A letter to John desired him to meet his aunt on the 8th, and accordingly he drove to the station at Westways Crossing, picking up Billy on the way. Mrs. Ann got out of the car followed by the conductor and brakeman carrying boxes and bundles, which Billy, greatly excited, stowed away under the seats of the Jersey wagon. Mrs. Penhallow distributed smiles and thanks to the men who made haste to assist, being one of the women who have no need to ask help from any man in sight.

"Now, Billy," she said, "be careful with those horses. When you attend, you drive very well."

She settled herself on the back seat with John, delighted to be again where her tireless sense of duty kept her busy — quite too busy at times, thought some of the village dames. "Your

Uncle James will soon be at home. Is his pet scamp any better?"

John did not know, but Josiah's rheumatism was quite well.

"Sister-in-law has a baby. Six trout I ketched; they're at the house for you — weighs seven pounds," said Billy without turning round.

"Trout or baby?" said Ann, laughing.

"Baby, ma'am."

"Thanks, but don't talk any more."

"Yes, ma'am."

"How is Leila?" asked John. "Does she like it at school?"

"No, not at all; but she will."

"I don't, Aunt Ann."

"I suppose not."

"Am I to be allowed to write to her?"

"I think not. There is some rule that letters, but —" and she laughed merrily. The rector, who worshipped her, said once that her laugh was like the spring song of birds. "But sometimes I may be naughty enough to let you slip a few lines into my letters."

"That is more than I hoped for. I am — I was so glad to get you back, Aunt Ann, that I forgot to tell you, Mr. George Grey has come."

"How delightful! He has been promising a visit for years. How pleased James will be! I wonder how the old bachelor ever made up his mind. I hope you made it pleasant, John."

"I tried to, aunt." Whether James Penhallow would like it was for John doubtful, but he said nothing further.

"The cities are wild about politics, and there is no end of trouble in Philadelphia over the case of a fugitive slave. I was glad to get away to Grey Pine."

John had never heard her mention this tender subject and was not surprised when she added quickly, "But I never talk politics, John, and you are too young to know anything about them." This was by no means true, as she well knew. "How are my chickens?" She asked endless questions of small moment.

"Got a new fishing-rod," said Billy, but to John's amusement did not pursue the story concerning which George Grey had gleefully enlightened him.

"Well, at last, Cousin George," she cried, as the cousin gave her his hand on the porch. "Glad to see you — most glad. Come in when you have finished your cigar."

She followed John into the hall. "Ah! the dear home." Then her eyes fell on the much used spittoon by the fireside. "Good gracious, John, a — a spittoon!"

"Yes, aunt. Mr. Grey chews."

"Indeed!" She looked at the box and went upstairs. For years to come and in the most incongruous surroundings John Penhallow now and then laughed as he saw again the look with which Mrs. Ann regarded the article so essential to Mr. Grey's comfort. She disliked all forms of tobacco use, and the law of the pipe had long ago been settled at Grey Pine as Mrs. Penhallow decreed, because that was always what James Penhallow decided to think desirable.

"But this! this!" murmured the little lady, as she came down the staircase ready for dinner. She rang for the maid. "Take that thing away and wash it well, and put in fresh sawdust twice a day."

"I hope John has been a good host," she said, as Grey entered the hall.

"Could n't be better, and I have had some delightful rides. I found the mills interesting — in fact, most instructive." He spoke in short childlike sentences unless excited by politics.

Mrs. Ann noted without surprise the free use of whisky, and later the appreciative frequency of resort to Penhallow's Madeira. A glass of wine at lunch and after dinner were her husband's sole indulgence. The larger potations of her cousin in no way affected him. He talked as usual to Mark Rivers and John about horses, crops and the weather, while Mrs. Ann listened to the flow of disconnected trifles in some wonder as to how James Penhallow would endure it. Grey for the time kept off the danger line of politics, having had of late such variously contributed knowledge as made him careful.

When to Mrs. Ann's relief dinner was over, the rector said his sermon for to-morrow must excuse him and went home. John decided that his rôle of host was over and retired to his algebra and to questions more easy to solve than of how to entertain Mr. George Grey. It was not difficult, as Mrs. Penhallow saw, to make Grey feel at home; all he required was whisky, cigars, and some mild appearance of interest in his talk. She had long anticipated his visit with pleasure, thinking that James Penhallow would be pleased and the better for some rational male society. Rivers had now deserted her, and she really would not sit with her kinsman's cigar a whole evening in the library. She said, "The night is warm for October, come out onto the porch, George."

"With all the pleasure in the world," said Grey, as he followed her.

By habit and training hospitable and now resigned to her fate, Mrs. Ann said, "Light your cigar, George; I do not mind it out-of-doors."

"I am greatly indebted — I was given to understand that it was disagreeable to you — like — politics — ah! Cousin Ann."

"We are not much given to talking politics," she said rather sharply.

"Not talk politics!" exclaimed Grey. "What else is there to talk about nowadays? But why not, Cousin Ann?"

"Well, merely because while I am Southern — and a Democrat, James has seen fit to abandon our party and become a Republican."

"Incomprehensible!" said Grey. "Ours is the party of gentlemen — of old traditions. I cannot understand it."

"Nor I," said she, "but now at least," and she laughed — "there will be one Republican gentleman. However, George, as we are both much in earnest, we keep politics out of the house."

"It must be rather awkward, Ann."

"What must be rather awkward?"

Did he really mean to discuss, to criticize her relations to James Penhallow? The darkness was for a time the grateful screen.

Grey, a courteous man, felt the reproof in her question, and replied, "I beg pardon, my dear Ann, I have heard of the captain's unfortunate change of opinion. I shall hope, however, to be able to convince him that to elect Fremont will be to break up the Union. I think I could put it so clearly that —"

Ann laughed low laughter as vastly amused she laid a hand on her cousin's arm. "You don't know James Penhallow. He has been from his youth a Democrat. There never was any question about how he would vote. But now, since 1850 —" and she paused, "in fact, I do not care to discuss with you what I will not with James." Her great love, her birth, training, education and respect for the character of her husband, made this discussion hateful. Her eyes filled, and, much troubled, she was glad of the mask of night.

"But answer me one question, Ann. Why did he change?"

"He was becoming dissatisfied and losing faith in his own party, but it was at last my own dear South and its friends at the North who drove him out." Again she paused.

"What do you mean, Ann?" asked Grey, still persistent.

"It began long ago, George. He said to me one day, 'That fool Fillmore has signed the Fugitive-Slave Act; it is hardly possible to obey it.' Then I said, 'Would you not, James?'"

I can never forget it. He said, ' Yes, I obey the law, Ann, but this should be labelled ' an act to exasperate the North.' I am done with the Democrat and all his ways. Obey the law! Yes, I was a soldier.' Then he said, ' Ann, we must never talk politics again.' We never do."

"And yet, Ann," said Grey, "that act was needed."

"Perhaps," she returned, and then followed a long silence, as with thought of James Penhallow she sat smiling in the darkness and watched the rare wandering lanterns of the belated fireflies.

The man at her side was troubled into unnatural silence. He had hoped to find an ally in his cousin's husband, and now what should he do? He had concluded that as an honest man he had done his duty when he had written to Woodburn; but now as a man of honour what should he say to James Penhallow? To conceal from his host what he had done was the obvious business-like course. This troubled a man who was usually able to see his way straight on all matters of social conduct and was sensitive on points of honour. While Ann sat still and wondered that her guest was so long silent, he was finding altogether unpleasant his conclusion that he must be frank with Penhallow. He felt sure, however, that Ann would naturally be on his side. He introduced the matter lightly with, " I chanced to see in the village a black man who is said to be a vagabond scamp. He is called Josiah — a runaway slave, I fancy."

Ann sat up in her chair. " Who said he was a scamp? "

" Oh, a man named Lamb." Then he suddenly remembered Mr. Swallow's characterization, and added, " not a very trustworthy witness, I presume."

Ann laughed. " Peter Lamb! He is a drunken, loafing fellow, who to his good fortune chances to have been James's foster-brother. As concerns Josiah, he turned up here some years ago, got work in the stables, and was set up by James as

the village barber. No one knew whence he came. I did, of
course, suspect him to be a runaway. He is honest and industrious. Last year I was ill when James was absent. We have
only maids in the house, and when I was recovering Josiah carried me up and downstairs until James returned. A year
after he came, Leila had an accident. Josiah stopped her
horse and got badly hurt —" Then with quick insight, she
added, " What interest have you in our barber, George? Is
it possible you know Josiah? "

Escape from truthful reply was impossible. " Yes, I do. He
is the property of my friend and neighbour Woodburn. I knew
him at once — he did not see me."

" Well! " she said coldly, " what next, George Grey? "

" I must inform his master. As a Southern woman you, of
course, see that no other course is possible. It is unpleasant,
but your sense of right must make you agree with me."

She returned, speaking slowly, " I do wish you would not
do it, George." Then she said quickly, " Have you taken any
steps in this matter? "

He was fairly cornered. " Yes, I wrote to Woodburn. He
will be here in a couple of days. I am sure he will lose no
time — and will take legal measures at once to reclaim his
property."

" I suppose it is all right," she said despairingly, " but I
am more than sorry — what James will say I do not know. I
hope he will not be called on to act — under the law he may."

" When does he return? " said Grey. " I shall, of course,
be frank with him."

" That will be advisable. He may be absent for a week
longer, or so he writes. I leave you to your cigar. I am tired,
and to-morrow is Sunday. Shall you go to church? "

" Certainly, Ann. Good-night."

At the door she turned back with a new and relieving thought,
" Suppose I — or we — buy this man's freedom."

"If I owned him that would not be required after what you have told me, but Woodburn is an obstinate, rather stern man, and will refuse, I fear, to sell —"

"What will he do with Josiah if he is returned to him as the Act orders?"

"Oh! once a runaway — and the man is no good — he would probably sell him to be sent South."

She rose and for a moment stood still in the darkness, and then crying, "The pity of it, my God, the pity of it!" went away without the usual courtesy of good-night.

George Grey, when left to his own company, somewhat amazed, began to wish he had never had a hand in this business. Ann Penhallow went up to her room, although it was as yet early, leaving John in the library and Grey with a neglected cigar on the porch. In the bedroom over his shop the man most concerned sat industriously reading the *Tribune*.

Ann sat down to think. The practical application of a creed to conduct is not always easy. All her young life had been among kindly considered slaves. Mr. Woodburn had a right to his property. The law provided for the return of slaves if they ran away. She suddenly realized that this man's future fate was in her power, and she both liked and respected him, and he had been hurt in their service. "Oh! why was not James at home? Could she sit still and let things go their way while the mechanism of the law worked." Between head and heart there was much argument. Her imagination pictured Josiah's future. "Had he deserved a fate so sad?" She fell on her knees and prayed for help. At last she rose and went down to the library. John laid down his book and stood up. The young face greeted her pleasantly, as she said, "Sit down, John, I want to talk to you. Can you keep a secret?"

"Why — yes — Aunt Ann. What is it?"

"I mean, John, keep it so that no one will guess you have a secret."

"I think I can," he replied, much surprised and very curious.

"You are young, John, but in your uncle's absence there is no one else to whom I can turn for help. Now, listen. Has Mr. Grey gone to bed?"

"Yes, aunt."

She leaned toward him, speaking low, almost in a whisper, "I do not want to explain, I only want to tell you something. Josiah is a runaway slave, John."

"Yes, aunt, he told me all about it."

"Did he, indeed!"

"Yes, we are great friends — I like him — and he trusted me. What's the matter now?" He was quick to understand that Josiah was in some danger. Naturally enough he remembered the man's talk and his one fear — recapture.

"George Grey has recognised Josiah as a runaway slave of a Mr. Woodburn —" She was most unwilling to say plainly, "Go and warn him."

He started up. "And they mean to take him back?"

She was silent. The indecisions of the habitually decisive are hard to deal with. The lad was puzzled by her failure to say more.

"It is dreadful, Aunt Ann. I think I ought to go and tell Josiah — now — to-night."

She made no comment except to say, "Arrest is not possible on Sunday — and he is safe until Monday or Tuesday."

John Penhallow looked at her for a moment surprised that she did not say go, or else forbid him to go; it was unlike her. He had no desire to wait for Sunday and was filled with anxiety. "I think I must go now — now," he said.

"Then I shall go to bed," she said, and kissing him went away slowly step by step up the stairs.

Staircases are apt to suggest reflections, and there are various ways of rendering the French phrase " *esprit de l'escalier.*" Aware that want of moral courage had made her uncertain what to do, or like the Indian, having two hearts, Ann had been unable to accept bravely the counsel of either. The loyal decisiveness of a lad of only sixteen years had settled the matter and relieved her of any need to personally warn Josiah. Some other influences aided to make her feel satisfied that there should be a warning. She was resentful because George Grey had put her in a position where she had been embarrassed by intense sectional sense of duty and by kindly personal regard for a man who not being criminal was to be deprived of all the safeguards against injustice provided by the common law. There were other and minor causes which helped to content her with what she well knew she had done to disappoint Mr. Woodburn of his prey. George Grey was really a bore of capacity to wreck the social patience of the most courteous. The rector fled from him, John always had lessons and how would James endure his vacuous talk. It all helped her to be comfortably angry, and there too was that horrible spittoon.

The young fellow who went with needless haste out of the house and down the avenue about eleven o'clock had no indecisions. Josiah trusted him, and he felt the compliment this implied.

CHAPTER X

ON the far side of the highroad Westways slumbered. Only in the rector's small house were lights burning. The town was in absolute darkness. Westways went to bed early. A pleased sense of the responsibility of his errand went with John as he came near to where Josiah's humble two-storey house stood back from the street line, marked by the well-known striped pole of the barber, of which Josiah was professionally proud. John paused in front of the door. He knew that he must awaken no one but Josiah. After a moment's thought he went along the side of the house to the small garden behind it where Josiah grew the melons no one else could grow, and which he delighted to take to Miss Leila or Mrs. Penhallow. In the novel the heroes threw pebbles at the window to call up fair damsels. John grinned; he might break a pane, but the noise — He was needlessly cautious. Josiah had built a trellis against the back of the house for grapevines which had not prospered. John began to climb up it with care and easily got within reach of the second-storey window. He tapped sharply on the glass, but getting no reply hesitated a moment. He could hear from within the sonorous assurance of deep slumber. Somehow he must waken him. He lifted the sash and called over and over in a low voice, "Josiah!" The snoring ceased, but not the sleep. The lad was resolute and still fearful of making a noise. He climbed with care into the dark room upsetting a little table. Instantly Josiah bounded out of bed and caught him in his strong grip, as John gasped, "Josiah!"

"My God!" cried the black in alarm, "anything wrong at the house?"

"No, sit down — I've got to tell you something. Your old master, Woodburn, is coming to catch you — he will be here soon — I know he won't be here for a day or two —"

"Is that so, Master John? It's awful — I've got to run. I always knowed sometime I'd have to run." He sat down on the bed; he was appalled. "God help me! — where can I go? I've got two hundred dollars and seventy-five cents saved up in the county bank, and I've not got fifty cents in the house. I can't get the money out — I'd be afraid to go there Monday. Oh, Lord!"

He began to dress in wild haste. John tried in vain to assure him that he would be safe on Sunday and Monday, or even later, but was in fact not sure, and the man was wailing like a child in distress, thinking over his easy, upright life and his little treasure, which seemed to him lost. He asked no questions; all other emotion was lost in one over-mastering terror.

John said at last, "If I write a cheque for you, can you sign your name to it?"

"Yes, sir."

"Then I will write a cheque for all of it and I'll get it out for you."

A candle was lighted and the cheque written. "Now write your name here, Josiah — so — that's right." He obeyed like a child, and John who had often collected cheques for his aunt of late, knew well enough how to word it to be paid to bearer. He put it in his pocket.

"But how will I ever get it?" said Josiah, "and where must I go? I'll get away Monday afternoon."

John was troubled, and then said, "I'll tell you. Go to the old cabin in the wood. That will be safe. I will bring you your money Monday afternoon."

The black reflected in silence and then said, "That will do — no man will take me alive, I know — my God, I know! Who set them on me? Who told? It was that drunken rascal, Peter. He told me he 'd tell if I did n't get him whisky. How did he know — Oh, Lord! He set 'em on me — I 'd like to kill him."

John was alarmed at the fierceness of the threat. "Oh! but you won't — promise me. I 've helped you, Josiah."

"I promise, Master John. I 'm a Christian man, thank the Lord. I 'd like to, but I won't — I won't."

"Now, that 's right," said John much relieved. "You 'll go to the cabin Monday — for sure."

"Yes — who told you to tell me?"

John, prudently cautious, refused to answer. "Now, let me out, I must go. I can't tell you how sorry I will be —" and he was tempted to add his aunt, but was wise in time. He had done his errand well, and was pleased with the success of his adventure and the flavour of peril in what he had done. He let himself into Grey Pine and went noiselessly upstairs. Then a window was closed and a waiting, anxious woman went to bed and lay long awake thinking.

John understood the unusual affection of his aunt's greeting when before breakfast she kissed him and started George Grey on his easy conversational trot. She had compromised with her political conscience and, notwithstanding, was strangely satisfied and a trifle ashamed that she had not been more distinctly courageous.

At church they had as usual a good congregation of the village folk and men from the mills, for Rivers was eminently a man's preacher and was much liked. John observed, however, that Josiah, who took care of the church, was not in his usual seat near the door. He was at home terribly alarmed and making ready for his departure on Monday. The rector missing him called after church, but his knock was not answered.

When Mr. Grey in the afternoon declared he would take a

walk and mail some letters, Mrs. Ann called John into the library. "Well," she said, "did you see Josiah?"

"Yes, aunt." It was characteristic of John Penhallow even thus early in life that he was modest and direct in statement. He said nothing of his mode of reaching Josiah. "I told him of his risk. He will hide in —"

"Do not tell me where," said Ann quickly; "I do not want to know."

He wondered why she desired to hear no more. He went on —" He has money in the county bank — two hundred dollars."

"He must have been saving — poor fellow!"

"I wrote a cheque for him, to bearer. I am to draw it to-morrow and take it to him in the afternoon. Then he will be able to get away."

Here indeed was something for Ann to think about. When Josiah was missed and legal measures taken, a pursuit organized, John having drawn his money might be questioned. This would never do — never. Oddly enough she had the thought, "Who will now shave James?" She smiled and said, "I must keep you out of the case — give me the cheque. Oh, I see it is drawn to bearer. I wonder if his owner could claim it. He may — he might — if it is left there."

"That would be mean," said John.

"Yes," she said thoughtfully. "Yes — I could give him the money. Let me think about it. Of course, I could draw on my account and leave Josiah's alone. But he has a right to his own money. I will keep the cheque, John. I will draw out his money and give it to you. Good gracious, boy! you are like James Penhallow."

"That's praise for a fellow!" said John.

Ann had the courage of her race and meant at last to see this thing through at all costs. The man had made his money and should have it. She was now resolute to take her share in the perilous matter she had started; and after all she was the wife of James Penhallow of Grey Pine; who would dare to question her? As to George Grey, she dismissed him with a low laugh and wondered when that long-desired guest would elect to leave Grey Pine.

At ten on Monday Billy, for choice, drove her over to the bank at the mills. The young cashier was asked about his sick sister, and then rather surprised as he took the cheque inquired, "How will you have it, ma'am? Josiah must be getting an investment."

"One hundred in fifties and the rest — oh, fifty in fives, the rest in ones."

She drove away, and in an hour gave the notes to John in an envelope, asking no questions. He set off in the afternoon to give Josiah his money.

Meanwhile on this Monday morning a strange scene in this drama was being acted in Josiah's little shop. He was at the door watchful and thinking of his past and too doubtful future, when he saw Peter Lamb pause near by. The man, fresh from the terrors of delirium tremens, had used the gift of Grey with some prudence and was in the happy condition of slight alcoholic excitement and good-humour.

"Halloa!" cried Peter. "How are you? I'm going to the mills to see my girl — want you to shave me — got over my joke; funny, was n't it?"

A sudden ferocious desire awoke in the good-natured barber — some long-past inheritance of African lust for the blood of an enemy.

"Don't like to kiss with a rough beard," said Peter. "I'll pay — got money — now."

"Come in," said Josiah. "Set down. I'll shut the door — it's a cold morning."

He spread the lather over the red face. "Head back a bit — that's right comfortable now, is n't it?"

" All right — go ahead."

Josiah took his razor. " Now, then," he said, as he set a big strong hand on the man's forehead, " if you move, I 'll cut your throat — keep quiet — don't you move. You told I was a slave — you ruined my life — I never did you no harm — I 'd kill you just as easy as that —" and he drew the blunt cold back of the razor across the hairy neck.

" My God! — I —" The man shuddered.

" Keep still — or you are a dead man."

" Oh, Lord! " groaned Lamb.

" I would kill you, but I don't want to be hanged. God will take care of you — He is sure. Some day you will do some wickedness worse than this — you just look at me."

There was for Peter fearful fascination in the black face of the man who stood looking down at him, the jaw moving, the white teeth showing, the eyes red, the face twitching with half-suppressed passion.

" Answer me now — and by God, if you lie, I will kill you. You set some one on me? Quick now! "

" I did."

" Who was it? No lies, now! "

" Mr. George Grey." Then Josiah fully realized his **danger.**

" Why did you? "

" You would n't help me to get whisky."

" Well, was that all? "

" You went and got the preacher to set Mr. Penhallow **on** me. He gave me the devil."

" My God, was that all? You 've ruined me for a drink of whisky — you 've got your revenge. I 'm lost — lost. Your day will come — I 'll be there. Now go and repent if you can — you 've been near to death. Go! " he cried.

He seized the terrified man with one strong hand, lifted him from the chair, cast open the door and hurled him out into the street. A little crowd gathered around Lamb as he rose on one elbow, dazed.

"Drunk!" said Pole, the butcher. "Drunk again!"

Josiah shut and locked the door. Then he tied up his bundle of clothes, filled a basket with food, and went out into his garden. He cast a look back at the neatly kept home he had recently made fresh with paint. He paused to pick a chilled rosebud and set it in his button-hole — a fashion copied from his adored captain. He glanced tearfully at the glass-framed covers of the yellowing melon vines. He had made money out of his melons, and next year would have been able to send a good many to Pittsburgh. As he turned to leave the little garden in which he took such pride, he heard an old rooster's challenge in his chicken-yard, which had been another means of money-making. He went back and opened the door, leaving the fowl their liberty. When in the lane behind his house, he walked along in the rear of the houses, and making sure that he was unobserved, crossed the road and entered the thick Penhallow forest. He walked rapidly for half an hour, and leaving the wood road found his way to the cabin the first Penhallow built. It was about half after one o'clock when the fugitive lay down on the earth of the cabin with his hands clasped behind his head. He stared upward, wondering where he could go to be safe. He would have to spend some of the carefully saved money. That seemed to him of all things the most cruel. He was not trained to consecutive thinking; memories old or new flitted through his mind. Now and then he said to himself that perhaps he had had no right to run away — and perhaps this was punishment. He had fled from the comforts of an easy life, where he had been fed, clothed and trusted. Not for a moment would he have gone back — but why had he run away? What message that soaring hawk had sent to him from his swift circling sweep overhead he was not able to put in words even if he had so desired. "That wicked hawk done it!" he said aloud.

At last, hearing steps outside, he bounded to his feet, a hand on the knife in his belt. He stood still waiting, ready as a crouching tiger, resolute, a man at bay with an unsated appetite for freedom. The door opened and John entered.

"You sort of scared me, Master John."

"You are safe here, Josiah, and here is your money."

He took it without a word, except, "I reckon, Master John, you know I'm thankful. Was there any one missing me?"

"No, no one."

"I'll get away to-night. I'll go down through Lonesome Man's Swamp and take my old bateau and run down the river. You might look after my muskrat traps. I was meaning to make a purse for the little missy. Now do you just go away, and may the Lord bless you. I guess we won't ever meet no more. You'll be mighty careful, Master John?"

"But you'll write, Josiah."

"I wouldn't dare to write — I'd be takin' risks. Think I'm safe here? Oh, Lord!"

"No one knows where you are — you'll go to-night?"

"Yes, after dark." He seemed more at ease as he said, "It was Peter Lamb set Mr. Grey on me. He must have seen me after that. I told you it was Peter."

"Yes,"— and then with the hopefulness of youth — "but you will come back, I am sure."

"No, sir — never no more — and the captain and Miss Leila — it's awful — where can I go?"

John could not help him further. "God bless you, Master John." They parted at length at the door of the cabin which had seen no other parting as sad.

The black lay down again. Now and then he swept his sleeve across tearful eyes. Then he stowed his money under his shirt in a linen bag hung to his neck, keeping out a few dollars, and at last fell sound asleep exhausted by emotion.

Josiah's customers were few in number. Westways was too poor to be able to afford a barber more than once a week, and then it was always in mid-morning when work ceased for an hour. Sometimes the Squire on his way to the mills came to town early, but as a rule Josiah went to Grey Pine and shaved him while they talked about colts and their training. As he was rarely needed in the afternoon, Josiah often closed his shop about two o'clock and went a-fishing or set traps on the river bank. His absence on this Monday afternoon gave rise, therefore, to no surprise, but when his little shop remained closed on Tuesday, his neighbours began to wonder. Peter Lamb wandering by rather more drunken than on Monday, stood a while looking at the shut door, then went on his devious way, thinking of the fierce eyes and the curse. Next came Swallow for his daily shave. He knocked at the door and tried to enter. It was locked. He heard no answer to his louder knock. He at once suspected that his prey had escaped him, and that the large fee he had counted on was to say the least doubtful. But who could have warned the black? Had Mr. Grey been imprudent? Lamb had been the person who had led Grey, as Swallow knew from that gentleman, to suspect Josiah as a runaway; but now as he saw Peter reeling up the street, he was aware that he was in no state to be questioned. He went away disappointed and found that no one he met knew whither Josiah had gone.

At Grey Pine Mrs. Ann, uneasily conscious of her share in the matter, asked John if he had given the money to Josiah. He said yes, and that the man was safe and by this time far away. Meanwhile, the little town buzzed with unwonted excitement and politics gave place about the grocer's door at evening to animated discussion, which was even more interesting when on Wednesday there was still no news and the town lamented the need to go unshaven.

On Thursday morning Billy was sent with a led horse to meet Penhallow at Westways Crossing. Penhallow had written that he must go on to a meeting of the directors of the bank at the mills and would not be at home until dinner-time. The afternoon train brought Mr. Woodburn, who as advised by Grey went at once to Swallow's house, where Mrs. Swallow gave him a note from her husband asking that if he came he would await the lawyer's return.

"Well, Billy, glad to see you," said Penhallow, as he settled himself in the saddle. "All well at Grey Pine?"

"Yes, sir."

The Squire was in high good-humour on having made two good contracts for iron rails. "How are politics, Billy?"

"Don't know, sir."

"Anything new at Westways?"

"Yes, sir," replied Billy with emphasis.

"Well, what is it?"

"Josiah's run away."

"Run away! Why?"

"Don't know — he's gone."

Penhallow was troubled, but asked no other questions, as he was late. He might learn more at home. He rode through the town and on to the mills. There he transacted some business and went thence to the bank. The board of well-to-do farmers was already in session, and Swallow — a member — was talking.

"What is that?" said Penhallow as he entered, hearing Josiah mentioned.

Some one said, "He has been missing since Monday." "He drew out all his money that morning," said Swallow, "all of it."

"Indeed," said Penhallow. "Did *he* draw it — I mean in person?"

"No," said the lawyer, who was well pleased to make mischief and hated Penhallow.

Penhallow was uneasily curious. "Who drew it?" he asked. "Josiah could hardly have known how to draw a cheque; I had once to help him write one."

"It was a cheque to bearer, I hear," said Swallow smiling. "Mrs. Penhallow drew the money. No doubt Josiah got it before he left."

Penhallow said, "You are insolent."

"You asked a question," returned Swallow, "and I answered it."

"And with a comment I permit no man to make. You said, 'no doubt he got it.' I want an apology at once." He went around the table to where Swallow sat.

The lawyer rose, saying, "Every one will know to-day that Josiah was a runaway slave. His master will be here this evening. Whoever warned him is liable under the Fugitive-Slave Act — Mrs. Penhallow drew the money and —"

"One word more, sir, of my wife, and I will thrash you. It is clear that you know all about the matter and connect my wife with this man's escape — you have insulted her."

"Oh, Mr. Penhallow," said the old farmer who presided, "I beg of you —"

"Keep quiet," said the Squire, "this is my business."

"I did not mean to insult Mrs. Penhallow," said Swallow; "I apologize — I —"

"You miserable dog," said Penhallow, "you are both a coward and a lying, usurious plunderer of hard-working men. You may be thankful that I am a good-tempered man — but take care."

"I shall ask this board to remember what has been said of me," said Swallow. "The law —"

"Law! The law of the cowhide is what you will get if I

hear again that you have used my wife's name. Good-day, gentlemen."

He went our furious and rode homeward at speed. Before the Squire reached Grey Pine he had recovered his temper and his habitual capacity to meet the difficulties of life with judicial calmness. He had long been sure that Josiah had been a slave and had run away. But after these years, that he should have been discovered in this remote little town seemed to him singular. The man was useful to him in several ways and had won his entire respect and liking, so that he felt personal annoyance because of this valuable servant having been scared away. That Ann had been in any way concerned in aiding his escape perplexed him, as he remembered how entire was her belief in the creed of the masters of slaves who with their Northern allies had so long been the controlling legislative power of the country.

"I am glad to be at home, my dear Ann," he said, as they met on the porch. "Ah! Grey, so you are come at last. It is not too late to say how very welcome you are; and John, I believe you have grown an inch since I left."

They went in, chatting and merry. The Squire cast an amused look at the big spittoon and then at his wife, and went upstairs to dress for dinner. At the meal no one for a variety of good reasons mentioned Josiah. The tall soldier with the readiness of helpless courtesy fell into the talk of politics which Grey desired. "Yes, Buchanan will carry the State, Grey, but by no large majority."

"And the general election?" asked the cousin.

"Yes, that is my fear. He will be elected."

Ann, who dreaded these discussions, had just now a reproachful political conscience. She glanced at her husband expecting him to defend his beliefs. He was silent, however, while Grey exclaimed, "Fear, sir — fear? You surely cannot mean to say — to imply that the election of a black Republican would be desirable." He laid down his fork and was about to become untimely eloquent — Rivers smiled — watching the Squire and his wife, as Penhallow said:

"Pardon me, Grey, but I cannot have my best mutton neglected."

"Oh, yes — yes — but a word — a word. Elect Fremont — and we secede. Elect Buchanan — and the Union is safe. There, sir, you have it in a nutshell."

"Ah, my dear Grey," said Penhallow, "this is rather of the nature of a threat — never a very digestible thing — for me, at least — and I am not very convincible. We will discuss it over our wine or a cigar." He turned to his wife, "Any news of Leila, Ann?"

"Yes, I had a letter to-day," she returned, somewhat relieved. "She seems to be better satisfied."

Grey accepted the interrupting hint and fell to critical talk of the Squire's horses. After the wine Penhallow carried off his guest to the library, and avoiding politics with difficulty was unutterably bored by the little gentleman's reminiscent nothings about himself, his crops, tobacco, wines, his habits of life, what agreed with him and what did not. At last, with some final whisky, Mr. Grey went to bed.

Ann, who was waiting anxiously, eager to get through with the talk she dreaded, went at once into the library. Penhallow rising threw his cigar into the fire. She laughed, but not in her usual merry way, and cried, "Do smoke, James, I shall not mind it; I am forever disciplined to any fate. There is a spittoon in the hall — a spittoon!"

The Squire laughed joyously, and kissed her. "I can wait for my pipe; we can't have any lapse in domestic discipline." Then he added, "I hear that my good Josiah has gone away — I may as well say, run away."

"Yes — he has gone, James." She hesitated greatly troubled.

"And you helped him — a runaway slave — you —" He smiled. It had for him an oddly humorous aspect.

"I did — I did —" and the little lady began to sob like a child. "It was — was wrong —" There was nothing comic in it for Ann Penhallow.

"You angel of goodness," he cried, as he caught her in his arms and held the weeping face against his shoulder, "my brave little lady!"

"I ought not to have done it — but I did — I did — oh, James! To think that my cousin should have brought this trouble on us — But I did — oh, James!"

"Listen, my dear. If I had been here, I should have done it. See what you have saved me. Now sit down and let us have it all out, my dear, all of it."

"And you really mean that?" she wailed piteously. "You won't think I did wrong — you won't think I have made trouble for you —"

"You have not," he replied, "you have helped me. But, dear, do sit down and just merely, as in these many years, trust my love. Now quiet yourself and let us talk it over calmly."

"Yes — yes." She wiped her eyes. "Do smoke, James — I like it."

"Oh, you dear liar," he said. "And so it was Grey?"

She looked up. "Yes, George Grey; but, James, he did not know how much we liked Josiah nor how good he had been to me, and how he got hurt when he stopped Leila's pony. He was sorry — but it was too late — oh, James! — you will not — oh, you will not —"

"Will not what, dear?" Penhallow was disgusted. A guest entertained in his own house to become a detective of an escaped slave in Westways, at his very gate! "My charity, Ann, hardly covers this kind of sin against the decencies of life. But I wish to hear all of it. Now, who betrayed the man — who told Grey?"

"I am sorry to say that it was Peter Lamb who first mentioned Josiah to George Grey as a runaway. When he spoke of his lost fingers, George was led to suspect who Josiah really was. Then he saw him, and as soon as he was sure, he wrote to a Mr. Woodburn, who was Josiah's old owner."

"I suppose he recognized Josiah readily?"

"Yes, he had been a servant of George's friend, Mr. Woodburn, and George says he was a man indulgently treated and much trusted."

"I infer from what I learned to-day that George told you all this and had already seen Swallow, so that the trap was set and Mr. Woodburn was to arrive. Did George imagine you would warn my poor barber —"

"But I — I did n't — I mean — I let John hear about it — and he told Josiah."

He listened. Here was another Mrs. Ann. There was in Ann at times a bewildering childlike simplicity with remarkable intelligence — a combination to be found in some of the nobler types of womanhood. He made no remark upon her way of betraying the trust implied in George Grey's commonplace confession.

"So, then, my dear, John went and gave the man a warning?"

"Yes, I would have gone, but it was at night and I thought it better to let John see him. How he did it I did not want to know — I preferred to know nothing about it."

This last sentence so appealed to Penhallow's not very ready sense of humour that he felt it needful to control his mirth as he saw her watching earnestness. "Grey, I presume, called on that rascal Swallow, Mr. Woodburn is sent for, and meanwhile Josiah is told and wisely runs away. He will never be caught. Anything else, my dear?"

"Yes, I said to George that we would buy Josiah's freedom — what amuses you, James?" He was smiling.

"Oh, the idea of buying a man's power to go and come, when he has been his own master for years. You were right, but it seems that you failed — or, so I infer."

"Yes. He said Mr. Woodburn was still angry and always had considered Josiah wickedly ungrateful." Penhallow looked at his wife. Her sense of the comedies of life was sometimes beyond his comprehension, but now — now was she not a little bit, half consciously, of the defrauded master's opinion?

"And so, when that failed, you went to bank and drew out the poor fellow's savings?" He meant to hear the whole story. There was worse yet, and he was sure she would speak of it. But now she was her courageous self and desired to confess her share in the matter. "Of course, he had to have money, Ann."

She wanted to get through with this, the most unpleasant part of the matter. "I want to tell you," she said. "I drew out his money with a cheque John made out and Josiah signed. John took him his two hundred dollars, as he knew where Josiah would hide — I — I did not want to know."

Her large part in this perilous business began to trouble the Squire. His face had long been to her an open book, and she saw in his silence the man's annoyance. She added instantly, "I could not let John draw it — and Josiah would not — he was too scared. He had to have his money. Was I wrong — was I foolish, James?"

"No — you were right. The cheque was in John's handwriting. You were the person to draw it. I would have drawn the money for him. He had a man's right to his honest savings. It will end here — so you may be quite at ease." Of this he was not altogether certain. He understood now why she had not given him of her own money, but Ann was clearly too agitated to make it well or wise to question her methods further. "Go to bed, dear, and sleep the sleep of the just — you did the right thing." He kissed her. "Good-night."

"One moment more, James. You know, of course — you

know that all my life I have believed with my brothers that slavery was wise and right. I had to believe that — to think so might exact from me and others what I never could have anticipated. I came face to face with a test of my creed, and I failed. I am glad I failed."

"My dear Ann," he said, "I am supposed to be a Christian man — I go to church, I have a creed of conduct. To-day I lost my temper and told a man I would thrash him if he dared to say a word more."

"It was at the bank, James?"

"Yes. That fellow Swallow spoke of your having drawn Josiah's money. He was insolent. You need have no anxiety about it — it is all over. I only mention it because I want you to feel that our creeds of conduct in life are not always our masters, and sometimes ought not to be. Let that comfort you a little. You know that to have been a silent looker-on at the return to slavery of a man to whom we owed so much was impossible. My wonder is that for a moment you could have hesitated. It makes me comprehend more charitably the attitude of the owners of men. Now, dear, we won't talk any more. Good-night — again — good-night."

He lighted a cigar and sat long in thought. He had meant not to speak to her of Swallow, but it had been, as he saw, of service. Then he wondered how long Mr. George Grey would remain and if he would not think it necessary to speak of Josiah. As concerned John, he would be in no hurry to talk to him of the barber; and how the lad had grown in mind and body! — a wonderful change and satisfactory.

When after breakfast Mr. Grey showed no desire to mention Josiah and prudently avoided talk about politics, Penhallow was greatly relieved. That his host did not open the question of Mr. Grey's conduct in the matter of the runaway was as satisfactory to the Maryland gentleman, whose sense of duty had created for him a situation which was increasingly disagreeable. He warmly welcomed Penhallow's invitation to look at some newly purchased horses, and expressed the most cordial approval of whatever he saw, somewhat to the amusement of Penhallow.

Penhallow left him when, declining to ride to the mills, Mr. Grey retired to the library and read the *Tribune,* with internal comment on its editorial columns. He laid the paper aside. Mr. Woodburn would probably have arrived in the afternoon, and would have arranged with Swallow for a consultation in which Mr. Grey would be expected to take part. It was plain that he really must talk to the Captain. He rose and went slowly down the avenue. A half-hour in Westways singularly relieved him. Swallow was not at home, and Josiah, the cause of Mr. Grey's perplexities, had certainly fled, nor did he learn that Mr. Woodburn had already arrived.

He was now shamefully eager to escape that interview with the captain, and relieved to find that there was no need to wait for the friend he had brought to Westways on a vain errand. Returning to Grey Pine, he explained to his cousin that letters from home made it necessary for him to leave on the mid-afternoon train. Never did Ann Penhallow more gratefully practise the virtue that speeds the parting guest. He was sorry to miss the captain and would have the pleasure of sending him a barrel of the best Maryland whisky; "and would you, my dear cousin, say, in your delightful way, to the good rector how much I enjoyed his conversation?"

Ann saw that the lunch was of the best and that the wagon was ready in more than ample season. As he left, she expressed all the regret she ought to have felt, and as the carriage disappeared at a turn of the avenue she sank down in a chair. Then she rang a bell. "Take away that thing," she said,—"that spittoon."

"If James Penhallow were here," she murmured, "I should ask him to say — damn! I wonder now if that man Woodburn will come, and if there will be a difficulty with James on my account." She sat long in thought, waiting to greet her husband, while Mr. Grey was left impatient at the station owing to the too hospitable desire of Ann to speed the parting guest.

When about dusk the Squire rode along the road through Westways, he came on the rector and dismounted, leaving his horse to be led home by Pole's boy. "Glad to see you, Mark. How goes it; and how did you like Mr. Grey?"

"To tell you the truth, Squire, I did not like him. I was forced into a talk about politics. We differed, as you may suppose. He was not quite pleasant. He seemed to have been so mixed up with this sad business about Josiah that I kept away at last, so that I might keep my temper. Billy drove him to the station after lunch."

"Indeed!" said Penhallow, pleased that Grey had gone. It was news to him and not unwelcome. Ann would no doubt explain. "What put Grey on the track of Josiah as a runaway? Was it a mere accidental encounter?" He desired to get some confirmatory information.

"No — I suspect not." Then he related what Josiah had told him of Peter's threats. "I may do that reprobate injustice, but — However, that is all I now know or feel justified in suspecting."

"Well, come up and dine to-day; we can talk it out after dinner."

"With pleasure," said Rivers.

Penhallow moodily walking up the street, his head bent in thought, was made aware that he was almost in collision with Swallow and a large man with a look of good-humoured amusement and the wide-open eyes and uplift of brow expressive of pleasure and surprise.

"By George, Woodburn!" said the Squire. "I heard some one of your name was here, but did not connect the name with you. I last heard of you as in a wild mix-up with the Sioux,

and I wished I was with you." As Penhallow spoke the two
men shook hands, Swallow meanwhile standing apart not overpleased as through the narrowed lids of near-sight he saw that
the two men must have known one another well and even inti-
mately, for Woodburn replied, "Thought you knew I'd left the
army, Jim. The last five years I've been running my wife's
plantation in Maryland."

The Squire's pleasure at his encounter with an old West
Point comrade for a moment caused him to forget that this was
the master who had been set on Josiah's track by Grey. It was
but for a moment. Then he drew up his soldierly figure and
said coldly, "I am sorry that you are here on what cannot be a
very agreeable errand."

"Oh!" said Woodburn cheerfully, "I came to get my old
servant, Cæsar. It seems to have been a fool's errand. He has
slipped away. I suppose that Grey as usual talked too freely.
But how the deuce does it concern you? I see that it does."

Penhallow laughed. "He was my barber."

"And mine," said Woodburn. "If you have missed him,
Jim, for a few days, I have missed him for three years and
more." Then both men laughed heartily at their inequality of
loss.

"I cannot understand why this fellow ran away. He was a
man I trusted and indulged to such an extent that my wife says
I spoiled him. She says he owned me quite as much as I owned
him — a darned ungrateful cuss! I came here pretty cross
when I got George's letter, and now I hear of an amount of
hostile feeling which rather surprised me."

"That you are surprised, Will, surprises me," said Penhallow. "The Fugitive-Slave Act will always meet with opposition at the North. It seems made to create irritation even
among people who really are not actively hostile to slavery. If
it became necessary to enforce it, I believe that I would obey
it, because it is the law — but it is making endless trouble.

May I ask what you propose to do about this present case?"

"Do — oh, nothing! I am advised to employ detectives and hunt the man down. I will not; I shall go home. It is not Mr. Swallow's advice."

"No, it is not," said the lawyer, who stood aside waiting a chance to speak. "Some one warned the man, and it is pretty generally suspected how he came to be told."

Penhallow turned to Woodburn, "Has Mr. Swallow ventured to connect me or any of my family with this matter?"

"No," said Woodburn, which was true. Swallow meant to keep in reserve Mrs. Penhallow's share in the escape until he learned how far an angry slave-owner was disposed to go. Woodburn had, however, let him understand that he was not of a mind to go further, and had paid in good-humour a bill he thought excessive. Grey had made it all seem easy, and then as Swallow now learned had gone away. He had also written to his own overseer, and thus among their neighbours a strong feeling prevailed that this was a case for prompt and easy action. The action had been prompt and had failed. Woodburn was going home to add more bitterness to the Southern sense of Northern injustice.

When Woodburn, much to Penhallow's relief, had said he was done with the case, the Squire returned, "Then, as you are through with Mr. Swallow, come home and dine with me. Where are you staying?"

"At Mr. Swallow's, but I leave by the night train."

"So soon! But come and dine. I will send for your bag and see that you get to your train."

The prospect of Swallow and his feeble, overdressed wife, and his comrade's urgency, decided Woodburn. He said, "Yes, if Mr. Swallow will excuse me."

Swallow said, "Oh, of course!" relieved to be rid of a dissatisfied client, and the two ex-soldiers went away together chatting of West Point life.

Half-way up the avenue Penhallow said, " Before we go in, a word or two —"

" What is it, Jim? "

" That fellow said nothing of Mrs. Penhallow, you are sure? "

" Yes," returned Woodburn, " not a word. I knew that you lived here, but neither of you nor of Mrs. Penhallow did he say a word in connection with this business. I meant to look you up this afternoon. Why do you speak of your wife? "

" Because — well — I could not let you join us without an honest word concerning what I was sure you would have heard from Swallow. Now if you had taken what I presume was his advice — to punish the people concerned in warning Josiah, you — indeed I — might hesitate —"

" What do you mean, Jim? " said his companion much amazed.

" I mean this: After our loose-tongued friend Grey told my wife that Josiah was in danger, she sent him word of the risk he ran, and then drew out of our bank for him his savings and enabled him to get away. Now don't say a word until I have done. Listen! This man turned up here over three years ago and was soon employed about my stables. He broke his leg in stopping a runaway and saved my wife's young niece, our adopted child, Leila Grey. There was some other kind and efficient service. That's all. Now, can you dine with me? "

" With all my heart, Jim. Damn Grey! Did he talk much? "

" Did he? No, he gabbled. But are you satisfied? "

" Yes, Jim. I am sorry I drove off your barber — and I shall hold my tongue when I get home — as far as I can."

" Then come. I have some of my father's Madeira, if Grey has left any. I shall say a word to Mrs. Penhallow. By George! I am glad to have you."

Penhallow showed Woodburn to a room, and feeling relieved and even elated, found his wife, who had tired of waiting and had gone to get ready to dine. He told her in a few words

enough to set her at ease with the new guest. Then Mark
Rivers came in and John Penhallow, who having heard about
the stranger's errand was puzzled when he became aware of the
cordial relations of his uncle and Mr. Woodburn.

The dinner was pleasant and unembarrassed. The lad whom
events had singularly matured listened to gay memories of West
Point and to talk of cadets whose names were to live in history
or who had been distinguished in our unrighteous war with
Mexico. When now and then the talk became quite calmly political, Ann listened to the good-natured debate and was longing to speak her mind. She was, however, wisely silent, and reflected half amused that she had lost the right to express herself on the question which was making politics ill-tempered but
was now being discussed at her table with such well-bred
courtesy. John soon ceased to follow the wandering talk, and
feeling what for him had the charm of romance in the flight of
Josiah sat thinking over the scene of the warning at night, the
scared fugitive in the cabin, and the lonely voyage down through
the darkness of the rapids of the river. Where would the man
go? Would they ever see him again? They were to meet in
far-away days and in hours far more perilous. Then he was
caught once more by gay stories of adventures on the plains and
memories of Indian battles, until the wine had been drunk and
the Squire took his friend to the library for an hour.

CHAPTER XI

PENHALLOW himself drove his guest to meet the night express to the East, and well pleased with his day returned to find his wife talking with Rivers and John. He sat down with them at the fire in the hall, saying, "I wanted to keep Woodburn longer, but he was wise not to stay. What are you two talking over — you were laughing?"

"I," said Rivers, "was hearing how that very courteous gentleman chanced to dine with these mortal enemies who stole his property. I kept quiet, Mrs. Penhallow said nothing, John ate his dinner, and no one quarrelled. I longed for Mr. Grey —"

"For shame," said Mrs. Ann. "Tell him why we were laughing — it was at nothing particular."

"It was about poor old Mrs. Burton."

"What about her? If you can make that widow interesting in any way, I shall be grateful."

"It was about her dead husband —"

"Am I to hear it or not?" said Penhallow. "What is it?"

"Why, what she said was that she was more than ever confirmed in her belief in special Providences, because Malcolm was so fond of tomatoes, and this year of his death not one of their tomatoes ripened."

The Squire's range of enjoyment of the comic had limitations, but this story was immensely enjoyed and to his taste. He laughed in his hearty way. "Did she tell you that, Mark, or has it improved in your hands?"

"No — no, I got it from Grace, and he had it from the widow. I do not think it seemed the least bit funny to Grace."

173

"But after all," said Mrs. Ann, "is it so very comic?"

"Oh, now," said Penhallow, "we are in for a discussion on special Providences. I can't stand it to-night; I want something more definite. My manager says sometimes, 'I want to close out this-here business.' Now I want to close out this abominable business about my poor Josiah. You and your aunt, John, have been, as you may know, breaking the law of your country —"

Rivers, surprised and still partially ignorant, looked from one to another.

"Oh, James!" remonstrated his wife, not overpleased.

"Wait a little, my dear Ann. Now, John, I want to hear precisely how you gave Josiah a warning and — well — all the rest. You ought to know that my little lady did as usual the right thing. The risks and whatever there might have been of danger were ours by right — a debt paid to a poor runaway who had made us his friends. Now, John!"

Rivers watched his pupil with the utmost interest. John stood up a little excited by this unexpected need to confess. He leaned against the side of the mantel and said, "Well, you see, Uncle Jim, I got in at the back —"

"I don't see at all. I want to be made to see — I want the whole story."

John had in mind that he had done a rather fine thing and ought to relate it as lightly as he had heard Woodburn tell of furious battles with Apaches. But, as his uncle wanted the whole story, he must have some good reason, and the young fellow was honestly delighted. Standing by the fire, watched by three people who loved him, and above all by the Captain, his ideal of what he felt he himself could never be, John Penhallow told of his entrance to Josiah's room and of his thought of the cabin as a hiding-place. When he hesitated, Penhallow said, "Oh, don't leave out, John Penhallow, I want all the details. I have my reasons, John."

Flushed and handsome, with his strong young face above the figure which was to have his uncle's athletic build, he related his story to the close. As he told of the parting with the frightened fugitive and the hunted man's last blessing, he was affected as he had not been at the time. "That's all, Uncle Jim. It was too bad — and he will never come back."

"He could," said Rivers.

"Yes — but he will not. I know the man," said Penhallow. "He has the courage of the minute, but the timidity of the slave. We shall see him no more, I fear."

The little group around the fire fell to silence, and John sat down. He wanted a word of approval, and got it. "I want you to know, John," said Penhallow, "that I think you behaved with courage and discretion. It was not an errand for a boy, but no man could have done better, and your aunt had no one else. I am glad she had not."

Then John Penhallow felt that he was shaky and that his eyes were uncomfortably filling. With a boy's dislike of showing emotion, he mastered his feelings and said, "Thank you, Uncle Jim."

"That is all," said the Squire, who too saw and comprehended what he saw, "go to bed, you breaker of the law —"

"And I," said Ann, "a wicked partner. Come, John."

They left the master of the house with the rector. Rivers looked at the clock, "I think I must go. I do not stand late hours. If I let the day capture the night, the day after is apt to find me dull."

"Well, stand it this once, Mark. I hate councils of war or peace without the pipe, and now, imagine it, my dear wife wanted me to smoke, and that was all along of that terrible spittoon and the long-expected cousin of whom I have heard from time to time. *Les absens n'ont pas toujours tort.* Now smoke and don't watch the clock. I said this abominable business was to be closed out —"

"And is it not?" asked Rivers.

"No. I do not talk about Peter Lamb to my wife, because she thinks my helping him so often has done the man more harm than good. It was not Grey alone who was responsible. He told Mrs. Penhallow that Peter had sent him to Josiah's shop. He told Grey too that Josiah must be a runaway slave and that any one would know him by his having lost two fingers. That at once set Grey on this mischievous track."

"I am only too sure that you are right," returned Rivers. "Peter tried a very futile blackmailing trick on Josiah. He wanted to get whisky, and told the poor negro that he must get it for him or he would let his master know where he was. Of course, the scamp knew what we all knew and no more, but it alarmed Josiah, who came to me at once. He was like a scared child. I told him to go home and that Peter had lied. He went away looking as if the old savagery in his blood might become practically active."

"I don't wonder," said Penhallow. "Did it end there?"

"No, I saw Peter next day, and he of course lied to me very cleverly, said it was only a joke on Josiah, and so on. I think, sir, and you will I hope excuse me — I do think that the man were better let alone. Every time you help him, he gets worse. When he was arrested and suspected of burning Robert's hayrick, you pleaded with the old farmer and got the man off. He boasted of it the next time he got drunk."

"I know — I know." The Squire had paid Robert's loss, and aware of his own folly was of no mind to confess to any one. "I have no wish or will to help him. I mean now to drop him altogether, and I must tell him so. But what a pity it is! He is intelligent, and was a good carpenter until he began to drink. I must talk to him."

"You will only make him more revengeful. He has what he calls 'got even' with Josiah, and he is capable of doing it with you or me. Let him alone."

" Not I," said the Squire; " if only for his mother's sake, I must see what I can do."

" Useless — quite useless," said Rivers. " You may think that strange advice for a clergyman, but I do sometimes despair of others and occasionally of Mark Rivers. Goodnight."

During these days the fugitive floated down the swift little river at night, and at dawn hid his frail boat and himself in the forests of a thinly settled land. He was brave enough, but his ignorance of geography added to his persistent terror. On the third day the broader waters brought him to farms and houses. Then he left his boat and struck out across the country until he came to a railway. In the station he made out that it led to Philadelphia. Knowing that he would be safe there, he bought a ticket and arrived in the city the next day — a free man with money, intelligence, and an honest liking for steady work.

The Squire had the good habit of second thought. His wife knew it well and had often found it valuable and to be trusted. At present he was thoroughly disgusted with the consequences of what he knew to be in some degree the result of his own feeling that he was bound to care for the man whose tie to him was one few men would have considered as in any serious degree obligatory. The night brought good counsel, and he made up his mind next morning simply to let the foster-brother alone. Fate decreed otherwise. In the morning he was asked by his wife to go with her to the village; she wanted some advice. He did not ask what, but said, " Of course. I am to try the barber's assistant I have brought from the mills to shave me, and what is more important — Westways. I have put him in our poor old Josiah's shop."

They went together to Pole's, and returning she stopped before the barn-like building where Grace gathered on Sundays a scant audience to hear the sermons which Rivers had told him had too much heart and too little head.

"What is it?" asked Penhallow.

"I have heard, James, that their chapel (she never called it church) is leaking — the roof, I mean. Could not you pay for a new roof?"

"Of course, my dear — of course. It can't cost much. I will see Grace about it."

"Thank you, James." On no account would she now have done this herself. She was out of touch for the time with the whole business of politics, and to have indulged her usual gentle desire to help others would have implied obligation on the part of the Baptist to accept her wish that he should vote and use his influence for Buchanan. Now the thing would be done without her aid. In time her desire to see the Democrats win in the interest of her dear South would revive, but at present what with Grey and the threat of the practical application of the Fugitive-Slave Act and her husband's disgust, she was disposed to let politics alone.

Presently, as they walked on, Peter Lamb stopped them. "I'd like to speak to you for a moment, Mr. Penhallow." Mrs. Penhallow walked on.

"What is it?" said the Squire.

"I'm all right now — I'll never drink again. I want some work — and mother's sick."

"We will see to her, but you get no more work from me."

"Why, what's the matter, sir?"

"Matter! You might ask Josiah if he were here. You know well enough what you did — and now I am done with you."

"So help me God, I never —"

"Oh! get out of my way. You are a miserable, lying, ungrateful man, and I have done with you."

He walked away conscious of having again lost his temper, which was rare. The red-faced man he left stood still, his lips parted, the large yellow teeth showing. "It's that damned parson," he said.

Penhallow rejoined his wife. "What did he want?" she asked.

"Oh, work," he said. "I told him he could get no more from me."

"Well, James," she said, "that is the first sensible thing you have ever done about that man. You have thoroughly spoiled him, and now it is very likely too late to discipline him."

"Yes — perhaps — you may be right." He knew her to be right, but he did not like her agreement with his decision to be connected with even her mild statement that it had been better if long before he had been more reasonably severe and treated Lamb as others would have treated him. In the minor affairs of life Ann Penhallow used the quick perception of a woman, and now and then brought the Squire's kindly excesses to the bar of common sense. Sometimes the sentence was never announced, but now and then annoyed at his over-indulgent charity she allowed her impatience the privilege of speech, and then, as on this occasion, was sorry to have spoken.

Dismissing his slight vexation, Penhallow said presently, "He told me his mother was sick."

"She was not yesterday. I took her our monthly allowance and some towels I wanted hemmed and marked. He lied to you, James. Did you believe him even for a moment?"

"But she might be sick, Ann. I meant you to stop and ask."

"I will, of course." This time she held her tongue, and left him at Grace's door.

The perfect sweetness of her husband's generous temperament was sometimes trying to Ann in its results, but now it had helped her out of an awkward position, and with pride and affection she watched his soldierly figure for a moment and then went on her way.

Intent with gladness on fulfilling his wife's errand, he went up the steps of the small two-storey house of the Baptist preacher. He had difficulty in making any one hear where there was no one to hear. If at Westways the use of the rare bells or more common knockers brought no one to the door, you were free to walk in and cry, " Where are you, Amanda Jane, and shall I come right up? " Penhallow had never set foot in the house, but had no hesitation in entering the front room close to the narrow hall which was known as the front entry. The details of men's surroundings did not usually interest Penhallow, but in the mills or the far past days of military service nothing escaped him that could be of use in the work of the hour. The stout little Baptist preacher, with his constant every-day jollity and violent sermons, of which he had heard from Rivers, in no way interested Penhallow. When he once said to Ann, " The man is unneat and common," she replied, " No, he is homely, but neither vulgar nor common. I hate his emotional performances, but the man is good, James." " Then I do wish, Ann, he would button his waistcoat and pull up his socks."

Now he looked about him with some unusual attention. There was no carpet. A set of oddly coloured chairs and settees which would have pleased Ann, a square mahogany table set on elephantine legs, completed the furnishings of a whitewashed room, where the flies, driven indoors by cool weather, buzzed on window glasses dull with dust. The back room had only a writing-table, a small case of theological books, and two or three much used volumes of American history. Penhallow looked around him with unusually awakened pity. The gathered dust, the battered chairs, the spider-webs in the darker corners, would have variously annoyed and disgusted Ann Penhallow. A well-worn Bible lay on the table, with a ragged vol-

ume of "Hiawatha" and "Bunyan's Holy War." There were
no other books. This form of poverty piteously appealed to him.

"By George!" he exclaimed, "that is sad. The man is book-
poor. Ann must have that library. I will ask him to use
mine." As he stood still in thought, he heard steps, and turned
to meet Dr. McGregor.

"Come to see Grace, sir?" said the doctor.

"Yes, I came about a little business, but there seems to be
no one in."

"Grace is in bed and pretty sick too."

"What is the matter?"

"Oh, had a baptism in the river — stood too long in the
water and got chilled. It has happened before. Come up and
see him — he'll like it."

The Squire hesitated and then followed the doctor. "Who
cares for him?" he asked as they moved up the stairs.

"Oh, his son. Rather a dull lad, but not a bad fellow. He
has no servant — cooks for himself. Ever try it, Squire?"

"I — often. But what a life!"

The stout little clergyman lay on a carved four-post bedstead
of old mahogany, which seemed to hint of better days. The
ragged patch-work quilt over him told too of busy woman-
hands long dead. The windows were closed, the air was sick
(as McGregor said later), and there was the indescribable com-
posite odour which only the sick chamber of poverty knows.
The boy, glad to escape, went out as they entered.

Grace sat up. "Now," he said cheerfully, "this is real good
of you to come and see me! Take a seat, sir."

The chairs were what the doctor once described as non-sit-
able, and wabbled as they sat down.

"You are better, I see, Grace," said the doctor. "I fetched
up the Squire for a consultation."

"Yes, I'm near about right." He had none of the common
feeling of the poor that he must excuse his surroundings to

these richer visitors, nor any least embarrassment. "It's good to see some one, Mr. Penhallow."

"I come on a pleasant errand," said Penhallow. "We will talk it over and then leave you to the doctor. Mrs. Penhallow wants me to roof your church. I came to say to you that I shall do it with pleasure. You will lose the use of it for one Sunday at least."

"Thank you, Squire," said Grace simply. "That's real good medicine."

"I will see to it at once."

The doctor opened a window, and Penhallow drew a grateful breath of fresh air.

"Don't go, sir," said Grace. The Squire sat down again while McGregor went through his examination of the sick man. Then he too rose to leave.

"Must you go?" said Grace. "It is such a pleasure to see some one from the outside." The doctor smiled and lingered.

"I suppose, Squire, you'll get Joe Boynton, the carpenter, to put on the roof? He's one of my flock."

"Yes," said Penhallow, "but he will want to put his old workman, Peter Lamb, on the job, and I have no desire to help that man any further. He gives his mother nothing, and every cent he makes goes for drink."

McGregor nodded approval, but wondered why at last the Squire's unfailing good-nature had struck for higher wages of virtue in the man he had ruined by kindness.

"I try to keep work in Westways," said Penhallow. "Joe shall roof the chapel, and like as not Peter will be too drunk to help. I can't quite make it a condition with Joe that he shall not employ Peter, but I should like to." McGregor's face grew smiling at Penhallow's conclusion when he added, "I hope he may get work elsewhere." Then the Squire went downstairs with the doctor, exchanging brevities of talk.

"Are you aware, Penhallow, that this wicked business about

Josiah has beaten Buchanan in Westways? Come to apply the Fugitive-Slave Act and people won't stand it. As long as it was just a matter of newspaper discussion Westways did n't feel it, but when it drove away our barber, Westways's conscience woke up to feel how wicked it was."

The Squire had had an illustration nearer home and kept thinking of it as he murmured monosyllabic contributions while the doctor went on — " My own belief is that if the November election were delayed six months, Fremont would carry Pennsylvania."

Penhallow recovered fuller consciousness and returned, " I distrust Fremont. I knew him in the West. But he represents, or rather he stands for, a party, and it is mine."

" I am glad to know that," said McGregor. " I am really glad. It is a relief to be sure about a man like you, Penhallow. I suppose you know that you are loved in the county as no one else is."

" Nonsense," exclaimed the Squire, laughing, but not ill-pleased.

" No, I am serious; but it leads up to this: Am I free to say you will vote the Republican ticket?"

" Yes — yes — you may say so."

" It will be of use, but could n't I persuade you to speak at the meeting next week at the mills?"

" No, McGregor. That is not in my line." He had other reasons for refusal. " Let us drop politics. What is that boy of yours going to do?"

" Study medicine," he says. " He has brains enough, and Mr. Rivers tells me he is studious. Our two lads fell out, it seems, and my boy got the worst of it. What I don't like is that he has not made up with John."

" No, that is bad; but boys get over their quarrels in time. However, I must go. If I can be of any use to Tom, you know that I am at your service."

"When were you not at everybody's service?" said the doctor, and they went out through the hall.

"Good-bye," said Penhallow, but the doctor stopped him.

"Penhallow, may I take the liberty to bother you with a bit of unasked advice?"

"A liberty, nonsense! What is it?"

"Well, then — let that drunken brute Peter alone. You said that you would not let the carpenter use him, but why not? Then you hoped he would get work. Let him alone."

"McGregor, I have a great charity for a drunkard's son — and the rest you know."

"Yes, too well."

"I try to put myself in his place — with his inheritance —"

"You can't. Nothing is more kind than that in some cases, and nothing more foolish in others or in this —"

"Perhaps. I will think it over, Doctor. Good-bye."

Meanwhile Grace lay in bed thoughtfully considering the situation. While her husband seemed practically inactive in politics, Mrs. Penhallow had been busy, and she had clearly hinted that the roofing of the chapel might depend on how Grace used his large influence in the electoral contest, but had said nothing very definite. He was well aware, however, that in his need for help he had bowed a little in the House of Rimmon. Then he had talked with Rivers and straightened up, and now did the Squire's offer imply any pledge on his own part? While he tried to solve this problem, Penhallow reappeared.

"I forgot something, Grace," he said. "Mrs. Penhallow will send Mrs. Lamb here for a few days, and some — oh, some little luxuries — ice and fresh milk."

The Baptist did not like it. Was this to keep him in the way he had resolved not to go. "Thank you and her," he returned, and then added abruptly, "How are you meaning to vote, Squire?"

"Oh, for Fremont," replied Penhallow, rather puzzled.

"Well, that will be good news in Westways." It was to him, too, and he felt himself free. "Is n't Mrs. Penhallow rather on the other side?"

He had no least idea that the question might be regarded as impertinent. Penhallow said coldly, "My wife and I are rather averse to talking politics. I came back to say that I want you to feel free to make use of my library — just as Rivers does."

"Now that will be good. I am book-starved except for Rivers's help. Thank you." He put out a fat hand and said, "God has been good to me this day; may He be as kind to you and yours."

The Squire went his way wondering what the deuce the man had to do with Ann Penhallow's politics.

Mrs. Lamb took charge of Grace, and Mrs. Penhallow saw that he was well supplied and gave no further thought to the incorrigible and changeful political views of Westways.

The excitement over the flight of Josiah lessened, and Westways settled down to the ordinary dull routine of a little community dependent on small farmers and the mill-men who boarded at the old tavern or with some of the townspeople.

The forests were rapidly changing colour except where pine and spruce stood darkly green amid the growing magnificence of maple and oak. It was the intermediate season in which were neither winter nor summer sports, and John Penhallow enjoying the pageant of autumn rode daily or took long walks, exploring the woods, missing Leila and giving free wing to a mind which felt the yearning, never to be satisfied, to translate into human speech its bird-song of enjoyment of nature.

On an afternoon in mid-October he saw Mr. Rivers, to his surprise, far away on the bank of the river. Well aware that the clergyman was rarely given to any form of exercise on foot,

John was a little surprised when he came upon the tall, stooping, pallid man with what Ann Penhallow called the "eloquent" eyes. He was lying on the bank lazily throwing stones into the river. As John broke through the alders and red willows above him, he turned at the sound and cried, as John jumped down the bank, "Glad to see you, John! I have been trying to settle a question no one can settle to the satisfaction of others or even himself. You might give me your opinion as to who wrote the Epistle to the Hebrews. Origen gave it up, and Philo had a theory about Apollos, and there is Tertullian, that's all any fellow knows; and so now I await your opinion. What nobody knows about, anybody's opinion is good about."

John laughed as he said, "I don't think I'll try."

"Did you ever read Hebrews, John? The epistle I mean."

"No."

"Then don't or not yet. The Bible books ought to be read at different ages of a man's life. I could arrange them. Your aunt reads to you or with you, I believe?"

"Yes — Acts just now, sir. She makes it so clear and interesting that it seems as if all might have happened now to some missionaries somewhere."

"That is an art. Some of the Bible stories require such help to make them seem real to modern folk. How does, or how did, Leila take Mrs. Ann's teachings?"

"Oh, Leila," he replied, as he began to pitch pebbles in the little river, "Leila — wriggled. You know, she really can't keep quiet, Mr. Rivers."

"Yes, I know well enough. But did what interested you interest Leila?"

"No — no, indeed, sir. It troubled Aunt Ann because she could not make her see things. Usually at night before bedtime we read some of the Gospels, and then once a week Acts. Every now and then Leila would sit still and ask such queer questions — about people."

"What kind of questions, John?" He was interested and curious.

"Oh, about Peter's mother and — I forget — oh, yes, once — I remember that because aunt did not like it and I really could n't see why."

"Well, what was it?"

"She wanted to know if Christ's brothers ever were married and if they had children."

"Did she, indeed! Well — well!"

"Aunt Ann asked her why she wanted to know that, and Leila said it was because she was thinking how Christ must have loved them, and maybe that was why He was so fond of little children. Now, I could n't have thought that."

"Nor I," said Rivers. "She will care more for people — oh, many people — and by and by for things, events and the large aspects of life, but she is as yet undeveloped."

John was clear that he did not want her to like many people, but he was inclined to keep this to himself and merely said, "I don't quite understand."

"No, perhaps I *was* a little vague. Leila is at the puzzling age. You will find her much altered in a year."

"I won't like that."

"Well, perhaps not. But you too have changed a good deal since you came. You were a queer young prig."

"I was — I was indeed."

Then they were silent a while. John thought of his mother who had left him to the care of tutors and schools while she led a wandering, unhappy, invalid life. He remembered the Alps and the *spas* and her fretful care of his very good health, and then the delight of being free and surrounded with all a boy desires, and at last Leila and the wonderful hair on the snow-drift.

"Look at the leaves, John," said Rivers. "What fleets of red and gold!"

"I wonder," said John, "how far they will drift, and if any of them will ever float to the sea. It is a long way."

"Yes," returned Rivers, "and so we too are drifting."

"Oh, no, sir," said John, with the confidence of youth, "we are not drifting, we are sailing — not just like the leaves anywhere the waves take them."

"More or less," added Rivers moodily, "more or less."

He looked at the boy as he spoke, conscious of a nature unlike his own. Then he laughed outright. "You may be sure we are a good deal hustled by circumstances — like the leaves."

"I should prefer to hustle circumstances," replied John gaily, and again the rector studied the young face and wondered what life had in store for this resolute nature.

"Come, let us go. I have walked too far for me, I am over-tired, John."

What it felt to be overtired, John hardly knew. He said, "I know a short cut, cater-cornered across the new clearing."

As they walked homeward, Rivers said, "What do you want to do, John? You are more than fit for the university — you should be thinking about it."

"I do not know."

"Would you like to be a clergyman?"

"No," said John decisively.

"Or a lawyer, or a doctor like Tom McGregor?"

"I do not know — I have not thought about it much, but I might like to go to West Point."

"Indeed!"

"Yes, but I am not sure."

CHAPTER XII

WHEN John was eager to hear what Leila wrote, his aunt laughed and said, "As you know, there is always a word of remembrance for you, but her letters would hardly interest you. They are about the girls and the teachers and new gowns. Write to her — I will enclose it, but you need expect no answer."

That Leila should have acquired interest in gowns seemed to him unlike that fearless playmate. He learned that the rules of the school forbade the writing of letters except to parents and near relatives. He was now to write to Leila the first letter he had written since his laborious epistles to his mother when at school. His compositions seemed to Rivers childlike long after he showed notable competence in speech.

"DEAR LEILA: It is very hard that you cannot write to me. We are all well here except Lucy, who is lame. It isn't very much.

"Of course you have heard about our good old Josiah. Isn't that slave law wicked? Westways is angry and all turned round for Fremont. Mr. Grace has been ill, and Uncle Jim is putting a roof on his chapel. Josiah left me his traps when he ran away. He meant to make you a muskrat skin bag. I found four in his traps, and I have caught four more, and when Mrs. Lamb makes a bag of them, I am to have for it a silver clasp which belonged to Great-grandmother Penhallow. No girl will have one like that. It was on account of Josiah the town will not vote for Buchanan.

"I wish I had asked you for a lock of your hair. I remember how it looked on the snow when Billy upset us."—

189

He had found his letter-writing hard work, and let it alone for a time. Before he finished it, he had more serious news to add.

The autumnal sunset of the year, the red and gold of maple, oak and sassafras, was new to the boy who had spent so many years in Europe, and more wonderful was it when in this late October on the uplands there fell softly upon the glowing colours of the woods a light covering of early snow. Once seen it is a spectacle never to be forgotten, and he had the gift of being charmed by the scenic ingenuities of nature.

The scripture reading was over and he was thinking late in the evening of what he had seen, when his aunt said, " Good-night, John — bed-time," and went up the stairway. John lay quiet, with closed eyes, seeing the sunlit snow lightly dusted on the red and yellows of the forest.

About eleven his uncle came from the library. " What, you scamp! — up so late! I meant to mail this letter to-day; run down and mail it. It ought to go when Billy takes the letters to Westways Crossing early to-morrow. I will wait up for you. Now use those long legs and hurry."

John took his cap and set off, liking the run over the snow, which was light and no longer falling. He raced down the avenue and climbed the gate, thinking of Leila. He dropped the letter into the post-office box, and decided to return by a short way through the Penhallow woods which faced the town. He moved eastward, climbed the fence, and stood still. He was some two hundred yards from the parsonage. His attention was arrested by a dull glow behind the house. He ran towards it as it flared upward a broad rush of flame, brilliantly lighting the expanse of snow and sending long prancing shafts of shadow through the woods as it struck on the tall spruces. Shouting, " Fire! Fire! " John came nearer.

The large store of dry pine and birch for winter-use piled in a shed against the back of Rivers's house was burning fiercely, with that look of ungoverned fury which gives such an expression of merciless, personal rage to a great fire. The terror of it at first possessed the lad, who was shouting himself hoarse. The flame was already running up and over the outer planking and curling down upon the thin snow of the shingled roof as he ran around the small garden and saw the front door open and Rivers come out. The rector said, "It is gone, John; I will go for your uncle. Run over to the Wayne and call up the men. Tell them to get out my books and what they can, but to run no risks. Quick, now! Wake up the town."

There was little need, for some one at the inn had heard John's cries. In a few minutes the village was awake and out of doors before Penhallow arriving took charge and scattered men through the easily lighted pines, in some dread of a forest fire. The snow on the floor of pine-needles and on the laden trees was, however, as he soon saw, an insurance against the peril from far-scattered sparks, and happily there was no wind. Little of what was of any value was saved, and in the absence of water there was nothing to do but to watch the fire complete its destructive work.

"There is nothing more we can do, Rivers," said Penhallow. "John was the first to see it. We will talk about it to-morrow — not now — not here."

The three Grey Pine people stood apart while books and clothes and little else were carried across the road and stored in the village houses. At last the flames rose high in the air and for a few minutes as the roof fell in, the beauty of the illumination was what impressed John and Rivers. The Squire now and then gave quick orders or stood still in thought. At last he said to the rector, "I want you to go to Grey Pine, call up Mrs. Penhallow and tell her, and then go to bed. You will like to stay here with me, John?"

"Yes, sir." The Squire walked away as Rivers left them.

"Fine sight, ain't it, Mr. John," said Billy, the one person who enjoyed the fire.

"Yes," said John, absently intent on the red-lighted snow spaces and the gigantic shadows of the thinly timbered verge of the forest as they were and were not. Then there was a moment of alarm. An old birch, loosely clad with dry, ragged bark stood near to the house. A flake of falling fire fell on it. Instantly the whole trunk-cover blazed up with a roar like that of a great beast in pain. It was sudden and for the instant terrible, but the snow-laden leaves still left on it failed to take fire, and what in summer would have been a calamity was at an end.

"Gosh!" exclaimed Billy, "did n't he howl?" John made no reply.

"Could n't wake Peter. I was out first." He had liked the fun of banging at the doors. "Old Woman Lamb said she could n't wake him."

"Drunk, I suppose," said John absently, stamping out a spark among the pine-needles at his feet, now freed from snow by the heat.

The night passed, and when the dawning came, the Squire leaving some orders went homeward with John, saying only, "Go to bed at once, we will talk about it later. I don't like it, John. You saw it first — where did it begin?"

"Outside, sir, in the wood-shed."

"Indeed! There has been some foul play. Who could it have been?" He said no more.

It was far into the morning when John awaking found that he had been allowed to make up for the lost sleep of the past night. His aunt smiling greeted him with a kiss, concerning which there is something to be said in regard to what commentary the assistant features make upon the kiss. "I would not have you called earlier," she said; "but now, here is your breakfast, you have earned it." She sat down and watched the disappearance of a meal which would have filled his mother with anxiety. Ann was really enjoying the young fellow's wholesome appetite and contrasting it with the apprehensive care concerning food he had shown when long before he had seemed to her husband and herself a human problem hard to solve. James Penhallow had been wise, and Leila a rough and efficient schoolmistress. "Do not hurry, John; have another cup?"

"Yes, please."

"Have you written that letter? I mean to be naughty enough to enclose it to Leila. I told you so."

"Yes, but it is not quite done, and now I must tell her about the fire. I wrote her that Josiah had gone away."

"The less of it the better. I mean about — well, about your warning him — and the rest — your share and mine."

"Of course not, Aunt Ann. I would not talk about myself. I mean, I could not write about it."

"You would talk of it if she were here — you would, I am sure."

"Yes, that's different — I suppose, I would," he returned. She was struck with this as being like what James Penhallow would have said and have, or not have, done.

"If you have finished, John, I think your uncle wants you."

"Why didn't you tell me, aunt?" he said, as he got up in haste.

"Oh, boys must be fed," she cried. She too rose from her seat, and went around the table and kissed him again, saying, "You are more and more like my captain, John."

Being a woman, as John was well aware, not given to express approval of what were merely acts of duty, he was surprised at what was, for her, excess of praise; nor was she as much given to kissing, as are many women. The lad felt, therefore, that what she thus said and did was unusual, and was what his Uncle Jim called one of Ann's rarely conferred brevets of affection.

"Yes," she repeated, "you are like him."

"What! I like Uncle Jim! I wish I were."

"Now go," she said, giving him a gentle push. She was shyly aware of a lapse into unhabitual emotion and of some closer

approach to the maternal relation fostered by his growing resemblance to James Penhallow.

"So," laughed his uncle as John entered the library, "you
have burned down the school and are on a holiday — you and
Rivers."

John grinned. "Yes, sir."

"Sit down. We are discussing that fire. You were the first
to see it, John. It was about eleven —"

"Yes, uncle, it struck as I left the hall."

"No one else was in sight, and in fact, Rivers, no one in
Westways is out of bed at ten. Both you and John are sure the
fire began outside where the wood was piled under a shed."

"Yes," said Rivers. "It was a well dried winter supply,
birch and pine. The shed, as you know, was alongside of the
kitchen door. I went over the house as usual about nine, after
old Susan, the maid, had gone home. I covered the kitchen
fire with ashes — a thing she is apt to neglect. I went to bed
at ten and wakened to hear the glass crack and to smell smoke.
The kitchen lay under my bedroom. I fear it was a deliberate
act of wickedness."

"That is certain," said Penhallow, "but who could have
wanted to do it. You and I, Rivers, know every one in Westways. Can you think of any one with malice enough to make
him want to burn a house and risk the possibility of murder?"

Rivers turned his lean pale face toward the Squire, unwilling
to speak out what was in the minds of both men. John listened,
looking from one serious face to the other.

"It seems to me quite incredible," said Penhallow, and then
Rivers knew surely that the older man had a pretty definite belief in regard to the person who had been concerned. He knew
too why the Squire was unwilling to accuse him, and waited to
hear what next Penhallow would say.

"It makes one feel uncomfortable," said Penhallow, and turning to John, "Who was first there after you came?"

"Billy, sir, I think, even before the men from the Wayne, but I am not sure. I told him to pound on the doors and wake up the town."

"Did he say anything?"

"Oh, just his usual silliness."

"Was Peter Lamb at the fire?"

"I think not. His mother opened a window and said that she could not waken Peter. It was Billy told me that. I told Billy, I supposed Peter was drunk. But he wasn't yesterday afternoon — I saw him."

"Oh, there was time enough for that," remarked Rivers.

Then the two men smoked and were silent, until at last the Squire said, "Of course, you must stay here, Rivers, and you know how glad we shall be — oh, don't protest. It is the only pleasant thing which comes out of this abominable matter. Ann will like it."

"Thank you," returned Rivers, "I too like it."

John went away to look at the ruin left by the fire, and the Squire said to his friend, "As I am absent in the mornings at the mills, you may keep school here, Rivers," and it was so settled.

Before going out Penhallow went to his wife's little room on the farther side of the hall. He had no desire to hide his conclusions from her. She saw how grave he looked. "What is it, James?" she asked, looking up from her desk.

"I am as sure as a man can be that Peter Lamb set fire to the parsonage. He has always been revengeful and he owed our friend, the Rector, a grudge. I have no direct evidence of his guilt, and what am I to do? You know why I have always stood by him. I suppose that I was wrong."

She knew only too well, but now his evident trouble troubled her and she loved him too well to accept the temptation to use the exasperating phrase, "I always told you so." "You can do nothing, James, without more certainty. You will not question his mother?"

"No, I can't do that, Ann; and yet I cannot quite let this go by and simply sit still."

"What do you propose to do?"

"I do not know," and with this he left her and rode to the mills. In the afternoon he called at Mrs. Lamb's and asked where he could find Peter.

She was evidently uneasy, as she said, "You gave him work on the new roof of the Baptist chapel with Boynton; he might be there."

He made no comment, and went on his way until reaching the chapel he called Peter down from the roof and said, "Come with me, I want to talk to you."

Peter was now sober and was sharply on guard. "Come away from the town," added the Squire. He crossed the street, entered his own woods and walked through them until he came in sight of the smoking relics of the parsonage, where at a distance some few persons were idly discussing what was also on Penhallow's mind. Here he turned on his foster-brother, and said, "You set that house on fire. I could get out of your mother enough to make it right to arrest you, but I will not bring her into the matter. Others suspect you. Now, what have you to say?"

"Say! I didn't do it — that's all. I was in bed."

"Why did you not get up and help?"

"Wasn't any of my business," he replied sulkily. "Everybody in this town's against me, and now when I've given up drinking, to say I set a house afire —"

"Well!" said Penhallow, "this is my last word, you may go. I shall not have you arrested, but I cannot answer for what others may do."

Peter walked away. He had been for several days enough under the influence of whisky to intensify what were for him

normal or at least habitually indulged characteristics. For them
he was only in part responsible. His mother had spoiled him.
He had been as a child the playmate of his breast-brother until
time and change had left him only in such a relation to Penhallow as would have meant little or nothing to most men. As
a result, out of the Squire's long and indulgent care of a lad
who grew up a very competent carpenter, and gradually more and
more an idle drunkard, Peter had come to overestimate the power
of his claim on Penhallow. What share in his evil qualities his
father's drunkenness had, is in no man's power to say. His desire to revenge the slightest ill-treatment or the abuse his evil
ways earned had the impelling force of a brute instinct. What
he called "getting even" kept him in difficulties, and when he
made things unpleasant or worse for the offenders, his constant
state of induced indifference to consequences left him careless
and satisfied. When there was not enough whisky to be had,
his wild acts of revengeful malice were succeeded by such childlike terror as Penhallow's words produced. 'The preacher
would have him arrested; the Squire would not interfere. Some
day he would get even with him too!' There was now, however,
no recourse but flight. He hastened home and finding his
mother absent searched roughly until by accident as he let fall
her Bible, a bank note dropped out. There were others, some
sixty dollars or more, her meagre savings. He took it all
without the least indecision. At dark after her return he ate
the supper she provided. When she had gone to bed, he packed
some clothes in a canvas bag and went quietly out upon the
highway. Opposite to the smoking ruin of the rectory he halted.
He muttered, "I've got even with him anyhow!"

As he murmured his satisfaction, a man left on guard crossed
the road. "Halloa! Where are you bound, Peter?"

"Goin' after a job. Bad fire, wasn't it — hard on the
preacher!"

"Hard. He's well lodged at the Squire's, and I do hear it

was insured. Nobody's much the worse, and it will make a
fine bit of work for some of us. Who done it, I wonder?"

"How should I know! Good-night."

When out of sight, he turned and said, "I ain't got even yet.
Them rich people's hard to beat. Damn the Squire! I'll get
even with him some day." He was bitterly disappointed.
"Gosh! I ran that nigger out, and now I'm a runaway too.
It's queer."

At Westways Crossing he waited until an empty freight train
was switched off to let the night express go by. Then he stowed
himself away in an open box-car and had a comfortable sense
of relief as it rolled eastward. He felt sure that the Squire's
last words meant that he might be arrested and that immediate
flight was his only chance of escape.

He thus passes, like Josiah, for some years out of my story.
He had money, was when sober a clever carpenter, and felt,
therefore, no fear of his future. He had the shrewd conviction
that the Squire at least would not be displeased to get rid of
him, and would not be very eager to have him pursued.

James Penhallow was disagreeably aware that it was his duty
to bring about the punishment of his drunken foster-brother,
but he did not like it. When the next morning he was about
to mount his horse, he saw Mrs. Lamb, now an aged woman,
coming slowly up the avenue. As she came to the steps of the
porch, Penhallow went to meet her, giving the help of his
hand.

"Good-morning, Ellen," he said, "what brings you here over
the snow this frosty day? Do you want to see Mrs. Penhallow?"

For a moment she was too breathless to answer. The withered
leanness of the weary old face moved in an effort to speak, but
was defeated by emotion. She gasped, "Let me set down."

He led her into the hall and gave her a chair. Then he called
his wife from her library-room. Ann at once knew that some-

thing more than the effect of exertion was to be read in the moving face. The dull grey eyes of age stared at James Penhallow and then at her, and again at him, as in the vigour of perfect health they looked down at his old nurse and with kindly patience waited. "Don't hurry, Ellen," said Mrs. Ann. "You are out of breath."

She seemed to Ann like some dumb animal that had no language but a look to tell the story of despair or pain. At last she found her voice and gasped out, "I came to tell you he has run away. He went last night. I'd like to be able to say, James Penhallow, that I don't know why he went away —"

"We will not talk of it, Ellen," said the Squire, with some sense of relief at the loss of need to do what he had felt to be a duty. "Come near to the fire," he added.

"No, I want to go home. I had to tell you. I just want to be alone. I'd have given it to him if he had asked me. I don't mind his taking the money, but he took it out of my Bible. I kept it there. It was like stealing from the Lord. It'll bring him bad luck. Mostly it was in the Gospels — just a bank-note here and there — sixty-one dollars and seventy-three cents it was." She seemed to be talking to herself rather than to the man and woman at her side. She went on — sometimes a babble they could not comprehend, as in pity and wonder they stood over her. Then again her voice rose, "He took it from the book of God. Oh, my son, my son! I must go."

She rose feebly tottering, and added, "It will follow him like a curse out of the Bible. He took it out of the Bible. I must go."

"No," said Penhallow, "wait and I will send you home."

She sat down again. "Thank you." Then with renewed strength, she said, "You won't have them go after him?"

"No, I will not."

He went away to order the carriage, and returning said, "You know, Ellen, that you will always be taken care of."

" Yes, I know, sir — I know.   But he took it out of my Bible — out of the book of God."   She was presently helped into the wagon and sent away murmuring incoherently.

" And so, James," said Ann, " she knew too much about the fire.   What a tragedy! "

" Yes, she knew.   I am glad that he has gone.   If he had faced it out and stayed, I must have done something.   I suppose it is better for her on the whole.   When he was drunk, he was brutal; when he was sober, he kept her worried.   I am glad he has gone."

" But," said Ann, " he was her son —"

" Yes, more 's the pity."

In a day or two it was known that Peter had disappeared. The town knew very well why and discussed it at evening, when as usual the men gathered for a talk.   Pole expressed the general opinion when he said, " It 's hard on the old woman, but I guess it 's a riddance of bad rubbish."   Then they fell to talking politics, the roofing of the chapel and the price of wheat and so Westways settled down again to its every-day quiet round of duties.

The excitement of the fire and Lamb's flight had been unfavourable to literary composition, but now John returned to his letter.   He continued:

" The reticule will have to be finished in town.   Uncle will take it after the election or send it to you.   If you remember your Latin, you will know that reticule comes from *reticulus,* a net.   But this is n't really a net.

" We have had a big excitement.   Some one set fire to the parsonage and it burnt down."   [He did not tell her who set it on fire, although he knew very well that it was Peter Lamb.]   " Lamb has run away, and I think we are well rid of him.

" I do miss you very much.   Mr. Rivers says you will be a

fashionable young lady when you come back and will never snow-ball any more. I don't believe it.

"Yours truly,

"JOHN PENHALLOW."

Mrs. Penhallow enclosed the letter in one of her own, and no answer came until she gave him a note at the end of October. Leila wrote:

"DEAR JOHN: It is against the rules to write to any one but parents, and I am breaking the rules when I enclose this to you. I do not think I ought to do it, and I will not again.

"You would not know me in my long skirts, and I wear my hair in two plaits. The girls are all from the South and are very angry when they talk about the North. I cannot answer them and am sorry I do not know more about politics, but I do know that Uncle Jim would not agree with them.

"I go on Saturdays and over Sundays to my cousins in Balti-more. They say that the South will secede if Fremont should be elected. I just hold my tongue and listen.

"Yours sincerely,

"LEILA GREY.

"P. S. I shall be **very** proud of the bag. I hope you are studying hard."

"Indeed!" muttered John. "Thanks, Miss Grey." There was no more of it.

John Penhallow had come by degrees to value the rare privi-lege of a walk with the too easily wearied clergyman, who had avenues of ready intellectual approach which invited the ad-venturous mind of the lad and were not in the mental topography of James Penhallow. The cool, hazy days of late October had come with their splendour of colour-contrasts such as only the artist nature could make acceptable, and this year the autumn was unusually brilliant.

"Do you enjoy it?" asked Rivers.

"Oh, yes, sir. I suppose every one does."

"In a measure, as some people do the great music, and as the poets usually do not. People presume that the ear for rhythm is the same as that for music. They are things apart. A few poets have had both."

"That seems strange," said John. "I have neither," and he was lost in thought until Rivers, as usual easily tired, said, "Let us sit down. How hazy the air is, John! It tenderly flatters these wild colour-contrasts. It is like a November day of the Indian summer."

"Why do they call it Indian summer?" asked John.

"I do not know. I tried in vain to run it down in the dictionaries. In Canada it is known as 'L'été de St. Martin.'"

"It seems," said John, "as if the decay of the year had ceased, in pity. It is so beautiful and so new to me. I feel sometimes when I am alone in these woods as if something was going to happen. Did you ever feel that, sir?"

Rivers was silent for a moment. The lad's power to state things in speech and his incapacity to put his thoughts in writing had often puzzled the tutor. "Why don't you put such reflections into verse, John? It's good practice in English."

"I can't — I've tried."

"Try again."

"No," said John decidedly. "Do look at those maples, Mr. Rivers — and the oaks — and the variety of colour in the sassafras. Did you ever notice how its leaves differ in shape?"

"I never did, but nothing is exactly the same as anything else. We talked of that once."

"Then since the world began there never was another me or Leila?"

"Never. There is only one of anything."

John was silent — in thought of his unresemblance to any other John. "But I am like Uncle Jim! Aunt says so."

" Yes, outwardly you are; but you have what he has not —
imagination. It is both friend and foe as may be. It may not
be a good gift for a soldier — at least one form of it. It may be
the parent of fear — of indecisions."

" But, Mr. Rivers, may it not work also for good and suggest possibilities — let you into seeing what other men may do? "

The reflection seemed to Rivers not like the thought of so
young a man. He returned, " But I said it might be a friend
and have practical uses in life. I have not found it that myself.
But some men have morbid imagination. Let us walk." They
went on again through the quiet splendour of the woodlands.

" Uncle Jim is going away after the election."

" Yes."

" He will see Leila. Don't you miss her? "

" Yes, but not as you do. However, she will grow up and go
by you and be a woman while you are more slowly maturing.
That is their way. And then she will marry."

" Good gracious! Leila marry! "

" Yes — it is a way they have. Let us go home."

John was disinclined to talk. Marry — yes — when I am
older, I shall ask her until she does!

November came in churlish humour and raged in storms of
wind and rain, until before their time to let fall their leaves the
woods were stripped of their gay colours. On the fourth day of
November the Squire voted the Fremont electoral ticket, and
understood that with the exception of Swallow and Pole, Westways had followed the master of Grey Pine. The other candidates did not trouble them. The sad case of Josiah and the
threat to capture their barber had lost Buchanan the twenty-
seven votes of the little town. Mr. Boynton, the carpenter,
fastening the last shingles on the chapel roof remarked to a
workman that it was an awful pity Josiah could n't know about
it and that the new barber was n't up to shaving a real stiff
beard.

The Squire wrote to his wife from Philadelphia on the ninth:

"DEAR ANN: We never talk politics because you were born a Democrat and consider Andrew Jackson a political saint. I begin to wish he might be reincarnated in the body of Buchanan. He will need backbone, I fear. He has carried our State by only three thousand majority in a vote of 433,000. I am told that the excitement here was so great that the peacemaking effect of a day of cold drizzle alone prevented riot and bloodshed. Mr. Buchanan said in October, 'We shall hear no more of "Bleeding Kansas."' Well, I hope so. Here we are at one. I should feel more regret at the defeat of my party if I had more belief in Fremont, but your man is, I am sure, elected, and we must hope for the best and try to think that hope reasonable.

"I have been fortunate in my contracts for rails with the two railroads. I shall finish this letter in Baltimore.—

"Baltimore.— I saw Leila, who has quite the air of a young lady and is well, handsome and reasonably contented. Dined with your brother Henry; and really, Ann, the cold-blooded way the men talked of secession was a little beyond endurance. I spoke my mind at last, and was heard with courteous disapproval. My friend, Lt.-Colonel Robert Lee of the Army, was the only man who was silent about our troubles. Two men earnestly advocated the re-opening of the slave-trade, and if as they say slavery is a blessing, the slave-trade is morally justified and logically desirable. I do want you to feel, my dear Ann, how extreme are the views of these pleasant gentlemen.

"The Madeira was good, and despite the half-hidden bitterness of opinion, I enjoyed my visit. Let John read this letter if you like to do so.

"Yours always and in all ways,
"JAMES PENHALLOW."

She did not like, but John heard all about this visit when the Squire came home.

The winter of 1856-7 went by without other incident at Westways, with Mrs. Ann's usual bountiful Christmas gifts to the children at the mills and Westways. Mr. Buchanan was inaugurated in March. The captain smiled grimly as he read in the same paper the message of the Governor of South Carolina recommending the re-opening of the trade in slaves, and the new President's hopes " that the long agitation over slavery is approaching its end." Nor did Penhallow fancy the Cabinet appointments, but he said nothing more of his opinions to Ann Penhallow.

CHAPTER XIII

IN the early days of May the Squire began to rebuild the parsonage, and near by it a large room for Sunday school and town-meetings. Ann desired to add a library-room for the town and would have set about this at once had not her husband resolutely set himself against any addition to the work with which she filled her usefully busy life. She yielded with reluctance, and the library plan was set aside to the regret of Rivers, who living in a spiritual atmosphere was slow to perceive what with the anxiety of a great love James Penhallow saw so clearly — the failure of Ann Penhallow's health.

When at last Penhallow sat down with McGregor in his office, the doctor knew at once that something serious was troubling his friend.

"Well, Penhallow," he said, "what can I do for you?"

"I want you to see my wife. She sleeps badly, tires easily, and worst of all is unwilling to consult you."

"Yes, that's serious. Of course, she does the work of two people, but has it ever occurred to you, Penhallow, that in the isolated life you lead she may be at times bored and want or need society, change?"

"My dear Doctor, if I propose to her to ask our friends from the cities to visit us, she says that entertaining women would only add to her burdens. How could she amuse them?" The Squire had the helplessness of a strong man who has to deal with the case of a woman who, when a doctor is thought to be necessary, feels that she has a right to an opinion as to whether or not it is worth while. She did not believe it to be necessary and felt that there was something unpleasant in this medical intrusion upon a life which had been one of unbroken health. To her husband's annoyance she begged him to wait, and on one pretext or another put off the consultation — it would do in a week, or 'she was better.' Her postponement and lack of decision added to the Squire's distress, but it was mid-June before she finally yielded and without a word to Penhallow wrote to ask McGregor to call.

In a week Leila would be at Grey Pine. The glad prospect of a summer's leisure filled John with happy anticipations. He had his boat put in order, looked after Lucy's condition, and had in mind a dozen plans for distant long-desired rides into the mountains, rides which now his uncle had promised to take with them. He soon learned that the medical providence which so often interferes with our plans in life had to be considered.

Mrs. Penhallow to John's surprise had of late gone to bed long before her accustomed hour, and one evening in this June of 1857 Penhallow seeing her go upstairs at nine o'clock called John into the library.

"Mr. Rivers," he said, "has gone to see some one in Westways, and I have a chance to talk to you. Sit down."

John obeyed, missing half consciously the ever-ready smile of the Squire.

"I am troubled about your aunt. Dr. McGregor assures me that she has no distinct ailment, but is simply so tired that she is sure to become ill if she stays at home. No one can make her lessen her work if she stays here. You are young, but you must have been aware of what she does for this town and at the mills — oh, for every one who is in need or in trouble. There is the every-day routine of the house, the sick in the village, the sewing class, the Sunday afternoon reading in the small hospital at our mills, letters — no end of them. How she has stood it so long, I cannot see."

"But she seems to like it, sir," said John. He could n't understand that what was so plainly enjoyed could be hurtful.

" Yes, she likes it, but — well, she has a heavenly soul in an earthly body, and now at last the body is in revolt against over-use, or that at least is the way McGregor puts it. I ought to have stopped it long ago." John was faintly amused at the idea of any one controlling Ann Penhallow where her despotic beliefs concerning duties were concerned.

The Squire was silent for a little while, and then said, " It has got to stop, John. I have talked to McGregor and to her. Leila is to meet us in Philadelphia. I shall take them to Cape May and leave them there for at least the two months of summer. You may know what that means for me and for her, and, I sup-pose, for you."

" Could I not go there for a while? "

" I think not. I really have not the courage to be left alone, John. I think of asking you to spend a part of the day at the mills this summer. You will have to learn the business, for as you know your own property, your aunt's and mine are largely invested in our works. I thought too of an engineering school for you in the fall, and then of the School of Mines in Paris. It is a long look ahead, but it would fit you to relieve me of my work. Think it over, my son. How does it look to you, or have you thought of what you mean or want to do? Don't an-swer me now — think it over. And now I have some letters to write. Good-night."

John went upstairs to bed with much to think about, and above all else of the disappointing summer before him and the wish he had long cherished, but which his uncle's last words had made it necessary for him to reconsider.

Ann Penhallow had made a characteristic fight against the combined forces of the doctor and her husband. She had de-clared she would give up this and that, if only she could be left at home. She showed to the doctor an irritability quite new to his experience of her and which he accepted as added evidence of need of change. Her bodily condition and her want of common sense in a matter so clear to him troubled the Squire and drove him to his usual resort when worried — long rides or hard tramps with his gun. After luncheon and a decisive talk with Mrs. Ann, she had pleaded that he ought to remain with them at the shore. She was sure he needed it and it would set her mind at ease. He told her what she knew well enough, how impossible it would be for him to leave the mills and be absent long. She who rarely manufactured difficulties now began to ask how this was to be done and that, until Rivers said at last, " I can promise to read at the hospital until I go away for my August holiday."

" You would not know the kind of things to read."

" No one could do it as well as you," said Rivers, " but I can try."

" Everything will be cared for, Ann," said Penhallow, " only don't worry."

" I never worry," she returned, rising. " You men think everything will run along easily without a woman's attention."

" Oh, but Ann, my dear Ann ! " exclaimed Penhallow, not knowing what more to say, annoyed at the discussion and at her display of unnecessary temper and the entire loss of her usual common sense.

She said, with a laugh in which there was no mirth, " I presume one of you will, of course, run my sewing-class ? "

" Ann — Ann ! " said the Squire.

Rivers understood her now in the comprehending sympathy of his own too frequent moods of melancholy. " Ah ! " he murmured, " if I could but teach her how to knit the ravelled sleeve of care."

" I presume," she added, " that I am to accept it as 'settled," and so went out.

" Come, John," said Penhallow an hour later, " get the guns : we will see if we can find a bird or two. It is early, but we will at least have a good tramp."

John kept pace with the rapid stride of the Squire, taking note of the reddening buds of the maples, for this year in the hills the spring came late.

"You must have seen your aunt's condition," said Penhallow. "I have seen it coming on ever since that miserable affair of Josiah. It troubled her greatly."

John had the puzzled feeling of the inexperienced young in regard to the matter of illness and its influential effect on temper, and was well pleased to converse on anything else, when his uncle asked, "Have you thought over what I said to you about your future?"

"Well?"

"I should like to go to West Point, Uncle Jim."

To his surprise Penhallow returned, pausing as he spoke, "I had thought of that, but as I did not know you had ever considered it, I did not mention it. It would in some ways please me. As a life-long career it would not. We are in no danger of war, and an idle existence at army-posts is not a very desirable thing for an able man."

"I had the idea, uncle, that I would not remain in the service."

"But you would have to serve two years after you were graduated — and still that was what I did, oh! and longer — much longer. As an education in discipline and much else, it is good — very good. Are you really in earnest about it?"

"Yes, sir."

"Well, it is better than college. I will think about it. If you go to the Point, it should be this coming fall.— See! there's a bird. Ah! you missed him. I wonder what Ann will say."

Then John knew that the Squire favoured what had been for a long time on his own mind. What had made him eager to go into the army was in part that tendency towards adventure which had been a family trait and his admiration for the soldier-uncle; nor did the mere student life and the quiet years of managing the iron-mills as yet appeal to him as desirable.

"I wish, Uncle Jim, that you could settle the matter."

This was so like his own dislike of unsettled affairs that the Squire laughed in his hearty way. "So far as I am concerned, you may regard it as decided; but securing a nomination to the Point is quite another matter. It may be difficult. I will see about it. Now we will let it drop. That dog is pointing. Ah! the rascal. It is a hare."

They saw no more birds, nor did the Squire expect to find anything in the woods except the peace of mind to be secured by violent exercise. He went on talking about the horses and the mills.

When near to the house, Penhallow said, "Your aunt is to go away to-morrow. Every day here seems to add to her difficulty in leaving home. I shall say nothing to her of West Point until it is settled one way or another. I shall, of course, go to the Cape for a day, unless your aunt's brother Charles will take my place when he brings Leila to Philadelphia to meet us. I may be gone a week, and you and Rivers are to keep bachelor's hall and watch the work on the parsonage. I shall ask Leila to write to you and to me about your aunt. Did I say that we go by the 9:30 A. M. express?"

"No, sir."

"Well, we do."

James Penhallow was pleased and amazed when he discovered that Mrs. Ann was quietly submissive to the arrangements made for her comfort on the journey. She appeared to have abruptly regained her good temper and, Penhallow thought, was unnaturally and excessively grateful for every small service. Being unused to the ways of sick women, he wondered as the train ran down the descent from the Alleghany Mountains how long a time was required to know any human being entirely. He had been introduced within two weeks to two Ann Penhal-

lows besides the Ann he had lived with these many years. He
concluded, as others have done, that people are hard to understand, and thus thinking he ran over in mind the group they left
on the platform at Westways Crossing.

There was Billy — apparently a simple character, abruptly
capable of doing unexpected things; useful to-day, useless to-
morrow. He called up to mind the very competent doctor;
John, and his friend the moody clergyman — beloved of all men.
The doctor had said of him, " a man living in the monastery of
himself — in our world, but not of it."

" What amuses you, James? " asked his wife.

This good sign of return to her normal curiosity was fa-
miliarly pleasant. " I was recalling, Ann, what McGregor said
of Rivers after that horrid time of sickness at Westways. You
may remember it."

" No, I do not."

" No! He said that Rivers was a round-shouldered angel."

" That does not seem to me amusing, James."

" Round-shouldered he is, Ann, and for the rest you at least
ought to recognize your heavenly fellow-citizens when you meet
them."

" Is that your poetry or your folly, James Penhallow? "

" Mine, my dear? No language is expansive enough for Mc-
Gregor when he talks about you."

" Nonsense, James. He knows how to please somebody. We
were discussing Mark Rivers."

" Were we? Then here is a nice little dose from the doctor
for you. Last Christmas, after you had personally sat up with
old Mrs. Lamb when she was so ill, and until I made a row about
it —"

" Yes — yes — I know." Her curiosity got the better of her
dislike of being praised for what to her was a simple duty, and
she added, " Well, what did he say? "

" Oh, that you and Rivers were like angels gone astray in the strange country called earth; and then that imp of a boy, John, who says queer things, said that it was like a bit of verse Rivers had read to him. He knew it too. I liked it and got him to write it out. I have it in my pocket-book. Like to see it?"

"No," she returned — and then —"yes," as she reflected that it must have originally applied to another than herself.

He was in the habit of storing in his pocket-book slips from the papers — news, receipts for stable-medicine, and rarely verse. Now and then he emptied them into the waste basket. He brought it out of his pocket-book and she read it:

> As when two angel citizens of Heaven
> Swift winged on errands of the Master's love
> Meet in some earthly guise.

"Is that all of it?"

"No, John could not remember the rest, and I did not ask Mark."

"I should suppose not. Thank you for believing it had any application to me. And, James, I have been a very cross angel of late."

"Oh, my dear Ann, Dr. McGregor said —"

"Never mind Dr. McGregor, James. Go and smoke your cigar. I am tired and I must not talk any more — talking on a train always tires me."

Two days after the departure of his aunt and uncle, John persuaded Rivers to walk with him on the holiday morning of Saturday. The clergyman caring little for the spring charm of the maiden summer, but much for John Penhallow's youth of promise, wandered on slowly through the woods, with head bent forward, stumbling now and then, lost to a world where his companion was joyfully conscious of the prettiness of new-born and translucent foliage.

Always pleased to sit down, Rivers dropped his thin length

of body upon the brown pine-needles near the cabin and settling his back against a fallen tree-trunk made himself comfortable. As usual, when at rest, he began to talk.

"John," he said, "you and Tom McGregor had a quarrel long ago — and a fight."

"Yes, sir," returned John wondering.

"I saw it — I did not interfere at once — I was wrong." ·

This greatly amused John. "You stopped it just in time for me — I was about done. for."

"Yes, but now, John, I have talked to Tom, and — I am afraid you have never made it up."

"No, he was insolent to Leila and rude. But we had a talk about it — oh, a good while ago — before she went away."

"Oh, had you! Well, what then?"

"Oh, he told me you had talked to him and he had seen Leila and told her he was sorry. She never said a word to me. I told him that he ought to have apologized to me — too."

Rivers was amused. "Apologies are not much in fashion among Westways boys. What did he say?"

"Oh, just that he did n't see that at all — and then he said that he was going away this fall to study medicine, and some day when he was a doctor he would have a chance to get even with me, and would n't he dose me well. Then we both laughed, and — I shook hands with him. That's all, sir."

"Well, I am pleased. He is by no means a bad fellow, and as you know he is clever — and can beat you in mathematics."

"Yes, but I licked him well, and he knows it."

"For shame, John. I wish my Baptist friend's boy would do better — he is dull."

"But I like him," said John. "He is so plucky."

"There is another matter I want to talk about. I had a long conversation about you with your uncle the night before he left. I heard with regret that you want to go into the army."

"May I ask why?" said John, as he lay on the ground lazily fingering the pine-needles.

"Is it because the hideous business called war attracts you?"

"No, but I like what I hear of the Point from Uncle Jim. I prefer it to any college life. Besides this, I do not expect to spend my life in the service, and after all it is simply a first rate training for anything I may want to do later — care of the mills, I mean. Uncle Jim is pleased, and as for war, Mr. Rivers, if that is what you dislike, what chance of war is there?"

"You have very likely forgotten my talk with Mr. George Grey. The North and the South will never put an end to their differences without bloodshed."

It seemed a strange opinion to John. He had thought so when he heard their talk, but now the clergyman's earnestness and some better understanding of the half-century's bitter feeling made him thoughtful. Rising to his feet, he said, "Uncle Jim does not agree with you, and Aunt Ann and her brother, Henry Grey, think that Mr. Buchanan will bring all our troubles to an end. Of course, sir, I don't know, but "— and his voice rose —" if there ever should be such a war, I am on Uncle Jim's side, and being out of West Point would not keep me out of the fight."

Rivers shook his head. "It will come, John. Few men think as I do, and your uncle considers me, I suspect, to be governed by my unhappy way of seeing the dark side of things. He says that I am a bewildered pessimist about politics. A pessimist I may be, but it is the habitually hopeful meliorist who is just now perplexed past power to think straight."

John's interest was caught for the moment by the word, "meliorist." "What is a meliorist, sir?" he asked.

"Oh, a wild insanity of hopefulness. You all have it. I dislike to talk about the sad future, and I wonder men at the North are so blind."

He fell again to mere musings, a self-absorbed man, while

John, attracted by a squirrel's gambols and used to the rector's long silences, wandered near by among the pines, with a vagabond mind on this or that, and watching the alert little acrobat of the forest. As he moved about, he recalled his first walks to the cabin with Leila and the wild thing he had said one day — and her reply. One ages fast at seventeen, and now he wondered if he had been quite wise, and with the wisdom and authority of a year and a half of mental growth punished his foolish boy-past with severity of reproach. He had failed for a time to hear, or at least to hear with attention, the low-voiced soliloquies in which Mr. Rivers sometimes indulged. McGregor, an observant man, said that Rivers's mind jumped from thought to thought, and that his talk had at times no connective tissue and was hard to follow.

Now he spoke louder. "No one, John, no one sees that every new compromise compromises principles and honour. Have you read any of the speeches of a man named Lincoln in Illinois? He got a considerable vote in that nominating convention."

"No, sir."

"Then read it — read him. A prophet of disaster! He says, 'A house divided against itself cannot stand. This government cannot endure permanently half slave, half free.' The man did not know that he was ignorantly quoting George Washington's opinion. It is so, and so it will be. I would let them go their way in peace, for the sin of man-owning is ours — was ours — and we are to suffer for it soon or late — a nation's debts have to be paid, and some are paid in blood."

The young fellow listened but had no comment ready, and indeed knew too little of the terrible questions for which time alone would have an answer to feel the full force of these awful texts. He did say, "I will read Mr. Lincoln's speeches. Uncle talks to me about Kansas and slavery and compromises, but it is sometimes too much for me."

"Yes, he will not talk of these things to your aunt, and is

not willing to talk to me. He thinks both of us are extremists. No, I won't walk any further. Let us go home."

The natural light-mindedness of a healthy lad easily disposes of the problems which disturb the older mind. John forgot it all for a time in the pleasant interest of a letter from Leila, received a day before his uncle's return.

" CAPE MAY, June 21st.

" MY DEAR JOHN: Here at last I am free to write to you when I please, and I have some rather strange news; but first of Aunt Ann. She is very well pleased and is already much better. Uncle Jim left us to-day, and I am to have Lucy here and one of the grooms. If only I could have you to ride with me on this splendid beach and see the great blue waves roll up like a vast army charging with white plumes and then rolling back in defeat."—

John paused. This was not like Leila. He felt in a vague way that she must be changing, and remembered the rector's predictions. Then he read on —

" Now for my adventure: Aunt Ann wanted some hair-wash, and I went to the barber's shop in the town to buy it. There was no one in but a black boy, because it was the bathing-time. He, I mean the boy, said he would call Mr. Johnson. In a moment there came out of a back room who do you think but our Josiah! He just stood still a moment — and then said, ' Good God! Miss Leila! Come into the back room — you did give me a turn.' I thought he seemed to be alarmed. Well, I went with him, and he asked me at once who was with me. I said, Aunt Ann, and that she was not well. Then I got out of him that he had wandered a while, and at last chosen this as a safe place. No one had told me fully about Cousin George Grey and why Josiah was scared and ran away, but now I got it all out of him — and how you warned him — and I do think it was splendid of a boy like you. He was dreadfully afraid of being taken back to be a slave. It seems he saved his money, and after working here bought out the shop when his master fell ill. I did not like it, but to quiet him I really had to say that I would not tell Aunt Ann, or he would have to run away again. I am sure aunt would not do anything to trouble him, but it was quite impossible to make him believe me, and he got me at last to promise him. I suppose there is really no harm in it, but I never did keep anything from Aunt Ann. I got the hair-wash and went away with his secret. Now, is n't that a story!

" I forgot one thing. As the Southern gentlemen come to be shaved and ask where he was born, they hear — think of it — that ' Mr. Johnson ' was born in Connecticut! His grandfather had been a slave. I shall see him again.

" This is the longest letter I ever wrote, and you are to feel duly complimented, Mr. Penhallow.

" Good-bye. Love from Aunt Ann.

" Yours truly,

" Leila Grey.

" P.S. I am sure that I may trust you not to speak of Josiah."

Mr. John Penhallow, as they said at Westways, " going on seventeen," gathered much of interest in reading and re-reading this letter from Miss Grey. To own a secret with Leila was pleasant. To hear of Josiah as " Mr. Johnson " amused him. That he was prosperous he liked, and that he was fearful with or without reason seemed strange. It was and had been hard for the young freeman to realize the ever-present state of mind of a man in terror of arrest without any crime on his conscience. There was perhaps a slight hint of doubt in Leila's request that he would be careful not to mention what she had said of Josiah, " as if I am really a boy and Leila older than I," murmured John. He knew, as he once more read her words, that he ought to tell his uncle, who could best decide what to do about Josiah and his terror of being reclaimed by his old owner.

During the early hours of a summer night Mark Rivers sat on the porch in a rocking-chair, which he declared gave him all the exercise he required. It was the only rocking-chair at Grey Pine, and nothing so disturbed the Squire as Mark Rivers rocking on that unpleasant piece of furniture and smoking as if it were a locomotive. It was an indulgence of Ann Penhallow, who knew that there had been a half-dozen rockers in the burned rectory.

John sat on the steps and listened to the shrill katydids or watched the devious lanterns of the fireflies. A bat darted over the head of Rivers, who ducked as it went by, watching its uncertain flight.

"I am terribly afraid of bats," said the rector. "Are you?"

"I — no. They 're harmless."

"Yes, I know that, but I am without reason afraid of them. I think of the demons as being like monstrous bats. But that is a silly use of imagination."

"Uncle Jim does n't like them, and you once told me that he had very little imagination."

"Yes. One can't explain these dislikes. Your uncle reasons well and has a clear logical mind, but he has neither creative nor receptive imagination."

"Receptive?" asked John.

"Yes, that is why he has none of your aunt's joy in poetry. When I read to her Wordsworth's 'Brougham Castle,' he said that he had never heard more silly nonsense."

"I remember it was that wonderful verse about the 'longing of the shield.'"

"Yes — I forgot you were there. Verse like that is a good test of a person's capacity to feel poetry — that kind, I mean."

"I hear Uncle Jim's horse."

"Yes. I can't see, John, why a man should want to have a horse sent to meet him instead of a comfortable wagon,"— and for emphasis, as usual with Rivers, the rocking-chair was swinging to the limits of its arc of safe motion.

The Squire dismounted and came up the steps with "Good-evening, Rivers,"— and to John, "I have good news for you — but order my supper at once, then we will talk." He was in his boyish mood of gaiety. "How far have you travelled on that rocker, Rivers?"

"Now, Squire — now, really —" It was a favourite subject of chaff.

"Why not have rocking-chairs in church, Mark? Think what a patient congregation you would have! Come, John, I am hungry." He fled laughing.

While the Squire ate in silence, John waited until his uncle said, "Come into the library." Here he filled his pipe and took the match John offered. "There are many curious varieties of man, John. There is the man who prefers a rocking-chair to the saddle. It's queer — very queer; and he is as much afraid of a horse as I am — of — I don't know what."

The Squire's memory failed to answer the call. "What are you grinning at, you young scamp?"

"Oh, Mr. Rivers did say, Uncle Jim, something about bats."

"Yes, that's it — bats — and I do suppose every one has his especial fear. Ah! quite inexplicable nonsense! — fears like mine about bats, or your aunt's about dogs, but also fears that make a man afraid that he will not face a danger that is a duty. When we had smallpox at the mills, soon after Rivers came here, he went to the mill-town and lived there a month, and nursed the sick and buried the dead. At last he took the disease lightly, but it left a mark or two on his forehead. That I call — well, heroic. Confound that rocking-chair! How it squeaks!"

John was too intently listening to hear anything but the

speaker who declared heroic the long lean man with the pale face and the eyes like search-lights. John waited; he wanted to hear something more.

"Did many die, uncle?"

"Oh, yes. The men had fought McGregor about vaccination. Many died. There was blindness too. Supplies failed — no one would come in from the farms."

John waited with the fear of defect in his ideal man. Then he ventured, "And Aunt Ann, was she here?"

"No, I sent her away when I went to Milltown."

"Oh! you were there too, sir?"

"Yes, damn it!" He rarely swore at all. "Where did you suppose I would be? But I lived in terror for a month — oh, in deadly fear!"

"Thank you, sir."

"Thank me, what for? Some forms of sudden danger make me gay, with all my faculties at their best, but not that. I had to nurse Rivers; that was the worst of it. You see, my son, I was a coward."

"I should like to be your kind of a coward, Uncle Jim."

"Well, it was awful. Let us talk of something else. I left your aunt better, went to Washington, saw our Congressman, got your nomination to West Point and a letter from Leila. Your aunt must be fast mending, for she was making a long list of furniture for the new parsonage, and 'would I see Ellen Lamb and'— eleven other things, the Lord knows what else, and 'when could she return?' McGregor said in September, and I so wrote to her; she will hate it. And she dislikes your going to West Point. I had to tell her, of course."

"I have had a letter from Leila, uncle. Did she write you anything about Josiah?"

"About Josiah! No. What was that?"

"She said I was not to tell, but I think you ought to know —"

"Of course, I should know. Go on. Let me see the letter."

"It is upstairs, sir, but this is what she wrote," and he went on to tell the story.

The Squire laughed. "I must let Mr. Johnson know, as Leila did not know, that it was Ann who really sent you to warn him. Poor fellow! I can understand his alarm, and how can I reassure him? George Grey is going to Cape May, or so says your aunt, and I am sure if Josiah knows that he is recognized, he will drop everything and run. I would run, John, and quickly too. Grey will be sure to write to Woodburn again."

"What then, sir?"

"Oh, he told your Aunt Ann and me that he would not go any further unless he chanced to know certainly where Josiah was. If he did, it would be his duty, as he said, to reclaim him. It is not a pleasant business, and I ought to warn Josiah, which you may not know is against the law. However, I will think it over. Ann did not say when Grey was coming, and he is just as apt not to go as to go. Confound him and all their ways."

John had nothing to say. The matter was in older and wiser hands than his. His uncle rose, "I must go to bed, but I have a word to say now about your examinations for admission. I must talk to Rivers. Good-night!"

CHAPTER XIV

O N Saturday the Squire asked John to ride with him. As they mounted, Billy came with the mail. Penhallow glanced at the letters and put them in his pocket.

As the horses walked away, John said, " I was in Westways yesterday, uncle, to get my hair cut. I heard that Pole has had chicken-pox, uncle."

" Funny that, for a butcher!" said the Squire. They chatted of the small village news. " They have quit discussing politics, Uncle Jim."

" Yes, every four years we settle down to the enjoyment of the belief that now everything will go right, or if we are of those who lost the fight, then there is the comfort of thinking things could not be worse, and that the other fellows are responsible."

" Uncle Jim, at Westways people talked about the election as if it were a horse-race, and did n't interest anybody when it was over."

" Yes, yes; but there are for the average American many things to think about, and he does n't bother himself about who is to be President or why, until, as McGregor says, events come along and kick him and say, ' Get up and think, or do something.' "

" When I talked to Mr. Rivers lately, he seemed very blue about the country. He seems to believe that everything is going wrong."

" Oh, Rivers!" exclaimed Penhallow, " what a great, noble soul! But, John, a half hour of talk with him about our national affairs leaves me tangled in a net of despair, and I hate it. You have a letter, I see."

"Yes, it is from Leila, sir."

"Let's hear it," said Penhallow.

John was inclined, he could hardly have told why, to consider this letter when alone, but now there was nothing possible except to do as he was bid.

"Read it. I want to hear it, John."

As they walked their horses along the road, John read:

"DEAR JOHN: I did not expect to write to you again until you wrote to me, but I have been perplexed to know what was best to do. I wanted — oh, so much — to consult Uncle Jim, or some older person than you, and so I ask you to send this to Uncle Jim if he is absent, or let him see it if he is at home. He is moving about and we do not know how to address him."—

"That's a big preface — go on."

"I did not see Josiah again until yesterday morning. Aunt Ann has been insisting that my hair needs singeing at the ends to make it grow. [It is too long now for comfort.]"—

"That's in brackets, Uncle Jim — the hair, I mean."

"Yes — what next?"

"Well, John, when Aunt Ann keeps on and on in her gently obstinate, I mean resolute, way, it is best to give up and make believe a little that you agree with her. My hair was to be singed — I gave up."—

"Oh, Leila!" exclaimed Penhallow, rocking in the saddle with laughter, while John looked up smiling. "Go on."

"So aunt's new maid got her orders, and while aunt was asleep in her room the maid brought up Josiah. It was as

good as a play. He was very civil and quiet. You know how
he loved to talk. He singed my hair, and it was horrid — like
the smell of singeing a plucked chicken. After that he sent the
maid to his shop for some hair-wash. As soon as she was gone,
he said, 'I'm done for, Miss Leila. I met Mr. George Grey
on the beach this morning. He knew me and I knew him.
He said, "What! you here, you rascally runaway horse-thief!"
I said, "I was n't a thief or a rascal." Then he said something
I did n't hear, for I just left him and — I can't stay here —
he'll do something, and I can't run no risks — oh, Lord!' "—

"I thought," said the Squire, "we were done with that tiresome fool, George Grey. Whether he will write again to Woodburn about Josiah or not, no one can say. Woodburn did tell
me that if at any time he could easily get hold of his slave, he
would feel it to be a duty to make use of the Fugitive-Slave
Law. I do not think he will be very eager, but after all it is
uncertain, and if I were Josiah, I would run away."

As he talked, the horses walked on through the forest wood-
roads. For a moment he said nothing, and then, "It is hard to
put yourself in another man's place; that means to be for the
time of decision that man with his inheritances, all his memories, all his hopes and all his fears."

This was felt by the lad to be somehow unlike his uncle, who
added, "I heard Mark Rivers say that about Peter, but it ap-
plies here. I would run. But go on with your letter. What
else does Leila say?"

John read on:

"Josiah was so scared that I could not even get him to listen
to me. He gathered up his barber things in haste, and kept
on saying over and over, 'I have got to go, missy.' Now he has
gone and his shop is shut up. I was so sorry for him, I must
have cried, for aunt's maid asked me what was the matter.

This is all. It is late. I shall mail this to-morrow. Aunt Ann has been expecting Mr. George Grey, my far-away cousin. I wish he was further away!"—

"Good gracious! Leila. Well, John, any more?"
"Yes, sir."

"He came in this morning, I mean Mr. Grey, and began to talk and was so pleased to see his dear cousin. Aunt Ann went on knitting and saying something pleasant now and then. At last he asked if she knew that runaway horse-thief we called Josiah was the barber here. He said that he must really write to that rascal's owner, and went over and over the same thing. Aunt Ann looked at me when he mentioned the barber. Then she sat up and said, 'If you have done talking, I desire to say a word.' Of course, he was at her service. You know, John, how he talks. Aunt Ann said, 'You made quite enough trouble, George, about this man at Westways. I told you then that he had done us a service I could never forget. I won't have him disturbed here. Mr. Woodburn behaved with discretion and courtesy. If you make any more trouble, I shall never forgive you. I won't have it, George Grey.' I never saw any one so embarrassed, John. He put his hat on the floor and picked it up, and then he sat down in his chair and, I call it, wilted. He said that he had not quite made up his mind. At this Aunt Ann stood up, letting her knitting drop, and said, 'Then you had better; you've got no mind.' After this he got up and said that she had insulted him. Aunt Ann was red and angry. She said, 'Tell James Penhallow that, Mr. Grey.' After this he went away, and Aunt Ann said to me, 'Tell Josiah if you can find him that he need not be afraid; the man will not write to Mr. Woodburn.' After that I told her all about Mr. Johnson and got a good scolding for not having told her before, and that Josiah had gone away scared. She was tired and angry and sent me away. That is all. Let Uncle Jim get this letter.

"Yours truly,

"LEILA.

"P.S. Oh, I forgot. Josiah gave me a letter for Uncle Jim. I enclose it. I did not give it to Aunt Ann; perhaps I ought to have done so. But it would have been useless because it is sealed, and you know the rule at Grey Pine."

"Poor Josiah!" said Penhallow, "I wonder where he has gone."

"He may say in his letter," said John.

"Read it to me, my son. I forgot my glasses."

"It is addressed to Captain Penhallow."

"Yes, I was always that to Josiah — always."

John opened the letter, which was carefully sealed with a large red wafer.

"It is well written, uncle."

"Yes — yes. Rivers taught him — and he speaks nearly as good English as George Grey."

John looked up from the letter. "Oh, that is funny! It begins, 'Respectable Sir.'"

"My dear John, that is n't funny at all — it 's old-fashioned. I have seen a letter from the great Dr. Rush in which the mother of Washington is mentioned as 'that respectable lady.' But now, sir, you will be good enough to let me hear that letter without your valuable comments."

The tone was impatient. John said, "Excuse me, uncle, but I could n't help it."

"Oh, read it."

"I am driven away again. I write this to thank you for all you done for me at Westways. Mr. Grey he met me here on the beach and I 'm afraid — I don't take no chances. I saved money here. I can get on anywhere. It 's awful to have to

run away, and that drunkard Peter Lamb all the while safe
with his mother. I can't get him out of my mind. I'm a
Christian man — and I tried to forgive him. I can't do it.
If I am quiet and let alone, I forget. I've got to get up and
go and hide, and I curse him that done it. Please, sir, not tell
Mr. Rivers what I say. I seen Miss Leila. I always said Miss
Leila would be a beauty. There ain't no young lady here can
hold a candle to her. I want to say I did have hope to see Mr.
John.

"God bless you, Captain.

"Your obedient servant,

"JOSIAH."

The Squire halted in the open pine forest on a wood-road
behind the cabin. He threw one leg over the pommel and sat
still with the ease of a horseman in any of the postures the
saddle affords. "Read me both of those letters again, and
slowly."

This time John made no remarks. When he came to the end
of Josiah's letter, he looked towards the silent figure seated side-
ways. The Squire made no comment, but searched his pockets
for the flint and steel he always carried. Lighting his pipe
he slid to the ground.

"Take the rein, John," he said, "or the mare will follow
me."

Penhallow was deep in the story these letters told, and he
thought best when walking. John sat in his saddle watching
the tall soldierly figure move up the road and back again to
the cabin his ancestors had held through one long night of fear.
John caught sight of the face as Penhallow came and then
turned away on his slow walk, smoking furiously. He sat still,
having learned to be respectful of the long silences to which at
times Penhallow was given. Now and then with a word he
quieted the uneasy mare — a favourite taught to follow the

master. At last Penhallow struck his pipe on a stone to empty it, and by habit carefully set a foot on the live coal. Then he came to the off side of his mare and took the rein. Facing John, he set an elbow on the horse's back and a hand on his own cheek. This was no unusual attitude. He did not mount, but stood still. The ruddy good-humoured face, clean-shaven and large of feature, had lost its look of constant good-humour. In fact, the feature language expressed the minute's mood in a way which any one less familiar with the man than John might have read with ease. Then he said, in an absent way, " Are we men of the North all cowards like Josiah? They think so — they do really think so. It is helping to make trouble." Then he lifted himself lightly into the saddle, with swift change of mood and an odd laugh of comment on his conclusion, as he broke into a gallop. " Let us get into the sun."

John followed him as they rode swiftly over a cross-road and out on to the highway. Again the horses were walking, and Penhallow said, " I suppose you may not have understood me. I was suddenly angry. It is a relief sometimes to let off steam. Well, I fancy time will answer me — or that is what I try not to believe — but it may — it may. Let us talk of something else. I must find out from Rivers just how well you are prepared for the Point. Then I mean to give you every night an hour or so of what he cannot teach. You ride well, you know French and German, you box — it may be of service, keep it up once a week at least. I envy you the young disciplined life — the simpleness of it — the want of responsibilities."

" Thank you, sir," returned John, " I hope to like it and to do you credit, uncle."

" You will, I am sure. Let us go to the mills."

John hesitated before he asked, " Could not I have, sir, a few days with Aunt Ann at the Cape? "

" No, I shall want you here."

John was silent and disappointed. The Squire saw it. " It

can't be helped — I do not feel able to be alone. Leila will be away a year more and you will be gone for several years. For your sake and mine I want you this summer. Take care! You lost a stirrup when Dixy shied. Oh! here are the mills. Good morning, McGregor. All well?"

"Yes, sir. Tom has gone to the city. He is to be in the office of a friend of mine this summer. I shall be alone."

"John goes to West Point this September, Doctor."

"Indeed! You too will be alone. Next it will be Leila. How the young birds are leaving the nests! Even that slow lad of Grace's is going. He is to learn farming with old Roberts. He has a broad back and the advantage of not being a thinking-machine."

"He may have made the best choice, McGregor."

"No, sir," said the Doctor, "my son has the best of it."

John laughed. "I don't think I should like either farm or medicine."

"No," returned the Doctor, with his queer way of stating things, "there must be some one to feed the people; Tom is to be trained to cure, and you to kill."

"I don't want to kill anybody," said John, laughing.

"But that is the business you are going to learn, young man." John was silent. The idea of killing anybody!

"Heard from Mrs. Penhallow lately?" asked the doctor.

"No, but from Leila to-day; and, you will be surprised, from Josiah too."

"Is that so?"

"Yes. Give him the two letters, John. Let me have them to-morrow, Doctor. Good-bye," and they rode on to the mills.

"It is a pity, John, Josiah gave no address," said Penhallow, —"a childlike man, intelligent, and with some underlying temper of the old African barbarian." The summer days ran on with plenty of work for John and without incidents of moment, until the rector went away as was his habit the first of

August, more moody than usual. If the rectory were finished, he would go there in September, and Mrs. Ann had written to him about the needed furniture.

On August 20th that lady wrote from Cape May that she must go home, and Leila that her aunt was well but homesick. The Squire, who missed her greatly, unreluctantly yielded, and on August 25th she was met at the station by Penhallow and John. To the surprise of both, she had brought Leila, as her school was not to begin until September 10th.

"My dear James," cried Mrs. Ann, "it is worth while to have been away to learn how good it is to get home again. I thought I would surprise you with Leila." As the Squire kissed her, Leila and the maid came from the car to the platform loaded with bundles.

John stood still. Nature had been busy with her artist-work. A year had gone by — the year of maturing growth of mind and body for a girl nearing sixteen. Unprepared for her change, John felt at once that this was a woman, who quickly smiling gave him a cordial greeting and her hand. "Why, John Penhallow," she said, "what a big boy you are grown!" It was as if an older person had spoken to a younger. A head taller than the little Mrs. Ann, she was in the bloom of maiden loveliness, rosy, joyous, a certain new stateliness in her movements. The gift of grace had been added by the fairy godmother nature.

John said, with gravity, "You are most welcome home, Leila," and then quickly aware of some coldness in his words, "Oh, I am so very glad to see you!" She had gone by him in the swift changes of life. Without so putting it distinctly into the words of a mental soliloquy, John was conscious that here was another Leila.

"Come, in with you," said the happy master of Grey Pine. "How well you look, Ann, and how young! The cart will bring your bundles."

John Penhallow on an August afternoon was of Billy's opinion that Leila had "growed a lot" as she came out upon the porch and gaily laughing cried, "At last, Aunt Ann has done with me."

They were both suffering from one of those dislocations of relation which even in adult life are felt when friends long apart come together again. The feeling of loss, as far as John was concerned, grew less as Leila with return of childlike joy roamed with him over the house and through the stables, and next day through Westways, with a pleasant word for every one and on busying errands for her aunt. He was himself occupied with study; but now the Squire had said it would be wise to drop his work.

With something of timidity he said to Leila, "I am free for this afternoon; come and see again our old playgrounds. It will be a long while before we can take another walk."

"Certainly, John. And isn't it a nice, good-natured day? The summer is over. Sometimes I wish we had no divisions of months, and the life of the year was one quiet flow of days — oh, with no names to remind you."

"But think, Leila, of losing all the poetry of the months. Why not have no day or night? Oh, come along. What do you want with a sunshade and a veil — we will be mostly in the woods."

"My complexion, Mr. Penhallow," cried Miss Grey gaily.

He watched her young figure as she went upstairs — the mass of darkened gold hair coiled in the classic fashion of the day on the back of her head. She looked around from the stair. "I shall be ready in a minute, John. It rained yesterday — will it be wet in the woods?"

"No," cried John, "and what does it matter?" He had a dull feeling of resentment, of loss, of consciousness of new barriers and of distance from the old comrade.

Their way led across the garden, which was showing signs

of feeling the chilly nights of the close of summer in this upland, where the seasons sometimes change abruptly.

"The garden has missed Aunt Ann," said Leila. "Uncle Jim looks at it from the porch, says 'How pretty!' and expects to see roses on his table every day. I do believe he considers a garden as merely a kind of flower-farm."

"Aunt Ann's garden interests her the way Westways does. There are sick flowers and weeds like human weeds, and bugs and diseases that need a flower-doctor, and flowers that are morbid or ill-humoured. That is not my wisdom, Leila, it is Mr. Rivers's."

"No, John, it isn't at all like you."

"Aunt Ann didn't like it, and yet I think he meant it to be a compliment, for he really considers Aunt Ann a model of what a woman ought to be."

"I know that pretty well," said Leila. "When I used to lose my temper over that horrid algebra, I was told to consider how Aunt Ann kept her temper no matter what happened, as if that had anything to do with algebra and equations. If he had seen her when she talked to George Grey about Josiah, he would have known Aunt Ann better. I was proud of her."

"Aunt Ann angry!" said John. "I should have liked to have seen that. Poor Josiah!"

They talked of the unlucky runaway, and were presently among the familiar pine and spruce, far beyond the garden bounds. "Do put up that veil," said John, "and you have not the least excuse for your parasol."

"Oh, if you like, John. Tell me about West Point. It was such a surprise."

"I will when I am there, if I am able to pass the examinations."

"You will — you will. Uncle Jim told me you would pass easily."

"Indeed! He never told me that. I have my doubts."

"And I have none," she returned, smiling. "Mr. Rivers dislikes it. He wrote to me about it just before he left. Do you know, he did really think that you ought to be a clergyman. He said you were so serious-minded for — for a boy."

John laughed. "A nice clergyman I'd have made." Did Leila too consider him a boy? "Oh! here we are at the old cabin. I never forget the first day we came here — and the graves. The older I grow, Leila, the more clearly I can see the fight and the rifle-flashes, and the rescue — and the night — I can feel their terror."

"Oh, we were mere children, John; and I do suppose that it is a pretty well decorated tradition." He looked at her with surprise, as she added, "I used to believe it all, now it seems strange to me, John — like a dream of childhood. I think you really are a good deal of a boy yet."

"No, I am not a boy. I sometimes fancy I never was a boy — I came here a child." And then, "I think you like to tease me, Leila," and this was true, although she was not pleased to be told so. "You think, Leila, that it teases me to be called a boy by your ladyship. I think it is because you remember what a boy once said to you here — right here."

"What do you mean?" She knew very well what he meant, but quickly repenting of her feminine fib, said, "Oh, I do know, but I wanted to forget — I wanted to pretend to forget, because you know what friends we have been, and it was really so foolish."

He had been lying at her feet; now he rose slowly. "You are not like my Leila to-day."

"Oh, John!"

"No — and it is hard, because I am going away — and — it will not be pleasant to think how you are changed."

"I wish you would n't say such things to me, John."

"I had to — because — I love you. If I was a boy when I

was, as you say, silly, I was in earnest. It was nonsense to ask you to say you would marry me some day. It was n't so very long ago after all; but I agree with you, it *was* foolish. Now I mean to make no such proposal."

"Please, John." She looked up at him as he stood over her so grave, so earnest — and so like Uncle Jim. For the time she got the fleeting impression of this being a man.

He hardly heard her appeal. "I want to say now that I love you." For a moment the 'boy's will, the wind's will,' blew a gale. "I love you and I always shall. Some day I shall ask you that foolish question again, and again."

She too was after all very young and had been playing a bit at being a woman. Now his expression of passion embarrassed her — because she had no answer ready; nor was it all entirely disagreeable.

He stood still a moment, and added, "That is all — I ask nothing now."

Then she stood up, having to say something and unwilling to hurt him — wanting not to say too much or too little, and ending by a childlike reply. "Oh, John, I do wish you would never say such things to me. I am too young to listen to such nonsense."

"And I am young too," he laughed. "Well — well — let us go home and confess like children."

"Now I know you are a fool, John Penhallow, and very disagreeable."

"When we were ever so young, Leila, and we quarrelled, we used to agree not to speak to one another for a day. Are you cross enough for that now?"

"No, I am not; but I want to feel sure that you will not say such things to me again."

"I make no promise, Leila; I should break it. If I gave you a boy's love, forget it, laugh at it; but if I give you a man's love, take care."

This odd drama — girl and woman, boy and maturing man — held the stage; now one, now the other.

"Take care, indeed!" she said, repeating his words and turning on him with sudden ungraciousness, "I think we have had enough of this nonsense."

She was in fact the more disturbed of the two, and knowing it let anger loose to chase away she knew not what, which was troubling her with emotion she could neither entirely control nor explain later as the result of what seemed to her mere foolishness. If he was himself disturbed by his storm of primitive passion, he did not show it as she did.

"Yes," he said in reply, "we have had for the present enough of this — enough talk, I mean —"

"We!" she exclaimed.

"Leila! do you want me to apologize?"

"No."

"Then — let us get those roses for Aunt Ann — what are left of them."

She was glad to escape further discussion — not sure of her capacity to keep in order this cousin who was now so young and now so alarmingly old. His abrupt use of self-control she recognised — liked and then disliked, for a little wrath in his reply would have made her feel more at ease. With well-reassumed good-humour, she said, "Now you are my nice old playmate, but never, never bother me that way again."

"Yes, ma'am," said John, laughing. "I can hear Aunt Ann say, 'Run, dears, and get me flowers — and — there will be cakes for you.'"

"No, bread and apple-butter, John." They went along merry, making believe to be at ease.

"The robins are gone," said Leila. "I haven't seen one to-day; and the warblers are getting uneasy and will be gone soon. I haven't seen a squirrel lately. Josiah used to say that meant an early winter."

" Oh, but the asters! What colour! And the golden-rod! Look at it close, Leila. Each little flower is a star of gold."

" How pretty! " She bent down over the flowers to pay the homage of honest pleasure. " How you always see, John, so easily, the pretty little wild beauties of the woods; I never could." She was " making up " as children say.

" Oh, you were the schoolmaster once," he laughed. " Come, we have enough; now for the garden."

They passed through the paling fence and along the disordered beds, where a night of too early frost had touched with chill fingers of disaster the latest buds. Leila moved about looking at the garden, fingering a bud here and there with gentle epitaphs of " late," " too late," or gathering the more matronly roses which had bloomed in time. John watched her bend over them, and then where there were none but frost-wilted buds stand still and fondle with tender touch the withered maidens of the garden.

He came to her side, " Well, Leila, I'll swap thoughts with you."

She looked up, " Your's first then."

" I was thinking it must be hard to die before you came to be a rose — like some other more human things."

" Is that a charade, John? You will be writing poems about the lament of the belated virgin roses that had not gathered more timely sunshine and were alas! too late."

He looked at her with a smile of pleased surprise. " Thanks, cousin; it is you who should be the laureate of the garden. Shelley would envy you."

" Indeed! I am flattered, sir, but I have not read any of Shelley as yet. You have, I suppose? He is supposed to be very wicked. Get me some more golden-rod, John." He went back to the edge of the wood and came again laden, rejoining her at the porch.

For two days her aunt kept her busy. Early in the week she

went away to be met in Philadelphia by her Uncle Charles, and to be returned to her Maryland school.

A day or two later John too left to undergo the dreaded examination at West Point. The two older people were left alone at Grey Pine with the rector, who had returned from his annual holiday later than usual. Always depressed at these seasons, he was now indisposed for the society of even the two people who were his most valued friends. He dined with them the day John went away and took up the many duties of his clerical life, until as was his custom, a week later he came in smiling for the Saturday dinner, saying, "Well, here comes the old house-dog for his bone."

They made him welcome as gaily. "Has the town wickedness accumulated in your absence, Mark?" said Penhallow.

"Mine has," said Ann Penhallow, "but I never confess except to myself."

"Ann Penhallow might be a severe confessor," said Rivers as they sat down. "How you must miss John and Leila. I shall most sadly."

"Oh, for my part," said Ann, "I have made up my mind not to lament the inevitable, but my husband is like a lost dog and — oh! — heart-hungry for Leila, and worried about that boy's examination — his passing."

"Have I said a word?" said the Squire indignantly. "Pass! Of course, he will pass."

"No one doubts that, James; but you are afraid he will not be near the top."

"You are a witch, Ann. How did you know that?"

"How?" and she laughed. "How long have we been married!"

"Nonsense, Ann! What has that got to do with the matter?"

"Well," said Rivers, a little amused, "we shall know in a day or two. He will pass high."

" Of course," said Penhallow.

Then the talk drifted away to the mills, the village and the farm work. When after dinner Rivers declined to smoke with the Squire, Ann walked with the clergyman down the avenue and said presently, " Dine with us on Monday, Mark, and as often as possible. My husband is really worrying about John."

" And you, dear lady? "

" I — oh, of course, I miss them greatly; but Leila needs the contact with the social life she now has in the weekly holiday at Baltimore; and as for John, did it never occur to you that he ought to be among men of his age — and social position — and women too, who will not, I fancy, count for much in the West Point education."

" Yes — yes, what you say is true of course, but ah! I dread for him the temptations of another life than this."

" Would you keep him here longer, if you could? " she asked.

" No. What would life be worth or how could character be developed without temptation? That is one of my puzzles about the world to come, a world where there would be no ' yes and no ' would hardly be worth while."

" And quite beyond me," cried Ann, laughing. " We have done our best for them. Let us pray that they will not forget. I have no fear for Leila. I do not know about John. I must go home. Come often. Good-night. I suppose the sermon takes you away so early."

" Yes — more or less, and I am poor company just now. Good-night."

CHAPTER XV

W HEN at breakfast on a Monday morning Penhallow said, "That mail is late again," his wife knew that he was still eager for news from John.

"The mail is always late on Monday morning, James. If you are in haste to get to the mills, I will send it after you."

"No, it is unimportant, Ann. Another cup, please. Ah! there it is now." He went out on to the porch. "You are late, Billy."

"I ain't late — it was Mrs. Crocker — she kept me."

Penhallow selected two letters postmarked West Point, and opening one as he went in to the breakfast-room, said, "My dear, it is rather satisfactory — quite as much as could be expected."

"Well, James! What is rather satisfactory? You are really exasperating at times."

"Am I? Well, John has passed in the first half dozen — he does not yet know just where —"

"And are you not entirely contented? You ought to be. What is the other letter?"

He opened it. "It is only a line from the old drawing-master to say that John did well and would have been second or third, they said, except for not being higher in mathematics." As he spoke he rose and put both letters in his pocket. "Now I must go."

"But let me see them, James."

"Oh, John's is only a half dozen lines, and I must go at once — I have an appointment at the mills — I want to look over the letters again, and shall write to him from the office." Ann was slightly annoyed, but said no more until on the porch before he mounted she took a mild revenge. " I know where you are going."

" Well, and where, please? " He fell into her trap.

" First, you will stop at the rectory and read those letters to Mark Rivers; then the belated mail will excuse a pause at the post-office to scold Mrs. Crocker. Tell Pole as you go by that last mutton was atrociously tough. Of course, you won't mention John."

" Well, are you done? " he said, as he mounted Dixy. " I can wait, Ann, until you read the letters."

" Thanks, I am in no hurry." He turned in the saddle and gave her the letters. She put aside her brief feeling of annoyance and stood beside him as she read them. " Thank you, James. What an uneasy old uncle you are. Now go. Oh, be off with you — and don't forget Dr. McGregor." As he rode away, she called after him, " James — James — I forgot something."

He turned, checking Dixy. " Oh, I forgot to say that you must not forget the office clerks, because you know they are all so fond of John."

" What a wretch you are, Ann Penhallow! Go in and repent."

" I don't," and laughing, joyously, she stood and looked after the tall figure as he rode away happy and gaily singing, as he was apt to do if pleased, the first army carol the satisfaction of the moment suggested:

> Come out to the stable
> As soon as you 're able,
> And see that the horses
> That they get some corn.
> For if you don't do it,
> The colonel will know it,
> And then you will rue it
> As sure as you 're born.

"Ah!" said his wife, "how he goes back — always goes back — to the wild army life when something pleases him. Thank God that can never come again." She recalled her first year of married life, the dull garrison routine, the weeks of her husband's absences, and when the troop came back and there were empty saddles and weeping women.

At dinner the Squire must needs drink the young cadet's health and express to Rivers his regret that there was not a West Point for Leila. Mrs. Ann was of opinion that she had had too much of it already. Rivers agreed with his hostess, and in one of his darkest days won the privilege of long silences by questioning the Squire in regard to the studies and life at West Point, while Mrs. Ann more socially observant than her husband saw how moody was Rivers and with what effort he manufactured an appearance of interest in the captain's enthusiasm concerning educative methods at the great army school. She was relieved when he carried off Rivers to the library.

"It is chilly, Mark; would you like a fire?" he asked.

"Yes, I am never too warm."

The Squire set the logs ablaze. "No pipe, Mark?"

"Not yet." He stretched out his lean length before the ruddy birch blaze and was silent. The Squire watched him and made no attempt to disturb the deep reverie in which the young clergyman remained. At last the great grey eyes turned from the fire, and Rivers sat up in his chair, as he said, "You must have seen how inconsiderately I have allowed my depression to dismiss the courtesies of life. I owe you and my dear Mrs. Penhallow both an apology and an explanation."—

"But really, Mark —"

"Oh, let me go on. I have long wanted to talk myself out, and as often my courage has failed. I have had a most unhappy life, Penhallow. All the pleasant things in it — the past few years — have been given me here. I married young —"

"One moment, Mark. Before you came to us the Bishop

wrote me in confidence of your life. Not even Mrs. Penhallow has seen that letter."

" Then you knew — but not all. Now I have had a sad relief. He told you of — well, of my life, of my mother's hopeless insanity — and the rest."

" Yes — yes — all, I believe — all."

" Not quite all. I have spent a part at least of every August with her; now at last she is dead. But my family story has left with me the fear of dying like my brothers or of becoming as she became. When I came to you I was a lonely soul, sick in mind and weak in body. I am better — far better — and now with some renewal of hope and courage I shall face my world again. You have had — you will have charity for my days of melancholy. I never believed that a priest should marry — and yet I did. I suffered, and never again can I dream of love. I am doubly armed by memory and by the horror of continuing a race doomed to disaster. There you have it all to my relief. There is some mysterious consolation in unloading one's mind. How good you have been to me! and I have been so useless — so little of what I might have been."

Penhallow rose, set a hand on Rivers's shoulder, seeing the sweat on his forehead and the appeal of the sad eyes turned up to meet his gaze. " What," he said, " would our children have been without you? God knows I have been a better man for your company, and the mills — the village — how can you fail to see what you have done —"

" No — no — I am a failure. It may be that the moods of self-reproach are morbid. That too torments me. Even to-day I was thinking of how Christ would have dealt with that miserable man, Peter Lamb, and how uncharitable I was, how crude, how void of sympathy —"

" You — you —" said Penhallow, as he moved away. " My own regret is that I did not turn him over to the law. Well, points of view do differ curiously. We will let him drop. He will come to grief some day. And now take my thanks and my dear Ann's for what you have told me. Let us drop that too. Take a pipe."

"No, I must go. I am the easier in my mind, but I am tired and not at all in the pipe mood." He went out through the hall, and with a hasty "good-night" to his hostess and "pleasant dreams — or none," went slowly down the avenue.

The woman he left, with her knitting needles at rest a moment, was considering the man and his moods with such intuitive sympathy and comprehension as belongs to the sex which is physiologically the more subject to abrupt changes in the climate of the mind. As her husband entered, she began anew the small steadying industry for which man has no substitute.

"Upon my word, James, when you desire to exchange confidences, you must get further away from me."

"You don't mean me to believe you overheard our talk in the library, with the door closed and the curtain across it." Her acuteness of hearing often puzzled him, and he had always to ask for proof.

She nodded gay assurance, and said again, ceasing to knit, "I overheard too much — oh, not all — bits — enough to trouble me. I moved away so as not to hear. All I care to know is how to be of real service to a friend to whom we owe so much."

"I want you — in fact, Mark wants you — to hear in full what you know in part."

"Well, James, I have very little curiosity about the details of the misfortunes of my friends unless to know is to obtain means of helpfulness."

"You won't get any here, I fear, but as he has been often strange and depressed and, as he says, unresponsive to your kindness, he does want you now to see what cause there was."

"Very well, if he wants it. I see you have a letter."

"Yes, I kept it. It was marked strictly confidential — I hate that —" She smiled as he added, " It seems to imply the possibility of indiscretion on my part."

" Oh, James! Oh, you dear man! " and she laughed outright, liking to tease where she deeply loved, knowing him through and through, as he never could know her. Then she saw that he was not in the mood for jesting with an edge to it; nor was she. " At all events, you did not let me see that letter — now I am to see it."

" Yes, you are to see it. You might at any time have seen it."

" Yes, read it to me."

" When our good Bishop sent Mark Rivers here to us, he wrote me this letter —"

" Well, go on."

" MY DEAR SIR: I send you the one of my young clergy with whom I am the most reluctant to part. You will soon learn why, and learning will be thankful. But to make clear to you why I urge him — in fact, order him to go — requires a word of explanation. He is now only twenty-six years of age but looks older. He married young and not wisely a woman who lived a childlike dissatisfied life, and died after two years. One of his brothers died an epileptic; the other, a promising lawyer, became insane and killed himself. This so affected their widowed mother that she fell into a speechless melancholy and has ever since been in the care of nurses in a farmer's family — a hopeless case. I became of late alarmed at his increasing depression and evident failure in bodily strength. He was advised to take a small country parish, and so I send him to you and my friend, Mrs. Penhallow, sure that he will give as much as he gets. I need not say more. He is well worth saving — one of God's best — with too exacting a conscience — learned, eloquent and earnest, and to end, a gentleman."

" There is a lot more about Indian missions, which I think are hopeless, but I sent him a cheque, of course."

" I supposed, James, that his depression was owing to his want of vigorous health. Now I see, but how very sorrowful it is! What else is there? I did not mean to listen, but something was said about his mother."

" Yes. He has spent with her a large part of every August — he called it his holiday. My God, Ann! Poor fellow! This August she died. It must be a relief."

" Perhaps."

" Oh, surely. This is all, Ann."

" I wish you had been less discreet long ago, James. I think that the Bishop knowing how sensitive, how very reticent Mark is, meant only that he should not learn what was confided to you."

" I never thought of that, Ann. You may be right."

She made no further comment, except to say, " But to know clears the air and leaves me free to talk to him at need." Penhallow felt that where he himself might be a useless confessor, his wife was surely to be trusted.

" If, Ann, the man could only be got on to the back of a horse —" She won the desirable relief of laughter, and the eyes that were full of the tears of pity for this disastrous life overflowed of a sudden with mirth at the Squire's one remedy for the troubles of this earthly existence.

" Oh, I am in earnest," he said. " Now I must write to John."

When after a week or more she did talk to Mark Rivers, he was the better for it and felt free to speak to her as a younger man may to an older woman and can rarely do to the closest of male friends, for, after all, most friendships have their personal limitations and the man who has not both men and women friends may at some time miss what the double intimacies alone can give.

The uneasy sense of something lost was more felt than men-

tioned that fall at Grey Pine, where quick feet on the stair and
the sound of young laughter were no longer heard. Rivers saw
too how distinctly the village folk missed these gay young
people. Mrs. Crocker, of the shop where everything was
to be bought, bewailed herself to Rivers, who was the receiver
of all manner of woes. " Mrs. Penhallow is getting to be so
particular no one knows where to find her. You would never
think it, sir, but she says my tea is not fit to drink, and she is
going to get her sugar from Philadelphia. It's awful! She
says it isn't as sweet as it used to be — as if sugar wasn't always the same —"

" Which it isn't," laughed Rivers.

" And my tea! — Then here comes in the Squire to get a
dog-collar, and roars to my poor deaf Job, ' that last tea was the
best we have ever had. Send five pounds to Dr. McGregor from
me — charge it to me — and a pound to Mrs. Lamb.' It wasn't
but ten minutes later. Do set down, Mr. Rivers." He accepted the chair she dusted with her apron and quietly enjoyed
the little drama. The facts were plain, the small influential
motives as clear.

Secure of her hearer, Mrs. Crocker went on: " I was saying
it wasn't ten minutes later that same morning Mrs. Penhallow
came down on me about the sugar and the tea — worst she ever
had. She — oh, Lord! — She wouldn't listen, and declared
that she would return the tea and get sugar from town."

" Pretty bad that," said Rivers, sympathetic. " Did she send
back the tea?"

" No, sir. In came Pole grinning that very evening. He
said she had made an awful row about the last leg of mutton he
sent. Pole said she was that bad — She didn't show no temper, but she kept on a sort of quiet mad about the mutton."

" Well, what did Pole do?"

" You'd never guess. It was one of the Squire's own sheep.
Pole he just sent her the other leg of the same sheep!"

Again the rector laughed. "Well, and what did Mrs. Penhallow do?"

"She told him that was all right. Pole he guessed I'd better send her a pound of the same tea."

"Did you?"

"I did — ain't heard yet. Now what would you advise? Never saw her this way before."

"Well," said Rivers, "tell her how the town misses Leila and John."

"They do. I do wonder if it's just missing those children upsets her so."

Whether his advice were taken or not, Rivers did not learn directly, but Mrs. Crocker said things were better when next they met, and the clergyman asked no questions.

Penhallow had his own distracting troubles. The financial condition which became serious in the spring and summer of 1857 was beginning to cause him alarm, and soon after the new year came in he felt obliged to talk over his affairs and to advise his wife to loan the mill company money not elsewhere to be had except at ruinous interest. She wished simply to give him the sum needed, but he said no, and made clear to her why he required help. She was pleased to be consulted, and showing, as usual, notable comprehension of the business situation, at once did as he desired.

Rivers not aware of what was so completely occupying Penhallow's mind, wondered later why he would not discuss the decision of the Supreme Court in the Dred Scott case and did not share his own indignation. "But," he urged, "it declares the Missouri Compromise not warranted by the Constitution!"

"I can't talk about it, Mark," said Penhallow, "I am too worried by my own affairs."

Then Rivers asked no further questions; he hoped he would read the masterly dissenting opinion of Justices McClean and Curtis. Penhallow returned impatiently that he had no time, and that the slavery question were better left to the decision of " Chief Justice Time."

It was unlike the Squire, and Rivers perplexed and more or less ignorant concerning his friend's affairs left him, in wonder that what was so angrily disturbing the Northern States should quite fail to interest Penhallow.

Meanwhile there were pleasant letters from Leila. She thought it hard to be denied correspondence with John, and wrote of the satisfaction felt by her Uncle Henry and his friends in regard to the Dred Scott decision. She had been wise enough to take her Uncle Charles's advice and to hold her Republican tongue, as he with a minority in Baltimore was wisely doing.

The money crisis came with full force while the affairs of Kansas were troubling both North and South. In August there was widespread ruin. Banks failed, money was held hard, contracts were broken and to avoid a worse calamity the Penhallow mills discharged half of the men. Meanwhile under Governor Walker's just and firm rule, for a brief season ' Bleeding Kansas ' was no longer heard of. To add to the confusion of parties, Douglas broke with the Administration and damaged the powerful Democratic machine when he came out with changed opinions and dauntless courage against the new Lecompton constitution.

In June Leila's school life came to a close, and to the delight of her relations she came home. When that afternoon Rivers came into the hall, a tall young woman rose of a sudden and swept him a curtsey, saying, " I am Leila Grey, sir. Please to be glad to see me."

" Good gracious, Leila! You are a woman! "

" And what else should I be? "

" Alas! what? My little friend and scholar — oh! the evil magic of time."

" Oh! Friend — friend! " she exclaimed, " then, now, and always." She gave him both hands.

" Yes, always," he said quickly. " And this," he said to himself, " is the child who used to give me the morning kiss. It is
very wonderful ! "

" I really think, Aunt Ann, that Mr. Rivers just for a moment
did not know me."

" Indeed ! That must have amused him."

" Oh, here is James." There was laughter at dinner and a
little gay venture into the politics of Leila's school, which appeared to have been disagreeable to Miss Grey.

Rivers watched the animated face as she gave her account of
how the school took a vote in the garden and were all Democrats.
The Squire a little puzzled by his wife's evident disinclination to
interfere with the dinner-table politics got a faint suspicion that
here had come into Grey Pine a new and positive influence. He
was more surprised that Mrs. Ann asked, " What did you say,
Leila ? "

" I ? Now, Aunt Ann, what would you have done or said ? "

" Oh, voted with the Democrats, of course."

" Oh, Mrs. Penhallow ! " cried the Rector.

The Squire much amused asked, " Well, Leila, did you run
away ? "

" I — Oh, Uncle Jim ! I said I was a democrat — I voted
the Democratic ticket."

" Did you ? " exclaimed Rivers.

" So James Penhallow and my brother Charles have lost a
Republican vote," laughed Ann.

" But, Aunt Ann, I added that I was a Douglas Democrat."

The Squire exploded into a peal of laughter. Ann said, " For
shame ! "

" They decided to lynch me, but no one of them could catch
me before Miss Mayo appeared on the playground and we all
became demure as pussy cats. She was cross."

" She was quite right," said her aunt. " I do not see why girls
should be discussing politics."

Rivers became silently regardant, and Penhallow frowning sat still. The anticipated bolt had fallen — it fell in vain. Leila did not accept the decree, but defended herself gaily. "Aunt Ann," she said, "Douglas is right, or at least half right. And do tell me how old must a girl be before she has a right to think?"

"Think! Oh, if you like, think. But, my dear Leila, your uncle, Mr. Rivers and I, although we think and hold very diverse opinions, feel that on such matters discussion only leaves a sting, and so we tacitly leave it out of our talk. There, my dear, you have my opinion."

There was a moment of silence. Leila looked up. "Oh, my dear Aunt Ann, if you were on the side of old Nick, Mr. Rivers would n't care a penny less for you, and I never could see why to differ in talk about politics is going to hurt past anything love could accept. Aunt Helen and Uncle Charles both talk politics and they do love one another, although Aunt Helen is tremendously Democratic."

"My dear Leila!"

"Oh, Aunt Ann! I will not say a word more if you want me to hold my tongue."

"Would n't the other way be more wholesome on the whole?" said Rivers.

"I have long thought so," said the Squire. "There are ways and ways —"

"Perhaps," said Ann. "Shall you ride with your uncle to-morrow, Leila?"

"Oh, shall I! I long for it — I dream about it. May I ride Dixy, Uncle Jim?"

"Yes, if you have a riding-habit you can wear. We will see to that. You have spread a good bit, but I fancy we can manage."

"And how is Pole, aunt; and the doctor and Crocker and his fat wife — oh, and everybody?"

"Oh, much as usual. We had a skirmish about mutton, but the last Pole sent is good — in fact, excellent. He needs watching."

Then the talk fell on the lessened work at the mills, and there being now four players the Squire had his whist again, and later carried Rivers away to smoke in the library, leaving Ann and Leila.

As the library door closed, Leila dropped on a cushion at her aunt's feet, and with her head in Ann's lap expressed her contentment by a few moments of silence. Then sitting up, she said, "I am so happy I should like to purr. I was naughty at dinner, but it was just because I wanted to make Uncle Jim laugh. He looks — Don't you think he looks worried, aunt? Is it the mills and — the men out of work? Dear Aunt Ann, how can one keep on not talking about politics and things that are next to one's religion — and concerning our country — my country?"

Ann made no direct reply, but went back to what was nearer than any creed of politics. "Yes, dear. When one big thing worries James, then everything worries him. The state of the money market makes all business difficult, and he feels uncomfortable because the mill company is in want of work, and because their debts are overdue and not likely to be paid in full or at all."

"I wish I could do something to help Uncle Jim."

"You can ride with him and I cannot. You can talk to him without limitations; I cannot. He is reasonable about this grave question of slavery. He does not think it right; I do — oh, good for master and best for the black. When, soon after our marriage, we spoke of it, he was positive and told me to read what Washington had said about slavery. We were both young and said angry things which left a pang of remembrance. After that we were careful. But now this terrible question comes up in the village and in every paper. It will get worse, and I see no end to it."

Leila was silent, remembering too her aunt's share in Josiah's escape. The advice implied in her aunt's frank talk she saw was to be accepted. " I will remember, Aunt Ann." At least she was free to talk to her uncle.

" Has any one heard of Josiah ? " asked Leila.

" No, I was sorry for him. He had so many good traits. I think he would have been more happy if he had remained with his master."

Leila had her doubts, but was self-advised to say no more than, " I often think of him. Now I shall go to bed."

" Yes, you must be tired."

" I am never tired, but to be free to sit up late or go to bed and read what I want to — and to ride! Good-night. I can write to John — now there 's another bit of freedom. Oh, dear, how delightful it all is ! " She went upstairs thinking how hard it would be to keep off of the forbidden ground, and after all was her aunt entirely wise ? Well, there was Uncle Jim and John.

While this talk went on the rector alone with his host said, " You are evidently to have a fresh and very positive factor in your household life —"

" Hush," said the Squire. " Talk low — Ann Penhallow has incredible hearing."

" True — quite true — I forgot. How amazingly the child has changed. She will be a useful ferment, I fancy. How strange it is always — this abrupt leap of the girl into the heritage of womanhood. The boy matures slowly, by imperceptible gradations. Now Leila seems to me years older than John, and the change is really somewhat startling; but then I have seen very little of young women. There is the girl, the maid, the woman."

" Oh, but there is boy, lad, and man."

" Not comparable, Squire; continuously growing in one case, and in the other developmental surprises and, ever after, fall and rise of energy. The general trouble about understanding women is that men judge them by some one well-known woman. I heard a famous doctor say that no man need pretend to understand women unless he had been familiar with sick women."

The Squire recalling the case of Ann Penhallow was silent. The clergyman thinking too of his own bitter experience lapsed into contemplative cleaning of a much valued meerschaum pipe. The Squire not given to morbid or other psychological studies made brief reply. " I hope that Leila will remain half boy."

" Too late, Squire — too late. You 've got a woman on your hands. There will be two heads to Grey Pine."

" And may I ask where do I come in? " He was at times almost dull-witted, and yet in danger swift to think and quick to act.

Rivers filling the well-cleaned pipe looked up. There was something of unwonted gaiety in the moving face-lines which frame the eyes and give to them the appearance of change of expression. " My dear friend, you were as dough that is kneaded in the hands of Leila, the girl; you will be no less so now in the hands of this splendid young woman."

" Oh, now — by George! Rivers, you must think me —"

" Think you! Oh, like other men. And as concerns Mrs. Ann, there will sometimes be a firm alliance with Leila before which you will wilt — or — no, I will not venture further."

" You had better not, or you may fail like other prophets."

" No, I was thinking as you spoke of the fact that Leila has seen a good deal of a very interesting society in Baltimore, and has had the chance, and I am sure the desire, to hear more of the wild Southern party-talk than most girls have."

" Yes, she has been in both camps."

" And always was and is, I fancy, eagerly curious in the best sense. More than my dear Mrs. Ann, she has wide intellectual sympathies — and appetites."

"That's a very fine phrase, Mark."

"Is n't it, Squire? I was also comparing in my mind John's want of association with men of his own social accident of position. He lived here with some rough country lads and with you and me. He has had no such chance as Leila's."

"Oh, the Point will mature him. Then two years on the Plains — and after that the mills."

"Perhaps — two years! But, Penhallow, who can dare to predict what God has in store for us. Two years!"

"Yes — too true — who can! Just now we are financially diseased, and men are thinking more of the bread and butter and debts of to-morrow than of Mr. Buchanan in the toils of his Southern Cabinet."

"That's so. Good-night."

Leila took upstairs with her John's last letter to her aunt, and sitting down read it eagerly:

"WEST POINT.

"MY DEAR AUNT: The life here, as I wrote you, is something almost monastic in its systematic regularity, and its despotic claims on one's time. It leaves small leisure for letters except on Sundays; and if a fellow means to be well placed, even then he is wise to do some work. The outside world seems far away, and we read and can read few papers.

"I am of Uncle Jim's politics, but although there are many pretty sensitive cadets from the South, some of them my friends, there is so pleasant a camaraderie among us that there are few quarrels, and certainly none of the bitterness of the two sections.

"I think I may have told you that we have no furlough until we have been here two years, but I hope some time for a visit from Uncle Jim and you, or at least from him and Leila. How she would enjoy it! The wonderful beauty of the great river in the embrace of these wooded mountains, the charm of the heroic lives it has nourished and the romance of its early history are delightful —"

"Enjoy it," murmured Leila, "oh, would I not indeed!" Then she read on:

"Tell Leila to write me all about the horses and the town, and if Josiah has been heard of. Tom McGregor writes me that after he is graduated next year, he means to try for a place in the army and get a year or two of army life before he settles down to help his father. So it takes only two years to learn how to keep people alive and four to learn how to kill them."

"I wonder who John means to kill." She sat in thought a while, and rising to undress said, "He must be greatly changed, my dear boy, Jack. Jack!"

CHAPTER XVI

THE widespread disapproval at the North of the Dred Scott Decision was somewhat less manifest in the middle months of the year because of the general financial distress, which diverted attention from what was so agreeable to the slave States, where in fact the stringency in the money market had been felt but little.

At Grey Pine, as elsewhere in Pennsylvania, the evil influence of the depression in trade was felt as never before. More men were discharged, and Penhallow and his wife practised economy which to him was difficult and distasteful. To limit expenditure on herself was of little moment to Ann Penhallow, but to have to limit her ability to give where more and more were needing help was to her at least a hard trial. With the spring of 1858, business had begun to revive, while more bitterness arose when in the senatorial contest Stephen Douglas encountered the soil-born vigorous intellect of the little known lawyer Lincoln. The debate put fresh life into the increasing power of the Republican party in the West.

"Listen to this," said Rivers to the Squire in July of 1858. "Here is a new choice. Long ago I got touch of this man, when he said, ' A house divided against itself cannot stand.' " He went on to read aloud parts of the famous speech.

Leila sitting with them on the porch looked round to hear her uncle's comment. He said, "It is too radical, Rivers. It leaves no chance for compromise — it is a declaration of war."

"It is God's truth," said Rivers.

"The Democrats will rejoice," said Penhallow. "The Administration will be as I am against Douglas and against this man's views."

" I wish he were even more of an abolitionist, Squire. The right to life, liberty and the pursuit of happiness, ought to apply to all men, black and white."

" Yes, but are there to be further applications. Shall your free black vote? Does he say that? "

" No, but I do."

" Good gracious! " exclaimed the Squire. " I move we adjourn. Here comes Ann."

Keen to have the last word, Rivers urged, " He is not against some fugitive-slave law — not for abolition of slavery in the District of Columbia — or the slave trade between the States."

" But," said Leila, " I read it all last night in my room. He said it was the right and duty of Congress to prohibit slavery in all the territories."

" The right," said Penhallow, " Miss Politician? "

" And the duty," returned Rivers. They rose as Ann came up the steps.

Billy was carrying the baskets she had emptied in the village, and as usual with Ann when there had been much to do, she came home, Rivers said, refreshed by the exercise of her gentle despotisms as a man may be by use of competent muscles. " You are all struck dumb," she cried. " I smell the sulphur of bad politics."

" I 'm for Buch and Breck," said Billy. " Misses she give me a dollar to vote for Buchanan, I know —"

Leila delightedly encouraged him. " Did you? "

" No, it was for poll-tax. Take in those baskets at once," said Ann.

" Yes, ma'am. Bought a fishing-pole."

The confusion of mind which had made this practical use of Ann's mild political contribution was new to the Squire, and deliciously funny to Leila. Penhallow laughed outright. Rivers was silent watching Mrs. Ann.

To his surprise, she said, " You are bad — all of you. If the women could vote we would cease to have trouble. It may please you all to know that since that idiot Pole has mortgaged his farm to Swallow and bought out the butcher at the mills, he has repented of his Democratic wickedness and says, 'After all the Squire was right.'"

"And where, my dear, did you get all this gossip?" asked Penhallow.

"It is complicated; ask Pole."

"I could guess," laughed Leila.

"And I," cried the Squire.

"You will all suffer," cried Ann, "and don't complain, James Penhallow, if tough beef is the final result of political complications." Whereupon she gathered her skirts and fled laughing.

"Pole will pay dearly," said the Squire, who was secretly securing meat for the discharged mill-hands and understood what had influenced Pole.

Grey Pine and Westways during the summer and fall of 1858 felt, like many in the Northern States, the need to live with economy. Want of employment added to the unrest, and the idle men found time to discuss the angry politics which rang through the debates in the Senate. The changed tariff on iron, to which Pennsylvania was always selfishly sensitive, affected the voting, and Penhallow was pleased when the Administration suffered disaster in the October elections. All parties — Republican, American and Douglas Democrats — united to cast discredit on the President's policy, but Penhallow knew that the change of duties on iron had little to do with the far-spread ruin of trade and manufactures the result of long credits and the careless finance of an over-prosperous people. The electoral results were looked upon as a Republican victory. He so explained it on a November afternoon, as he rode through the still forest with Leila Grey, when the faint haze and warmer days told of that mysterious arrest of decay we call the Indian summer.

As they rode, the long lapses into silence told of the pleasant relations of two people entirely at ease with one another. Now it was a question asked — and now quick discussion. She had slowly won with maidenhood what few children have, more or less of the varied forms of imagination, which once had rather amused or puzzled her in John Penhallow. Her uncle, who thought slowly unless in danger, rode on with his mind upon a small order for rails and was far from feeling the mystery of the autumn days. The girl beside him was reading into the slow rocking to and fro of the falling leaves some reluctance to become forever a part of the decaying mould.

"Please, Uncle Jim, don't trot. Let them walk. It is so full of tender deaths."

"What do you mean, Leila? — as if death were ever beautiful or tender. You and your aunt bother me with your absurd manufacture of some relation to nature —"

"Oh, Uncle Jim! Once I saw you pat a big pine and say 'how are you, old fellow?' I told John it was nonsense, but he said it was fine."

"Oh, but that was a tree."

Leila laughed. "Of that there can be no doubt."

"Well, and what of it? It was half fun. You and John and your aunt sit up and explode into enthusiasm over verse, when it could all be said far better in simple prose."

"I should like to put that to the test some night."

"Not I, Miss Grey. I have no poetry in me. I am cold prose through and through."

"You — you!" she cried. "Some people like poetry — some people are poetry."

"What — what?"

"Wasn't your hero Cromwell just magnificent, stately blank verse?"

"What confounded nonsense!" She glanced at the manly figure with the cavalry seat, erect, handsome, to her heroic — an ideal gentleman in all his ways. "Stuff and nonsense!" he added.

"Well, Uncle Jim — to talk prose — the elections please you?"

"Yes. The North is stiffening up. It is as well. Did you see what Seward said, 'An irrepressible conflict,' and that man Lincoln, 'The house divided against itself cannot stand'? Now I should like to think them both wrong."

"And do you not?" she asked.

"No. Some devilish fate seems to be at the helm, as Rivers says. We avoid one rock to fall into wild breakers of exasperation; with fugitive-slave cases on one side, and on the other importations of slaves. Where will it end?"

"But what would you do, uncle?"

"Oh, amend the Fugitive-Slave Law. Try the cases by jury. Let slavery alone to cure itself, as it would in time. It would if we let it alone."

"And Kansas?" asked Leila.

"Oh, Douglas is right, but his view of the matter will never satisfy the South nor the extreme men at the North. My dear Leila, the days are dark and will be darker, and worst of all they really think we are afraid." His face grew stern. "I hate to talk about it. Have you heard from John lately?"

"Yes, only last week."

"And you write to him, of course?"

"Yes, I answer his letters. Aunt Ann writes every Sunday. Are things better at the mills?"

"Rather. Now for a gallop — it puts me always in a more hopeful humour. Don't let your aunt overwork you, Leila; she will."

"She can't, Uncle Jim." It was true. Leila gently rebelled against incessant good works — sewing-classes for the village girls, Sunday school, and the endless errands which left no time for books. Her occasional walks with Marks Rivers enabled her to form some clear idea of the difference of opinion which so sharply divided parties north of Maryland. His own belief was that slavery was a sinful thing with which there should be no truce and no patient waiting upon the influence of time. He combated the Squire's equally simple creed — the unbroken union of the States. She fought the rector hard, to his delight. Far more pleasant on three afternoons in the week were the lessons in Italian with her aunt, and Rivers's brilliant commentary on Dante. The months ran on into and through the winter, with an economical Christmas to Ann's regret.

As a rule the political contests of our country go on without deeply affecting the peace of families. In the cotton States opinion was or had to appear to be at one. In the North the bitterness and unreason of limited groups of anti-slavery people excited the anger of men who saw in their ways and speeches continual sources of irritation, which made all compromise difficult. The strife of parties where now men were earnest as they never were before since revolutionary days was felt most seriously in the border States.

"James," said Ann after breakfast, when Leila had gone to dress for a ride, "I think I ought to tell you that I have had this morning letters from both my brothers. I wrote, you know, asking them to bring the girls to us. Leila is too much alone. They both decline. Charles has come out for the Republicans, and now — it is too dreadful — they do not speak. Charles tells me there is a strong minority with him and that the State is not all for the South. I cannot believe it."

"Indeed!" He was not altogether displeased. "I am sorry for you, Ann, as their sister."

" And as a man, you are not! Where will it all end? There is neither charity nor reason at the North. I am disturbed for our country."

" You ask where it will all end. Where will it end? God alone knows. Let us at least wait quietly the course of events we cannot control. I at least try to be reasonable." He left her standing in tears, for which he had no comfort in thought or word. Over all the land, North and South, there were such differences of opinion between wife and husband, brothers, friends and kinsmen. As he stood at the door about to ride to the mills he looked back and heard her delayed comment.

" One moment, James —"

" Oh, what is the matter?" cried Leila at the foot of the stairs. To see Ann Penhallow in tears was strange indeed.

Her uncle standing with his hand on his wife's shoulder had just spoken. Turning to Leila, he said: " Your aunt and I have had some unpleasant news from your uncles in Baltimore — a political quarrel."

" I knew it in the spring, Uncle Jim."

The girl's thoughtful reticence surprised him. Neither to him nor to Ann had she said a word of this family feud.

" Thank you, Leila," murmured her aunt. The Squire wondered why, as her aunt added, " I am greatly troubled. We have always been a most united family; but, dear, this — this has brought home to me, as nothing else has, the breaking up of the ties which bound the South and North together. It is only the sign of worse things to come."

" But, Ann," said Penhallow, " I must say "— A sharp grip on his arm by Leila's hand stopped him. He checked himself in time —" it is all very sad, but neither you nor I can help it."

" That is too true, James. I should not have said what I did. I want to see one of the men at the mills. His children are ill, his wife is in great distress."

"I will drive you myself this morning. I will send Dixy away and order the gig."

"Thank you; I shall like that, James."

Meanwhile Leila rode away, having in a moment of tactful interference made her influence felt. She was well aware of it and smiled as she walked her horse down the avenue, murmuring,

"I suppose I shall catch it from Uncle Jim." And then, "No, he will be glad I pinched him, but he did look cross for a moment." No word of the family dissension reached John in their ever cheerful letters.

On a wild windy afternoon in February, the snow falling heavily, Leila on her way to the village rang at the Rector's door. Getting no answer, she went in and passing through the front room knocked at the library door.

"Come in." Rivers was at his table in a room littered with books and newspapers. The gentle smile of his usual greeting was missing. She saw at once that he was in one of his moods of melancholy — rare of late. Her eyes quick to see when she was interested noted that where he sat there was neither book nor paper in front of him. He rose as she entered, tall, stooping, lean, and so thin-featured that his large eyes were the more notable.

"Aunt Ann has a cold, and Joe Grace was at the house to say that his father is ill, and aunt wishes you to go with me and see what is wanted. He has no way to send for the doctor; and so you see, as he is in bed, you must go with me."

"Oh, I saw him this morning. It is of no moment. I did what was needed."

"But I have to see Mrs. Lamb too. Come for the walk. It is blowing a gale and the snow is splendid — do come."

Of late he had rarely walked with her. He hesitated.

"Do come."

"If I die of cold, Leila."

" Die! You do not take exercise enough to keep your blood in motion. Come, please! "

He said no more except " Wait a moment," and returned fitly clad. A fury of charging battalions of snow met them in the avenue. She faced it gallantly, joyous and rosy. He bent to avoid the sting of the driven snow, shivering, and more at ease when in the town the houses broke the force of the gale.

" You won't need to go to Grace's," he urged.

" I am under orders. Don't you know Aunt Ann? "

Presently plunging through the snow-drifts they came into the dreary disordered back room which had so troubled Penhallow. It was cold with that indoor cold which is so unpleasant. Joe Grace came in — a big strapping young fellow. " I came from the farm and found father in bed and no wood in the stack. Some one has just fetched a load." He began to make a fire.

" Go up to your father," said Rivers. " Make a fire in his room. You ought to have come sooner. Oh, that poor helpless Baptist saint — there is n't much wrong, but the man is half frozen — and it is so needless."

" Come," said Leila. " Does he require anything? "

" No, I saw to that." As he spoke, he piled log on log and warmed his long thin hands. " Wait a little, Leila." She sat down, while the loose casements rattled.

" Leila," he said, " there is no chance to talk to you at Grey Pine. I am troubled about these, my friends. What I now have of health and mental wholesomeness in my life, I owe to them. I came hither a broken, hopeless man. Now they are in trouble." She looked up at him in some surprise at his confession. " I want to help them. Your uncle told me of your aunt's new distress and the cause. Then I made him talk business, and asked him to let me lend him thirty thousand dollars. He said no, but I did see how it pleased him. He said that it would be lost. At all events his refusal was decisive."

"But," said Leila, increasingly surprised, "that was noble of you."

"Nonsense, my dear Leila; I have more than I need — enough to help others — and would still have enough."

She had a feeling of astonishment at the idea of his being so well-off, and now from his words some explanation of the mysterious aid which had so helped at the mills and so puzzled Mrs. Ann. Why had he talked to her? He himself could not have told why. As he stood at the fire he went on talking, while she made her quick mental comments.

"You call it noble. It is a rather strange thing; but to go to a friend in financial despair with a cheque-book is a test of friendship before which many friendships fail. Before my uncle left me rich beyond my needs, I had an unpleasant experience on a small scale, but it was a useful example in the conduct of life." He paused for a moment, and then said, "I shall try the Squire again."

"I think you will fail — I know Uncle Jim. But what you tell me — is it very bad? I mean, is he — are the mills — likely to fail?"

"That depends as I see it on the summer nominations and the fall elections, and their result no one can predict. The future looks to me full of peril."

"But why?" she asked, and had some surprise when he said, "I have lived in the South. I taught school in Macon. I know the South, its increasing belief in the despotic power of cotton and tobacco, its splendid courage, and the sense of mastery given by the ownership of man. Why do I talk my despair out to a young life like yours? I suppose confession to be a relief — the tears of the soul. I suppose it is easier to talk to a woman." "Then why not to Aunt Ann?" thought Leila, as he went on to say, "I have often asked myself why confession is such a relief." He smiled as he added, "I wonder if St.

Francis ever confessed to Monica." Then he was silent, turning round before the fire, unwilling to leave it.

Leila had been but recently introduced to the knowledge of St. Francis, and was struck with the oddity of representing Monica; and the tall, gaunt figure with the sad eyes, as the joyful St. Francis.

"Now, I must go home," he said.

"Indeed, no! You are to go with me to the post-office and then to see Mrs. Lamb."

He had some pleasant sense of liking to be ordered about by this young woman. As they faced the snow, he asked, "How tall are you, Leila?"

"Five feet ten inches and — to be accurate — a quarter. Why do you ask?"

"Idle curiosity."

"Curiosity is never idle, Mr. Rivers. It is industrious. I proved that in a composition I wrote at school. It did bother Miss Mayo."

"I should think it might," said Rivers. "Any letters, Mrs. Crocker?"

"No, sir; none for Squire's folk. Two newspapers. Awful cold, Miss Leila. Molasses so hard to-day, had to be chopped —"

"Oh, now, Mrs. Crocker!"

The fat post-mistress was still handling the pile of finger-soiled letters. "Oh, there's one for Mrs. Lamb."

"We are going there. I'll take it."

"Thanks, miss. She's right constant in coming for letters, but the letters they don't come, and now here's one at last." Leila tucked it into her belt. "I tell you, Miss Leila, a post-office is a place to make you laugh one day and cry the next. When you see a girl from the country come here twice a week for maybe two months and then go away trying that hard to make believe it wasn't of any account. There ought to be some one to write 'em letters — just to say, 'Don't cry, he'll come.' It might be a queer letter."

Rivers wondered at the very abrupt and very American introduction of unexpected sentiment and humour.

"Let me know and I'll write them, Mrs. Crocker," cried Leila. She had the very youthful reflection that it was odd for such a fat woman to be sentimental.

"I should like to open all the letters for a week, Mrs. Crocker," said Rivers.

"Wouldn't Uncle Sam make a row?"

"He would, indeed!"

"Idle curiosity," laughed Leila, as they went out into the storm.

He made no reply and reflected on this young woman's developmental change and the gaiety which he so lacked.

Leila, wondering what Peter wrote to the lonely old widow, went to look for her in the kitchen, while Rivers sat down in the neatly kept front room. He waited long. At last Leila came out alone, and as they walked away she said, "The letter was from Peter."

"Indeed!"

"Yes, I got it all out of her."

"Got what?"

"She gets three dollars a week from Aunt Ann and all her vegetables from Aunt Ann, and she is all the time complaining to Uncle Jim. Then, of course, Uncle Jim gives her more money — and Peter gets it —"

"Where is he?"

"Oh, in Philadelphia, and here and there."

"You should tell the Squire."

"No, I think not."

"Perhaps — yes — perhaps you are right." And facing the wild norther she left him at his door and went homewards with a new burden of thought on her mind.

The winter broke up and late in May Penhallow left home on business. He wrote from Philadelphia:

"MY DEAR ANN: Trade is dead, money still locked up, and the railways hesitating to give orders for much-needed rails. I have one small order, which will keep us going, but will hardly pay.

"I never talk of the political disorder, but now you will feel as I do a certain dismay at the action of the Vicksburg Convention in the interest of the slave States. Not all were represented — Tennessee and Florida voted against the resolution that all State and Federal laws prohibiting the African slave trade ought to be repealed. South Carolina to my surprise divided its vote; there were forty for, nineteen against this resolution. It seems made to exasperate the North and build up the Republican party. I who am simply for the Union most deeply regret this action.

"I want Leila to meet me here to-day week. We will take the steamer and go to West Point, let her see the place, and bring John home for his month of furlough.

"I have talked here to the Mayor and other moderate Union men, and find them more hopeful than I of a peaceful ending.

"Yours always,

"JAMES PENHALLOW."

CHAPTER XVII

WHEN Leila sat upon the upper deck of the great Hudson River steamer, she was in a condition of excitement natural to an imaginative nature unused to travel. Her mind was like a fresh canvas ready for the hand of the artist. She was wondering at times what John Penhallow would look like after over two years of absence and hardly heard the murmur of talk around her, and was as unconscious of the interested glances of the young men attracted by the tall figure standing in the bow as the great river opened before her.

"That," said her uncle, "is Weehawken. There — just there — Hamilton was killed by Burr, and near by Hamilton's son four years before was killed in a duel — a political quarrel."

She knew the sad story well, and with the gift of visualization saw the scene and the red pistol-flashes which meant the death of a statesman of genius.

"And there are the palisades, Leila." The young summer was clothing the banks with leafage not yet dark green, and translucent in the morning sun. No railroads marred the loveliness of the lawns on the East bank, and the grey architecture of the palisades rose in solemn grandeur to westward.

"It is full of history, Leila. There is Tarrytown, where André was taken." She listened in silence. The day ran on — the palisades fell away. "Dobbs's Ferry, my dear;" and pointing across the river, "on that hill André died."

Presently the mountains rose before them, and in the afternoon they drew up at the old wharf. "We stay at Cozzen's Hotel, Leila. I will send on the baggage and we will walk up to the Point."

She hardly heard him. A tall young man in white panta-loons and blue jacket stood on the pier. "Good gracious, Uncle Jim, it is John!" A strange sense of disappointed remem-brance possessed her. The boy playmate of her youth was gone. He gave both hands of welcome, as he said, "By George, Leila, I am glad to see you."

"You may thank uncle for our visit. Aunt Ann was not very willing to part with me."

He was about to make the obvious reply of the man, but re-frained. They talked lightly of the place, of her journey, and at last he said very quietly, even coldly, as if it were merely a natural history observation, "You are amazingly grown, Cousin Leila. It is as well for cadets and officers that your stay is to be brief."

"John, I have been in Baltimore. You will have to put it stronger than that — I am used to it."

"I will see if I can improve on it, Leila."

Now this was not at all the way she meant to meet him, nor these the words they meant to use — or rather, she — for John Penhallow had given it no thought, except to be glad as a child promised a gift and then embarrassed into a word of simple descriptive admiration. When John Penhallow said, with a curious gravity and a little of his old formal manner, "I will reflect on it," she knew with the quick perception of her sex that here was a new masculine study for the great naturalist woman. The boy — the lad — she knew were no more.

"Who is that with Uncle James?" she asked.

"The Commandant."

"My niece, Miss Grey. Colonel Beauregard, my dear. Let us walk up to the Point." The Commandant, who made good his name, took possession of the delighted young woman and carried her away to his home with Penhallow, leaving the cadet to return to his routine of duty. As they parted, he said, "I am set free to-morrow, Leila, at five, and excused from the afternoon parade. If you and Uncle Jim will walk up to Fort Putnam, I will join you."

"I will tell Uncle Jim. You will be at the hop of course? I have been thinking of nothing else for a week."

"I may be late."

"Oh, why?"

"We are in the midst of our examinations. Even to get time for a walk with you and uncle was hard. I wrote Uncle Jim not to come now. He must have missed it."

"And so I am to suffer."

"I doubt the anguish," he returned, laughing, as he touched his cap, and left her to brief consideration of the cadet cousin.

"Uncle Jim might have been just like that — looked like that. They are very unlike too. I used to be able to tell just what Jack would do when we were children — don't think I can now. How tall he is and how handsome. The uniform is becoming. I wonder if I too am so greatly changed."

It is well here to betray the secrets of the novelists' confessional. Leila Grey had seen in the South much of an interesting society where love affairs were brief, lightly taken, easily ended, or hardly more than the mid-air flirtations of butterflies. No such perilous approaches to the most intimate relations of men and women were for this young woman, on whom the love and tactful friendship of the married life of Grey Pine had left a lasting impression. One must have known her well to become aware of the sense of duty to her ideals which lay behind her alert appearance of joyous gaiety and capacity to see the mirthful aspects of life. Once long ago the lad's moment of passionate longing had but lightly stirred the dreamless sleep of unawakened power to love. Even the memory of John's boy-folly had faded with time. Her relation to him had been little more than warm friendship. Even that tie — and she was abruptly aware of it — had become less close. She was directly conscious of the fact and wondered if this grave young man felt as she did. She lay awake that night and wondered too if his ideals of heroism and ambition were still actively present, and where too was his imagination — ever on the wing and far beyond her mental flight? She also had changed. Did he know it or care? Then she dismissed him and fell asleep.

As John Penhallow near to noon came out a little weary and anxious from the examination ordeal, he chanced on his uncle and Leila waiting with the officer of the day, who said to him, "After dinner you are free for the rest of the afternoon. Mr. Penhallow has asked me to relieve you."

As he bade them good-morning, his uncle said, "How goes the examination?"

"Don't ask me yet, sir; but I cannot go home until the end of next week. Then I shall know the result."

"But what examination remains?" persisted the Squire.

"Don't ask him, Uncle Jim."

"Well — all right."

"Thank you, Leila. I am worn out. I am glad of a let-up. I dream equations and pontoon bridges — and I must do some work after dinner. Then I will find you and Uncle Jim on Fort Putnam, at five."

"I want to talk with Beauregard," said Penhallow, "about the South. Leila can find her way."

"I can," she said. "I want to sketch the river, and that will give me time."

"Oh, there goes the dinner call. Come in at a quarter to one with Uncle Jim. I have leave to admit you. There will be something to interest you."

"And what, John — men eating?"

"No. One of my best friends, Gresham from South Carolina, has been ordered home by his father."

"And why?" asked Penhallow.

"Oh, merely because his people are very bitter, and, as he tells me, they write about secession as if it were merely needed to say to the North 'We mean to cut loose'— and go; it is just to be as simple as 'Good-bye, children.' I think I wrote you, uncle, that we do not talk politics here, but this quiet assumption of being able to do with us what they please is not the ordinary tone of the Southern cadets. Now and then there is a row —"

Leila listened with interest and some presently gratified desire to hear her cousin declare his own political creed. She spoke, as they stood beside the staff from which the flag was streaming in the north wind, "Would it not be better, John, as Mr. Rivers desires, to let the Southern States go in peace?" As she spoke, she was aware of something more than being merely anxious that he should make the one gallant answer to the words that challenged opinion. The Squire caught on to some comprehension of the earnestness with which she put the question.

To his uncle's surprise, the cadet said, "Ah, my dear Leila, that is really asking me on which side I should be if we come to an open rupture."

"I did not mean quite that, John, and I spoke rather lightly; but you do not answer."

He somewhat resented this inquisition, but as he saw his uncle turn, apparently expectant, he said quietly and speaking with the low voice which may be so surpassingly expressive, "I hardly see, Leila, why you put such a question to me here under the flag. If there is to be war — secession, I shall stand by the flag, my country, and an unbroken union." The young face flushed a little, the mouth, which was of singular beauty, closed with a grip on the strong jaw. Then, to Leila's surprise, the Captain and John suddenly uncovered as music rang out from the quarters of the band.

"Why do you do that, Uncle Jim?"

"Don't you hear, Leila? It is the 'Star-Spangled Banner'—

we all uncover." Here and there on the parade ground, far and near, officers, cadets and soldiers, stood still an instant bareheaded.

"Oh," murmured Leila. "How wonderful! How beautiful!" Surprised at the affect of this ceremonial usage upon herself, she stood a moment with that sense of constriction in the throat which is so common a signal of emotion. The music ceased, and as they moved on Penhallow asked, "What about Gresham, your friend?"

"Oh, you know, uncle, when a cadet resigns for any cause which involves no dishonour, we have a little ceremony. I want you to see it. No college has that kind of thing. Don't be late. I will join you in time."

The captain and Leila attracted much attention from the cadets at dinner in the Mess Hall. "Now, dear, look!" said Penhallow. At the end of the long table a cadet rose — the captain of the corps in charge of the battalion. There was absolute silence. The young officer spoke:

"You all know that to our regret one of us leaves to-day. Mr. Gresham, you have the privilege of calling the battalion to attention."

A slightly built young fellow in citizen's dress rose at his side. For a moment he could not fully command his voice; then his tones rang clear: "Most unwillingly I take my farewell. I am given the privilege of those who depart with honour. Battalion! Attention! God bless you! Good-bye!"

The class filed out, and lifting the departing man on their shoulders bore him down to the old south dock and bade him farewell.

Penhallow looked after them. "There goes the first, Leila. There will be more — many more — to follow, unless things greatly change — and they will not. I hoped to take John home with us, but he will come in a week. I must leave to-morrow morning. John is in the dumps just now, but Beauregard has only pleasant things to say of him. I wish he were as agreeable about the politics of his own State."

" Are they so bad? "

" Don't ask me, Leila."

The capital of available energy in the young may be so exhausted by mental labour, when accompanied by anxiety, that the whole body for a time feels the effect. Muscular action becomes overconscious, and intense use of the mind seems to rob the motor centres of easy capacity to use the muscles. John Penhallow walked slowly up the rough road to where the ruined bastions of Fort Putnam rose high above the Hudson. He was aware of being tired as he had not been for years. The hot close air and the long hours of concentration of mind left him discouraged as well as exhausted. He was still in the toils of the might-have-been, of that wasting process — an examination, and turning over in his mind logistics, logarithms, trajectories, equations, and a mob of disconnected questions. " Oh, by George ! " he exclaimed, " what's the worth while of it? " All the pleasantly estimated assets of life and love and friendship became unavailable securities in the presence of a mood of depression which came of breathing air which had lost its vitalizing ozone. And now at a turn in the road nature fed her child with a freshening change of horizon.

Looking up he saw a hawk in circling flight set against the blue sky. He never saw this without thinking of Josiah, and then of prisoned things like a young hawk he had seen sitting dejected in a cage in the barracks. Did he have dreams of airy freedom? It had affected him as an image of caged energy — of useless power. With contrasted remembrance he went back to the guarded procession of boys from the lyceum in France, the flower-stalls, and the bird-market, the larks singing merrily in their small wicker cages. Yes, he had them —

the two lines he wanted — a poet's condensed statement of the
thought he could not fully phrase:

> Ah! the lark!
> He hath the heaven which he sings,—
> But my poor hawk hath only wings.

The success of the capture of this final perfection of statement of his own thought refreshed him in a way which is one
of the mysteries of that wild charlatan imagination, who now
and then administers tonics to the weary which are of inexplicable value. John Penhallow felt the sudden uplift and
quickened his pace until he paused within the bastion lines of the
fort. Before him, with her back to him, sat Leila. Her hat
lay beside her finished sketch. She was thinking that John Penhallow, the boy friend, was to-day in its accepted sense but an
acquaintance, of whom she desired, without knowing why, to
know more. That he had changed was obvious. In fact, he had
only developed on the lines of his inherited character, while in
the revolutionary alterations of perfected womanhood she had
undergone a far more radical transformation.

The young woman, whom now he watched unseen, rose and
stood on the crumbling wall. A roughly caressing northwest
wind blew back her skirts. She threw out her wide-sleeved arms
in exultant pleasure at the magnificence of the vast river,
with its forest boundaries, and the rock-ribbed heights of
Crow's Nest. As she stood looking "taller than human," she
reminded him of the figure of victory he had seen as a boy on
the stairway of the Louvre. He stood still — again refreshed.
The figure he then saw lived with him through life, strangely
recurrent in moments of peril, on the march, or in the loneliness
of his tent.

"Good evening," he said as he came near. She sat down
on the low wall and he at her feet. "Ah, it is good to get
you alone for a quiet talk, Leila."

She was aware of a wild desire to lay a hand among the curls his cadet-cropped hair still left over his forehead. "Do you really like the life here, John?"

"Oh, yes. It is so definite — its duties are so plain — nothing is left to choice. Like it? Yes, I like it."

"But, is n't it very limited?"

"All good education must be — it is only a preparation; but one's imagination is free — as to a man's future, and as to ambitions. There one can use one's wings."

She continued her investigation. "Then you have ambitions. Yes, you must have," she cried with animation. "Oh, I want you to have them — ideals too of life. We used to discuss them."

He looked up. "You think I have changed. You want to know how. It is all vague — very vague. Yet, I could put my creed of what conduct is desirable in life in a phrase — in a text."

"Do, John." She leaned over in her interest.

"Render unto Cæsar the things which are Cæsar's and to God the things which are God's." The seriousness of the upturned face for a moment kept her silently reflective.

"Cæsar! What of Cæsar, John?"

"My country, of course; that is simple. The rest, Leila, covers all — almost all of life and needs no comment. But how serious we are. Tell me all about home and the village and the horses and Uncle Jim. He has some grey hairs."

"He may well have grey hairs, John. The times are bad. He is worried. Imagine Uncle Jim economical!"

"Incredible."

"Yes. He told me that his talk with Colonel Beauregard had made him despair of a peaceful ending, and usually he is hopeful."

"Well, don't make me talk politics. We rarely do. Is n't this outlook beautiful? People rarely come here and it often gives me a chance to be alone and to think."

" And what do you think about, John? " She was again curious.

" Oh, many things, big and little. Uncle Jim, Aunt Ann, Mr. Rivers, Dixy — hornets, muskrats," he laughed. She noted the omission of Leila Grey.

" And what else? "

" Oh, the tragedy of Arnold,— the pathos of Washington's despair,— his words, ' Who is there now I can trust?' "

" It came home to me, John, this morning when Colonel Beauregard showed us the portraits of the major-generals of the Revolution. I saw a vacant place and a tablet like the rest, but with ' Major General — Born 1740 ' and no name! I asked what it meant. The Colonel said only, ' Arnold.' That is too pitiful — and his wife — I read somewhere that she was young, beautiful, and innocent of his horrible treason."

" Yes, what crime could be worse than his, and, too, such a gallant soldier. Let us walk around the fort. Oh, by the way, I found here last week two Continental buttons, Third Pennsylvania Infantry. Like to have them, Leila? I thought you might."

" Would I like? " She took them eagerly. " They ought to be gilded and used as sleeve-links." But where she kept them John Penhallow never knew. They did not make the sleeve-links for which she agreed they were so suitable.

" Is n't there a walk down through the woods? " asked Leila.

" Yes, this way." Leaving the road they followed a rough trail through the woods to a more open space half-way down the hill. Here he paused. " This is our last chance to talk until I am at Grey Pine."

" That will be very soon, John." She sat down amid numberless violets, adding, " There will be the hop to-night, as you call it."

" Yes, the hop. I forgot. You will give me the first dance? "

To her surprise he asked no others. " Cadets have to learn to dance, but Baltimore may have left you critical."

Still on her investigation track, she returned, " Oh, Baltimore! It seems odd to me that I should have seen so much of the world of men and women and you who are older so little in this military monastery."

He laughed outright. " We have the officers' families, and if we are allowed to visit, the Kembles and Gouverneurs and Pauldings across the river — no better social life anywhere. And as for young women — sisters, cousins — *embarras de choix,* Miss Grey. They come in flocks like the blackbirds. I assure you that this branch of natural history is pretty well illustrated at the Point. We are apt to be rather over-supplied in June."

" Indeed! — all sorts, I suppose."

" Yes, a variety, and just now three charming young women from the South."

" Rather a strong adjective — charming. I might hesitate to apply it to a whole flock. I think men are more apt to use it than women."

" I stand by my adjective. Take care of your laurels, Miss Grey. I am lucky enough to have two dances with Miss Ramsay. Her brother is a cadet."

" Introduce him to me. What myriads of violets! "

" Do you remember how, when we were small, we used to fight violets? "

" How long ago it seems, John. It must have been the first June after you appeared in that amazing cap and — the cane. I have it yet. Let's fight violets. It may have a charm to make me look young again — I feel so old sometimes."

Intent on her game, she was already gathering the flowers in her lap, while the young man a little puzzled and a little amused watched the face which she described for his benefit as needing to look young. She ran on gaily, " You will pick five and I will pick five. I never heard of any other children fighting violets. It is a neglected branch of education. I got it from the Westways children. Now, fair play, John Penhallow." He was carelessly taking his five violets, while Leila was testing hers, choosing them with care. The charm she sought was working — they were children again.

"That's not fair, Leila."

"Why not?"

"You are testing yours. It is a mean advantage. I would scorn to do such a thing. It is just like a woman — the way you do about dress. All women ought to dress alike — then the competition would be fair."

Leila looked up from her lap full of violets. "I should like to see *your* Miss Ramsay in one of my gowns."

"*My* Miss Ramsay! No such luck."

"You're a goose, Jack."

"You're a silly, Leila."

"Oh, now, we are children, John. This is the magic of the June violets."

"And you are just fourteen, Leila. The wrinkles of age are gone — they used to be dimples."

"Nonsense! Let's play."

They hooked together the bent stems of the flowers. Then there was a quick jerk, and one violet was decapitated. "One for you, Leila; — and another."

"You are not paying any attention to the game. Please to keep young a little while." He was watching the sunlight as it fell upon her neck when it bent over the flowers.

"And how am I to keep young, Miss Grey?"

"Oh, any woman can answer that — ask Miss Ramsay."

"I will. There! you have won, Leila, three to two. There used always to be a forfeit. What must I pay?"

"Now, John, what terrible task shall I put upon you? I have it. You shall ask me to give you the third dance."

"That is Miss Ramsay's. I am sorry."

" Oh, one girl is as good as another."

" Perhaps — for women." He did not ask of her any other dances. " But really, Leila, the better bred of these Southern girls we see here are most pleasant acquaintances, more socially easy of acquaintance than Northern girls. As they are butter-flies of the hour — their frank ways are valuable in what you call our monastery."

" Yes, I know them well. There may be time here for some brief flirtations. I used to see them in Maryland, and once when Aunt Margaret took me on visits to some old Virginia homes. These pleasant girls take to it with no more conscience than birds in the spring. I used to see it in Maryland."

" Oh, yes," he said, " but it means very little; — quite harm-less — mere practice, like our fencing bouts."

" Did you ever kiss a woman, John — just for practice? " " Why did I say that! " thought Leila. " Come, sir, confess! "

" Yes," he said, not liking it and far from any conception of the little mob of motives which betrayed to her a state of mind he had not the daring to guess. " Did I? That requires cour-age. Have I — ever kissed a woman? Yes, often —"

" Oh, I did not ask who."

" Aunt Ann — and a girl once —"

" Indeed! "

" Yes — Leila Grey, aged fifteen — and got my ears boxed. This confession being at an end, I want absolution." The air was cleared.

" How about the first polka as absolution? " said Leila.

" It is unusual, but as penance it may answer."

" The penance may be mine. I shall know better after the first round, Mr. Penhallow."

" You are complimentary, Miss Grey," he added, with the whimsical display of mirth which was more than a smile and not a laugh, and was singularly attractive.

In place of keeping up the gay game of trifles as shuttle-cocks,

Leila stood still upon the edge of the wood, " I don't think you liked what I asked."

" What, about kissing? I did not, but upon my honour I answered you truly." He was grave as he replied.

" You did not think it impertinent, Jack? "

" I don't know what I thought it." And then, as if to avoid need to defend or explain contradictory statements, he said, " Put yourself in my place. Suppose I had dared to ask you if ever a man had kissed you—"

" Oh, that's the difference between kissing and being kissed."

" Then put it my way."

" John Penhallow, I should dearly like to box your ears. Once a man did kiss me. He was tall, handsome, and had the formal courtly manners you have at times. He was General Winfield Scott. He kissed my hand."

" You minx! " cried John, " you are no better than you used to be. There goes the bugle! " And laughing as he deserted her, he ran down the hill and across the parade ground.

" He is not really handsome," said the young woman, " but no man ought to have so beautiful a mouth — I could have made him do it in a minute. Why did I not? What's the matter? I merely could n't. He has n't the remotest idea that if he were to kiss me — I —" She reddened at the thought and went with quick steps of " virgin liberty " to take tea with the Commandant.

In New York, on his way home, Penhallow received a tele-gram, " I am third. John Penhallow." Then the Squire pre-sented Leila with a bracelet, to the belated indignation of Aunt Ann, who was practising the most disagreeable economy. Her husband wrote her that the best policy for a man financially in peril was to be extravagant enough to discredit belief in his need to lessen expenditure. He was, moreover, pleasantly aware that the improving conditions of trade this summer of 1859 had enabled him to collect some large outstanding debts. He encouraged Leila to remember their old village friends, but when he proposed a set of furs for Ann Penhallow's winter wear Leila became ingeniously impossible about choice, and the Squire's too lavish generosity somehow failed to materialize; but why or how was not clear to him because of their being feminine diplomatic ways — which attain results and leave with the male a mildly felt resentment without apparent cause of defeat.

As Cadet No. 3 of his class in this year's studies made the railway journey of a warm June day, he recalled with wondering amusement his first lonely railway travel. " I was a perfect little snob." The formal, too old-mannered politeness of his childhood had left, if the child is father of the man, an inheritance of pleasant courtesy which was unusual and had varied values in the intercourse of life. Rivers said of him later that the manner of John Penhallow's manners had the mystery of charm. Even when younger, at Grey Pine, he liked to talk to people, with curiosity about their lives and their work. Now, as the train moved on, he fell into chat with the country folk who got on the train for short travel. Soon or late they all talked politics, but 'generally guessed things would be settled somehow'— which is the easily reached conclusion of the American. When the old conductor, with the confidence John's manner invited, asked what uniform he wore, John said, laughing, " Do you not remember the boy with a cane who got out at Westways Crossing? "

" You ain't him — not really? Why it 's years ago! You are quite a bit changed."

" For the better, I hope."

" Well, here 's your station, and Miss Grey waiting."

" Oh, John, glad to see you! I told aunt no one must go for you but me. Get in. And Billy, look out how you drive."

Billy, bewildered by the tall figure in cadet jacket and grey pantaloons, needed the warning.

Then there was the avenue, the big grey pine, home, and
Aunt Ann's kiss of welcome. The old familiar life was again
his. He rode with the Squire or Leila, swam, and talked to
Rivers whenever he could induce the too easily tired man to
walk with him. He was best pleased to do so when Leila was
of the party. Then at least the talk was free and wandered
from poetry and village news to discussion of the last addition
to the causes of quarrel between the North and South. When
tempted to speak at length, Rivers sat down.

"How can a man venture to speak, John, like Mr. Jefferson
Davis? Have you read his speech?"

"No, sir."

"Well, he says the importation of Africans ought to be left
to the States — and the President. He thinks that as Cuba
is the only spot in the civilized world where the African
slave-trade is permitted, its cession to us would put an end
to that blot on civilization. An end to it, indeed! Think
of it!" His voice rose as he spoke. "End slavery and
you end that accursed trade. And to think that a woman
like Ann Penhallow should think it right!" Neither John
nor Leila were willing to discuss their aunt's definitely held
views.

"I think," said Leila, who had listened silently, "Aunt Ann
has lost or put aside her interest in politics."

"I wish I could," said John. "But what do you mean,
Leila? She has never said so."

"It's just this. Aunt Ann told me two weeks ago that
Uncle Henry Grey was talked of as a delegate to the Democratic Convention to meet next year. Now her newspapers
remain unopened. They are feeding these dissensions North
and South. No wonder she is tired of it all. I am with Uncle
Jim, but I hate to wrangle over politics like Senator Davis and
this new man Lincoln — oh, and the rest. No good comes of
it. I can't see it as you do, Mr. Rivers."

"And yet, I am right," said Rivers gravely. "God knows. It is in His hands."

"What Aunt Ann thinks right," said Leila, "can't be so unpardonably wicked." She spoke softly. "Oh, John, look at that squirrel. She is carrying a young one on her back — how pretty! She has to do it. What a lovely instinct. It must be heavy."

"I suppose," said Rivers, "we all have loads we must carry, are born to carry —"

"Like the South, sir," said John. "We can help neither the squirrel nor the South. You think we can throw stones at the chipmunk and make her drop it — and —"

"Bad logic, John," returned Rivers. "But soon there will be stones thrown."

"And who will cast the first stone?" rejoined Leila, rising.

"It is an ancient crime," said Rivers. "It was once ours, and it will be ours to end it. Now I leave you to finish your walk; I am tired." As they moved away, he looked after them. "Beauty, intelligence, perfect health — oh, my God!"

In August with ever resisted temptation John Penhallow went back to West Point to take up his work again.

The autumn came, and in October, at night, the Squire read with dismay and anger of the tragic attempt of John Brown at Harper's Ferry. "My poor Ann," he exclaimed. He went at once from his library back to the hall, where Leila was reading aloud. "Ann," he said, "have you seen the papers to-day?"

"I have read no paper for a month, James. They only fill me with grief and the sense of how helpless I am — even — even — with those I love. What is it now, James?"

"An insane murderer named John Brown has made an attack on Harper's Ferry with a dozen or so of infatuated followers." He went on to tell briefly the miserable story of a madman's folly.

"The whole North is mad," said Ann, not looking up, but knitting faster as she spoke, "mad — the abolitionists of Boston are behind it." It was too miserably true. "Thank you, James, for wanting to make me see in this only insanity."

The Squire stood still, watched by the pitiful gaze of Leila. "I want you, Ann — I wanted you to see, dear, to feel how every thoughtful man in the North condemns the wickedness of this, and of any, attempt to cause insurrection among the slaves."

"Yes — yes, of course — no doubt — but it is the natural result of Northern sentiment."

"Oh, Aunt Ann!"

"Keep quiet, child!"

"You should not have talked politics to me, James."

"But, my God, Ann, this is not politics!" He looked down at her flushed face and with the fatal newspaper in his hand stood still a moment, and then went back to his library. There he stayed before the fire, distressed beyond measure. "Just so," he said, "the South will take it — just so."

Ann Penhallow said, "Where did you leave off, Leila? Go on, my dear, with the book."

"I can't. You were cruel to Uncle Jim — and he was so dear and sweet."

"If you can't read, you had better go to bed." Leila broke into tears and stumbled up the stairs with half-blinded eyes.

Ann sat long, hearing Penhallow's steps as he walked to and fro. Then she let fall her knitting, rose, and went into the library.

"James, forgive me. I was unjust to say such things — I was —"

"Please don't," he cried, and took her in his arms. "Oh, my love," he said, "we have darker days than this before us. If only there was between North and South love like ours —

there is not. We at least shall love on to the end — no matter what happens."

The tearful face looked up, "And you do forgive me?"

"Forgive! There is no need for any such word in the dictionary of love." Between half-hysterical laughter and ready tears, she gasped, "Where did you get that prettiness?"

"Read it in a book, you goosey. Go to bed."

"No, not yet. This crime or craze will make mischief?"

"Yes, Ann, out of all proportion to the thing. The South will be in a frenzy, and the North filled with regret and horror. Now go to bed — we have behaved like naughty children."

"Oh, James, must I be put in a corner?"

"Yes — of my heart. Now, good night."

November passed. The man who had sinned was fairly tried, and on December 2nd went to a well-deserved death. Penhallow refused to talk of him to Rivers, who praised the courage of his last hours.

"Mark," he said, "I have been twice or thrice sure I was to die — and I have seen two murderers hanged, and I do assure you that neither they nor I were visibly disturbed. The fact is, when a fellow is sure to be put to death, he is either dramatic — as this madman was — or quietly undemonstrative. Martyr! Nonsense! It was simply stupid. I don't want to talk about it. Those mischief-makers in Congress will howl over it." They did, and secession was ever in the air.

CHAPTER XVIII

THE figure of Lincoln had been set on the by-ways of State politics by his debate with Douglas. His address in New York in February of 1860 set him on the highways of the nation's life. Meanwhile there were no talks about politics at Grey Pine. The Christmas Season had again gone by with unwonted economies.

While Douglas defined his opinions in the Senate and Jefferson Davis made plain that the Union would be dissolved if a radical Republican were elected, it became clear that the Democratic party which in April was to nominate candidates would be other than of one mind. Penhallow in Washington heard Seward in the Senate. Of this memorable occasion he wrote with such enthusiasm to Leila as he rarely showed:

"I may not write to your aunt, and I am moved to write to you by the effect Mr. Seward's speech had on me. He is not much of a man in his make-up. His voice is husky and his gestures are awkward and have no relation to what he says. It seemed a dried-up sort of talk, but he held the Senate and galleries to fascinated attention for two hours, and was so appealing, so moderate. The questions at issue were handled with what Rivers calls and never uses — the eloquence of moderation. I suppose he will be the nominee of the Republican party. It won't please the abolitionists at all. I wish you could have heard it.

"I came here to see two Southern Senators who have been counsel for us in regard to debts owing the mills by Southern railways. I gathered easily that my well-known Republican views made collection difficult. I was about to say something

289

angry — it would have done no good, and I am opposed to use-less anger. It is all pretty bad, because the South has hardly felt the panic, or its continued effect on our trade.

"I am wrong to trouble you with my troubles. We shall pull through.

"Yours,

"JAMES PENHALLOW."

"P. S. I should have been prepared for my failure to get fair treatment. I had learned in New York that lists of aboli-tion houses have been published in the South, and Southern buyers warned not to place orders with them. I wonder if I am thus listed. Our agent in Savannah writes that it is quite useless to solicit orders on account of the prevalent sentiment, and he is leaving the town."

Penhallow went home disappointed and discouraged, and called a private meeting of his Pittsburgh partners. He set before them the state of their affairs. There would be no debts collectible in the South. He smiled as he added that he had collected certain vague promises, which could hardly be used to pay notes. These could and would be met, they said, but finally agreed with him that unless they had other orders, it might be necessary to further reduce their small force. His partners were richer than he, but indisposed to take risks until the fall conventions were over. It was so agreed. As they were leaving, Penhallow said, "But there will be our workmen — what will become of them?" They were sure times would get better, and did not feel his nearness of responsibility for workmen he knew so long and so well.

He rode home at a walk. The situation of his firm was like that of many others, and now this April of 1860 business doubts, sectional feeling and love of country seemed to intensify the interest with which all classes looked forward to the Charleston Democratic Convention.

The Convention met on April 23rd. It was grave and able. There were daily prayers in the churches of Charleston for the success of Southern principles. Henry Grey, a delegate, wrote to his sister:

" The Douglas platform was adopted and at once the delegations of six cotton States withdrew. We who cannot accept Douglas meet in Richmond. It means secession unless the Republicans are reasonable when they nominate in Chicago. Mr. Alexander Stephens predicts a civil war, which most men I meet here consider very unlikely."

Ann handed this letter to her husband, saying, " This will interest you."

He read it twice, and then said, " There is at least one man in the South who believes the North will fight — Stephens."

" But will it, James? " A predictive spectre of fear rose before her.

Slowly folding the letter he said, " Yes, the South does not know us." She walked away.

On May 16th the Republicans met in Chicago. The news of the nomination of Lincoln came to the Squire as riding from the mills he met Dr. McGregor afoot.

" What, walking! " he said. " I never before saw you afoot — away from that saint of a mare."

" Yes, my old mare got bit by something yesterday and kicked the gig to smithereens, and lamed her off hind-leg."

" I will lend you a horse and a gig," said Penhallow.

" Thanks," said McGregor simply. " I am sweating through my coat."

" But don't leave my horse half a day tied to a post — any animal with horse-sense would kick."

" As if I ever did — but when the ladies keep me waiting. Heard the good news? No — We have nominated Lincoln — and Hamlin."

"I preferred Seward. You surprise me. What of the platform?"

"Oh, good! The Union, tariff, free soil. You will like it. The October elections in Pennsylvania will tell us who will win — later you will have to take an active part."

"No. Come up to-morrow and get that horse — No, I'll send it."

The Squire met Rivers on the avenue. As he walked beside the horse, he said, "I am going to dine with you."

"That is always good, but be on your guard about politics at Grey Pine. Lincoln is nominated."

"Thank God! What do you think of it, Squire?"

"I think with you. This is definite — no more wabbling. But rest assured, it means, if he is elected, secession, and in the end war. We will try to avert it. We will invent compromises, at which the South will laugh; at last, we will fight, Mark. But we are a quiet commercial people and will not fight if we can avoid it. They believe nothing will make us fight. The average, every-day Northerner thinks the threat of secession is mere bluff."

"Do you recall, Squire, what Thucydides said of the Greeks at the time of the Peloponnesian War?"

"I — how the deuce should I? — what did he say?"

"He said the Greeks did not understand each other any longer, although they spoke the same language. The same words in Boston and in Charleston have different meanings."

"But," said Penhallow, "we never did understand one another."

"No, never. War — even war — is better than to keep up a partnership in slavery — a sleeping partnership. Oh, I would let them go — or accept the gage of battle."

"Pretty well that, for a clergyman, Mark. As for me, having seen war, I want never to see it again. This may please you." As he spoke, he extracted a slip of paper from his pocket-book, where to Leila's amusement queer bits of all kinds of matters were collected. Now it was verse. " Read that. You might have written it. I kept it for you. There is Ann on the porch. Don't read it now."

Late that evening Rivers sat down to think over the sermon of the next Sunday. The Squire had once said to him, " War brings out all that is best and all that is worst in a nation." He read the verses, and then read them aloud.

> They say that war is hell, the great accursed,
>   The sin impossible to be forgiven;
> Yet I can look beyond it at its worst
>   And still find blue in Heaven.
>
> And as I note how nobly natures form
>   Under the war's red reign, I deem it true
> That He who made the earthquake and the storm
>   Perchance makes battles too.
>
> The life He loves is not the life of span
>   Abbreviated by each passing breath;
> It is the true humanity of man
>   Victorious over death.

" No great thing in the way of poetry — but — a thought — a thought. Oh, I should like to preach of men's duty to their country just now. I envy Grace his freedom. If I preached as he does, people would say it was none of a preacher's business to apply Christ's creed of conduct to a question like slavery. Mrs. Penhallow would walk out of the church. But before long men will blame the preacher who does not say, ' Thou shalt love thy country as thyself '— ah, and better, yes, and preach it too."

During the early summer of 1860, James Penhallow guarded an awkward silence about politics. Leila found that her uncle would not talk of what the closing months of Buchanan's administration might contribute to insure peaceful settlement. John Penhallow was as averse to answering her eager questions. Their silence on matters which concerned a nation's possible dismemberment and her aunt's too evident distress weighed heavily upon Leila. The newspapers bewildered her. The *Tribune* was for peaceful separation, and then later was against it. Uncle Jim had said he was too worried about the mills to talk politics, "Don't ask me, Leila." At last, an errand to Dr. McGregor's gave her the chance she desired.

"Yes," said the doctor, "I'll come to-day. One of the maids? Well, what else, Leila?" seeing that she still lingered.

"I want to know something about all this tangle of politics. There's Breckinridge, Douglas, Bell and Lincoln — four candidates. Uncle Jim gets almost cross when I ask him what they all stand for. Mr. Rivers told me to be thankful I have no vote. If there is to be war, have I no interest? There is Uncle Jim — and — and John."

The doctor said, "Sit down, Leila. Your uncle could answer you. He won't talk. I don't believe John Penhallow owns any politics except a soldier's blind creed of devotion to the Flag."

"Oh, the Flag, Doctor! But it is a symbol — it is history. I won't write to a man any more who has no certain opinions. He never answers."

"Well, my dear, see how hard it is to know what to think! One State after another is seceding. The old juggle of compromises goes on in that circus we call Congress. The audience is grimly silent. Crittenden's compromise has failed. The President is at last against secession — and makes no vigorous effort to reinforce Fort Sumter. The Cabinet was distinctly with the South — the new men came in too late. You — a girl — may well call it a tangle. It is a diabolical cat's-cradle. My only hope, my dear, is in a new and practically untried man — Abraham Lincoln. The South is one in opinion — we are perplexed by the fears of commerce and are split. There you have all my wisdom. Read the news, but not the weathercock essays called editorials. Oh! I forgot to tell the Squire that

Tom, my young doctor, has passed the Army Board and is awaiting orders in Washington. By-bye!"

"Tom as a doctor — and in uniform," Leila murmured, as her horse walked away. "How these boys go on and on, and we women just wait and wait while men dispose of our fates."

In February the Confederacy of the South was organising, and in March of 1861 Mr. Lincoln was President. Penhallow groaned over Cameron as Secretary of War, smiled approval of the Cabinet with Seward and Chase and anxiously waited to see what Lincoln would do.

Events followed fast in those eventful days. On the thirteenth of April Ann Penhallow sat in the spring sunshine on the porch, while Leila read aloud to her with entranced attention "The Marble Faun." The advent of an early spring in the uplands was to be seen in the ruddy colour of the maples. Bees were busy among the young flowers. There was noiseless peace in the moveless infant foliage.

"How still it is!" said Leila looking up from the book. They were far from the madding crowd. "What is it, Billy?"

He was red, breathless, excited, and suddenly broke out in his thin boy-like voice, "Hurrah! They've fired on the flag."

"Who — what flag?"

"Don't know." He had no least idea of what his words meant. "Don't know," and crying "Hurrah! They've fired on the flag," fled away.

Ann said, "Go to the village and find out what that idiot meant."

In a half hour Leila came back. "Well, what is it?"

"The Charleston troops have fired on Fort Sumter — My God! Aunt Ann — on the flag — our flag!"

Ann rose, gathered up her work, hesitated a moment, and saying, "That is bad news, indeed," went into the house.

Leila sat down on the step of the porch and broke into a

passion of tears, as James Penhallow coming through the woods dismounted at her side. "What is the matter, my dear child?"

"They have fired on the flag at Sumter — it is an insult!"

"Yes, my child, that — and much more. A blunder too! Mr. Lincoln should thank God to-day. He will have with him now the North as one man. Colonel Anderson must surrender; he will be helpless. Alas for his wife, a Georgia woman! — and my Ann, my dear Ann."

There are few alive to-day who recall the effect caused in the States of the North by what thousands of men and women, rich and poor, felt to be an insult, and for the hour, far more to them than the material consequences which were to follow.

When Rivers saw the working people of the little town passionately enraged, the women in tears, he read in this outbreak of a class not given to sentimental emotion what was felt when the fatal news came home to lonely farms or great cities over all the North and West.

Memorable events followed in bewildering succession during the early spring and summer of 1861. John wrote that Beauregard and all but a score of Southern cadets had left the Point. Robert Lee's decision to resign from the army was to the Squire far more sorrowfully important.

When Lincoln's call to arms was followed in July by the defeat of Bull Run, James Penhallow wrote to his nephew:

"MY DEAR JOHN: Your aunt is beyond measure disturbed. I have been more at ease now that this terrible decision as to whether we are to be one or God knows how many is to be settled by the ordeal of battle. I am amazed that no one has dwelt upon what would have followed accepted secession. We should have had a long frontier of custom houses, endless rows over escaping slaves, and the outlet of the Mississippi in the possession of a foreign country. Within ten years war would have followed; better let it come now.

"I am offered a regiment by Governor Curtin. To accept would be fatal to our interests in the mills. It may become an imperative duty to accept; but this war will last long, or I much underestimate the difficulties of overcoming a gallant people waging a defensive war in a country where every road and creek is familiar.

"Yours, in haste,
"JAMES PENHALLOW."

John wrote later:

"MY DEAR UNCLE: Here is news for you! All of my class are ordered to Washington. I shall be in the engineer corps. I see General McClellan is put in command of the army. I will write again from Washington."

Ann Penhallow heard the letter, and saying merely, "It had to come!" made the bitter forecast that it would be James Penhallow's turn next.

John wrote again as he had promised, but now to Leila:

"At last we are in this crowded city. We get our uniforms in a day or two. I am a lieutenant of engineers. We are now in tents. On arrival we were marched to General Scott's headquarters, and while drawn up in line Mr. Lincoln came out. He said a few words to us. His appearance was strange to me. A tall stooping figure, in what our village calls 'store clothes,' but very neat; the face big, homely, with a look of sadness in the eyes. He shook hands with each of us in turn, saying a word of encouragement. Why he spoke specially to me, I do not know. He asked my name. I said 'Penhallow.' 'Oh,' he said, 'a Cornish name — the great iron-works. Do you know the Cornish rhyme? It rings right true.' I said, 'No, sir.' 'Well, it is good. Do your duty. There is a whole creed in the word — man needs no other. God bless you, boys.' It was great, Leila. What is the Cornish rhyme? Ask Uncle Jim. Write me care of the Engineer Camp.

"I put this on a separate slip for you. In Baltimore we were delayed and I had an hour's leave. I called on your uncle, Charles Grey. He is Union through and through. His brother Henry has gone South. While I was walking with Mr. Charles Grey, a lady went by us, drawing away her skirts with quite unmistakable contempt and staring at your uncle in a way which was so singular that I asked what it all meant. He replied, 'It is your United States cadet uniform — and the lady is Mrs. Henry Grey. I am not of their acquaintance.' This, Leila, was my first taste of the bitterness of feeling here. It is the worse for the uprising of union feeling all over Maryland.

"My class-mates are rather jolly about their commissions and the prospect of active war. I have myself a certain sense of being a mere cipher, a dread too of failure. I can say so to you and to no one else. I am going where death is in the air — and there are things which make me eager to live — and — to be able to live to feel that I have done my duty. Thinking of how intensely you feel and how you grieve over being unable to do more than pray, I mean to pet a little the idea that I am your substitute."

At this point she sat a while with the letter on her lap. Then she read on:

"I hoped for a brief furlough, but got none, and so I shall apply to memory and imagination for frequent leave of absence, — from duty.

"Yours,
"JOHN PENHALLOW."

"To pet a little the idea! That is so like John. Well, yes — I don't mind being petted as a substitute and at a distance. It's rather confusing."

CHAPTER XIX

IT was late in October and ten at night, when Leila with her uncle was endeavouring to discover on one of the large maps, then so much in demand, the situation of the many small conflicts which local feeling brought about.

"It all wants a head — one head, Leila. Now it is here, there and everywhere, useless gain or loss — and no large scheme. John left Washington two weeks ago. You saw his letter?"

"No."

"Then I may have told you — I am sure I did. Damn it, Leila! I am so bothered. I did tell Ann, I suppose."

"Why, of course, Uncle Jim. I wish I could help you. Is it the mills?"

"Yes. Your little property, part of John's — your aunt's — are all in the family business. Ann says, 'What's the difference? Nothing matters now.' It isn't like her."

"I'm sure I don't care, Uncle Jim."

"Don't talk nonsense. In a month we shall know if we are bankrupt. I did not mean to trouble you. I did mean to tell you that to my relief John is out of Washington and ordered to report to General Grant at Cairo. See, dear, there is a pin marking it on the map."

"Do you know this General?"

"Yes. He took no special rank at the Point, but — who can tell! Generals are born, not made. I saw a beautiful water-colour by him at the Point. That's all I know of him. Now, go to bed — and don't take with you my worries and fight battles in your dreams."

There was in fact no one on whom he could willingly unload all of his burdens. The need to relieve the hands out of work — two-thirds of his force — was growing less of late, as men drifted off into the State force which the able Governor Curtin was sending to McClellan. Penhallow's friends in Pittsburgh had been able to secure a mortgage on Grey Pine, and thus aided by his partners he won a little relief, while Rivers watched him with increasing anxiety.

On the 17th of January, 1862, he walked into McGregor's office and said to his stout friend, "McGregor, I am in the utmost distress about my wife. Inside my home and at the mills I am beset with enough difficulties to drive a man wild. We have a meeting in half an hour to decide what we shall do. I used to talk to Ann of my affairs. No one has or had a clearer head. Now, I can't."

"Why not, my friend?"

"She will not talk. Henry Grey is in the Confederate service; Charles is out and out for the Union; we have no later news of John. We miserably sit and eat and manufacture feeble talk at table. It is pitiful. Her duties she does, as you may know, but comes home worn out and goes to bed at nine. Even the village people see it and ask me about her. If it were not for Leila, I should have no one to talk to."

A boy came in. "You are wanted, sir, at the mill office."

"Say I will come at once. I 'll see you after the meeting, McGregor."

"One moment, Squire. Here's a bit of good news for you. Cameron has resigned, and Edwin Stanton is Secretary of War."

"Stanton! Indeed! Thank Heaven for that. Now things will move, I am sure."

The Squire found in his office Sibley, one of his partners, a heavy old man, who carried the indifferent manners of a farmer's son into a middle age of successful business. He sat with his chair tilted back, a huge Cabana cigar hanging unlighted from the corner of his mouth. He made no movement towards rising, but gave his hand as he sat, and said: "There, Penhallow, just read that!"

As the Squire took the telegram, Sibley scratched a match on the back of his pantaloons and waiting for the sulphur to burn out lit his cigar. Ever after the smell of sulphur brought to the Squire of Grey Pine the sense of some pleasant association and then a less agreeable remembrance.

"Read it — read it out loud, Penhallow! It was a near thing. Wardlow could n't meet us — be here at noon. Read it — I 've read it about ten times — want to hear it again. I 've been as near broke as you — but that 's an old story. When you 're at your last dollar, buy a fast pair of trotters — one thousand-dollar pair — and drive them. Up goes your credit! Told you that once."

Penhallow looked up from the telegram. "Is this certain?"

"Yes, it has been repeated — you can rely on it."

"WASHINGTON, Willard's Hotel.

"Mr. Stanton has given contract for field artillery to the Penhallow Mills.

"RICHARD AINSELEY."

Penhallow had read it aloud as he stood. Then he sat down. "Don't speak to me for a moment, Sibley. Thank God!" he murmured, while the care-wrinkled face of the veteran speculator looked at him with a faint smile of affectionate regard.

"Well," said Penhallow, "is this all?"

"No. While Cameron was in office the contract was drawn in favour of the Lancaster Works. We have been urging our own claims, and their Washington agent, your very particular friend, Mr. Swallow, would have had the job in a week more. When Stanton saw our bid and that it was really a more advantageous offer, he sent first for Swallow and then for Ainseley and settled it at once. I believe your name and well-known character did the business. Do you know — do you realize what it means to us?"

"Hardly. I had no hope while Cameron was in office. I left it to you and Ainseley."

"Well, you will see the contract to-morrow." He wriggled on to one leg of the frail office chair and came down with a crash. He gathered up his two hundred pounds and laughing said, as he looked at the wreck, "That's what we would have been to-morrow but for that bit of yellow paper. In six months you will be a rich man, my friend. Cannon — shells — the whole outfit. We must get to work at once. An ordnance officer will be here to-morrow with specifications, and your own knowledge will be invaluable. I'd like to see Swallow again. He was so darned sure!"

Wardlow turned up by the noon train, and they worked until dusk, when his partners left him to secure hands in Pittsburgh, while the good news spread among the men still at work. Penhallow rode home through the woods humming his old army songs — a relieved and happy man.

The Doctor waited a half-hour in vain, and after his noonday dinner was about to go out when Mrs. Penhallow was driven to his door. Somewhat surprised, he went back with her.

"Sit down," he said. "What can I do for you?"

"Oh, for me nothing! I want to talk about my husband. He is ill, I am sure — he is ill. He eats little, he sleeps badly, he has lost — oh, altogether lost — his natural gaiety. He hardly speaks at all."

The Doctor was silent.

"Well," she said.

"Can you bear a little frank talk?" he asked.

"Yes — why not?"

"Do you know that he is on the verge of complete financial ruin?"

"What does that matter? I can — I can bear anything — give up anything —"

"You have the woman's — the good woman's — indifference about money. Do you talk to him about it?"

"No. We get on at once to the causes of trouble — this unrighteous war — that I can't stand."

"Ah, Mrs. Penhallow, there must be in the North and South many families divided in opinion; what do you suppose they do? This absolute silence is fatal. You two are drifting apart —"

"Oh, not that! Surely not that!"

"Yes! The man is worried past endurance. If he really were to fall ill — a serious typhoid, for instance, the South and your brother and John, everything would be forgotten — there would be only James Penhallow. It would be better to talk of the war — to quarrel over it — to make him talk business — oh, anything rather than to live as you are living. He is not ill. Go home and comfort him. He needs it. He has become a lonely man, and it is your fault. He was here to-day in the utmost distress about you —"

"About me?"

"Yes."

"There is nothing the matter with me!"

"Yes, there is — oh, with both of you. This war will last for years — and so will you. All I have to say is that my friend, James Penhallow, is worth all the South, and that soon or late he will stand it no longer and will go where he ought to be — into the army."

"You are talking nonsense — he will never leave the mills." He had called up her constant fear.

"It is not nonsense. When he is a broken man and you and he are become irritable over a war you did not make and cannot end, he will choose absence and imperative duty as his only relief."

As she stood up, red and angry, she said, "You have only hurt and not helped me." She said no other word as he went with her to the wagon. He looked after her a moment.

"Well, well! There are many kinds of fools — an intelligent fool is the worst. I did n't help her any, and by George! I am sorry."

When at twilight the doctor came home from distant visits to farms, he met Leila near to his door. "I want to see you a minute," she said, as she slipped out of her saddle.

"A woman's minute or a man's minute?"

"A man's."

She secured her mare as he said, "Well, come in. It 's rather amusing, Leila. Sit down. I 've had James Penhallow here to say his wife 's breaking down. I 've had Mrs. Penhallow here to say James Penhallow is ill. Except the maids and the cats and you, all Grey Pine is diagnosing one another. And now, you come! Don't tell me you 're ill — I won't have it."

"Please don't joke, Doctor. I am troubled about these dear people. I talked to Mr. Rivers about it, and he is troubled and says it is the mills and money. I know that, but at the bottom of it all is the war. Now Aunt Ann is reading the papers again — I think it is very strange; it 's confusing, Doctor."

"Here," reflected the doctor, "is at least one person with some sense."

She went on, speaking slowly, " Uncle Jim comes home tired. Aunt Ann eats her dinner and reads, and is in bed by nine. The house is as melancholy as — I feel as if I were in a mouse-trap —"

"Why mouse-trap, my dear?"

"It sounds all right. The mouse is waiting for something awful to happen — and so am I. Uncle Jim talked of asking people to stay with us. It 's just to please Aunt Ann. She said, ' No, James, I don't want any one.' He wished to please her. She really thinks of nothing but the war and Uncle Jim, and when Uncle Jim is away she will spend an hour alone over his maps. She has — what do you call it — ? "

" Is obsession the word you want? "

" Yes — that's it."

" Now, Leila, neither you nor I nor Mark Rivers can help those two people we love. Don't cry, Leila; or cry if it will help you. When you marry, be sure to ask, ' what are your politics, Jeremiah?'" His diversion answered his purpose.

" I never would marry a man named Jeremiah."

" I recommend a well-trained widower."

" I prefer to attend to my husband's education myself. I should like a man who is single-minded when I marry him."

" Well, for perversion of English you are quite unequalled. Go and flirt a bit for relief of mind with Mark Rivers."

" I would as soon flirt with an undertaker. Why not with Dr. McGregor? "

" It would be comparable, Leila, to a flirtation between a June rose and a frost-bitten cabbage. Now, go away. These people's fates are on the lap of the gods."

" Of the god of war, I fear," said Leila.

" Yes, more or less." He sent her away mysteriously relieved, she knew not why. " A little humour," he reflected, " is as the Indians say, *big medicine.*"

Whether the good doctor's advisory prescription would have served as useful a purpose in the case of Ann Penhallow, he doubted. That heart-sick little lady was driven swiftly homeward, the sleigh-runners creaking on the frozen snow: " Walk the horses," she said to Billy, as they entered the long avenue, " and quit talking."

While with the doctor and when angrily leaving him, she was the easy victim of a storm of emotions. As she felt the healthy sting of the dry cold, she began the process of re-adjustment we are wise to practise after a time of passion when by degrees facts and motives begin to reassume more just proportions. He had said, the war would last long. That she had not believed. Could she and James live for years afraid to speak of what was going on? The fact that her much-loved Maryland did not rise as one man and join the Confederacy had disturbed her with her first doubt as to the final result of the great conflict. She thought it over with lessening anger at the terrible thing McGregor had said, "You two are drifting apart." This sentence kept saying itself over and over.

"Stop, Billy." She was back again in the world of everyday. "Get in, Mr. Rivers. We are both late for our Dante." As she spoke, an oppressed pine below which he stood under a big umbrella was of a mind to bear its load no longer and let fall a bushel or so of snow on the clergyman's cover. His look of bewilderment and his upward glance as if for some human explanation routed from Ann's mind everything except amusement over this calamity.

"You must not mind if I laugh." She took for granted the leave to laugh, as he said, "I don't see where the fun comes in. It is most disagreeable." The eloquent eyes expressed calamity. It was really felt as if it had been a personal attack.

"It was a punishment for your utterly abominable politics." For the first time for months she was her unfettered self. His mind was still on his calamity. "I really staggered under it."

"Shake it off and get in to the sleigh. My husband ought to have all the big pines cut down." Rivers's mind had many levels. Sometimes they were on spiritual heights, or as now — almost childlike.

"To stay indoors would be on the whole more reasonable," he said, "or to have these trees along the avenue shaken."

"I'd like the job," ventured Billy.

"Keep quiet," said Mrs. Ann.

"It is most uncomfortable as it melts," said Rivers.

Ann thought of John Penhallow's early adventure in the snow, and seeing how strangely real was Mark Rivers's discomfort, remarked to herself that he was like a cat for dislike of being wet, and was thankful for her privilege of laughing inwardly.

Billy, who was, as Leila said, an unexpectable person, contributed to Ann Penhallow's sense of there being still some available fun in a world where men were feebly imitating the vast slaughters of nature. He considered the crushed umbrella, the felt hat awry, and the disconsolate figure. "Parson do look crosser than a wet hen."

Then too Rivers's laugh set free her mirth, and Ann Penhallow laughed as she had not done for many a day. "That is about my condition," said Rivers. "I shall go home and get into dry clothes. Billy, you're a poet."

"Don't like nobody to call me names," grunted Billy.

"I wish James had heard that," cried Ann, while Rivers gathered up the remains of his umbrella.

As Billy drove away, Mrs. Penhallow called back, "You will come to dinner to-day?"

"Thank you, but not to-day."

As Ann came down the stairs to the hall, Penhallow was in the man's attitude, with his back to the fire. Leila with a hand on the mantel and a foot on the fender was talking to her uncle, an open letter in her hand. Ann heard him say, "That was in October"— and then —"Why this must be a month old!"

"It must have been delayed. He wrote a note after the fight at Belmont, and that was in October. He did write once since then, but it was hardly worth sending. As a letter writer, John is rather a failure, but this is longer." She laughed gaily as she spread open the letter.

"He has got a new hero, uncle — General Grant. John is strong on heroes — he began with you."

"Stuff and nonsense," said the Squire. "Read it."

Leila hesitated.

"Oh, let's hear it," cried her aunt.

" Go on, dear," said the Squire.

Leila still hesitated. Usually Ann Penhallow carried away John's rare letters to be read when alone. Now she said, with unnatural deliberation. " Read it; one may as well hear his news; we can't always just ignore what goes on."

Leila a little puzzled glanced at her aunt. The Squire pleased and astonished said, " Go on, my dear."

Turning to the candles on the hall table, Leila read the letter: —" Why how long it has been ! It is dated November 20th."

" DEAR LEILA : We have been moving from place to place, and although I know or guess why, it is best left out of letters. At Belmont General Grant had a narrow escape from capture. He was the last man on board the boat. He is a slightly built, grave, tired-looking man, middle-aged, carelessly dressed and eternally smoking. I was in the thick of the row — a sort of aide, as there was no engineer work. He was as cool as a cucumber —"

" Why are cucumbers cool ? " asked Leila, looking up.

" Oh, bother ! Go on ! " said Penhallow.

" We shall move soon. Good-bye.

" JOHN PENHALLOW."

Ann made no comment. The Squire said, " It might have been longer. Come, there 's dinner, and I am hungry."

Ann looked at him. He was gay, and laughed at her account of Rivers's disaster.

" I have some good news for you, Ann. I shall keep it until after dinner. Then we can talk it over at leisure. It concerns all of us, even John."

" I don't see how I am to wait," said Leila.

" You will have to."

Ann made an effort to meet the tone of gaiety in her husband's talk, and when the wine was set before him, he said, " Now, Ann, a glass — and Leila, ' To our good news and good luck — and to John.' "

They followed him into the library, and being in sacrificial mood, Ann filled a pipe, lighted a match, and said, " I want you to smoke, James."

" Not yet, dear. Sit down."

" No, I want to stand." She stood beside the fire, a little lady, with an arm around the waist of her niece. The Squire seated was enjoying the suspense of his eager audience.

" You know, dear Ann, that for two years or more the mills have been without large orders. We have been in the most embarrassing situation. Our debts "— he was about to say, ' in the South '—" unpaid. I had to ask you to help us."

This was news to Leila. " Why mention that, James ? " said her aunt.

" Well, we long ago lessened our force. To shut down entirely was ruin, but when we met to-day we were to decide whether it was honest to borrow more money and stagger on, or as I thought, honourable to close the mills and realize for our creditors all we could."

Ann sat down with some feeling of remorse. Why had she not known all this ? Was it her fault ? He had borne it for the most part without her knowledge — alone. " My God ! It is true," she reflected, " we have drifted apart." He had hopefully waited, not wanting to trouble a woman already so obviously sorrow-laden. He seemed to echo her thought.

" You see, dear," and the strong face grew tender, " I did not mean to disturb you until it became inevitable. I am glad I waited."

Ann, about to speak, was checked by his lifted hand. " Now, dear, all my troubles are over. Mr. Stanton, the new Secretary of War, has signed a contract with our firm for field ar-

tillery. It is a fortune. Our bid was low. A year's work —
shot, shell — and so on. Congratulate me, Ann."

"My God!" he cried, "what is the matter?"

Ann Penhallow turned quickly, a hand on the table staying
herself. "And you — you are to make cannon — you — and
I — and with my money!" she laughed hysterical laughter —
"to kill my people the North has robbed and driven into war
and insulted for years — I — I —" her voice broke — she stood
speechless, pale and more pale.

Penhallow was appalled. He ran to catch her as she swayed.

"Don't touch me," she cried. "I feared for — you — the
army — but never this — this!" Despite her resistance, he
laid her on the lounge.

"Leila," she said, "I want to go upstairs to bed." The face
became white; she had fainted.

"Is she dead?" he said hoarsely, looking down at her pale
face.

"No — no. Carry her upstairs, uncle." He picked up the
slight form and presently laid her on her bed. "Leave her
to me, Uncle Jim. I have seen girls in hysterics. Send up
a maid — the doctor! No, I will come down when she is un-
dressed. See, her colour is better."

He went downstairs, reluctant to leave her. In the library
he sat down and waited. An hour passed by, and at last Leila
reappeared. She kissed him with more than her usual tenderness, saying, "She is quiet now. I will lie down on her lounge
to-night. Don't worry, Uncle Jim."

This advice so often given was felt by him to be out of his
power to follow. He knew very well that this he would have
now to consider was not only a mere business affair. It ceased
to be that when he heard with the shock of bewilderment his
wife's outburst of angry protest. He loved her as few men love
after many years of married life, and his affection was still
singularly young. His desire to content her had made him un-

wisely avoid talk about differences of opinion. In fact his normal attitude was dictated by such gentle solicitude as is not uncommon in very virile men, who have long memory for the careless or casual sharp word. To the end of his days he never suspected that to have been less the lover and more the clear-sighted outspoken friend would have been better for her and for him. He sat into the night smoking pipe after pipe, grappling with a situation which would have presented no difficulties to a coarser nature. At last he went upstairs, listened a moment at Ann's chamber door, and having smoked too much spent a thought-tormented night, out of which he won one con-clusion — the need to discuss his trouble with some friend. At six he rose and dressed, asked the astonished cook for an egg and coffee, went to the stables, and ordered a groom to saddle horses and follow him.

A wild gallop over perilously slippery roads brought him to McGregor's door, a quarter of a mile from the mills. The doctor was at breakfast, and rose up astonished. "What's wrong now, Penhallow?" he said.

"Oh, everything — everything."

"Then sit down and let us talk. What is it?"

The Squire took himself in hand and quietly related his story of the contract and his wife's reception of what had been to him so agreeable until she had spoken.

"Can you bear — I said it yesterday to Mrs. Penhallow — a frank opinion?"

"Yes, from you — anything."

"Have no alarm about her health, my friend. It is only the hysteria of a woman a little spoiled by too tender indulgence."

The Squire did not like it, but said, "Oh, perhaps! But now — the rest — the rest — what am I to do?" The doctor sat still a while in perplexed thought. "Take your time," said Penhallow. "I have sent the horses to the stable at the mills, where my partners are to meet me early to-day."

The doctor said, " Mrs. Penhallow will be more or less her-self to-day. I will see her early. There are several ways of dealing with this matter. You can take out of the business her share of the stock."

" That would be simple. My partners would take it now and gladly."

" What else you do depends on her condition of mind and the extent to which you are willing to give way before the per-sistency of a woman who feels and does not or can not reason."

" Then I am not now to do anything but tell her that I will take her stock out of the business."

" That may relieve her. So far I can go with you. But, my dear Penhallow, she may be utterly unreasonable about your manufacture of cannon, and what then you may do I cannot say. How long will it be before you begin to turn out cannon ? "

" Oh, two months or more. Many changes will be needed, but we have meanwhile an order for rails from the Baltimore and Ohio."

" Then we can wait. Now I am off for Grey Pine. See me about noon. Don't go back home now. That 's all."

While the Squire walked away to the mills, McGregor was uneasily moving his ponderous bulk to and fro in the room.

" It 's his damn tender, soft-hearted ways that will win in the end. My old Indian guide used to say, ' Much stick, good squaw.' Ann Penhallow has never in her whole life had any stick. Damn these sugar plum husbands ! I 'd like to know what Miss Leila Grey thinks of this performance. Now, there 's a woman ! "

When after a night of deep sleep Ann woke to find Leila standing by her bed, she rose on an elbow saying, " What time is it ? Why are you here ? "

" It is eight, aunt. You were ill last night; I stayed on your lounge."

Now her aunt sat up. " I was ill, you say — something happened." The thing pieced itself together — ragged bits of memories storm-scattered by emotion were reassembled, vague at first, then quickly more clear. She broke into unnaturally rapid speech, reddening darkly, with ominous dilatation of the pupils of her large blue eyes. "And so James Penhallow is to be made rich by making cannon to kill my people — oh, I remember!" It seemed absurdly childlike to Leila, who heard her with amazement. "And with my money — it is easy to stay at home and murder — and be paid for it. Let him go and — fight. That's bad enough — I —"

"God of Heaven, Aunt Ann!" the girl broke in, "don't dare to say that to Uncle Jim. Are you crazy — to say such things."

"I don't know what I am. Oh, those cannon! I hear them. He shall not do it — do you hear me? Now send me up a cup of tea — and don't come in again. I want James — tell him — tell him."

"He went away to the mills at six o'clock."

"I know. He is afraid to talk to me — I want to see him — send for him at once. I said at once — do you hear! Now go."

As Leila turned to leave, she heard a knock at the door, said "Come in," and to her relief saw enter large and smiling the trusted doctor. As he neared the bed, Ann fell back speechless and rigid.

"Ah, Leila! That makes it all plain. There is no danger. Close the blinds; I want the room darkened. So! Come into the back room — leave the door ajar." He selected a trustworthy chair and sat down with deliberate care. "Now listen to me, my dear. This is pure hysteria. It may last for days or weeks — it will get well. It is the natural result of birth, education, worry, etc.— and a lot of darned et ceteras. When you let loose a mob of emotions, you get into trouble — they smash things, and this is what has become of one of God's sweetest, purest souls."

"It is most dreadful, Doctor; but what shall we do with Uncle Jim. If she has a mere cold in the head, he is troubled."

"Yes — yes." The doctor took counsel with himself. "I will send up old Mrs. Lamb to help you — she is wise in the ways of sick women. Take your rides — and don't fret over this suicide of reason." He was pleased with his phrase. "Let her see Penhallow if she asks for him, but not if you can help it. It is all as plain as day. She has been living of late a life of unwholesome suppression. She has been alarmed by Penhallow's looks, hurt by her brothers' quarrels, and heart-sick about the war and John. Then your uncle springs on her this contract business and there is an explosion."

After giving careful orders, he went away. To Penhallow he said, "When you are at home keep out of her room. If you have to see her, tell her nothing has been done or will be for months. The time will come when you will have to discuss matters."

CHAPTER XX

L EILA GREY never forgot the month which followed. Penhallow was mercifully spared the sight of the drama of hysteria, and when not at the mills went about the house and farm like a lost dog; or, if Leila was busy, took refuge with Rivers. Even the war maps claimed no present interest until a letter came from John after the capture of Fort Donaldson. At evening they found the place on the map.

"Well, now let's hear it. Ann is better, McGregor says." He was as readily elated as depressed. "Does she ask for me?"

"No," said Leila, "at first she did, but not now."

"Read the letter, my dear."

"DEAR LEILA: I wrote to Aunt Ann and Uncle Jim a fortnight ago —"

"Never came," said Penhallow.

"I am called an engineer, but there is no engineering required, so I am any General's nigger. I have been frozen and thawed over and over. No camp fires allowed, and our frozen 15,000 besieged 21,000 men. General S. T. Smith picked me up as an aide, and on the 15th personally led a charge on the Rebel lines, walking quietly in front of our men to keep them from firing. It did not prevent the Rebs from abusing our neutrality. It was not very agreeable, but we stormed their lines and I got off with a bit out of my left shoulder — nothing of moment. Now we have them. If this war goes on, Grant will be the man who will end it. I am too cold to write more. Love to all.

"General Smith desires to be remembered to Uncle Jim, and told me he was more than satisfied with

"Yours,

"JAMES PENHALLOW."

"Is n't that delightful, Uncle Jim? But every night I think
of it — this facing of death. I see battles and storming parties.
Don't you see things before you fall asleep? I can see whatever I want to see — or don't want to."

"Never saw anything of the kind — I just go to sleep."

"I thought everybody could see things as I do."

"See John too, Leila? Wish I could."

"Yes," she said, "sometimes." In fact, she could see at
will the man who was so near and so dear and a friend to-day
— and in that very lonely time when the house was still and
the mind going off guard, the something indefinitely more.

The Squire, who had been studying the map, was now standing before the fire looking up where hung over the mantel his
sword and the heavy army pistols. He turned away as he said,
"Life is pretty hard, Leila. I ought to be here — here making
guns. I want to be where my class-mates are in the field. I
can't see my way, Leila. When I see a duty clearly, I can do
it. Now here I have to decide what is my duty. There is no
devil like indecision. What would you do?"

"It is a question as to what you will do, not I — and — oh,
dear Uncle Jim, it is, you know, what we call in that horrid
algebra the X of the equation."

"I must see your Aunt Ann. Is she "— and he hesitated —
"is she herself?"— he would not say, quite, sane.

"She is not at all times."

"How far must I consider her, or be guided by the effect my
decision will have on her? There are my partners to consider.
The money does not influence me — it is Ann — Ann." Then
she knew that he would make any sacrifice necessary to set Ann
Penhallow at ease. "I think," she said as she rose, "that we
had better go to bed."

"I suppose so," he said. "Wait a moment. Your aunt
told me that I had better go where there was war — she could
not have guessed that I have lived for months with that tempta-

tion. I shall end by accepting a command. Now since her reproach I shall feel that war offers the bribe of ease and relief from care."

"I know, the call of duty — you will have to go. But, oh, my God! it is very terrible."

"The fact is, this sudden good fortune for a time so set me at ease that I lost sight of my honest craving for action. Now I ought to thank Ann for making me see what I ought to do — must do. But how — how? It will clear up somehow. Goodnight."

It was the end of March before McGregor told Penhallow that Mrs. Penhallow insisted on seeing him. "Now, Squire," he said, "you will be shocked at her appearance, but she is really well in body, and this thing has got to be set at rest. She talks of it incessantly."

Penhallow entered the dimly lighted room and passed his old nurse, Mrs. Lamb, as she whispered, "Don't stay long, sir." He was shocked as he won clearer vision in the dim light.

"Oh, James!" she said, "they would n't let me see you. Open the shutters." He obeyed, and kneeling kissed the wasted face he loved so well. The commonplaces of life came to his aid as he kissed her again, and she said, "Dear me, James, you have n't shaved to-day."

"No, I am going to stop at the barber's — but I miss Josiah."

She smiled. "Yes, poor Josiah."

Then he took courage, fearfully timid as men are when they confront the illness of women. "I want to say to you, Ann, that having your power of attorney I have withdrawn your fifty thousand dollars you had lent to the mills. My partners were glad to take it." He said nothing of their surprise at the offer.

"Thank you," she returned feebly. "And you are going on with the business?" her voice rising as she spoke.

"We will talk of that later, Ann. I was told not to let you

talk long. I shall endeavour to invest your money so as to give you a reasonable return — it will take time."

He did not succeed in diverting her attention. She put out a thin hand and caught his sleeve. "Do you think me unreasonable, James?"

"Yes," he said, and it needed courage.

"I was sure you would say so." The great blue eyes, larger for the wasted setting of nature's wonderful jewels, looked up at him in dumb appeal. "Won't you think a little of how I feel — and — and shall feel?"

"Think a little — a little?" he returned; "I have done nothing else but think."

"You don't answer me, James." There was the old quiet, persistent way he had known in many happy days, reinforced by hysteric incapacity to comprehend the maze of difficulties in which he was caught.

"It is a pity I did not die," she said, "that would have saved you all this trouble."

He felt the cruelty of her words as he broke away and left the room. McGregor had waited, and hearing his story said, "It will pass. You must not mind it — she is hardly sane."

James Penhallow mounted and rode to the village, was duly shaved, and went on to the post-office. Mrs. Crocker rotund and rosy came out and handed him as he sat in the saddle a sheaf of letters. "Yes, Mrs. Penhallow is better, thank you." As he rode away the reins on Dixy's neck, he read his letters and stuffed them in his pocket until he came to one, over which he lingered long. It ran thus:

"MY DEAR SIR: Will you not reconsider the offer of the colonelcy of a regiment? It will not require your presence until July. There is no need to reply at once. There is no one else so entirely fit for such a charge, and the Attorney-General,

your friend Meredith, unites with me in my appeal to you.
The State and the country need you.

> " Yours truly,
> " ANDREW CURTIN."

He reached but one conclusion as he turned the tempting
offer over in his mind, and acting on it wrote the Governor from
his office that his wife was at present too ill for him to consider
the offer of a command.

As day by day he sat with Ann, to his relief she ceased to dwell
on the matter which had so disturbed her, and rapidly regain-
ing health, flesh and strength, began to ask about the house and
the village people.   It was a happy day when in May he carried
her down to a hammock on the porch.   A week later she spoke
again, " What conclusion have you reached? " she said.

" About the mills? "

" Yes."

" Ask me in a week, Ann.   Do you want to read John's
letters?   There are several — one about a battle at Pittsburgh
Landing in Tennessee."

" I want to hear nothing of the war.   Is he well? "

" Yes, thank God."   The news of McClellan's army was
anything but satisfactory, and more and more the soldier longed
to be in the field.

Early in June, Penhallow on his way to meet his partners
paused at McGregor's house to ask his opinion of his wife.
" How do I find her?   Better every day — more herself.   But
what of you? "

" Of me?   I can stand it no longer, Doctor.   I cannot see
this war in Virginia go on to the end without taking part
in it.   I must — do anything — anything — make any sacrifice."

" But your wife — the mills —"

" I have but one answer — my country!   I told you I had

refused Governor Curtin's offer — what to do about our contract I do not yet know. They are reorganizing the artillery service."

"And you would like that best?"

"Yes. What amuses you?"

The doctor smiled often, but as Mrs. Crocker said, when he did laugh it was as good as a Fourth of July celebration and the house shook. As the Squire watched him, the smile broadened out in circles from the mouth like the ripples cast by a stone on still water; then the eyes grew merrily busy and the big frame shook with laughter.

"Well, now, Squire! To give up making guns and go in for using them — well — well!"

"Don't chaff me, McGregor; I mean to be in it, cost what it may. I am to meet my partners — good-bye."

The doctor wondered what Ann Penhallow would do or say. It was past guessing but he saw clearly that Penhallow was glad of any excuse to get into the field.

"Glad to see you, Ainseley," said Penhallow. "Good morning, Sibley. You will find things moving. Many casting moulds will be ready by this day week."

"Last night," said Sibley, the richer member of the firm, " I had a telegram from Austin, the iron-man. He asks what we would take to transfer our contract. I replied that we did not deal that way with Government contracts. To-day I got this other — read it."

"On what terms will you take me in? My ore, as you know, is not hematite and is better than yours."

Penhallow sat still reading the telegram again and again. Here was an unlooked-for way out of his troubles. At last he looked up, and to their surprise said, " My capital in the business is one hundred and fifty thousand dollars, and you — the firm — pay me a rental of ten thousand."

"Not last year," said Ainseley; "we could not, as you know."

"Yes. Our partnership ends this July 1st. Wire Austin that I will sell him my share and go out. You may ask him what bonus you please — I mean, I will sell to you at one hundred and fifty thousand dollars — the rental will go on, of course."

"My heavens!" cried Sibley, "what do you mean? It is throwing away a fortune, man — a fortune."

Penhallow laughed. "And yet I mean to do it. The work is ready to go on. You will have ordnance officers here — you won't miss me."

They argued with him in vain. Waldron not altogether dissatisfied sat still, wondering how much bonus Austin would stand, while Ainseley and Sibley troubled for their friend and not well pleased, fought his decision. "Are you fully resolved on this, Penhallow?" said Sibley.

"I am. I cannot take out the small amount of money John Penhallow owns. It must remain, at least for a time, and will be a convenience to you. My wife's money is already out. It was only a loan."

"But why should not you sell out to Austin," said Sibley, "if you mean to leave us, and get out of him a profit — and why after all this act of supreme folly? Pardon me, it is that — really that"

Penhallow smiled. "I go out of this business because I simply cannot stay out of the army. I could not be a soldier and accept continuous profits from a Government contract. Imagine what would be said! For the same reason I cannot sell to Austin at an advance. That is clear — is it not?"

"Yes," said Ainseley, "and I am sorry. Think it over."

"I have done my thinking. It will take the lawyers and you at least two months to settle it and make out the papers. After July 1st I shall not come to the mills. I mean to leave no occasion for unpleasant comment when I re-enter the service. Of course, you will advertise your new partnership and make plain my position. I am sorry to leave you, but most glad to leave you prosperous. I will put it all on paper, with a condition that at the close of the war — I give it three years — I shall be free to replace Austin — that is, if the Rebs don't kill me."

As he mounted at evening to ride home, he was aware of Leila. "Halloa, Uncle Jim! As Mr. Rivers was reading Dante to Aunt Ann, I begged off, and so here I am — thought I would catch you. I have n't been on a horse for a week. The mare knows it and enjoyed the holiday. She kicked Pole's bull terrier into the middle of next week."

"A notable feat. I wish some one would kick me into the middle of August."

"What 's wrong, Uncle Jim? Aunt Ann is every day better; John is well; you don't look unhappy. Oh, I know when anything really is the matter."

"No, I am happier than I have been for many a day. You know what Rivers says, 'In the Inn of Decision there is rest,' — some oriental nonsense. Well, I am a guest in the Inn of Decision, but I 've got to pay the bill."

"Please not to talk riddles, uncle. I have gone through so much this spring — what with aunt and this terrible war — and where John is we don't know. I heard from Aunt Margaret. She says that we escape the endless reminders of war — the extras called at night, heard in church, great battle on the Potomac, lists of killed and wounded. It must be awful. You buy a paper — and find there was no battle."

"Yes, we escape that at least. I have made arrangements to close my partnership on July 1st."

"Oh, Uncle Jim!"

"The President, I hear, will call for three hundred thousand men — I can stand it no longer — I am eating my heart out. I refused a regiment some time ago; now I shall ask for one. I wrote at once to the Governor."

She leaned over, laid a hand on his arm and said, " Is not one dear life enough? "

" My child, John had to go. I could, of course, find some excuse for not going. I set myself free to-day. But now I am to settle with Ann. Except for that I would be supremely contented. You would not keep me here if you had the power, nor would you bring home John if you could, dear."

"No," she said faintly. Some quickly dismissed suspicion rose to consciousness as he stole a glance at her face. " I understand," she added, " it is a question of honour — you must go."

" It is a question of duty, dear; but what Ann will say I do not know — but I shall go."

She turned. " Uncle Jim, if you did not go and the war went on to — God alone knows what end — she would be sick with shame. I know. You see I am a woman and I know. She will suffer, but she will not break down again and she will not try to hold you back. But this house without you and John will be rather lonely. How did you get out of the mills, uncle? "

He answered her at length as they rode homeward with more to think of than was pleasant. At the avenue gate she said earnestly, " Don't wait too long before telling Aunt Ann."

" Upon my word, I am sorry," returned the Squire, " for the unfortunate man who may become your husband. If you undertake to offer advice at your tender years, what will you do when you are older? "

" My husband-that-is-to-be sends you his compliments," laughed Leila, " and says — I don't know what he says, but it is exactly the right thing, Captain Penhallow. But really, don't wait, uncle."

" You are quite right, my dear." Nevertheless he waited. Decisiveness in affairs and in moments of peril he had, but where Ann was concerned he became easily unsure, and as Mc-Gregor said, "wabbled awful." This was to Leila. "What gets the matter with men? The finer they are, the braver — the more can a woman bother their judgment. He wires for a regimental command — gets it; and, by George, throws away a fortune to get the privilege of firing a cannon at Mrs. Ann's beloved Rebels. He must n't make guns it seems — he tries not to believe her hysterics at all affected by his tossing away this big contract."

"Now, Doctor, you are in one of your cynical moods. I hate you to talk this way about the finest gentleman I ever knew, or ever shall know. You delight to tease me."

"Yes — you are so real. No one could get hysterics out of you. Now why do you suppose James Penhallow wants to plunge into this chaotic war?"

"Or your son, Tom? Why do you get up of a winter night to ride miles to see some poor woman who will never pay you a penny?"

"Pure habit."

"Nonsense. You go — and Uncle Jim goes — because to go is duty."

"Then I think duty is a woman — that accounts for it, Leila. I retire beaten."

"You are very bad to-day — but make Uncle Jim talk it all out to Aunt Ann."

"He will, and soon. He has been routed by a dozen excuses. I told him at last that the mill business has leaked out and the village is saying things. I told him it must not come to her except through him, and that he could not now use her health as an excuse for delay. It is strange a man should be so timid."

And still Penhallow lingered, finding more or less of reason in the delays created by the lawyers. Meanwhile he had accepted the command of the 129th Pennsylvania infantry which was being drilled at Harrisburg, so that he was told there was no occasion for haste in assuming charge. But at last he felt that he must no longer delay.

The sun was setting on an afternoon in July when Penhallow, seeing as she sat on the porch how the roses of the spring of health were blooming on his wife's cheeks, said, " I want to talk to you alone, Ann. Can you walk to the river? "

" Yes, I was there yesterday."

The cat-birds, most delightful of the love-poets of summer, were singing in the hedges, and as they walked through the garden Penhallow said, " The rose crop is promising, Ann."

" Yes." She was silent until they sat on the bank above the little river. Then she said, " You are keeping something from me, James. No news can trouble me as much as — as to be sure that I am kept in the dark about your affairs."

" I meant to be frank, Ann, but I have felt so alarmed about your health —"

" You need not be — I can bear anything but not to know —"

" That is why I brought you here, my dear. You are aware that I took out of the business the money you loaned to us."

" Yes — yes — I know."

" I have given up my partnership and withdrawn my capital. The business will go on without me."

" Was this because — I ? — but no matter. Go on, please."

He was incapable of concealing the truth from her, however much he might have disguised it from others. " You had your share in causing me to give up, but for a year since this war has gone on from one disaster to another, I have known that as a soldier I must be in it."

She was perfectly calm. " I have long known it would come, James. To have you and John and my brother Henry — all in it, is a hard fate."

" My dear, Charles writes me that Henry has left the army and gone to Europe on business for the Confederates."

"Indeed." Some feeling of annoyance troubled her. "Then he at least is in no danger."

"None, my dear."

"When do you go?"

"I am to command the 129th Infantry, and I shall leave about August 1st."

"So soon!" She sat still, thinking over what Grey Pine would be without him. He explained as she sat that all details of his affairs would be put for her clearly on paper. He ended by saying, "Ask me any questions you want answered."

"Then, James, there will be no income from the mills — from — from that contract?"

"None, except my rental. With that you may do as you please. There will be also, of course, at your disposal the income from my re-invested capital."

"Thank you, James." She was by far the less moved of the two.

"Have I greatly troubled you?" he asked. He was distressed for her.

"No, James. I knew it would come." As the shadows darkened on the forest floor and gathered overhead, she rose to her feet. "Whatever happens, James — whoever wins — I am the loser. I want you to be sorry for me."

"And, my dear Ann, whichever way this contest ends, I too lose."

She returned with tender sadness, "Yes, I did not think of that. Give me your arm, James — I am — tired."

He wondered that she had said nothing of the immense sacrifice few men would have made; nor did she seem to have realized what urgency of added motives she had contributed to bring about his decision.

CHAPTER XXI

THROUGH the great heat of July, 1862, the war went on its inconclusive way. In Westways, as elsewhere, the call of the people's President for three hundred thousand men was felt the more thoughtfully because now it was, of course, known that Penhallow was Colonel of the 129th Infantry; that he had made a great sacrifice of money was also known, but not understood, and Ann Penhallow's half-forgotten politics were again discussed when the village evening parliament met in front of the post-office.

Mrs. Crocker, off duty, stood framed in the door, cooling her round face with a palmetto fan and listening with interest to the talk or taking part in the discussion in so positive a way as was felt to be indiscreetly feminine, but respected on account of her official representation of a husband too deaf to fulfil his duties.

The Doctor got out of his gig. "Any letters from my boy?"

"Yes, two. Wanted to send them by Billy, but he's war-wild and would n't go." The Doctor looked over his letters.

"All right, I hope," said Mrs. Crocker.

Pole in his shirt sleeves listening said, "Of course, he is all right — doctors don't fight none."

"Send your son, Pole, before you talk nonsense," said Mc-Gregor. "My boy got a ball in his leg at Malvern Hill."

"My son's going along with the Squire," returned Pole, "leaves me short of help, and my wife's about crazy over it."

"What about Mrs. Penhallow?" said Mrs. Crocker. "I guess she's the kind that don't show what she feels."

"Oh, money's a great comforter," returned the butcher. "What I'm to do, I don't know."

327

"Well, I'm going too," said Joe Grace, "and father says I'm right."

"Oh, here's the parson," said Pole, as Rivers approached. "He's like the rest of them — all for war."

"Well, Pole," said Rivers, "how are you and Mrs. Crocker? I think you are getting thin this hot weather."

"Am I? No such good luck. We are talking war, Mr. Rivers. I do hear that what with the mill-boys and country fellows there's some thirty going into the Colonel's regiment."

"So I hear. On Sunday I mean to talk to them after service. You might say so."

"I will. If I had a boy, he should go," said Mrs. Crocker.

"It's easy talking when you have n't none," said Pole. "We are gettin' licked, and some day Lee will be over the border. It's just useless to spend money and cripple men."

There was a moment of silence, when Mrs. Crocker spoke. "Pole, you are n't ever sure of your legs. You were all for Buchanan, and then all for Lincoln. Now you're uneasy on the top rail of the fence and the rail ain't round." The parliament broke into laughter, and with more talk dissolved after some critical wisdom about the war.

It was July 30th, after ten at night, the day before the final Sunday of the month. The Colonel of the 129th stood with Leila before a big war map. "This fight at Malvern Hill"— he put a pin on the place —"was a mistake on the part of Lee, and yet he is a master of the game. He was terribly beaten — an aggressive general would have attacked at once."

"Would he have won, uncle?"

"I think so — but after a defeat these armies are as dangerous as a cornered cat."

"But, dear Uncle Jim, what is the matter with us? — We have men, money and courage."

"Well, this is how I see it. Neither side has a broad-minded

General in command of the whole field of war. Every day sees bits of fights, skirmishes, useless loss of life. There is on neither side any connected scheme of war. God knows how it will end. I do not yet see the man. If Robert Lee were in absolute command of all the effective force of the South, we would have trouble."

"But if he is so good a soldier, why did he make what you call a frontal attack on entrenched troops at Malvern?"

"My dear, when two men spar and neither can quite end the fight, one gets angry or over-confident and loses his head, then he does something wild — and pays for it."

"I see. You leave on Monday?"

"Yes — early."

"Mr. Rivers means to talk after service to the men who are enlisting."

"So he told me. I begged him to be moderate."

"He asked me for a text, uncle."

"Well!"

"I gave him the one about Cæsar and God."

"What put that into your head — it does not seem suitable?"

"Oh, do you think so? Some one once mentioned it to me. I could preach on it myself, but texts grow wonderfully in his hands. They glow — oh, they get halos about them. He ought to be in a great city."

"Oh, my dear, Mark Rivers has his limitations like all of us. He would die. Even here he has to be watched. McGregor told him last year that he was suffering from the contagion of other people's wickedness with occasional acute fits of over-conscientiousness. Rivers said it was incomprehensible nonsense; he was almost angry."

"And yet it is true, Uncle Jim."

"I'm glad I haven't the disease. I told McGregor as much. By George! he said my variety of the disorder was about other folk's stupidity. Then, when I said that I did n't understand him, he laughed. He makes me furious when he only laughs and won't answer — and won't explain."

"Why, uncle! I love to see him laugh. He laughs all over — he shakes. I told him it was a mirthquake. That set him off again. Was Tom McGregor badly hurt?"

"No, not badly."

"Will aunt go to church to-morrow?"

"No."

"I thought she would not. I should love to see you in uniform."

"Not here, my dear, but I will send you a daguerreotype."

When on this Sunday long remembered in Westways, the tall figure of Mark Rivers rose to open the service, he saw the little church crowded, the aisles filled, and in the front pews Penhallow, his niece, and behind them the young men who were to join his regiment. Grace had asked his own people to be present, and here and there were the mothers and sisters of the recruits, and a few men on crutches or wasted by the fevers of the Virginia marshes. Mark Rivers read the morning service as few men know how to read it. He rarely needed the prayer-book — he knew it all. He gave to it the freshness of a new message of love and helpfulness. More than ever on this Sunday Leila felt a sense of spiritual soaring, of personally sharing the praises of the angel choir when, looking upwards, he said: "Therefore with angels and archangels and all the company of heaven we laud and magnify Thy glorious name." She recalled that John had said, "When Mark Rivers says 'angels and archangels' it is like the clash of silver cymbals."

He gave out at the close his favourite hymn, "Lead, Kindly Light." It was well and sweetly sung by the girl-choir. As the music closed he rose — a figure of command, his spare frame looking larger for his robes. For a silent moment his eloquent eyes wandered over the crowd, gathering the attentive gaze of young and old, then he said: "I want to talk on this unusual occasion for a little while, to you who are answering the call of a man who is like a father calling his sons to a task of danger. My text is: 'Render, therefore, unto Cæsar the things which are Cæsar's and unto God the things which are God's.' The wonder of the great texts is that they have many applications as time runs on. You know the familiar story. Payment of the tax meant obedience to the Government, to law, to order. I would that I had the power to make you see with me the scene. It is to me so very distinct. The Pharisees desire to tempt him, a Jew, into a statement treasonable to the Roman rule they had accepted. Was it right for the Jew to pay the tax which sustained this Government? He had, as you may remember, already paid it for Peter and himself. He asks for the penny bearing Cæsar's head and answers them in the words of the text, 'Render unto Cæsar, therefore, the things which are Cæsar's.' He returns the penny. I wonder where that little coin is to-day? It has gone, but the lesson it read remains forever; nor even to-day is the Pharisee gone with his invidious temptations. *You* are to-day obeying a greater than Cæsar. *You* are meeting the material obligations of a day of discouragement — and for some a day of doubt.

"The nobler applications which lie within the meaning of the latter part of the text He answers more fully than was asked: 'Render unto God the things which are God's.' What are these things which are at need to be rendered to Him? What larger tax? Ease — comfort — home — the strong bodies which make work safe and pleasant. He asks of you the exercise of unusual qualities — the courage which looks death in the face and will not take the bribe of safety, of life, at the cost of dishonour. Ah! not in battle is my fear for you. In the long idleness of camps will come your hours of temptation. Think then of those at home who believe in you. It is a great thing to have an outside conscience — wife, mother, sister. Those are hours when it is hard to render unto God what he gave.

"We are now, as I said, at a time of discouragement. There are cowards who would yield — who would compromise — men who want peace at any cost. You answer them nobly. Here, in this sacred cause, if He asks it, we render life or the easy competencies of youth in its day of vigour."

The man paused. The strange power of the eyes spoke to them in this moment of silence. "Oh! I said the cause was sacred — an unbroken land. *He* gave you that, just for wide-world uses. Keep it! Guard it! — with all that Union of the States meant and still means to-day. *You* are not to blame for this necessity — war. The man who bends unpaid over the master's cotton-field is the innocent cause of all this bloodshed. If there were no slavery, there would have been no war. But let there be no hatred in the brave hearts you carry. God did not slay Saul, the earnest — I might say — the honest persecutor. He made him blind for a time. The awful charity of God is nowhere else so wonderful. These gallant people you are going to meet will some day see that God was opening their eyes to better days and nobler ways. They too are honest in the belief that God is on their side. Therefore, let there be no bitterness.

"Some of you are what we call religious. Do not be ashamed of it. The hardest fighters the world has known were men who went to battle with arms invisible to man. A word more and I have done. I have the hope — indeed the certainty — that I shall be sent to the field on errands of mercy and helpfulness. We may meet again. And now, take with you the earnest will to render unto God what things He gave for His highest uses. Now let us offer the prayer for the volunteers our great Bishop desires the Church to use. Let us pray."

In unusual silence the congregation moved away, a silence

shared by Leila and her uncle. At last she said, "Uncle Jim, I wish Aunt Ann could have heard that sermon — it could not have hurt her."

"Perhaps not."

"I wonder why she has so great a respect for him, so real a friendship. He thinks slavery the sin of sins. He has very little charity about it — oh, none — and Aunt Ann is as sure it is a divinely appointed relation."

"They fought it out, my dear, in his early days at Westways, and when they both found that they were clad in the armour of changeless beliefs no arguments could penetrate, they gave up and took of two fine natures what was left for life's uses and became friends. At least, that is how McGregor put it. He sometimes states things well."

"I see," said Leila thoughtfully, and set herself to thinking whether if she had radical differences of opinion with some one, she could settle into a condition of armed neutrality. Then she wondered if war made changes in the character of a man.

Presently she asked, "Why, Uncle Jim, are you suddenly in such haste to go?"

"There is need of haste. I could not tell Ann; I can tell you. We were never worse off since the war began. The Governor asks me to meet him in Harrisburg. What he fears is that in September Lee will cross the Potomac, with the hope of Maryland rising. Our Governor will call out fifty thousand militia. He wants me to take a command; I shall take it, but Lee's veterans would brush our militia away like summer flies. If he finds the Army of the Potomac before him, there may be a different story. I hope, please God, to be with it. There you have all I know, but it is for you alone. My regiment will go to the front before the end of the month."

"You will write to me, uncle."

"Yes, when I can. Your aunt asks me to write often, but

not to write about the war, as if — well, no matter. But I can
write to you. Good night — and be brave, dear — and Ann!
You will watch over her? "

"Yes, surely."

Ann Penhallow having sorrowfully made up her mind that
her husband's honour required his return to the army saw to it
with her usual efficiency that everything he might need was carefully provided. At bed-time of that Sunday she said quietly,
"Good night and good-bye, James. I do not want to be called
to-morrow to say good-bye. You will be off by six. Leila will
give you your breakfast. Write often." She was to appearance
cheerful and even gay, as she paused on the stairs laughing.
"These men," she cried, " I wonder how they do without women
orderlies. At the last moment I found you had left your razors
— good-night! "

The Colonel's eyes followed her slight form a little puzzled and
not entirely pleased at this easy dismissal of sentiment, when he
knew what he himself would have done if she had flown the
least signal of distress. He turned to Leila. " I am very much
relieved, my dear, to see that your aunt is taking my departure
quietly. I was afraid of another breakdown, and I could not
have stayed a day longer."

Leila who had watched this parting with some anxiety said,
"I was a little uneasy myself, but really Aunt Ann was great."
She could have made the well-loved Colonel miserable by trans-
lating for him into the tongue of man the language of the
actress on the stairs. " I wonder," she reflected, " if all men are
that blind, or only the heroic or unimaginative."

Colonel Penhallow was detained by consultations with the
Governor and by regimental work until near the close of August,
when his command was hurried forward to join McClellan's
army. He followed it a day later. He wrote long notes to his

wife almost daily and then in September after the battle of Antietam more freely to Leila: —

"DEAR LEILA: You will be surprised to hear from me as at Washington on this September 19th. I overtook my command at noon, in Philadelphia, where the regiment was being well fed in the big building known as the Cooper Shop. I was pleased with the look of the men, who have been long drilled in camp. After the meal I went outside and mounted Dixy, who was as rebellious as if he knew he was on the side to which his name did not belong. A soldier was vainly trying to mount my mare. He lost his temper and struck her. I saw a black man interfering, and rode forward seeing there was some trouble. By George! it was Josiah. I shook hands with him and said, 'Where did you come from? He said, 'Saw your name, sir, in the paper and just quit my work. I'm goin' along with you — I'm your servant. I've been thinkin' this long while I'd go back to Westways, but I've been doin' well here, and I just kep' a puttin' it off. I'm goin' with you.' I said, 'All right, get on that horse.' He patted the uneasy mare and in a moment was in the saddle and I a well pleased man. Tell your aunt I am well cared for.

"We were hurried forward, and I had the pleasure of seeing my men behave well when we stormed South Mountain — a very gallant affair. Joe Grace was hurt, but not badly, and was left behind. As to the killed, none are from Westways. At Antietam we were with the reserve, which I thought should have been used and was not. It was an attack on an interior line as seems always to be our luck. McClellan will follow Lee, of course. My regiment is to be with the Sixth Corps, but I was ordered by the Secretary of War to report to him in Washington. It is disgusting! But orders are orders. The Lieutenant-Colonel will have my place, and I hope to get back soon. Josiah was caught in the thick of the fight at Fox Gap. He was scared a sort of green. He will get over it — I know the signs. It was pure nervousness. His explanation was very perfect, ' I just laid down flat because I was afraid of gittin' this servant of yours killed.' We grinned mutual approval of the excuse.

"Yours ever,

"JAMES PENHALLOW."

"P. S. You will have found this letter very unsatisfactory, but the fact is that only people of ample leisure make good correspondents. But now to sum up: Yesterday I saw Stanton, had a glimpse of Swallow, saw Mr. Lincoln, and had an adventure so out of the common that it was like one of the stories of adventure in which Jack used to delight. Now I cannot — should not tell it — but some day — yes. Send this P. S., bit of good news, on its way. Read it first."

"Well, that is exasperating? Surely men are most unsatisfactory letter writers. No woman with an interesting subject could be so uninteresting. John is as bad or worse."

She found enclosed a postscript slip for Mr. Grace.

"DEAR SIR: That boy of yours is not badly hurt. He behaved with intelligent courage when for a moment a part of our charging line hesitated. I was proud of him; I have made him a Corporal.

"Yours truly,

"JAMES PENHALLOW."

The order to report to the former counsel of his firm, Secretary Stanton, brought an unhappy Colonel to the War Department. He sent in his card, and was asked to follow an orderly. As he was about to enter the private office of the War Minister, to his amazement Swallow came out. With a curt good morning, Penhallow went by him. The great Secretary rose to greet him, saying, "You are very welcome, Penhallow — never more welcome."

"You look worn out, Stanton," said the Colonel.

"No, not yet; but, my God! Penhallow, my life is one to kill the toughest. What with army mishaps, inefficiency, contractors backed by Congressmen — all the scum that war brings to the top. Do you know why I sent for you?"

"No. It was an order — I ask no questions. I am at your service."

"You were disappointed, of course."

"Yes, I was."

"Well, there were two reasons. One is frankly this. Your firm has a contract for field artillery — and now you are in the service."

"I see! It is not now my firm. I gave up my partnership."

"So I saw, but who of these hungry contractors will believe that you gave up — a fortune — to enter the army! The facts are either not well known or have been misstated."

"Very likely. I gave up what you speak of as a fortune as you gave up a great income at the bar, and for the same reason I withdrew all my capital. Even the rental of my mills will go to the Sanitary Commission. I could not leave a doubt or the least cause for suspicion."

"I was sure of you, but this has been a well-nursed scandal, due to an influential lot of disappointed contractors who would have controlled the giving of that contract had I not come into office. I shall kill it dead. Trust that to me."

"Thank you, Stanton, I could have stood it."

"Yes, but you do not know, my dear Penhallow, what Washington is at present. Well, let it go. It is now my business. Do you know this Mr. Swallow?"

"Know him? Yes— a usurious scamp of a lawyer, who to our relief has left Westways. Do not trust him. I presume that I owe this talk about me to him."

"Well, yes, to him and his associates."

"What does he want now?"

"What he will not get. Let him go. I said I had two

reasons for ordering you here. One I have stated. I want some one I can entirely trust, not merely for honesty and loyalty, but also because of business competence. All manner of work for the Government is going on here and elsewhere. I want some one to report on it from time to time. It will keep you here this winter. You do not like it?"

"No, but it was an order."

"Yes, I am sorry to take you for a time out of active service, but trust me this war will last long. This winter I want you for a variety of inspection work here or elsewhere. It will be mere business, dull, unexciting, with unending watchfulness, and advisory technical help and advice. I want not only personal character — I can get that, but not easily the combination of technical training and business capacity." He unrolled a bundle of papers. "There for example, Colonel, are plans for a new form of ambulance and pontoon wagons ready for approval. I want a report on both." He went on to speak of the ambulances with amazing knowledge of the details of their build. Penhallow watched this earnest, overtasked man, and began to comprehend the vastness of his daily toil, the weight of his mighty load of care. As he talked, cards were brought in, messages sent or received, telegrams — the talk was dropped — resumed — and the Colonel simply listened. At last the Secretary said, "That will do for to-day. You have room No. 27, and such clerks and orderlies as you may need. You will find on your table these specifications — and more — others. And now, how is your beautiful Grey Pine and its mistress and Leila? You will assure them of my undiminished affection. And John — where is he?"

"With General Grant, but where just now I cannot say."

As he spoke, the door opened and an officer announced — "The President." The ungainly length of Lincoln appeared. A quiet smile lingered on the large-featured face, with some humorous appreciation of the War Secretary's evident annoyance at this abrupt visit. Mr. Stanton's greeting as he rose was as the Colonel thought coldly civil.

"My friend, Colonel Penhallow, sir."

"Glad to see you," said Lincoln, and then with a certain simplicity explained, "You see, Colonel, sometimes I run away out of the back of the White House — just to get free of the guards. Don't look so bothered, Stanton. I'm too fine a failure for any one to want to kill me. Any news?"

"None," said the secretary, as he stood not too well pleased; "Colonel Penhallow is to be in my office on inspection duty."

"Indeed! Glad to see you." The huge hand closed on Penhallow's with innocent use of its power. "Name sounds familiar. Yes — there was a cadet of your name last year. Your son, I suppose?"

"No, my nephew — in the engineers with General Grant."

"Tell him I asked for him — handsome fellow. Anything I can do for him?"

"Nothing, sir."

"Anything I can do for you?"

"Nothing, sir."

"Don't let Stanton kill you. He ought to have a brevet, Stanton. He is the only man in Washington don't want anything." Even the weary face of the Secretary smiled under his heavy beard. "Just stepped in to divide growls with you. Come with me, Colonel, or Stanton will have a brigade of officers to escort me. Wait for me at the outer door — I'll join you."

Penhallow pleased and amused, went out taking with him the sense of puzzle felt by so many over this unusual personage. At the main entrance the Colonel came on Swallow.

"A word with you," he said very quietly. "You have been lying about me to the Secretary and elsewhere. Be careful. I am sometimes short of temper. You have hurt yourself, not me, and you will get no contracts here."

" Well, we will see about that," said Swallow, and was about to say more when the President appeared.

" Come, Colonel," he said. Swallow fell back and Penhallow walked away as men touched their hats. For a block or more Lincoln did not speak, and respecting his silence the soldier was as silent. Then, with his amazing frankness, Lincoln spoke.

" Does the Emancipation Proclamation please you? "

" As a war measure, yes."

" And not otherwise? "

" It is none of my business to criticize my Commander-in-Chief."

" Well, I won't make it an order, but I wish McClellan was of your way of thinking." Again there was silence. Penhallow was astonished at this outspoken statement, being aware as few men were of the fact that the General in question had been disinclined to announce the emancipation message to the army until he found that his corps commanders were not cordially with him in opinion.

As they stopped at the gate of the railing around the White House, Lincoln said, " When you don't want anything, come and see me — or if you do." Then, becoming grave, he asked, " What effect will my proclamation of emancipation have in the South? It takes effect in January, you know." It was like Lincoln. He asked this question of all manner of people. " I want to know," he added, as Penhallow hesitated.

" I am not in a position, sir, to have any opinion about how the Rebels will be affected by it."

" Oh, Confederates! Colonel — not Rebels. Calling names only hurts, and don't ever help. Better to be amiable about labels."

" It was a slip of the tongue, Mr. President. I usually say Confederates."

" Quite right — tongue very slippery organ. Reckon my small truant holiday's over. Everybody generally is letting me know what effect that emancipation-thunder will have." A strangely tender smile grew upon the large features. "You see, Colonel, you and I are the only ignorant people in Washington. Good-bye."

CHAPTER XXII

SALUTING the Commander-in-Chief, Penhallow turned away in absent mood thinking of the burdened man who had passed from sight into the White House. As he crossed Lafayette Square, he suddenly remembered that the President's request for his company had caused him to forget to look over the papers in his office of which the Secretary had spoken. It was desirable to revisit the War Department. As he walked around the statue of Andrew Jackson, he came suddenly face to face with his wife's brother, Henry Grey. For a moment he was in doubt. The man was in United States uniform, with an army cloak over his shoulders — but it was Grey. Something like consternation possessed the Federal officer. The Confederate faced him smiling, as Penhallow said, "My God! Grey, you here! a spy in our uniform! Many people know you — detection and arrest would mean —"

"Don't talk so loud, James. You are excited, and there is really no reason."

Penhallow said quietly, "I have good reason to be excited. You will walk on in front of me to Willard's Hotel. I will go with you to my rooms, where we can talk freely. Now, sir."

Grey stood still. "And suppose I decline to obey my rather positive brother-in-law."

"You are not a fool. If you were to try to escape me, and you are thinking of it, I would set on you at once any half dozen of the soldiers within call."

"In that case my revolver would settle my earthly accounts — and pleasantly relieve you."

342

"Don't talk. Go on ahead of me." He would not walk beside him.

"As you please." No more words passed. They moved up Pennsylvania Avenue, now at mid-day crowded with officers, soldiers, and clerks going to lunch. Grey was courteously saluting the officers he passed. This particularly enraged the man who was following him and was hopelessly trying to see how with regard to his own honour he could save this easy-going and well-loved brother of Ann Penhallow. If the Confederate had made his escape, he would have been relieved, but he gave him no least chance, nor was Grey at all meaning to take any risks. He knew or believed that his captor could not give him up to justice. He had never much liked the steady, self-controlled business man, the master of Grey Pine. Himself a light-hearted, thoughtless character, he quite failed to comprehend the agony of indecision which was harassing the federal officer. In fact, then and later in their talk, he found something amusing in the personal embarrassment Penhallow's recognition had brought upon him.

As they approached the hotel, the Confederate had become certain that he was in no kind of danger. The trapper less at ease than the trapped was after his habit becoming cool, competent and intensely watchful. The one man was more and more his careless, rather egotistic self; the other was of a sudden the rare self of an hour of peril — in a word, dangerous. As they reached the second floor, Penhallow said, "This way." Josiah in the dimly lighted corridor was putting the last shine on a pair of riding-boots. As he rose, his master said, "Stay here — I am not at home — to anybody — to any one."

He led the way into his sitting-room; Grey following said, "Excuse me," as he locked the door.

"You are quite safe," remarked his host, rather annoyed.

"Oh, that I take for granted."

James Penhallow said, " Sit down. There are cigars."

" A match please. Cigars are rare luxuries with us."

As the Confederate waited for the sulphur of the match to pass away, Penhallow took note of the slight, delicate figure, the blue eyes like Ann's, the well-bred face. Filling his own pipe he sat down with his back to the window, facing his brother-in-law.

" You are very comfortable here, James. How is my sister, and your beauty, Leila ? "

" Well — very well. But let us talk a little. You are a spy in our uniform."

" That is obvious enough. I am one of many in your Departments and outside of them. What do you propose? I am sorry we met."

" My duty is to turn you over to the Provost-marshal."

" Of course, but alas! my dear James, there is my sister — you won't do it — no one would under the circumstances. What the deuce made you speak to me? You put us both in an awkward position. You became responsible for a duty you can't fulfil. I am really most sorry for you. It was a bit of bad luck."

Penhallow rose to get a match and moved about the room uneasily as Henry Grey went on talking lightly of the situation which involved for him possibilities of death as a spy, and for Penhallow a dilemma in which Grey saw his own safety.

" Rather disagreeable all round, James. But I trust you won't let it worry you. I always think a man must be worried when he lets his pipe go out. There is no need to worry, and after all "— he added smiling —" you created a situation which might have been avoided. No one would have known — in a day or two we would have been talking to General Lee. An excellent cigar, James."

While his brother-in-law chatted lightly, apparently unconcerned, the Union officer was considering this way or that out of the toils woven of duty, affection and honour; but as he kept on seeking a mode of escape, he was also hearing and watching the man before him with attention which missed no word. He was barely conscious that the younger man appeared enough at ease to dare to use language which the Federal officer felt to be meant to annoy. A single word used by Grey stopped the Colonel's mental mechanism as if a forceful brake had been applied. The man before him had said carelessly, "*We — we* would have been talking to General Lee." The word "we" repeated itself in his mind like an echo. He too lightly despised Grey's capacity as a spy, but he had said "we." There were, it seemed, others; how many? — what had they done? This terribly simplified the game. To arrest Grey would or might be useless. Who were his companions and where were they? Once missing this confident Confederate they might escape. To question Grey would be in vain. To give him any hint that he had been imprudent would be to lose an advantage. He was so intent on the question of how to carry out a decisive purpose that he missed for the moment Grey's easy-minded talk, and then was suddenly aware that Grey was really amusing himself with a cat-and-mouse game. But now he too was at ease and became quietly civil as he filled another pipe, and with an air of despair which altogether deceived Grey said, "I see that I can do nothing, Henry. There is no reason to protract an unpleasant matter."

"I supposed you would reach this very obvious conclusion." Then unable to resist a chance to annoy a man who had given him a needless half hour not free from unpleasant possibilities, Grey rose and remarked, smiling, "I hope when we occupy this town to meet you under more agreeable circumstances."

"Sir," said Penhallow, "the painful situation in which I am placed does not give you the freedom to insult me."

The Confederate was quite unaware that the Colonel was becoming more and more a man to fear. "I beg pardon, James," he said, "I was only anticipating history." As he spoke, he stood securing a neglected button of his neat uniform. This act strangely exasperated the Colonel. "I will see you out," he said. "The buttons of the Massachusetts Third might attract attention."

"Oh, my cloak covers it," and he threw it carelessly over his shoulders.

Penhallow said, "I have confessed defeat — you may thank Ann Penhallow."

"Yes — an unfortunate situation, James. May I have another cigar? Thanks."

"Sorry I have no whisky, Grey."

"And I — How it pours! What a downfall!"

The Colonel was becoming more and more outwardly polite.

"Good-bye, Henry."

"*Au revoir*," said the younger man.

Penhallow went with his brother-in-law down the long corridor, neither man speaking again. As they passed Josiah, Penhallow said, "I shall want my horse at five, and shall want you with me." At the head of the stairs he dismissed his visitor without a further word. Then he turned back quickly to Josiah and said in a low voice, "Follow that man — don't lose him. Take your time. It is important — a matter of life and death to me — to know where he lives. Quick now — I trust you."

"Yes, sir." He was gone.

Grey feeling entirely safe walked away in the heavy rain with a mind at ease and a little sorry as a soldier for the hapless situation with which Penhallow had had to struggle. When we have known men only in the every-day business of life or in ordinary social relations, we may quite fail to credit them with qualities which are never called into activity except by unusual circumstances. Grey, an able engineer, regarded Penhallow as a rather slow thinker, a good man of business, and now as a commonplace, well-mannered officer. He smiled as he thought how his sister had made her husband in this present predicament what algebraists call a "negligible quantity." He would have been less easy had he known that the man he left felt keenly a sense of imperilled honour and of insult which his relation to Grey forbade him to avenge. He had become a man alert, observant, and quick to see his way and to act.

Josiah, with all his hunting instincts aroused, loitered idly after Grey in the rain, one of the scores of lazy, unnoticeable negroes. He was gone all the afternoon, and at eight o'clock found Penhallow in his room. "Did you find where he lives?" asked the Colonel.

"That man, he lives at 229 Sixteenth Street. Two more live there. They was in and out all day — and he went to shops and carried things away —"

"What kind of shops?"

"Where they sell paper and pens — and 'pothecaries."

"Sit down — you look tired." It was plain that they were soon about to move and were buying what was needed in the South — quinine, of course. But what had been their errand? He said, "Get some supper and come back soon."

Then he sat down to think. An engineer of competence lately back from Europe! His errand — their errand — must be of moment. He took a small revolver out of a drawer, put in shells, placed it in his breast pocket, and secured a box of matches. About nine, in a summer thunder-shower of wind and rain, he followed Josiah and walked to No. 229 Sixteenth Street. As he stood he asked,

"How did those men get in, Josiah?"

"All had keys. Want to get in, Colonel?"

"Yes, I want to get in. Are there any others in the house — servants — any one?"

" No, sir," Josiah said. " I went round to an alley at the
back of the house. There are lights on the second storey. You
can get in easy at the back, sir."

Seeing a policeman on the opposite pavement, Penhallow at
once changed his plan of entrance, and crossing the street
said to the policeman, " Is this your beat? "

" Yes, sir."

" Very good! You see I am in uniform. Here is my card.
I am on duty at the War Department. Here is my general
pass from the Provost-marshal General. Come to the gas lamp
and read it. Here are ten dollars. I have to get into No.
229 on Government business. If I do not come out in thirty
minutes, give the alarm, call others and go in. Who lives
there? "

" It is a gambling house — or was — not now."

" Very good. This is my servant, Josiah. If I get out
safely, come to Willard's to-morrow at nine — use my card
— ask for me — and you will not be sorry to have helped me."

" You want to get in! "

" Yes."

" No use to ring, sir," said Josiah. " There ain't any servants and the gentlemen, they ate outside. Lord, how it rains! "

The policeman hesitated. Another ten dollar note changed
owners. " Well, it is n't police duty — and you 're not a bur-
glar —"

The Colonel laughed. " If I were, I 'd have been in that
house without your aid."

" Well, yes, sir. Burglars don't usually take the police into
their confidence. There are no lights except in the second
storey. If your man 's not afraid and it 's an honest Government job, let him go through that side alley, get over the
fence — I 'll help him — and either through a window or by
the cellar he can get in and open the front door for you."

Josiah laughed low laughter as he crossed the street with

the officer and was lost to view. The Colonel waited at the door. In a few minutes the man returning said, " Want me with you? He got in easily."

" No, but take the time when. I enter and keep near." They waited.

" Nine-thirty now, sir."

" Give me the full time."

Penhallow went up the steps and knocked at the door. It was opened and he went in. " Shut the door quietly, Josiah — open if the policeman knocks. Now, be quiet, and if you hear a shot, or a big row call the police."

The house below-stairs was in darkness. He took off his shoes and went into a room on the first floor. Striking a match, he saw only ordinary furniture. The room back of it revealed to his failing match a roulette table. He went out into the hall and up the stairs with the utmost caution to avoid noise. On the second floor the door of the front room was ajar. They must be careless and confident, he reflected as he entered. A lighted candle on a pine table dimly illuminated a room in some confusion. On the floor were two small bags half full of clothes which he swiftly searched, without revealing anything of moment. A third, smaller bag lay open on the table. It contained a number of small rolls of very thin paper, and on the table there were spread out two others. As he looked, he knew they were admirably drawn sketches of the forts and the lines of connecting works which defended the city. Making sure no more papers were to be found, he thrust all of them within his waistcoat, buttoned it securely, felt for his revolver, and listened.

In the closed back room there was much mirth and the clink of glasses. He drew near the door and felt certain that Grey was relating with comic additions his interview of the morning. Without hesitation he threw open the door as three men sprang to their feet and Grey covered him with a revolver. He said quietly, "Sorry to disturb you, gentlemen. Put down that toy, Grey."

"No, by Heaven! — not till —"

"My dear Grey, between me and that pistol stands a woman — as she stood for your safety this morning. Men who talk, don't shoot. You are all three in deadly peril — you had better hear me. I could have covered you all with my revolver. Put down that thing!"

"Put it down," said the older of the three. Grey laid the weapon on the table.

"This is not war," said Penhallow, "and you are three to one. Sit down." He set the example. "It is clear that you are all Confederate officers and spies. Let us talk a little. I came on Mr. Grey to-day by accident. It was my duty to have him arrested; but he is my wife's brother. If a pistol is heard or I am not out of this, safe, in a few minutes, the police now on guard will enter — and you are doomed men. I am presumably on Government business. Now, gentlemen, will you leave at once or in an hour or less?"

"I for one accept," said the man who had been silent.

"And I," said the elder of the party.

"On your honour?"

"Yes."

Grey laughed lightly, "Oh, of course. Our work is done. Speed the parting guest!"

"I wish," said the Colonel, rising, "to leave no misapprehension on your minds — or on that of Mr. Grey. Those admirable sketches left carelessly on the table are in my pocket. Were they not, you would all three be lost men. Did you think, Grey, that to save your life or my own I would permit you to escape with your work? Had I not these papers, your chance of death would not weigh with me a moment."

Grey started up. "Don't be foolish, Grey," said the older man. "We have played and lost. There has been much carelessness — and we have suffered for it. I accept defeat, Colonel."

Penhallow looked at the watch in his hand. "You have ten minutes grace — no, rather less. May I ask of you one thing? You are every hour in danger, but I too am aware that if this interview be talked about in Richmond or you are caught, my name may be so used as to make trouble for me, for how could I explain that to save my wife's brother I connived at the escape of Confederate officers acting as spies? I ask no pledge, gentlemen. I merely leave my honour as a soldier in your hands. Good-night, and don't delay."

Grey was silent. The older man said, "I permit myself to hope we may meet some time under more pleasant circumstances — for me, I mean,"— he added, laughing. "Good-night."

Penhallow withdrew quickly and found Josiah on guard. He said, "It is all right — but for sport it beats possum-hunting. Open the door." The rain was still falling in torrents. "All right," he said to the policeman, "come and see me to-morrow early."

"What was the matter, sir? I've got to make my report."

Then Penhallow saw the possibility of trouble and as quickly that to bribe further might only make mischief. "Do not come to the hotel, but at eleven sharp call on me at the War Department on Seventeenth Street. You have my card. By that time I shall have talked the matter over with the Secretary. I am not at liberty to talk of it now — and you had better not. It is a Government affair. You go off duty, when?"

"At six. You said eleven, sir?"

"Yes, good-night. Go home, Josiah."

The Colonel was so wet that the added contributions of water were of no moment. The soldier in uniform may not carry an umbrella — for reasons unknown to me.

Before breakfast next morning Josiah brought him a letter,

left at the hotel too late in the night for delivery. He read
it with some amusement and with an uncertain amount of
satisfaction:

"MY DEAR J: When by evil luck I encountered you, I was
sure of three things. First, that I was safe; then, that we had
secured what we wanted; and last, that our way home was
assured. If in my satisfaction I played the bluff game rather
lightly — well, in a way to annoy you — I beg now to apologize.
That I should so stupidly have given away a game already won
is sufficiently humiliating, and the dog on top may readily
forgive. You spoilt a gallant venture, but, by Jove, you did it
well! I can't imagine how you found me! Accept my congratulations.

                              " Yours sincerely,
                                        " G."

"Confound him! What I suffered don't count. He's just
the man he always was — brave, of course, quixotically chiv-
alrous, a light weight. Ann used to say he was a grown-up
boy and small for his age. Well, he has had his spanking.
Confound him!" He went on thinking of this gay, clever,
inconsiderate, not unlovable man. If by mishap he were captured while trying to escape, what then? He would be fool
enough to make the venture in our uniform. There would be
swift justice; and only the final appeal to Cæsar. He was
with good reason ill at ease. I might indeed have to ask the
President for something."

He reconsidered his own relation to the adventure as he sat
at breakfast, and saw in it some remainder of danger. At ten
o'clock he was with the Secretary.

"I want," he said, "to talk to you as my old friend. You
are my official superior and may order me to the North Pole,
but now may I re-assume the other position for a minute and
make a confidential statement?"

"Certainly, Penhallow. I am always free to advise you."

"I want to say something and to be asked no questions. Am I clear?"

"Certainly."

"Thank you. I had an extraordinary adventure yesterday. I am not at liberty to do more than say that it put me in possession of these plans." He spread on the table well-drawn sketches of the forts around Washington.

Stanton's grim, bearded face grew stern. "You have my word, Penhallow. If I had not too easily given it we would have been placed in a disagreeable position. I am debarred from asking you how you came into possession of these papers. The spies who made them would have been in my power early this morning — and not even the President's weakness would have saved their necks."

Penhallow was silent, but was anxiously watching the angry Secretary, who swept the papers aside with an impatient gesture, feeling that he had been so dealt with as to be left without even the relief he too often found in outbursts of violent language. Penhallow's quiet attitude reminded him that he could not now take advantage of his official position to say what was on his mind.

"Colonel," he said, "I want a report on some better method of getting remounts for the cavalry."

"I will consider it, sir."

"What about that contract for ambulances?"

"I shall have my report ready to-morrow."

"That is all." It is to be feared that the next visitor suffered what Penhallow escaped.

With no other orders the Colonel left, rewarded the punctual policeman and went home to write to his wife, infinitely disgusted with the life before him and behind him, and desiring no more adventures.

CHAPTER XXIII

THE winter of 1862-63 went by with Sherman's defeat at Vicksburg and Rosecrans's inconclusive battle of Stone River. The unpopular Conscription Act in February, 1863, and last of all the discreditable defeat of Hooker in May at Chancellorsville, disheartened the most hopeful.

Meanwhile, Penhallow wrote to his wife with no word of the war, and poured out his annoyance to Leila with less restraint.

"DEAR LEILA: I get brief notes from John, who is with the one General (Grant) who has any luck. The list of discredited commanders good and bad increases. I am weary beyond measure of the kind of life I lead. I learn to-day, May 18th, of the progress of the investment of Vicksburg, and of John as busy at last with his proper work of bridges, corduroy roads and the siege approaches.

"The drift homeward of our crippled men, you tell of, is indeed sad. I am glad that Grace's boy is well; and so Rivers has gone to the army again. Pole's lad, with the lost arm, must have some work at the mills. Say I ask it. Good-bye.

"Yours, JAMES PENHALLOW."

On the 16th of June the Secretary said to Penhallow, "You know that Lee has crossed the Potomac. General Hunt has asked to have you put in charge of the reserve artillery of the Potomac army. I shall relieve you here and give the order, but I want you for a week longer to clear up matters."

Penhallow worked hard up to the time set by Stanton, and meanwhile made his arrangements to leave for the field. "Now that you are going away," said Stanton, "I wish to express my warm thanks for admirable service. I may say to you that Hooker has been removed and Meade put in command."

"That is good news, indeed, sir. Now the Potomac army will be handled by a soldier."

The Secretary had risen to say his parting words, and Penhallow as he held his hand saw how reluctant he was to let him go. They had long been friends, and now the Colonel observing his worn face felt for him the utmost anxiety. A stern, grave man, passionately devoted to his country, he was the impatient slave of duty. Sometimes hasty, unjust, or even ungenerous, he was indifferent to the enmities he too needlessly created, and was hated by many and not loved even by those who respected his devotion and competence. He spared neither his subordinates nor, least of all, Edwin Stanton, and spendthrift of vital force and energy went his way, one of the great war ministers like Carnot and Pitt. Now, as they stood about to part, he showed feeling with which few would have given him credit, and for which Penhallow was unprepared.

"Well," he said, "you are going. I shall miss your help in a life sometimes lonely, and overcrowded with work. You have been far more useful here than you could have been in the field. Living and working as you have done, you have made enemies. The more enmities an honest gentleman collects the richer he is. You are glad to go — well, don't think this town a mere great gambling place. It is a focal point — all that is bad in war seems to be represented here — spies, cheating contractors, political generals, generals as meek as missionaries. You have seen the worst of it — the worst. But my dear Penhallow, there is one comfort, Richmond is just as foul with thieving contractors, extravagance, intrigue, and spies who report to us with almost the regularity of the post; and, as with us, there is also honour, honesty, religion, belief in their cause." The Secretary had spoken at unusual length and in an unusual mood. When once, before the war, he had

spent a few happy days at Grey Pine, Mrs. Crocker character-
ized him as "a yes-and-no kind of man." Now as he walked
with his friend to the door, he said, "Does Mrs. Penhallow
know of your change of duty? I am aware of her feeling about
this unhappy strife."

"No. There will be a battle — time enough — soon enough
to write afterwards, if there should be any earthly afterwards."

"You are quite right," said the Secretary. "Good-bye. I
envy you your active share in this game."

Penhallow, as for the last time he went down the outer steps,
looked back at the old brick war-office on Seventeenth Street.
He felt the satisfaction of disagreeable duty well done. Then
he recalled with some sense of it as being rather ridiculous his
adventure with Henry Grey. In a far distant day he would tell
Ann. As he halted at the foot of the steps, he thought of his
only interview with Lincoln. The tall figure with the sombre
face left in his memory that haunting sense of the unusual of
which others had spoken and which was apt to disappear upon
more familiar acquaintance.

On the morning of June 28 in this year 1863, Leila riding
from the mills paused a minute to take note of the hillside
burial-ground, dotted here and there with pitiful little linen
flags, sole memorials of son or father — the victims of war.
"One never can get away from it," she murmured, and rode
on into Westways. Sitting in the saddle she waited patiently
at the door of the post-office. Mrs. Crocker was distributing
letters and newspapers. An old Quaker farmer was reading
aloud on the pavement the latest news.

"There ain't no list of killed and wounded," he said. Forgetful of the creed of his sect, his son was with the army. He
read, "The Rebels have got York — that's sure — and Carlisle
too. They are near Harrisburg."

"Oh, but we have burned the bridge over the Susquehanna,"
said some one.

Another and younger man with his arm in a sling asked, "Are they only cavalry?"

"No, General Ewell is in command. There are infantry."

"Where is Lee?"

"I don't make that out." They went away one by one, sharing the uneasiness felt in the great cities.

Leila called out, "Any letters, Mrs. Crocker? This is bad news."

"Here's one for you — it came in a letter to me. I was to give it to you alone."

Leila tore it open and read it. "Any bad news, Leila?"

"Yes, Uncle James is with the army. I should not have told you. General Meade is in command. Aunt Ann is not to know. There will be a battle — after that he will write — after it. Please not to mention where Uncle Jim is. When is your nephew to be buried — at the mills?"

"At eleven to-morrow."

"I shall be there. Aunt Ann will send flowers. Poor boy! he has lingered long."

"And he did so want to go back to the army. You see, he was that weak he cried. He was in the colour-guard and asked to have the flag hung on the wall. Any news of our John? I dreamed about him last night, only he had long curly locks — like he used to have."

"No, not a word."

"Has Mr. Rivers got back?"

"No, he is still with the army. You know, aunt sends him with money for the Sanitary."

"Yes, the Sanitary Commission — we all know."

Leila turned homeward seeing the curly locks. "Oh, to be a man now!" she murmured. She was bearing the woman's burden.

Mrs. Crocker called after her, "You forgot the papers."

".Burn them," said Leila. "I have heard enough — and more than enough, and Aunt Ann never reads them."

Penhallow had found time to visit his home twice in the winter, but found there little to please him. His wife was obviously feeling the varied strain of war, and Leila showed plainly that she too was suffering. He returned to his work unhappy, a discontented and resolutely dutiful man, hard driven by a relentless superior. Now, at last, the relief of action had come.

No one who has not lived through those years of war can imagine the variety of suffering which darkened countless homes throughout the land. At Grey Pine, Ann Penhallow living in a neighbourhood which was hostile to her own political creed was deeply distressed by the fact that on both sides were men dear to her. It must have been a too common addition to the misery of war and was not in some cases without passionate resentment. There were Northern men in the service of the Confederacy, and of the Southern graduates from West Point nearly fifty per cent. had remained loyal to the flag, as they elected to understand loyalty. The student of human motives may well be puzzled, for example, to explain why two of the most eminent soldiers of the war, both being men of the highest character and both Virginians should have decided to take different sides.

Some such reflection occupied Leila Grey's mind as she rode away. Many of the officers now in one of the two armies had dined or stayed a few pleasant days at Grey Pine. For one of them, Robert Lee, Penhallow had a warm regard. She remembered too General Scott, a Virginian, and her aunt's Southern friend Drayton, the man whom a poet has since described when with Farragut as "courtly, gallant and wise." "Ah, me!" she murmured, "duty must be at times a costly luxury.— A costly necessity," she concluded, was better — that left no privilege of choice. She smiled, dismissing the mental problem, and rode on full of anxiety for those she loved and her unfortunate country. Our most profound emotions are for the greater souls dumb and have no language if it be not that of prayer, or the tearful overflow which means so much and is so mysteriously helpful. She found both forms of expression when she knelt that night.

In the afternoon the refreshing upland coolness of evening followed on the humid heat of a hot June day. Towards sunset Ann Penhallow, to her niece's surprise, drew on her shawl and said she would like to walk down to the little river. Any proposal to break the routine of a life unwholesome in its monotony was agreeable to Leila. No talk of the war was possible. When Ann Penhallow now more and more rarely and with effort went on her too frequently needed errands of relief or consolation, the village people understood her silence about the war, and accepting her bounty somewhat resented an attitude of mind which forbade the pleasant old familiarity of approach.

The life was unhealthy for Leila, and McGregor watched its influence with affection and some professional apprehension. Glad of any change, Leila walked with her aunt through the garden among the roses in which now her aunt took no interest. They heard the catbirds carolling in the hedges, and Ann thought of the day a year ago when she listened to them with James Penhallow at her side. They reached in silence an open space above the broad quiet backwater. Beyond a low beach the river flowed by, wide and smooth, a swift stream. From the western side the sunset light fell in widening shafts of scarlet across the water.

"Let us sit here," said the elder woman. "I am too weak to walk further"— for her a strange confession. As they sat down on the mossy carpet, Leila caught the passive hand of her aunt.

"I suppose you still swim here every morning, Leila? I used to like it — I have now no heart for anything."

Leila could only say, " Why not, aunt? "

" How can you ask me! I think — I dream of nothing but this unnatural war."

" Is that wise, aunt? or as Dr. McGregor would say, ' wholesome '? "

" It is not; but I cannot help it — it darkens my whole life. Billy was up at the house this morning talking in his wild way. I did not even try to understand, but "— and she hesitated —" I suppose I had better know."

This was strange to Leila, who too hesitated, and then concluding to be frank returned, " It might have been better, aunt, if you had known all along what was going on —"

" What would have been the use? " said her aunt in a tone of languid indifference. " It can end in but one way."

A sensation of anger rose dominant in the mind of the girl. It was hard to bear. She broke out into words of passionate resentment — the first revolt. " You think only of your dear South — of your friends — your brother —"

" Leila ! "

She was past self-control or other control. " Well, then, be glad Lee is in Pennsylvania — General Ewell has taken York and Hagerstown — there will be a great battle. May God help the right — my country ! "

" General Lee," cried Ann; " Lee in Pennsylvania! Then that will end the war. I am glad James is safe in Washington." Leila already self-reproachful, was silent.

To tell her he was with the army of the North would be cruel and was what James Penhallow had forbidden.

" He is in Washington? " asked Ann anxiously.

" When last I heard, he was in Washington, aunt, and as you know, John is before Vicksburg with General Grant."

" They will never take it — never."

" Perhaps not, Aunt Ann," said Leila, penitent. The younger woman was disinclined to talk and sat quiet, one of the millions who were wondering what the next few days would bring.

The light to westward was slowly fading as she remained with hands clasped about her knees and put aside the useless longing to know what none could know. Her anger was gone as she caught with a side glance the frail look of Ann Penhallow. She felt too the soothing benediction of the day's most sacred hour.

Of a sudden Ann Penhallow bounded to her feet. A thunderous roar broke on the evening stillness. The smooth backwater shivered and the cat-tails and reeds swayed, as the sound struck echoes from the hills and died away. Leila caught and stayed the swaying figure. "It is only the first of the great new siege guns they are trying on the lower meadows. Sit down, dear, for a moment. Do be careful — you are getting" — she hesitated —"hysterical. There will be another presently. Do sit down, dear aunt. Don't be nervous." She was alarmed by her aunt's silent statuesque position. She could have applied no wiser remedy than her warning advice. No woman likes to be told she is nervous or hysterical and now it acted with the certainty of a charm.

"I am not nervous — it was so sudden. I was startled." She turned away with a quick movement of annoyance, releasing herself from Leila's arm. "Let's go home. Oh, my God!" she cried, as once again the cannon-roar shook the leaves on the upward slope before them. "It is the voice of war. Can I never get away from it — never — never?"

"You will not be troubled again to-day," said the girl, "and the smaller guns on the further meadow we hardly notice at the house."

Ann's steps quickened. She had been scared at her own realization of her want of self-government and was once more in command of her emotions. "Do not talk to me, Leila. I was quite upset — I am all right now."

The great guns were sent away next day on their errands of destruction. Then the two lonely women waited as the whole country waited for news which whatever it might be would carry grief to countless homes.

On the second day of July, 1863, under a heavy cloud of dust which hung high in air over the approach of the Baltimore Pike to Gettysburg, the long column of the reserve artillery of the Potomac army rumbled along the road, and more and more clearly the weary men heard the sound of cannon. About ten in the morning the advance guard was checked and the line came to a halt. James Penhallow, who since dawn had been urging on his command, rode in haste along the side of the cumbered road to where a hurrying brigade of infantry crossing his way explained why his guns were thus brought to a standstill. He saw that he must wait for the foot soldiers to go by. The cannoneers dismounted from the horses or dropped off the caissons, and glad of a rest lit their pipes and lay down or wandered about in search of water.

The Colonel, pleased to be on time, was in gay good-humour as he talked to the men or listened to the musketry fire far to the left. He said to a group of men, " We are all as grey as the Rebs, boys, but it is good Pennsylvania dust." As he spoke a roar of laughter was heard from the neighbourhood of the village cemetery on his right. He rode near it and saw the men gathered before an old notice board. He read: " Any person found using fire arms in this vicinity will be prosecuted according to law." Penhallow shook with laughter. " Guess we 'll have to be right careful, Colonel," said a sergeant.

" You will, indeed."

" It 's an awful warning, boys," said a private. " Should n't wonder if Bob Lee set it up to scare us."

" I 'd like to take it home." They chaffed the passing infantry, and were answered in kind. Penhallow impatient saw that the road would soon be clear. As he issued quick orders and men mounted in haste, a young aide rode up, saluted, and said, " I have orders, Colonel, from General Hunt to guide you to where he desires your guns to be parked."

" One moment," said Penhallow; " the road is a tangle of wagons: " and to a captain, " Ride on and side-track those wagons; be quick too." Then he said to the aide, " We have a few minutes — how are things going? I heard of General Reynolds's death, and little more."

" Yes, we were outnumbered yesterday and — well licked. Why they did not rush us, the Lord knows! "

" Give me some idea of our position."

" Well, sir, here to our right is Cemetery Hill, strongly held; to your left the line turns east and then south in a loop to wooded hills — one Culp's, they call it. That is our right. There is a row on there as you can hear. Before us as we stand our position runs south along a low ridge and ends on two pretty high-wooded hills they call Round Tops. That 's our left. From our front the ground slopes down some forty feet or so, and about a mile away the Rebs hold the town seminary and a long low rise facing us."

" Thank you, that seems pretty clear. There is firing over beyond the cemetery? "

" Yes, the skirmishers get cross now and then. The road seems clear, sir."

Orders rang out and the guns rattled up the pike like some monstrous articulated insect, all encumbering wagons being swept aside to make way for the privileged guns.

" You are to park here, sir, on the open between this and the Taneytown road. There is a brook — a creek."

" Thanks, that is clear."

The ground thus chosen lay some hundred yards behind the low crest held midway of our line by the Second Corps, whence the ground fell away in a gentle slope. The space back of our line was in what to a layman's eye would have seemed the wildest confusion of wagons, ambulances, ammunition mules, cattle, and wandering men. It was slowly assuming some order as the Provost Guard, dusty, despotic and cross, ranged the wagons, drove back stragglers, and left wide lanes for the artillery to move at need to the front.

The colonel spent some hours in getting his guns placed and in seeing that no least detail was lacking. With orders about instant readiness, with a word of praise here, of sharp criticism there, he turned away a well-contented man and walked up the slope in search of the headquarters. As he approached the front, he saw the bushy ridge in which, or back of which, the men lay at rest. Behind them were surgeons selecting partially protected places for immediate aid, stretcher-bearers, ambulances and all the mechanism of help for the wounded. Officers were making sure that men had at hand one hundred rounds of ammunition.

Some three hundred yards behind the mid-centre of the Second Corps, on the Taneytown road, Penhallow was directed to a small, rather shabby one-storey farm-house. "By George," he murmured, "here is one general who means to be near the front." He was met at the door by the tall handsome figure of General Hancock, a blue-eyed man with a slight moustache over a square expressively firm jaw.

"Glad to see you, Penhallow. Meade was anxious — I knew you would be on time. Come in."

Penhallow saw before him a mean little room, on one side a wide bed with a gaudy coverlet, on a pine table in the centre a bucket of water, a tin cup, and a candle-stick. Five rickety rush-covered chairs completed the furnishings.

Meade rose from study of the map an engineer officer was explaining. He was unknown to Penhallow, who observed him with interest — a tall spare man with grey-sprinkled dark hair a large Roman nose and spectacles over wide blue eyes; a gentleman of the best, modest, unassuming, and now carelessly clad.

"Colonel Penhallow," said Hancock.

"Glad to see you." He turned to receive with evident pleasure a report of the morning's fight on the right wing, glanced without obvious interest at the captured flag of the Stonewall Brigade, and greeted the colonel warmly. "I can only offer you water," he said. "Sit down. You may like to look over this map."

While the Commander wrote orders and despatched aide after aide, Penhallow bent over the map. "You see," said Hancock, "we have unusual luck for us in a short interior line. I judge from the moving guidons that Lee is extending his front — it may be six miles long."

"And ours?"

"Well, from wing to wing across the loop to right, not half of that."

"I see," said Penhallow, and accepting a drink of tepid water he went out to find and report to the chief of artillery, General Hunt.

He met him with General John Gibbon and two aides a few yards from the door, and making his brief report learned as he moved away that there was some trouble on the left wing. Meade coming out with Hancock, they mounted and rode away in haste, too late to correct General Sickles' unfortunate decision to improve General Meade's battle-line. It was not Penhallow's business, nor did he then fully understand that costly blunder. Returning to his guns, he sent, as Hunt had ordered, two of his reserve batteries up to the back of the line of the Second Corps, and finding General Gibbon temporarily in command walked with him to what is now called the "Crest" and stood among Cushing's guns. Alertly interested, Penhallow saw to the left, half hidden by bushes and a clump of trees, a long line of infantry lying at ease, their muskets in glittering stacks behind them. To the right the ground was more open. A broken stone fence lay in front of the Second Corps. It was patched with fence rails and added stone, and where the clump of trees projected in advance of the line made a right angle and extended thence in front of the batteries on the Crest about thirty yards. Then it met a like right angle of stone fencing and followed the line far to the right. Behind these rude walls lay the Pennsylvania and New York men, three small regiments. Further back on a little higher ground was the silent array of cannon, thus able at need to fire over the heads of the guarding infantry, now idly lying at rest in the baking heat of a July morning. The men about the cannon lounged at ease on the ground in the forty foot interspaces between the batteries, some eighteen pieces in all.

Suddenly an aide rode up, and saying, " See you again, Penhallow," Gibbon rode away in haste. Penhallow, who was carefully gathering in all that could then be seen from the locality, moved over to where a young battery captain was leaning against a cannon wheel wiping the sweat from his face or gazing over the vale below him, apparently lost in thought. " Captain Cushing, I believe," said the colonel. " I am Colonel Penhallow, in command of the reserve artillery."

" Indeed ! " said the young officer. " These are some of your guns —"

" Not mine — I was out of it long ago. They still carry the brand of my old iron-mills."

" We shall see, sir, that they do honour to your name."

" I am sure of that," returned the colonel, looking at the face of the officer, who as he spoke patted the gun beside him in an affectionate way.

" It seems very peaceful," he said.

" Yes, yes," returned Penhallow, " very."

They looked for a moment of silence down the vale before

them, where a mile away the ground rose to a low ridge, beyond which in woody shelters lay the hostile lines.

"What road is that?" asked Penhallow. "It leaves our right and crosses to enter Lee's right."

"The Emmitsburg Pike, sir."

The Colonel's glass searched the space before him. "I see some fine farm-houses — deserted, of course, and wheat fields no man will reap this year." He spoke thoughtfully, and as Woodruff of the nearer battery joined them, the roar of cannon broke the stillness.

"Far on our left," said Woodruff. At the sound, the men sprang to their feet and took their stations. Smoke rose and clouded their view of the distant field where on our left a fury of battle raged, while the rattle of infantry volleys became continuous. No more words were spoken. Through the long afternoon the unseen fight went on in front of the Round Tops. As it came nearer and the grey lines were visible, the guns on the Crest opened a lively fire and kept up their destructive business until the approach of the enemy ceased to extend towards our centre and fell away in death or disorderly flight. About sunset this varied noise subsided and the remote sound of cheering was heard.

"We must have won," said General Webb, the brigade commander. "It was a flanking movement. How little any one man knows of a battle!"

"By George! I am glad of a let up," said the young Captain. "I am vilely dirty." He wiped the grime and sweat from his face and threw himself on the ground as Generals Hunt and Gibbon rode up.

"No great damage here, I see, Webb. They got awfully licked, but it was near to something else."

Questioned by Penhallow, they heard the news of our needless loss and final triumphant repulse of the enemy. Hunt said emphatic things about political generals and their ways. "He lost a leg," said Gibbon, "and I think to have lost his life would have been fortunate. They are at it still on the right, but the Twelfth Corps has gone back to Culp's Hill and Ewell will get his share of pounding — if it be his corps."

"Then we may get some sleep," said Penhallow, as he moved away. "I have had very little for two nights."

CHAPTER XXIV

IT was near to seven when he went down to his parked guns,
seeing as he went that the ways were kept clear, and finding ready hot coffee and broiled chicken.

"Where did you get this, Josiah?" he asked.

"Kind of came in, sir — know'd he was wanted — laid two
eggs." The colonel laughed and asked no further questions.

"Pull off my boots. Horses all right?"

"Yes, sir."

Without undressing he fell on his camp-bed and, towards
dusk thinking with grim humour of his wife and the Penhallow
guns, fell asleep. About four in the morning the mad clamour
of battle awakened him. He got up and went out of the tent.
The night air was hot and oppressive. Far to our right there
was the rattle of musketry and the occasional upward flare of
cannon flashes against low-lying clouds. From the farthest
side of the Taneytown road at the rear he heard the rattle of
ambulances arriving from the field of fight to leave the
wounded in tent hospitals. They came slowly, marked by their
flickering lanterns, and were away again more swiftly. He
gave some vague thought to the wounded and to the surgeons,
for whom the night was as the day. At sunrise he went up
past the already busy headquarters and came to the bush-hidden
lines, where six thousand men of the Second Corps along a half
mile of the irregular far-stretched Crest were up and busy.
Fires were lighted, coffee boiled and biscuits munched. An air
of confidence and gaiety among the men pleased him as he
paused to give a sergeant a pipe light and divided his tobacco

among a thankful group of ragged soldiers. All was quiet. An outpost skirmish on the right, as a man said, "was petering out." He paused here and there to talk to the men, and was interested to hear them discussing with intelligence the advantage of our short line. Now and then the guns far to left or right quarrelled, but at eleven in the morning this third of July all was quiet except the murmurous noise of thousands of men who talked or lay at rest in the bushes or contrived a refuge from the sun under shelter of a canvas hung on ramrods.

Generals Gibbon and Webb, coming near, promised him a late breakfast, and he went with them to the little peach orchard near the headquarters on the Taneytown road. They sat down on mess-chests or cracker-boxes, and to Penhallow's amusement Josiah appeared with John, the servant of Gibbon, for Josiah was, as he said, on easy terms with every black servant in the line. Presently Hancock rode up with Meade. Generals Newton and Pleasanton also appeared, and with their aides joined them. These men were officially Penhallow's superiors, and although Hancock and Gibbon were his friends, he made no effort to take part in the discussion in regard to what the passing day would bring. He had his own opinion, but no one asked for it and he smoked in an undisturbed private council of war.

At last, as he rose, Newton said, "You knew John Reynolds well, Penhallow. A moment before he fell, his aide had begged him to fall back to a less dangerous position."

"He was my friend — a soldier of the best."

"The Pennsylvanians are in force to-day — you and I and —"

"Oh, colonels don't count," laughed Penhallow; "but there are Meade, Hancock, Gregg, Humphreys, Hays, Gibbon, Geary, Crawford —"

Hancock said, "We Pennsylvanians hold the lowest and

weakest point of our line — all Pennsylvanians on their own soil."

"Yes, but they will not attack here," said Newton.

"Oh, do you think so?" said Hancock. "Wait a little."

The headquarters' ambulance drove up with further supplies. The chickens were of mature age, but every one was hungry. Cigars and pipes were lighted, and Newton chaffed Gibbon as the arrogant young brigadier in command for the time of Hancock's Corps. The talk soon fell again upon the probabilities of the day. Penhallow listened. Meade grave and silent sat on a cracker-box and ate in an absent way, or scribbled orders, and at last directed that the picked body of men, the provost's guards, should join their regimental commands. About a quarter to noon the generals one by one rode away.

Having no especial duty, Penhallow walked to where on the Crest the eighteen guns were drawn up. The sky was clear as yet, a windless, hot day. Gibbon joined him.

"What next?" said Gibbon, as Penhallow clambered up and stood a tall figure on the limber of one of Cushing's guns, his field glass searching the valley and the enemy's position. "Is n't it like a big chess-board?"

"Yes — their skirmishers look like grey posts, and our own blue. They seem uneasy."

"Are n't they just like pawns in the game!" remarked Captain Haskell of the Staff.

Penhallow, intent, hardly heard them, but said presently, "There are guidons moving fast to their right."

"Oh, artillery taking position. We shall hear from them," returned Gibbon. "Hancock thinks that being beaten on both flanks, Lee will attack our centre, and this is the lowest point."

"Well," said Haskell, "it would be madness — can Lee remember Malvern Hill?"

"I wonder what Grant is doing?" remarked Gibbon. At that time, seated under an oak, watched at a distance by John

Penhallow and a group of officers, he was dictating to unlucky Pemberton the terms of Vicksburg's surrender.

Penhallow got down from his perch and wandered among the other guns, talking to the men who were lying on the sod, or interested in the battery horses behind the shelter of trees quietly munching the thin grasses. He returned to Cushing's guns, and being in the mental attitude of intense attention to things he would not usually have noticed, he was struck with the young captain's manly build, and then with his delicacy of feature, something girl-like and gentle in his ways.

Penhallow remarked that the guns so hot already from the sun would be too easily overheated when they were put to use. "Ah," returned Cushing, "but will they be asked to talk to-day?" The innocent looking smile and the quick flash of wide-opened eyes told of his wish to send messages across the vale.

"Yes, I think so," said the colonel; "I think so,"— and again observant he saw the slight figure straighten and a quite other look of tender sadness come upon his face.

"How quiet they are — how very quiet!" Then he laughed merrily. "See that dog on the Emmitsburg road. He does n't know which side he 's on."

Penhallow looked at his watch. "It is one o'clock." Then his glass was up. "Ah!" he exclaimed, as he closed it, "now we shall catch it. I thought as much."

A mile away, far on Lee's right, on the low ridge in front of his position, a flash of light was seen. As the round ring of smoke shot out from the cannon, the colonel remembered the little Leila's delight when he blew smoke rings as they sat on the porch. Instantly a second gun spoke. The two shells flew over our line and lit far to the rear, while at once along Lee's position a hundred and fifty guns rang out and were instantly answered by our own artillery from Round Top to Cemetery Hill. General Hunt beside him replying to the quick questions he put, said, "We could not place over seventy-five guns — not room enough."

"Is that all? They are distributing their favours along our whole front."

At once a vast shroud of smoke rose and hid both lines, while out of it flew countless shell and roundshot. At first most of the Confederate missiles flew high and fell far behind our Crest. The two officers were coolly critical as they stood between the batteries.

"He must think our men are back of the guns like his own. The wall and bushes hide them."

"The fuses are too long," said Hunt quietly. "That's better and worse," he added, as a shell exploded near by and one of Woodruff's guns went out of action and the ground was strewn with the dead and wounded. "We shall want some of your guns."

Penhallow went in haste to the rear. What he saw was terrible. The iron hail of shells fell fast around him on the wide open space or even as far away as the hospital tents. On or near the Taneytown road terror-stricken wagon-drivers were flying, ammunition mules were torn to pieces or lying mangled; a shell exploded in a wagon,— driver, horses and a load of bread were gone. Horses lay about, dead or horribly torn; one horse hitched to a tree went on cropping grass. Penhallow missed nothing. He was in the mood peril always brought. Men said he was a slow, sure thinker, and missed seeing things which did not interest him. Now he was gay, tuned to the highest pitch of automatic watchfulness, as this far-sent storm of bursting shells went over and past the troops it was meant to destroy. Hurrying through it he saw the wide slope clear rapidly of what was left of active life. He laughed as a round shot knocked a knapsack off a man's back. The man unhurt did not stay to look for it. Once the colonel dropped as a shell lit near him. It did not explode. He ejaculated, "Pshaw," and went on. He came near the Taneytown road to find that his artillery had suffered. A score of harnessed horses lay dead or horribly mangled. His quick orders sent up to the front a dozen guns. Some were horsed, some were pulled with ropes by the cheering, eager cannoneers. Their way was up the deserted slope, "well cleared by the enemy," thought Penhallow with a smile. Once he looked back and saw the far flight of a shell end in or near an ambulance of the wounded beyond the Taneytown road.

During his absence gun after gun had been disabled and a caisson exploded; the gun crews lay dead or wounded. What more horribly disturbed Penhallow was the hideous screams of the battery horses. "Ah! the pity of it. They had no cause to die for — no duty — no choice." As he assisted in replacing the wreckage of the guns, he still heard the cries of the animals who so dumb in peace found in torture voices of anguish unheard before — unnatural, strange. The appalling tempest of shells screamed on and on, while the most of them fell beyond the Crest. Penhallow looked up to note their flight. They darted overhead shrill-voiced or hissing. There was a white puff of smoke, a red flash, and an explosion.

General Gibbon, coming back from the long line of his corps, said, "My men have suffered very little, but the headquarters behind them are in ruin. Meade has moved back." As he spoke the shells began to fall on the Crest.

"They seem to be more attentive to us," said the battery Captain Woodruff. "Thought we'd catch it!"

"Horrible! — Those horses, Gibbon," said Penhallow.

At last there seemed to be more concentrated firing on the Crest. Many shells fell near the imperfect wall-shelter of the crouching men, while others exploded among the lines to left or right in the bushes.

"They are doing better now, confound them!" said the young general coolly. "Our men at the wall seem disturbed.

Come with me," he said to Penhallow and Haskell of the Staff, who had just joined them.

They went down in front of the guns to where behind the low wall lay the two thin lines of the Pennsylvania regiments. He spoke to the Colonel of the 71st, who with other officers was afoot encouraging the men.

"Keep cool, boys," said Gibbon.

The men laughed. "Oh, we're all right, General, but we ain't cool."

Gibbon laughed. "Let us go over the wall and try to see a little better," said Penhallow.

A hundred yards beyond the lines they sat down. The ceaseless rain of shot and shell from both sides went over them, the canopy of smoke being so high above that the interspace between the lines was now more or less visible. Far beyond them our skirmish outposts were still motionless on guard; and yet further farms and houses, some smoking in ruin, lay among the green fields along the Emmitsburg Pike.

"It is pretty safe here," said the Corps Commander, while far above them the shells sang their war notes.

Penhallow looked back. "They've got the range — there goes one of the guns — oh! and another."

"Let's go back," said Gibbon, rising, "we are too safe here." They laughed at his reason and followed him, Haskell remarking on the lessening of the fire. As they moved about the forty-foot spaces between the disabled batteries, the last cannon-ball rolled by them and bounded down the slope harmless. At once there was movement,— quick orders, officers busy, as fresh cannon replaced the wrecked pieces. Many of the unhurt cannoneers lay down utterly exhausted. The dead were drawn aside, while the wounded crawled away or were cared for by the stretcher-bearers and surgeons. Meanwhile the dense, hot, smoke-pall rose slowly and drifted away. The field-glasses were at once in use.

"It is half-past two," said General Hunt; "what next? Oh! our skirmishers are falling back."

"They are going to attack," said Haskell, "and can they mean our whole line — or where?"

The cannoneers were called to their pieces, and silently expectant the little group waited on the fateful hour, while the orderly quiet of discipline was to be seen on the Crest. The field-glasses of the officers were searching with intense interest the more and more visible vale.

"Pretty plain now, Gibbon," said Hunt.

"Yes, we are in for it."

"They are forming," said Penhallow. A line appeared from the low swell of ground in front of Lee's position — then a second and a third. Muskets and bayonets flashed in the sun.

"Can you make out their flags?" asked Gibbon, "or their numbers?"

"Not the flags." He waited intent, watchful. No one spoke — minute after minute went by. At last Penhallow answered. "A long line — a good half mile — quite twelve thousand — oh, more — more. Now they are advancing *en échelon*."

To left, to right, along our lines was heard the thud, thud, of the ramrods, and percussion-cap boxes were slid around the waist to be handy. Penhallow and others drew their pistols. The cannon were now fully replaced, the regimental flags unrolled, and on the front line, long motionless, the trefoil guidons of the two divisions of the Second Corps fluttered feebly. The long row of skirmishers firing fell back more and more rapidly, and came at last into our lines.

Penhallow said, turning to Gibbon, "They have — I think — they have no supporting batteries — that is strange." Haskell and Gibbon had gone as he spoke and the low crest was free at this point of all but the artillery force. To left, the projecting clump of trees and the lines of the Second Corps — all he could see — were ominously quiet.

Gibbon came back to the crest. He said, "We may need backing if they concentrate on us; here our line is too thin." And still the orderly grey columns came on silently, without their usual charging-yell.

"Ah!" exclaimed Penhallow without lowering his glass, as he gazed to our left. The clamour of cannon broke out from little Round Top.

"Rifles!" exclaimed Gibbon. "Good!" Their left made no reply, but seemed to draw away from the fire.

"I can see no more," said the Colonel, "but they stopped at the Emmitsburg road."

The acrid odour of musketry drifted across the field as he turned to gaze at the left wing of the fast coming onset. Far to our right they came under the fire of Cemetery Hill and of an advanced Massachusetts regiment. He saw the blue flags of Virginia sway, fall, and rise no more, while scattered and broken the Confederates fled or fell under the fury of the death messages from above the long-buried dead of the village graves. "Now then, Cushing!" cried Hunt, and the guns on the Crest opened fire.

It was plain that the long Confederate lines, frayed on each flank, had crowded together making a vast wedge of attack. Then all along our miles of troops a crackle of musketry broke out, the big guns bellowing. The field was mostly lost to view in the dense smoke, under which the charging-force halted and steadily returned the fire.

"I can't see," cried Cushing near by.

"Quite three hundred yards or more," said the colonel, "and you are hurt, Cushing. Go to the rear." The blood was streaming down his leg.

"Not I — it is nothing. Hang those fellows!" A New

York battery gallantly run in between disabled guns crowded Cushing's cannon. He cried, " Section one to the front, by hand ! "

He was instantly obeyed. As he went with it to the front near to the wall, followed by Penhallow, he said, " It is my last canister, colonel. I can't see well."

Dimly seen figures in the dense smoke were visible here and there some two hundred yards away, with flutter of reeling battle-flags in the smoke, while more and more swiftly the wedge of men came on, losing terribly by the fire of the men at the wall along the lines.

Cushing stood with the lanyard of the percussion trigger in his hand. It seems inconceivable, but the two men smiled. Then he cried, " My God ! "— his figure swayed, he held his left hand over a ghastly wound in his side, and as he reeled pulled the lanyard. He may have seen the red flash, and then with a bullet through the open mouth fell dead across the prolonge of his gun.

For a moment Penhallow was the only officer of rank near the silent battery. Where Cushing's two guns came too near the wall, the men moved away to the sides leaving an unguarded space. Checked everywhere to right and left, the assailants crowded on to the clump of trees and to where the Pennsylvania line held the stone wall. Ignorant of the ruin behind them, the grey mass came on with a rush through the smoke. The men in blue, losing terribly, fell back from a part of the wall in confusion — a mere mob — sweeping Webb, Penhallow and others with them, swearing and furious. Two or three hundred feet back they stopped, a confused mass. General Webb, Haskell and other officers rallied them. The red flags gathered thicker, where the small units of many commands stood fast under the shelter of a portion of the lost wall. Penhallow looked back and saw the Massachusetts flags — our centre alone had given way. The flanks of the broken regiments still held the wall and poured in a murderous fire where the splendid courage of the onset halted, unwilling to fly, unable to go on.

Webb, furious, rallied his men, while Penhallow, Haskell and Gibbon vainly urged an advance. A colour-sergeant ran forward and fell dead. A corporal caught up the flag and dropped. A Confederate general leaped over the deserted wall and laid a hand on Cushing's gun. He fell instantly at the side of the dead captain, as with a sudden roar of fury the broken Pennsylvanians rolled in a disordered mass of men and officers against the disorganized valour which held the wall.

The smoke held — still holds, the secret of how many met the Northern men at the wall; how long they fought among Cushing's guns, on and over the wall, no man who came out of it could tell. Penhallow emptied his revolver and seizing a musket fought the brute battle with the men who used fists, stones, gun-rammers — a howling mob of blue and grey. And so the swaying flags fell down under trampling men and the lost wall was won. The fight was over. Men fell in scores, asking quarter. The flanking fires had been merciless, and the slope was populous with dead and wounded men, while far away the smoke half hid the sullen retreat of the survivors. The prearranged mechanism of war became active. Thousands of prisoners were being ordered to the rear. Men stood still, gasping, breathless or dazed. As Penhallow stood breathing hard, from the right wing, among the long silent dead of Cemetery Hill, arose a wild hurrah. It gathered volume, rolled down the long line of corps after corps, and died away among the echoes of the Pennsylvania hills. He looked about him trying to recover interest. Some one said that Hancock and Gibbon were wounded. The rush of the *mêlée* had carried him far down the track of the charge, and having no instant duty he sat down, his clothes in tatters. As he recovered strength, he was aware of General Meade on horseback with an aide. The general, white and grave, said to Haskell, " How has it gone here? "

An officer cried, " They are beaten," showing two flags he held.

Meade said sharply: " Damn the flags! Are the men gone?"

" Yes, sir, the attack is over."

He uncovered, said only, " Thank God!" gave some rapid orders and rode away beside the death-swath, careful, as Penhallow saw, to keep his horse off of the thirty scattered flags, many lying under or over the brave who had fought and lost in this memorable charge.

Penhallow could have known of the battle only what he had seen, but a few words from an officer told him that nowhere except at this part of the line of the Second Corps had the attack been at all fortunate.

On the wide field of attack our ambulance corps was rescuing the hundreds of wounded Confederates, many of them buried, helpless, beneath the bodies of the motionless dead. Two soldiers stood near him derisively flaunting flags.

" Quit that," cried the Colonel, " drop them!" The men obeyed.

" Death captured them — not we," said Penhallow, and saw that he was speaking to a boyish Confederate lieutenant, who had just dragged himself limping out of the ghastly heap of dead.

Touching his forehead in salute, he said, " Thank you, sir. Where shall I go?"

" Up there," replied the colonel. " You will be cared for."

The man limped away followed by Penhallow, who glanced at the torn Confederate banners lying blood-stained about the wall and beyond it. He read their labels — Manassas, Chancellorsville, Sharpsburg. One marked Fredericksburg lay gripped in the hand of a dead sergeant. He crossed the wall to look for the body of the captain of the battery; men were lifting it. " My God! — Poor boy!" murmured the colonel, as he looked on the white face of death. He asked who was the Rebel general who had fallen beside Cushing.

"General Armistead," said an officer —"mortally wounded, they say."

Penhallow turned and went down the slope again. Far away, widely scattered, he caught glimpses of this rash and gallant attack. He was aware of that strange complex odour which rises from a battlefield. It affected him as horrible and as unlike any other unpleasant smell. Feeling better, he busied himself directing those who were aiding the wounded. A general officer he did not know said to him, " Stop the firing from that regiment."

A number of still excited men of one of the flanking brigades on our right were firing uselessly at the dimly seen and remote mass of the enemy. Penhallow went quickly to the right, and as he drew near shouted, " Stop those men — quit firing ! " He raised his hand to call attention to his order. The firing lessened, and seeing that he was understood he turned away. At the moment he was not fifty feet from the flanking line, and had moved far down the slope as one of the final shots rang out. He felt something like a blow on his right temple, and as he staggered was aware of the gush of blood down his face. " What fool did that ? " he exclaimed as he reeled and fell. He rose, fell, rose again, and managed to tie a handkerchief around his head. He stumbled to the wall and lay down, his head aching. He could go no further. " Queer, that," he murmured; " they might have seen." He sat up; things around him were doubled to his view.

" Are you hit ? " said Haskell, who was directing stretcher-bearers and sending prisoners to the rear.

" Not badly." He was giddy and in great pain. Then he was aware of the anxious face of Josiah.

" My God ! you hurt, sir ? Come to look for you — can you ride ? I fetched Dixy — mare 's killed."

"I am not badly hurt. Tighten this handkerchief and give me your arm — I can't ride."

He arose, and amazed at his weakness, dragged himself down the slope, through the reforming lines, the thousands of prisoners, the reinforcing cannon and the wreckage of the hillside. He fell on his couch, and more at ease began to think, with some difficulty in controlling his thoughts. At last he said, "I shall be up to-morrow," and lay still, seeing, as the late afternoon went by, Grey Pine and Ann Penhallow. Then he was aware of Captain Haskell and a surgeon, who dressed his wound and said, "It was mere shock — there is no fracture. The ball cut the artery and tore the scalp. You'll be all right in a day or two."

Penhallow said, "Please to direct my servant to the Sanitary Commission. I think my friend, the Rev. Mark Rivers, is with them."

He slept none. It was early dawn when Rivers came in anxious and troubled. For the first time in years of acquaintance he found Penhallow depressed, and amazed because so small a wound made him weak and unable to think clearly or to give orders. "And it was some stupid boy from our line," he said.

His incapacity made Rivers uneasy, and although Penhallow broke out to his surprise in angry remonstrance, he convinced him at last that he must return to Grey Pine on sick leave. He asked no question about the army. Insisting that he was too well to give up his command, nevertheless he talked much of headache and lack of bodily power. He was, as Rivers saw, no longer the good-humoured, quiet gentleman, with no thought of self. In a week he was stronger, but as his watchful friend realized, there was something mysteriously wrong with his mental and moral mechanism.

On the day after the battle Penhallow asked to have his wife telegraphed that he was slightly wounded, and that she must not come to him. Rivers wrote also a brief and guarded letter to Leila of their early return to Grey Pine.

In a vain effort to interest the colonel, he told him of the surrender of Vicksburg.— He asked where it was and was n't John there, but somewhat later became more clear-minded and eager to go home.

CHAPTER XXV

RIVERS gathered no comfort from a consultation of surgeons, who talked of the long-lasting effects of concussion of the brain. Made careful by the sad change he had observed in Ann Penhallow when last seen, he sent his telegram for Leila to the care of the post-mistress, and a day later a brief letter.

Understanding the mode of address, Mrs. Crocker walked at once to Grey Pine, and found Leila in the garden. "Where is your aunt?" she asked.

"Lying down in her room. I got your kind note about the fight last evening. Is it true? Is the news confirmed?"

"Yes. There was a terrible battle at Gettysburg. The Rebels were defeated by General Meade and are retreating."

"I did not tell Aunt Ann anything. I waited to hear, as I was sure I would from Uncle James. Is there evil news?"

"I don't know. Here is a telegram to my care for you from Mr. Rivers. It must have been delayed — and then came this letter to Mrs. Penhallow from him."

"Then — then — there is bad news," she cried as she tore open the telegram and stood still.

"What is it? — you know how we all love him."

"Uncle Jim is wounded — not seriously — and will be here shortly."

"Oh, but I am sorry — and glad."

"Yes — yes — I must tell aunt at once. She has not left her room for two days, and I forbade the maids to talk of the victory until it was sure — now she must know all. I must tell her at once."

"Why not get Dr. McGregor?"

"No — no," she returned with decision. "I shall know best how to tell — it wants a woman."

The ruddy, stout post-mistress looked at the tall young woman with sudden appreciation of her self-command and mental growth. "Maybe you're about right, but I thought — well, fact is, I've seen of late so many people just tear open a letter — and go all to pieces."

Leila smiled. "You don't know my aunt. Now I must go. Oh, this war — this war! To-morrow will scatter joy and grief over all the land."

"Yes, I've been near about mobbed to-day. Good-bye."

The messenger of evil news went straight from the garden path, where the roses were in unusual abundance. To her surprise she saw her aunt on the back porch. As Leila hesitated, she said, "I saw Mrs. Crocker from my window, Leila. She gave you something — a letter — or a telegram. What is it? I suppose after what I have heard of the Confederates at York and Carlisle, they may be in Harrisburg by this time and the railroad to the west cut off. It may be well to know." She spoke rapidly as she came down the steps to meet her niece. "It is as well James Penhallow is not in it."

The two women stood facing one another in one of those immeasurably brief silences which are to timeless thought as are ages. Her husband safe, General Lee victorious — some slight look of satisfaction could be seen in her face — a faint smile, too easily read — and then —

"Well, dear, your news?"

Anger, tenderness, love, pity — all dictated answers. "Aunt Ann, I have bad news."

"Of course, dear. It was to be expected. You won't believe me, but I am sorry for you and for James."

The face of the tall young woman flushed hot. She had meant to spare her — to be tender. She said, "General Lee is retreating after losing a great battle at Gettysburg."

Her aunt said quickly, "But James Penhallow — he is in Washington?"

"No, he was in the army — he is wounded — not seriously — and he is coming home."

"I might have known it." A great illumination came over her face not understood by Leila. She was strangely glad for him that he had been in the field and not in peaceful safety at Washington. With abrupt change of expression, she added, "Wounded? Not seriously. That is n't like him to come home for a slight wound. You or Mark Rivers are hiding something."

"Not I, aunt; but any wound that kept him off duty would be better cared for here. Lee's defeat leaves him free for a time — I mean at ease —"

"Don't talk nonsense!" she cried. "What do I care for Lee — or Meade — or battles! James Penhallow is all the world to me. Victory!" — she flamed with mounting colour — "it is I am the victor! He comes back with honour — I have no duties — no country — I have only my love. Oh, my God! if he had died — if — if — I should have hated! —" She spoke with harsh vehemence, and of a sudden stopped, and breathing fast gasped in low-voiced broken tones, "Don't stare at me — I am not a fool — I am — I am — only the fool of a great love. You don't know what it means. My God! I have no child — James Penhallow is to me children, husband — all — everything." She stood still, wide-eyed, staring down the garden paths, a wonder of yearning tenderness in her face, with Rivers's letter in her hand.

"Read your letter, Aunt."

"Yes — yes — I forgot it." She read it, and said, "It only confirms the telegram."

The storm of passionate emotion was over. Leila amazed and fearful of results — twice seen before — watched her. "You have seen," she said in a low voice, "the soul of a great love laid bare. May you too some day, my child, love as I do!

Have no fear for me — I see it in your looks. Come in — I have to see to things — I have to give some orders — there will be much to do." She was at once quiet, and composedly led the way into the house, the astonished girl following her.

In the hall Mrs. Penhallow said, "I fear, dear, I have left too much of the management of the house to you — of late, I mean. What with the farms and stables, I am not surprised that things have not been quite as James would desire. I am going to relieve you a little. I suppose the stables are all right."

"They are," returned Leila, feeling hurt. Her aunt had not been in the kitchen or given an order for nearly a month, and house, farm and stables, had been by degrees allowed to slip into Leila's well-trained and competent hands. Meanwhile Ann Penhallow had gradually failed in health and lost interest in duties which had been to her, as Rivers said, what social pleasures were to some women. She yielded by degrees and not without resistance to mere physical weakness, and under the emotional stress of war, and above all the absence of the man on whom she depended, had lapsed to McGregor's dismay into a state of mind and body for which he had no remedy.

Every physician of large experience must have seen cases of self-created, unresisted invalidism end with mysterious abruptness and the return of mental, moral and physical competence, under the influence of some call upon their sense of duty made by calamity, such as an acute illness in the household, financial ruin, or the death of a husband. The return of a wounded man and the need to care for him acted thus upon Ann Penhallow.

Leila looked on in surprise. Her aunt's astounding indifference to the results of defeat for her beloved South when she learned of her husband's injury left the younger woman utterly bewildered. Nothing in her own nature, as she thought it all over, enabled her to understand it, nor was her aunt's rapid gain in health and cheerfulness during the next few days more easy to explain. At first with effort, but very soon with increase of ability, she gradually became more and more her old self.

Ann Penhallow spent the remainder of the next day in one of those household inspections which let no failure in neatness or order escape attention. James Penhallow's library was to be cleaned and cared for in a way to distress any man-minded man, while Leila looked on. Had her aunt's recent look of ill-health represented nothing but the depressing influence of a year of anxiety? And, if so, why under the distress of a nearer and more material disaster should she grow so quickly active, and apparently strong in place of becoming more feeble. She followed her aunt about the house trying to be helpful, and a little amused at her return to some of the ways which at times annoyed Penhallow into positive revolt. As she thought of it, Ann was standing over a battered army-chest, open and half full of well-worn cavalry uniforms.

"Really, Leila," she said, "these old army clothes had better be disposed of — and that shabby smoking-jacket — I have not seen it for years. Why do men keep their useless, shabby clothes?"

"I think Uncle Jim would n't like those old army uniforms given away, aunt; and don't you remember how he looked like an old Van Dyke portrait in that lovely brown velvet jacket?"

Ann, standing with the much used garment in her hand, let it drop into the chest, saying, "I really cannot see the use of keeping things as men love to do —"

"And women never!" cried Leila, closing the lid of the box, and remarking that he would like to find things as he left them; and had Aunt Ann noticed that there were moths about the bear skins. Now a moth has the power of singularly exciting some women — the diversion proved effectual.

And still as the week went by Ann seemed to be gaining in strength.

At lunch, a telegram from Charles Grey, Baltimore, said, "Penhallow here, doing well. Will return on the 14th, by afternoon train, with Rivers and servant."

"Read that, dear — I want you, Leila, to ride to the mills and tell Dr. McGregor that I will send the carriage for him in time for him to meet your uncle at the station. I had better not meet him — and there will be Mark Rivers and Josiah and — but you will see to all that."

"Certainly, aunt."

"It will be the day after to-morrow. Be sure that the doctor makes no mistake. There are two trains — he will be on the four o'clock express." This was in the manner of her Aunt Ann of former days. "Shall I write it down?"

Leila cried, "No," and fled, laughing.

The next day to Leila's surprise and pleasure her aunt came down to breakfast and quietly took her place as mistress of the tea-urn. The talent of common sense as applicable to the lesser social commerce of life was one of Leila's gifts, and she made no comment on her aunt's amazing resumption of her old habits. Ann herself felt some inclination to explain her rapid recovery of health, and said as she took the long-vacant seat at the breakfast table, "I think, Leila, the doctor's last tonic has been of use to me — I feel quite like myself." Having thus anticipated her too sharp-eyed niece's congratulations, Leila's expression of pleasure came in accordant place. Whereupon they both smiled across the table, having that delicate appreciation of the needs of the situation which is rarely at the service of the blundering mind of man.

The moment of gentle hypocrisy passed, the mistress of Grey Pine took up her memoranda for the day, and said with some attempt at being just her usual self, "I shall walk to Westways after breakfast — Pole needs to be talked to. The meats have been of his worst lately." Then with a glance at the paper, "Your uncle's books must be dusted; I quite forgot it; I will set Susan to work this morning."

"But," said Leila, "he does hate that, Aunt Ann. The last time she succeeded in setting together 'Don Juan' and 'St. Thomas à Kempis.'"

Ann laughed, and said with some of her old sense of humour, "It might do them both good — dust them yourself."

"I will," said Leila, liking the task.

"And when you ride this afternoon, see Mrs. Lamb. The cook tells me that she hears of that scamp, her son, as in the army — a nice kind of soldier." A half-dozen other errands were mentioned, and they parted, Ann adding, "There is no mail to-day."

They met again at lunch. "It is too bad, Leila, Billy was given the letters and forgot them and went a-fishing. There was a letter for you from Mark Rivers about your uncle. Does he think me a child? I read it."

"You read it, Aunt!" exclaimed Leila astonished at this infraction of their household law.

"Of course I read it. I knew it must be about James." Leila made no reply, but did not like it.

"Here it is, my dear. I fear James is in a more serious state than I was led to believe by their first letters. There is also a letter from John to you." She did not ask to see it, and Leila took both missives and presently went away to the stables. Even John, as was plain, was forgotten in her aunt's anxiety in regard to her husband.

Her many errands over, Leila riding slowly through the lonely wood-roads read the letters:

"My Dear Leila," wrote Rivers, "you had better let your aunt know that the Colonel's wound must have so shocked the brain, though there is no fracture, as to have left him in a mental state which gives me the utmost anxiety. You will sadly realize my meaning when you see him. Be careful how you tell your aunt.

"Yours truly,
"MARK RIVERS."

Here indeed was trouble. Leila's eyes filled and tears fell on the paper. She rode on deep in thought, and at last securing the message of calamity in her belt opened John's letter.

"I write you, dear Leila, from my tent near Vicksburg, this 5th of July. The prisoners from Pemberton's army are passing as I write. Our men are giving them bread and tobacco, and there is no least sign of enmity or triumph. I am pretty well worn out, as the few engineers have been worked hard and the constant nearness of death in the trenches within five to one hundred feet of the Rebel lines was a situation to make a man think — not of course while in immediate danger, but afterwards. I had some narrow escapes — we all had. But, dear Leila, it has been a splendid thing to see how this man Grant, with the expressionless face, struck swiftly one army after another and returned to secure his prey.

"I cannot even now get a leave of absence, and I am beyond words anxious to hear about dear Uncle Jim. Just a line from him makes me think he was to be with General Meade and in that great battle we won. A telegram to the Engineers' Camp, Vicksburg, will relieve me.

"It is unlikely, if we go South, that I shall see you for many a day. All leaves are, I find, denied. War — intense war like this — seems to me to change men in wonderful ways. It makes some men bad or reckless or drunkards or hard and cruel; it makes others thoughtful, dutiful and religious. This is more often the case among the men than you may think it would be. Certainly it does age a fellow fast. I seem to have passed many years since I sat with you at West Point and you made me feel how young I was and how little I had seen of life. It was true, but now I have seen life at its worst and its best. I have had too the education of battle, the lessons read by thousands of deaths and all the many temptations of camp life. I believe, and I can say it to you, I am the better for it all, and think less and less of the man who was fool enough to do what with more humility he will surely do once more, if it please God that he come out of this terrible war alive.

"When you see me again, you will at least respect my years, for one lives fast here, and the months seem years and the family Bible a vain record, as I remember that the statement of births comes after the Apocrypha which leaves room for doubt."—

Leila smiled. "How like him," she murmured.

"I said months. There are (there were once last week) minutes when one felt an insolent contempt of death, although the bullets were singing by like our brave hornets. Is that courage? I used as a boy to wonder how I would feel in danger. Don't tell, but on going under fire I shiver, and then am at once in quiet possession of all my capacities, whatever they be worth. A man drops by my side — and I am surprised; then another — and I am sure I won't be hit. But I *was* three weeks ago in my leg! It made me furious, and I still limp a bit. It was only a nip — a spent bullet. I wanted to get at that anonymous rascal who did it.

"Do wire me, and write fully.

"Yours,
"JOHN.

"P.S. I wonder where Tom McGregor is, and Pole's boy and Joe Grace, and those Greys who went diverse ways. As you never talk of yourself when you write those brief letters on notepaper the size of a postage stamp, you might at least tell me all about these good people in Westways."

She telegraphed him, " Uncle Jim slightly wounded, is coming home. Will write. Leila Grey."

About four in the afternoon of this July 14th Ann Penhallow kissed her husband as he came up the porch steps. He was leaning heavily on Mark Rivers's arm. He said, " It is quite a long time, Ann. How long is it? " Then he shook off Rivers, saying, " I am quite well," and going by his wife went through the open door, moving like one dazed. He stood still a moment looking about him, turned back and speaking to his wife said, " I understand now. At first it seemed strange to me and as if I had never been here before. Ever feel that way, Ann? "

" Oh, often, James." No signal of her anguish showed on the gallantly carried face of the little woman.

" Quiet, is n't it? When was it I was hit? It was — was n't it in May? Rivers says it was July — I do not like contradiction." His appreciation of time and recognition of locality were alike disordered, as Rivers had observed with distress and a too constant desire to set him right. With better appreciation of his condition, Ann accepted his statement.

" Yes — yes, of course, dear — it is just so."

" I knew you would understand me. I should like to go to bed — I want Josiah — no one else."

" Yes, dear," and this above all else made clear to the unhappy little lady how far was the sturdy soldier who had left her from the broken man in undress uniform who clung to the rail, as he went slowly up the stairway with his servant. In the hall he had seen Leila, but gave her no word, not even his habitual smile of recognition.

Ann stared after them a moment, motioned Rivers away with uplifted hand, and hastening into the library sat down and wept like a child. She had been unprepared for the change in his appearance and ways. More closely observant, Leila saw that the lines of decisiveness were gone, the humorous circles about the mouth and eyes, as it were, flattened out, and that the whole face, with the lips a little languidly parted, had become expressionless. It was many days before she could see the altered visage without emotion, or talk of him to her aunt with any of the amazing hopefulness with which the older woman dwelt on her husband's intervals of resemblance to his former self.

He would not ride or enter the stables, but his life was otherwise a childlike resumption of his ordinary habits, except that when annoyed by Ann's too obvious anxiety or excess of carefulness, he became irritable at times and even violent in language. He so plainly preferred Leila's company in his short walks as to make the wife jealous and vexed that she was not wanted during every minute of his altered life. He read no books as of old, but would have Leila read to him the war news until he fell asleep, when she quietly slipped away.

Mark Rivers resumed his duties for a time, unwilling to abandon these dear friends for whom McGregor, puzzled and perplexed, had no word of consolation, except the assurance that his condition did not grow worse.

At times Penhallow was dimly aware of his state; at others he resented any effort to control him and was so angry when the doctor proposed a consultation that the idea was too easily given up, for always in this as in everything his wife agreed with him and indulged him as women indulge a sick child. The village grieved for the Colonel who rode no more through Westways with a gay word of greeting for all he met. The ironmills were busy. The great guns tested on the meadows now and then shook the panes in the western windows of Grey Pine. They no longer disturbed Ann Penhallow. The war went its thunderous way unheeded by her. Unendingly hopeful, the oppression of disaster seemed only to confirm and strengthen her finest qualities. Like the pine-tree winning vigour from its rock-clasped roots, she gathered such hardening strength of soul and body from his condition as the more happy years had never put at her command.

"No letters to-day, Miss Leila," said the post-mistress standing beside the younger woman's horse. "Just only them papers with their lists of killed and wounded."

"I must always be Leila, not Miss Leila," said the horsewoman.

"Well — well — I like that better. How's the Colonel?"

"Much the same — certainly no worse. It is wonderful how my aunt stands it."

"Don't you notice, Leila, how she has kind of softened? Me and Joe was talking of it yesterday. She always was good, but folks did use to say she was sort of hard and — positive. Now, she's kind of gentled — noticed that?"

"Yes, I have noticed it; but I must go. Give me the papers. You love a talk."

"There's no news of John?"

"None of late. He is with General Grant — but where we do not know."

"It's right pleasant to have Josiah back. Lord! but he's strong on war stories — ought to hear him. He was always good at stories."

"Yes, I suppose so. Good-bye."

James Penhallow sat on the back porch in the after luncheon hour to get with the freshness of October what sunshine the westering sun was sifting through the red and gold of the maples beyond the garden walls. He was in the undress uniform of the artillery, and still wore the trefoil of the Second Corps. An effort by Ann to remove his soiled army garb and substitute his lay dress caused an outbreak of anger which left him speechless and feeble, and her in an agony of regretful penitence. Josiah, wiser than she, ventured to tell her what had happened once before when his badge of the glorious Second Corps had been missing. "After all, what does it matter?" she said to herself, and made no effort to repair the ragged bullet tear South Mountain left in his jacket, and in which he had at his worst times such childlike pride as in another and well-known general had once amused him.

He was just now in one of his best conditions and was clearly enjoying the pipe he used but rarely. Ann at his feet on the porch-step read aloud to him with indifference to all but the man she now and then looked up to with the loving tenderness his brief betterment fed with illusory hope.

"What's that, Ann?" he exclaimed; "Grant at Chattanooga! That's John's ideal General. Didn't he write about him at — where was it? Oh! Belmont."

"Yes, after Belmont, James."

"When does Mark Rivers go back?"

"To-morrow. He is always so out of spirits here that I am really relieved when he returns to the Sanitary Commission." He made no reply, and she continued her reading.

"Isn't that Leila with Rivers, Ann?"

"Yes. He likes to walk with her."

"So would any man." A faint smile — very rare of late — showed in her pleased upward look at the face — the changed face — she loved.

The pair of whom they spoke were lost to view in the forest.

"And you are glad to go?" said Leila to Rivers.

"Yes, I am. I can hardly say glad, but now that your uncle is, so to speak, lost to me and your aunt absorbed in her one task and the duties she has taken up again, our pleasant Dante lessons are set aside, and what is there left of the old intellectual life which is gone — gone?"

"But," said Leila gaily, "you have the church and my humble society. Why, you are really learning to walk, as you did not until of late."

Making no reply to her personal remark, he was silent for a moment, and then said with slow articulation and to her surprise, for he rarely spoke of himself, " Nine years ago I came here, a man broken in mind and body. This life and these dear friends have made me as strong as I can ever hope to be. But the rest — the rest. I know what power God has given me to bring souls to him. I can influence men — the lowly and — well, others, as few can. I cannot live in cities — I dare not risk the failure in health; and yet, I want — I want a larger field. I found it when your aunt's liberality sent me to the army. There in my poor way I can serve my country — and that is much to me." He was silent.

" But," she said, " is there not work enough here? and the war cannot last much longer. Don't think you must ever leave us."

" I shall — I must. There are limitations I cannot talk of even — above all to you. Your aunt knows this — and your uncle did — long ago."

" What limitations? " she asked rashly.

" You are the last person, Leila Grey, to whom I could speak of them. I have said too much, but "— and he paused —" I am tired — I will leave you to finish your walk." The great beautiful eyes turned on him for a moment. " Oh, my God ! " he exclaimed, and reproaching his brief human weakness left her abruptly, walking slowly away through the drifting red and gold of leaves rocking in air as they sauntered to earth, and was at last lost to view in the woodland.

Leila stood still, puzzled and sorrowful, as she watched the tall stooping form. " How old he looks," she murmured. " What did he mean? I must ask Aunt Ann." But she never did, feeling that what he had said was something like a cautiously hinted confession. In the early morning he was gone again to the field of war.

CHAPTER XXVI

THROUGH the winter of 1863-4 at Grey Pine things remained unaltered, and McGregor concluded that there was no hope for happier change. Rare letters came from John Penhallow to his aunt, who sent no replies, and to Leila, who wrote impersonal letters, as did John. Once he wrote that his uncle might like to know, that after that pontoon business in the night at Chattanooga and General Farrar Smith's brilliant action, he, John Penhallow, was to be addressed as *Captain*. As the war went on, he was across the Rapidan with Grant in May.

At Grey Pine after breakfast the windows and both doors of the hall were open to let the western breezes enter. They lingered in the garden to stir the mothers of unborn flowers and swept through the hall, bearing as they passed some gentle intimation of the ending of a cold spring.

The mail had been given to the colonel, as he insisted it should be. With some appearance of interest he said, " From Mark, for you, Ann."

" None for me, Uncle? " asked Leila, as she went around the table. " Let me help you. How many there are." She captured her own share, and for a moment stood curious as she sorted the mail. " Army trash, Uncle! What a lot of paper is needed to carry on war! Here is one — I have seen him before — he is marked ' Respectfully referred.' "

The colonel released a smile, which stirred Ann like a pleasant memory, and fed one of the little hopes she was ever on the watch to find. " What is your letter, Ann? " he asked.

Looking up she replied, " It is only to acknowledge receipt of my draft. He is in Washington. I gather that he does not mean to come back until the war is over." " Over! " she

398

thought; "Lee is not Pemberton, as Grant will learn." It was of more moment to her that Penhallow was easier to interest, and ate as he used to do.

"Is your letter from John, Leila?" he said. "I don't like concealments."

"But, I did n't conceal anything!"

"Don't contradict me!"

"No, sir."

Ann's face grew watchful, fearing one of the outbreaks which left him weak and querulous.

"Well," said the colonel, "read us John's letter. There is as much fuss about it as if it were a love-letter."

There is no way as yet discovered to victoriously suppress a blush, but time — a little fraction of time — is helpful, and there are ways of hiding what cannot be conquered. The letter fell on the floor, and being recovered was opened and read with a certain something in the voice which caused Ann critically to use her eyes.

"DEAR LEILA: I am just now with the Second Corps, but where you will know in a week; now I must not say.—"

"What 's the date?" asked Penhallow.

"There is none."

"Look at the envelope."

"I tore it up, sir."

"Never throw away an envelope until you have read the letter." Ann looked pleased — that was James Penhallow, his old self. Leila read on.

"I am glad to be under canvas, and you know my faith in General Grant.

"Tell Aunt Ann I have had three servants in two weeks. These newly freed blacks are like mere children and quite use-

less, or else — well — one was brutal to my horse. I sometimes
wish Josiah was twins and I had one of him.—"

"What's that?" asked Penhallow. "Twins — I don't understand."

"He wishes he had a servant like Josiah, Uncle."

"Well, let him go to John," said the Colonel, with something
of his old positive manner.

"But you would miss him, James."

"I will not," he returned, and then —" What else is there?"

"Oh — nothing — except that he will write again soon, and
that he met Mr. Rivers in Washington. That is all — a very
unsatisfactory letter."

For a day or two the colonel said no more of Josiah, and
then asked if he had gone, and was so obviously annoyed that
Ann gave way as usual and talked of her husband's wish to
Josiah. The old life of Westways and Grey Pine was over, and
Josiah was allowed by Ann to do so little for Penhallow that
the black was not ill-pleased to leave home again for the army
life and to be with the man whom as a lad he had trusted and
who had helped him in a day of peril.

No one thought of any need for a pass. He was amply supplied with money and bade them good-bye. He put what he
required in a knapsack, and leaving Westways for the second
time and with a lighter heart, set off afoot to catch the train
at Westways Crossing. The old slave was thus put upon a way
which was to lead to renewed and unpleasant acquaintance
with one of the minor characters of my story.

Tired of unaccustomed idleness Josiah grinned as he went
across country thinking of the directions he had received from
Leila of how he was to find John Penhallow.

"You know he is captain of engineers, Josiah. Now how
are you going to find him? An army is as big as a great city,
and in motion too."

"Well, missy," said Josiah, "the way I'll find him is the way dog Cæsar finds you in the woods." He would hear no more and left her.

Josiah knew many people in Washington, black and white, and after some disappointments went with a lot of remounts for cavalry to join the army in the Wilderness, where he served variously with the army teams. On an afternoon late in May, 1864, he strode on, passing by the long lines of marching men who filled the roadways on their way to the crossing of the North Anna River. He had been chaffed, misdirected, laughed at or civilly treated, as he questioned men about the engineers. He took it all with good-humour. About three, he came near to a house on the wayside, where a halt had been ordered to give the men a brief rest. The soldiers dust-grey and thirsty scattered over the clearing or lay in the shadow of the scrub oaks. Some thronged about a well or a wayside spring, or draining their canteens caught a brief joy from the lighted pipe so dear to the soldier. Josiah looked about him, and knew the log-cabins some distance away from the better house to have been the slave-quarters. Beyond them was a better built log-house. Apparently all were deserted — men, cattle and horses, were gone. He lay down a little way from the road and listened to the talk of the men seated in front of him. He heard a private say, "A halt is as bad as a march, the dust is a foot deep, and what between flies and mosquitoes, they're as bad as the Rebs."

"Ah!" said an old corporal, "just you wait a bit. These are only a skirmish line. July and Chickahominy mosquitoes will get you when your baccy's out."

"It's out now."

Josiah was eager to question some one and was aware of the value of tobacco as a social solvent. He said, "I've got some baccy, corporal."

The men in front of him turned. "For sale — how much?"

"No," said Josiah. "My pouch is full. Help yourselves."

This liberal contribution was warmly appreciated, and the private, who was the son of a New York banker, interested in the black man, asked, "What are you doing in this big circus?" It was the opening for which Josiah waited.

"Looking for an engineer-captain."

The corporal said, "Well, like enough he 'll be at the bridge of the North Anna — but the engineers are here, there and anywhere. What is his name?"

"Thank you, sir. My master is Captain Penhallow."

"Well, good luck to you."

"Take another pipe load," returned Josiah, grateful for the unusual interest.

"Thank you," said the private, "with pleasure. Tobacco is as scarce as hen's teeth."

"That 's so. Who 's that officer on the big horse? He 's a rider whoever he is."

"That 's the ring-master of this show," laughed the private.

"Not General Grant!"

"Yes." Josiah considered him with interest.

There was of a sudden some disturbance about the larger of the more remote cabins; a soldier ran out followed by a screaming young woman. Her wild cries attracted attention to the man, who was at once caught and held while he vainly protested. The men about Josiah sat up or got on their feet. The young woman ran here and there among the groups of soldiers like one distracted. At last, near the larger house at the roadside she fell on her knees and rocked backwards and forwards sobbing. Josiah at a distance saw only that a soldier had been caught trying to escape notice as a young woman followed him out of the house. It was too well understood by the angry men who crowded around the captive.

The general said to his staff, "Wait here, gentlemen." He rode through the crowd of soldiers, saying, "Keep back, my men; keep away — all of you." Then he dismounted and walked to where the girl — she was hardly more — still knelt wailing and beating the air with uplifted hands. " Stand up, my good girl, and tell me what is wrong."

The voice was low and of a certain gentleness, rarely rising even in moments of peril. She stood up, " I can't — I can't — let me go — I want to die!"

The figure, still slight of build in those days, bent over her pitiful. " I am General Grant. Look up at me. There shall be justice done, but I must know."

She looked up a moment at the kind grave face, then with bent head and hands over her eyes she sobbed out what none but the general could hear. His voice grew even more distinctly soft as touching her shoulder he said, " Look at that man. Oh, bring him near — nearer. Now, be sure, is that the man? Look again! I must be certain."

With a quick motion she pushed his hand from her shoulder as she stood, and pointing to the brute held by two soldiers cried, " That 's him — oh, my God! Take him away — kill him. Le' me go. Don't you keep me." She looked about like some hopelessly trapped, wild-eyed animal.

" You may go, of course," said the low-voiced man. " I will set a guard over your house."

" Don't want no Yankee guard — le' me go — I 've got nothin' to guard — I want to die." She darted away and through the parting groups of men who were clear enough about what they knew had happened and what should be done.

The dark grey eyes of the General followed her flight for a pitying instant. Then he remounted, and said to the scared captive, " What have you got to say?"

" It 's all a lie."

The general's face grew stern. He turned and asked for an officer of the Provost Guard. A captain rode up and saluted. " I have no time to lose in trying this scoundrel. We can't take along the only witness." He hesitated a moment. "Let your men tie him to a tree near the road. Let two of the guard watch him until the rear has gone by. Put a paper on his breast — make his crime clear, clear." He said a word or two more to the officer, and then "put on it, ' *Left to the justice of General Lee.*' "

" Is that all, sir? " said the amazed officer.

" No — put below, ' *U. S. Grant.*' The girl will tell her story. When the cavalry pass, leave him. Now, gentlemen, the men have had a rest, let us ride on."

Josiah a hundred feet away heard, " Fall in — fall in." The tired soldiers rose reluctant and the long line tramped away. Josiah interested sat still and saw them go by under the dust-laden air. The girl had gone past her home and into the woods. The guards curiously watched by the marching men passed near Josiah with their prisoner and busied themselves with looking among the hazel, scrub oak and sassafras for a large enough tree near to the road. As they went by, he saw the man.

" My God! " he exclaimed, " it 's Peter Lamb." He moved away and lay down well hidden in the brush. It was a very simple mind which considered this meeting with the only being the black man hated. The unusual never appealed to him as it would have done to a more imaginative person. The coming thus on his enemy was only what he had angrily predicted when he had Peter in his power and had said to him that some day God would punish him. It had come true.

The men who had arrested Peter and were near enough to hear the brief sentence, understood it, and being eagerly questioned soon spread among the moving ranks the story of the crime and this unexampled punishment. It was plain to Josiah, but what was to follow he did not know, as he rose, lingered about, and following the Provost's party considered the wonderful fact of his fulfilled prediction. The coincidence of being himself present did not cause the surprise which what we call coincidences awaken in minds which crave explanations of the uncommon. It was just what was sure to happen somehow, some day, when God settled Josiah's personal account with a wicked man. He had, however, an urgent curiosity to see how it would end and a remainder of far-descended savagery in the wish to let his one enemy know that he was a witness of his punishment. Thinking thus, Josiah went through the wayside scrub to see how the guard would dispose of their prisoner.

The man who had sinned was presently tied to a tree facing the road. His hands were securely tied behind it, and his feet as rudely dealt with. He said no word as they pinned the label on his breast. Then the two guards sat down between Peter and the roadway. Men of the passing brigades asked them questions. They replied briefly and smoked with entire unconcern as to their prisoner, or speculated in regard to what the Rebs would say or do to him. The mosquitoes tormented him, and once he shuddered when one of the guards guessed that perhaps the girl would come back and see him tied up. The story of Grant's unusual punishment was told over and over to men as the regiments went by. Now and then soldiers left the ranks to read the sentence of what must mean death. Some as they read were as silent as the doomed wretch; others laughed or cursed him for dishonouring the army in which this one crime was almost unknown. A sergeant tore the corps mark from his coat, and still he said no word. The long-drawn array went on and on; the evening shadows lengthened; miles of wagon trains rumbled by; whips cracked over mules; the cavalry guard bringing up the rear was lost in the dust left by tramping thousands; the setting sun shone through it ruddy; and last came the squadron net of the Provost-marshal gathering in the stragglers. Tired men were helped by a grip on the stirrup leather. The lazy loiterers were urged forward with language unquotable, the mildest being "darned coffee-coolers." At last, all had gone.

Josiah rose from his hiding place and listened as the clank of steel and the sound of hurried horsemen died away. No other noises broke the twilight stillness. He walked back to the roadside, and stood before the pinioned and now lonely man. "You're caught at last, Peter Lamb."

"Oh, Lord!" cried the captive. "It's Josiah. For God's sake, let me loose."

"Reckon I won't," said Josiah.

"I'm in agony — my arms — I shall die — and I am innocent. I did not do anything. Won't you help me?"

"No — the Rebs will come and hang you."

The man's cunning awoke. He said the one thing, made the one plea which, as he spoke, troubled Josiah's decision. "Is the Squire alive?"

"Why should n't he be alive?" asked Josiah, surprised.

"Oh, I saw in a paper that he was wounded at Gettysburg. Now, Josiah, if he was here — if he was to know you left me to die."

Josiah was uncertain what he would have done. His simple-minded view of things was disturbed, and his tendency to be forgiving kindly assisted to give potency to the appeal. He said, "I won't set you free, but I'll do this much," and he tore the paper from Peter's breast, saying, "You'll get off with some lie when the Rebs come." Then he turned and walked away, tearing up the death warrant and hearing the wild pleas of the painfully bound man.

The night had come, but save for the faintly heard complaint of some far-distant dog, there was nothing to break the quiet of the deserted land which lay between the two armies. Having torn to pieces and carefully scattered the bits of paper, Josiah, who while doing one thing could not think of another, began to reflect on what he had done. He had been too long in servitude not to respect authority. If any one knew — but no one could know. He himself had said that what had come upon Lamb was a judgment — the act of one who had said, " I will repay." It troubled a mind whose machinery was of childlike incapacity to deal with problems involving the moral aspects of conduct. Perhaps this had been a chance to give Lamb an opportunity to repent by setting him free; but there had already been interference with the judgment of God. More personally material events relieved the black from responsibility. His quick ear caught the sound of troopers, the sharp notes of steel clinking; he had no mind to be picked up by the enemy's horse, and dismissing all other considerations he took to the woods and walked rapidly away. Late in the evening he crossed the North Anna with a train of wagons, as driver of an unruly mule team, one of which had rewarded his driver in kind for brutal use of the whip and perverted English. The man groaning in the wagon informed Josiah concerning mules and their ways. After a day or two he was pleased to get back on his legs, for when bullets were not flying the army life was full of interest. A man who could cook well, shave an officer or shoe a horse, never lacked the friends of an hour; and too, his unfailing good-humour was always helpful. An officer of the line would have been easy to find, but the engineers were continually in motion and hard to locate. He got no news of John Penhallow until the 29th of May, when he came on General Wilson's cavalry division left on the north side of the Pamunkey River to cover the crossing of the trains. These troopers were rather particular about straggling negroes, and Josiah sharply questioned told the simple truth as he moved toward the bridge, answering the questions of a young officer. A horse tied to a sapling at the roadside for reasons unknown kicked the passing cavalry man's horse. The officer moved on swearing a very original mixture of the over-ripe English of armies. Swearing was a highly cultivated accomplishment in the cavalry; no infantry profanity approached it in originality. The officer occupied with his uneasy horse dropped Josiah as he rode on. A small, dark-skinned negro, rather neatly dressed, spoke to Josiah in the dialect of the Southern slave, which I shall not try to put on paper. He spoke reflectively and as if from long consideration of the subject, entering at once into the intimacies of a relation with the man of his own colour.

" That horse is the meanest I ever saw — I know him."

" He 's near thoroughbred," said Josiah, " and been badly handled, I reckon. It 's no good cussin' horses or mules — a good horseman don't ever do it — horses know."

" Well, the officer that rides that horse now is about the only man can ride him. That horse pretty nearly killed one of my general's staff. He sold him mighty sudden."

" Who 's your General?" queries Josiah.

" Why, General Grant — I 'm his headquarter man — they call me Bill — everybody knows me."

He rose at once in Josiah's estimation. " Who owns that horse?" asked Josiah. " I 'd like well to handle his beast."

" He 's an engineer-officer, name of Penhallow. He 's down yonder somewhere about that pontoon bridge. I 'm left here to hunt up a headquarter wagon."

" Penhallow!" exclaimed Josiah, delighted. " Why, I 'm down here to be his servant."

" Well, let 's go to the bridge. You 'll get a chance to cross after the wagons get over. I 've just found mine." They moved to one side and sat down. " That 's Wilson's cavalry on guard. Worst dust I ever saw. Infantry dust 's bad, but cavalry dust don't ever settle. The Ninth Corps 's gone over. There come the wagons." With cracking of whip and imprecations the wagons went over the swaying pontoons. Bill left him, and Josiah waited to cross behind the wagons.

On the bridge midway, a young officer in the dark dress and black-striped pantaloons of the engineers moved beside the teams anxiously observing some loosened flooring. A wagon wheel gave way, and the wagon lurching over struck the officer, who fell into the muddy water of the Pamunkey. Always amused at an officer's mishap, cavalry men and drivers laughed. The young man struck out for the farther shore, and came on to a shelving slope of slimy mud, and was vainly struggling to get a footing when an officer ran down the bank and gave him a needed hand. Thus aided, Penhallow gained firm ground. With a look of disgust at his condition, as he faced the laughing troopers he said, with his somewhat formal way, " To whom am I indebted? "

" Roland Blake is my name. Isn't it Captain Penhallow of the engineers? "

" Yes, well disguised with Rebel mud. What a mess! But, by George! not worse than you when I first saw you."

" Where was it? " asked Blake.

" I can give a good guess. You were quite as lovely as Mr. Penhallow." It was a third officer who spoke. " By the bye," he added, " as Blake doesn't present me, I am Philip Francis."

" I can't even offer to shake hands," returned Penhallow, laughing, as he scraped the flakes of mud from his face. " I saw you both at the Bloody Angle. I think I could describe you."

" Don't," said Francis.

" Some people are modest," said Blake. " I think you will soon dry to dust in this sun. I have offered myself that consolation before. It's the only certainty in this land of the unexpected."

" The wagons are over; here comes the guard," said Francis. " It's our beastly business now. Call up the men, Roland."

" Provost duty, I suppose," said Penhallow. " I prefer my mud."

" Yes," growled Francis, " human scavengers — army police. I'm out of it this week, thank Heaven."

The last wagon came creaking over the bridge, the long line of cavalry trotted after them, the Provost Guard mounted to fall in at the rear and gather in the stragglers.

"Sorry I can't give you a mount," said Blake, as he turned to recross the bridge.

"Thank you, I have a horse on the other side." As he spoke a breeze stirred the dead atmosphere and shook down from the trees their gathered load of dust.

Francis said, "It's half of Virginia!"

Blake murmured, "Dust to dust — a queer reminder."

"Oh, shut up!" cried Francis.

The young engineer laughed and said to himself, "If Aunt Ann could see me. It's like being tarred and feathered. See you soon again, I hope, Mr. Blake. I am deep in your debt." They passed out of sight. No one remained but the bridge-guard.

The engineer sat down and devoted his entire energies to the difficult task of pulling off boots full of mud and water. Meanwhile as the provost-officers rode back over the pontoons Francis said, "I remember that man, Penhallow, at the Bloody Angle. He was the only man I saw who wasn't fight-crazy, he insisted on my going to the rear. You know I was bleeding like a stuck pig. It was between the two attacks. I said, 'Oh, go to H——!' He said, 'There is no need to go far.' I am sure he did not remember me. A rather cool hand — West Point, of course."

"What struck me," said Blake, "was that he did not swear."

"Then," said Francis, "he is the only man in the army who would have failed to damn those grinning troopers."

"Except Grant," said Blake.

"So they say.— It's hard to believe, but I suppose the Staff knows. Wonder if Lee swears. Two army commanders who don't swear? It's incredible!"

As Penhallow, left alone, tugged at a reluctant boot, he heard, " Good Lord! Master John, that's my business."

He looked up to seize Josiah by the hand, exclaiming, " How did you get here? — I am glad to see you. Pull off this boot. How are they all? "

" The Colonel he sent me."

" Indeed! How is he? I 've not heard for a month."

" He 's bad, Master John, bad — kind of forgets things — and swears."

" That's strange for him."

" The doctors they can't seem to make it out. He has n't put a leg over a horse, not since he was wounded." Evidently this was for Josiah the most serious evidence of change from former health.

" How is Aunt Ann? "

Tugging at the boots Josiah answered, " She 's just a wonder — and Miss Leila, she 's just as pretty as a pansy."

Penhallow smiled; it left a large choice to the imagination. " Pansy — pansy — why is she like a pansy, Josiah? "

" Well, Master John, it 's because she 's so many kinds of pretty. You see I used to raise pansies. That boot 's a tough one."

" Have you any letters for me? "

" No, sir. They said I was n't as sure as the army-post. Got a note from Dr. McGregor in my sack. Had n't I better get your horse over the bridge — I liked his looks, and I asked a man named Bill who owned that horse. He said you did, and that 's how I found you. He said that horse was a bad one. He said he was called ' Hoodoo.' That's unlucky! "

" Yes, he 's mine, Josiah. You would like to change his name? "

" Yes, sir, I would. This boot 's the worst! "

Penhallow laughed. " That horse, Josiah, has every virtue a

horse ought to have and every vice he ought not to have. He 'll be as good as Aunt Ann one day, and as mean and bad as Peter Lamb the next day. Halloa there, guard! let my man cross over."

Hoodoo came quietly, and as Penhallow walked his horse, Josiah related the village news, and then more and more plainly the captain gathered some clear idea of his uncle's condition and of the influence the younger woman was exerting on a household over which hung the feeling of inexorable doom. As he read McGregor's letter he knew too well that were he with them he could be of no practical use.

The next few days John Penhallow was kept busy, and on June 2nd having to report with some sketch-maps he found the headquarters at Bethesda Church. The pews had been taken out and set under trees. The staff was scattered about at ease. General Grant, to John's amusement, was petting a stray kitten with one hand and writing despatches with the other. At last he began to talk with members of the Christian Commission about their work. Among them John was aware of Mark Rivers. A few minutes later he had his chance and took the clergyman away to the tents of the engineers for a long and disheartening talk of home. They met no more for many days, and soon he was too busy to think of asking the leave of absence he so much desired.

CHAPTER XXVII

THE effort to crush Lee's army by a frontal attack led to the disastrous defeat of Cold Harbor, and Grant who was never personally routed resolved to throw his army south of the James River. It involved a concealed night march, while his lines were in many places but thirty to one hundred feet from the watchful Confederates. The utmost secrecy was used in regard to the bold movement intended, but preparations for it demanded frequent reconnaissances and map-sketching on the part of the engineers. A night of map-making after a long day in the saddle left John Penhallow on June 6th a weary man lying on his camp-bed too tired to sleep. He heard Blake ask, "Are you at home, Penhallow?" Few men would have been as welcome as the serious-minded New England captain who had met Penhallow from time to time since the engineer's mud-bath in the Pamunkey River.

"Glad to get you by yourself," said Blake. "You look used up. Do keep quiet!"

"I will, but sit down and take a pipe. Coffee, Josiah!" he called out. "I am quite too popular by reason of Josiah's amazing ability to forage. If the Headquarters are within reach, he and Bill — that's the general's man — hunt together. The results are surprising! But I learned long ago from my uncle, Colonel Penhallow, that in the army it is well to ask no unnecessary questions. My man is very intelligent, and as I keep him in tobacco and greenbacks, I sometimes fancy that Headquarters does not always get the best out of the raids of these two contrabands."

"I have profited by it, Penhallow. I have personal memories of that young roast pig, I think your man called it a shoat. Your corps must have caught it hard these last days. I suppose we are in for something unusual. You are the only man I know who does n't grumble. Francis says it 's as natural to the beast called an army as barking is to a dog."

"Of course, the habit is stupid, Blake. I mean the constant growl about the unavoidable discomforts of war; but this last week has got me near the growling point. I have had two ague chills and quinine enough to ring chimes in my head. I have n't had a decent wash for a week, and really war is a disgustingly dirty business. You don't realize that in history, in fiction, or in pictures. It 's filthy! Oh, you may laugh!"

"Who could help laughing?"

"I can to-day. To-morrow I shall grin at it all, but just now I am half dead. What with laying corduroys and bridging creeks, to be burnt up next day, and Chickahominy flies — oh, Lord! If there is nothing else on hand in the way of copies of maps, some general like Barnard has an insane curiosity to reconnoitre. Then the Rebs wake up — and amuse themselves."

Blake laughed. "You are getting pretty near to that growl."

"Am I? I have more than impossible demands to bother me. What with some despondent letters — I told you about my uncle's wound and the results, I should have a fierce attack of home-sickness if I had leisure to think at all."

Blake had found in Penhallow much that he liked and qualities which were responsive to his own high ideal of the man and the soldier. He looked him over as the young engineer lay on his camp-bed. "Get anything but home-sick, Penhallow! I get faint fits of it. The quinine of 'Get up, captain, and put out those pickets' dismisses it, or bullets. Lord, but we have had them in over-doses of late. Francis has been hit twice but not seriously. He says that Lee is an irregular practitioner. It is strange that some men are hit in every skirmish; it would bleed the courage out of me."

"Would it? I have had two flesh wounds. They made me furiously angry. You were speaking of Lee — my uncle greatly admired him. I should like to know more about him. I had a little chance when we were trying to arrange a truce to care for the wounded. You remember it failed, but I had a few minute's talk with a Rebel captain. He liked it when I told him how much we admired his general. That led him to talk, and among other things he told me that Lee had no sense of humour and I gathered was a man rather difficult of approach."

"He might apply to Grant for the rest of his qualities," said Blake. "He would get it; but what made you ask about sense of the humorous? I have too little, Francis too much."

"Oh," laughed Penhallow, "from saint to sinner it is a good medicine — even for home-sickness."

"And the desperate malady of love," returned Blake. "I shall not venture to diagnose your need. How is that?"

"I? — nonsense," laughed the engineer. "But seriously, Blake, about home-sickness; one of my best men has it badly — not the mild malady you and I may have."

"You are quite right. It accounts for some desertions — not to the enemy, of course. I talked lately of this condition to a Dr. McGregor —"

"McGregor!" returned Penhallow, sitting up. "Where is he? I'd like to see him — an old comrade."

"He is with our brigade."

"Tell him to look me up. The engineers are easily found just now. He was an old schoolmate."

"I'll tell him. By the way, Penhallow, when asking for my mail to-day, I persuaded the post-master to give me your letters. Don't mind me — you will want to read them — quite a batch of them."

"Oh, they can wait. Don't go. Ah! here's Josiah with coffee."

"How it does set a fellow up, Penhallow. Another cup,

please. I had to wait a long time for our letters and yours. Really that place was more tragic than a battlefield."

"Why so? I send Josiah for my mail."

"Oh, there were three cold-blooded men-machines returning letters. I watched them marking the letters —'not found'— 'missing'— and so on."

"Killed, I suppose — or prisoners."

"Yes, awful, indeed — most sorrowful! Imagine it! Others were forwarding letters — heaps of them — from men who may be dead. You know how apt men are to write letters before a battle."

"I wait till it is over," said Penhallow.

"That post-office gave me a fit of craving for home and peace."

"Home-sickness! What, you, Blake!"

"Oh, that worst kind; home-sickness for a home when you have no home. I wonder if in that other world we shall be home-sick for this."

"That depends. Ah! here comes a reminder that we are in this world just now — and just as we have begun one of our real talks."

An orderly appeared with a note. Penhallow read it. He was on his feet at once. "Saddle Hoodoo, Josiah. I must go. Come soon again, Blake. We have had a good talk — or a bit of one."

At four in the morning of June 14th, when John Penhallow with a group of older engineers looked across the twenty-one hundred feet of the James River they were to bridge, he realized the courage and capacity of the soldier who had so completely deceived his wary antagonist. Before eleven that night a hundred pontoons stayed by barges bridged the wide stream from shore to shore. Already the Second Corps under Hancock had been hastily ferried over the river. The work on the bridge had been hard, and the young Captain had had neither

food nor rest. Late at night, the work being over, he recrossed
the bridge, and after a hasty meal lay down on the bluff above
the James with others of his Corps and slept the uneasy sleep
of an overtired man. At dawn he was awakened by the multi-
ple noises of an army moving on the low-lying meadows
below the bluff. Refreshed and free from any demand on his
time, he breakfasted at ease, and lighting his pipe was
at once deeply interested in what he saw. As he looked about
him, he was aware of General Grant standing alone on the
higher ground. He saw the general throw away his cigar and
with hands clasped behind him remain watching in rapt
silence the scene below him. " I wonder," thought Penhallow,
" of what he is thinking." The face was grave, the man motionless. The engineer turned to look at the matchless spectacle
below him. The sound of bands rose in gay music from the
approaches to the river, where vast masses of infantry lay waiting their turn to cross. The guns of batteries gleamed in the
sun, endless wagon-trains and ambulances moved or were at rest.
Here and there the wind of morning fluttered the flags and
guidons with flashes of colour. The hum of a great army, the
multitudinous murmurs of men talking, the crack of whips,
the sharp rattle of wagons and of moving artillery, made a
strange orchestra. Over all rose the warning shrieks of the
gun-boat signals. Far or near on the fertile meadows the
ripened corn and grain showed in green squares between the
masses of men and stirred in the morning breeze or lay trampled
in ruin by the rude feet of war. It was an hour and a scene to
excite the dullest mind, and Penhallow intensely interested
sat fascinated by a spectacle at once splendid and fateful. The
snake-like procession of infantry wagons and batteries moved
across the bridge and was lost to view in the forest. Penhallow
turned again to look at his general, who remained statuesque
and motionless. Then, suddenly the master of this might of
men and guns looked up, listened to Warren's artillery far

beyond the river, and with the same expressionless face called for his horse and rode away followed by his staff.

The battle-summer of 1864 went on with the wearisome siege of Petersburg and the frequent efforts to cut the railways which enabled the Confederates to draw supplies from states which as yet had hardly felt the stress of war.

Late in the year the army became a city of huts, and there was the unexampled spectacle of this great host voting quietly in the election which gave to Lincoln another evidence of the trust reposed in him. The engineers had little to do in connection with the larger movements of the army, and save for the siege work were at times idle critics of their superiors. The closing month of 1864 brought weather which made the wooden huts, usually shared by two officers, more comfortable than tents. The construction of these long streets of sheltering quarters brought out much ingenuity, and Penhallow profited by Josiah's clever devices and watchful care. As the army was in winter-quarters, there was time enough for pleasant visiting, and for the engineers more than enough of danger in the trenches or when called on to accompany some general officer as an aide during Grant's obstinate efforts to cut the railways on which Lee relied. Francis, not gravely wounded, was at home repairing damages; but now, with snow on the ground and ease of intercourse, Blake was a frequent visitor in the engineer quarters. When Rivers also turned up, the two young men found the talk unrivalled, for never had the tall clergyman seemed more attractive or as happy.

Of an afternoon late in November Penhallow was toasting himself by the small fire-place and deep in thought. He had had a long day in the intrenchments and one moment of that feeling of imminent nearness to death which affects men in various ways. A shell neatly dropped in a trench within a few feet of where he stood, rolled over, spitting red flashes. The men cried, " Down, down, sir! " and fell flat. Something

like the fascination a snake exercises held him motionless; he
never was able to explain his folly. The fuse went out as he
watched it — the shell was a dead thing and harmless. The
men as they rose eyed him curiously.

"A near thing," he said, and with unusual care moved along
a traverse, his duty over for the day. He took with him a
feeling of mental confusion and of annoyed wonder.

He found Josiah picking a chicken as he sat whistling in
front of the tent. "There's been a fight, sir, about three
o'clock, on our left. Bill says we beat."

"Indeed!" It was too common news to interest him. He
felt some singular completeness of exhaustion, and was troubled
because of there being no explanation which satisfied him.
Asking for whisky to Josiah's surprise, he took it and lay down,
as the servant said, "There's letters, sir, on the table."

"Very well. Close the tent and say I'm not well; I won't
see any one."

"Yes, sir. Nothing serious?"

"No." He fell asleep as if drugged.

Outside Josiah picked his lean chicken and whistled with such
peculiar sweetness as is possible only to the black man. Everything interested him. Now and then he listened to the varied
notes of the missiles far away and attracting little attention
unless men were so near that the war-cries of shot and
shell became of material moment. The day was cold, and an
early November snow lay on the ground and covered the long
rows of cabins. Far to the rear a band was practising. Josiah
listened, and with a negative head-shake of disapproving criticism returned to the feather picking and sang as he picked:

> I wish I was in Dixie land,
> In Dixie land, in Dixie land.

He held up the plucked fowl and said, "Must have been on
short rations."

The early evening was quiet. Now and then a cloaked horseman went by noiseless on the snow. Josiah looked up, laid down the chicken, and listened to the irregular tramp of a body of men. Then, as the head of a long column came near and passed before him between the rows of huts, he stood up to watch them. "Prisoners," he said. Many were battle-grimed and in tatters, without caps and ill-shod. Here and there among them a captured officer marched on looking straight ahead. The larger part were dejected and plodded on in silence, with heads down, while others stared about them curious and from the cabins near by a few officers came out and many soldiers gathered. As usual there were no comments, no sign of triumph and only the silence of respect.

Josiah asked a guard where they came from. "Oh, Hancock's fight at Hatcher's Run — got about nine hundred."

The crowd of observers increased in number as the end of the line drew near. Josiah lost interest and sat down. "Got to singe that chicken," he murmured, with the habit of open speech of the man who had lived long alone. Suddenly he let the bird drop and exclaimed under his breath, "Jehoshaphat!" — his only substitute for an oath —"it's him!" Among the last of the line of captured men he saw one with head bent down looking neither to the right nor the left — it was Peter Lamb! At this moment two soldiers ran forward and shouted out something to the officer bringing up the rear. He cried, "Halt! take out that man." There was a little confusion, and Peter was roughly haled out of the mass. The officer called a sergeant. "Guard this fellow well," and he bade the men who had detected Lamb go with the guard.

Soldiers crowded in on them. "What's the matter — who is he?" they asked.

"Back, there!" cried the Lieutenant.

"A deserter," said some one. "Damn him."

Lamb was silent while between the two guards he was taken

to the rear. Josiah forgot his chicken and followed them at a distance. He saw Lamb handcuffed and vainly protesting as he was thrust into the prison-hut of the provostry.

Josiah asked one of the men who had brought about the arrest, "Who is that man?"

"Oh, he was a good while ago in my regiment — in our company too, the 71st Pennsylvania — a drunken beast — name of Stacy — Joe Stacy. We missed him when we were near the North Anna — at roll-call."

"What will they do with him?"

"Shoot him, I hope. His hands were powder blacked. He was caught on the skirmish line."

"Thank you." Josiah walked away deep in thought. He soon settled to the conclusion that the Rebs had found Peter and that perhaps he had had no choice of what he would do and had had to enlist. What explanatory lie Peter had told he could not guess.

Josiah went slowly back to the tent. His chicken was gone. He laid this loss on Peter, saying, "He always did bring me bad luck." Penhallow was still asleep. Ought he to tell him of Peter Lamb. He decided not to do so, or at least to wait. Inborn kindliness acted as it had done before, and conscious of his own helplessness, he was at a loss. Near to dusk he lighted a pipe and sat down outside of Penhallow's hut. Servants of engineer officers spoke as they passed, or chaffed him. His readiness for a verbal duel was wanting and he replied curtly. He was trying to make out to his own satisfaction whether he could or ought to do anything but hold his tongue and let this man die and so disappear. He knew that he himself could do nothing, nor did he believe anything could be done to help the man. He felt, however, that because he hated Peter, he was bound by his simply held creed to want to do something. He did not want to do anything, but then in confusing urgency there was the old mother, the colonel's indulgent care of this drunken animal, and at last some personal realization of the loneliness of this man so near to death. Then he remembered that Mark Rivers was within reach. To get this clergyman to see Peter would relieve him of the singular feeling of responsibility he could not altogether set aside. He was the only person who could identify Lamb. That, at least, he did not mean to do. He would find Mr. Rivers and leave to him to act as he thought best. He heard Penhallow calling, and went in to find him reading his letters. After providing for his wants, he set out to find the clergyman. His pass carried him wherever he desired to go, and after ten at night he found Mark Rivers with the Christian Commission.

"What is it?" asked Rivers. "Is John ill?"

"No, sir," and he told in a few sentences the miserable story, to the clergyman's amazement.

"I will go with you," he said. "I must get leave to see him, but you had better not speak of Peter to any one."

Josiah was already somewhat indisposed to tell to others the story of the North Anna incident, and walked on in silence over the snow until at the provost-marshal's quarters Rivers dismissed him.

In a brief talk with the provost-marshal, Rivers learned that there had been a hastily summoned court-martial, and in the presence of very clear evidence a verdict approved by General Grant. The man would be shot at seven the next morning. "A hopeless case, Mr. Rivers," said the Provost, "any appeal for reprieve will be useless — utterly useless — there will be no time given for appeal to Mr. Lincoln. We have had too much of this lately."

Rivers said nothing of his acquaintance with the condemned man. He too had reached the conviction, now made more definite, that needless pain for the old mother could be avoided by letting Peter die with the name he had assumed.

It was after twelve at night when the provost's pass admitted him to a small wooden prison. One candle dimly lighted the hut, where a manacled man crouched by a failing fire. The soldier on guard passed out as the clergyman entered. When the door closed behind him, Rivers said, "Peter."

"My God! Mr. Rivers. They say I 'll be shot. You won't let them shoot me — they can't do it — I don't want to die."

"I came here because Josiah recognized you and brought me."

"He must have told on me."

"Told what? He did not tell anything. Now listen to me. You are certain to be shot at seven to-morrow morning. I have asked for delay — none will be given. I come only to entreat you to make your peace with God — to tell you that you have but these few hours in which to repent. Let me pray with you — for you. There is nothing else I can do for you; I have tried and failed. Indeed I tried most earnestly."

"You can help if you will! You were always against me. You can telegraph Colonel Penhallow. He will answer — he won't let them shoot me."

Rivers who stood over the crouched figure laid a hand on his shoulder. "If he were here he could do nothing. And even if I did telegraph him, he is in no condition to answer. He was wounded at Gettysburg and his mind is clouded. It would only trouble him and your mother, and not help you. Your mother would hear, and you should at least have the manliness to accept in silence what you have earned."

"But it 's my life — my life — I can't die." Rivers was silent. "You won't telegraph?"

"No. It is useless."

"But you might do something — you 're cruel. I am innocent. God let me be born of a drunken father — I had to drink too — I had to. The Squire would n't give me work — no one helped me. I enlisted in a New York regiment. I got drunk and ran away and enlisted in the 71st Pennsylvania. I stole chickens, and near to the North Anna I was cruelly punished. Then the Rebs caught me. I had to enlist. Oh, Lord! I am unfortunate. If I only could have a little whisky."

Mark Rivers for a moment barren of answer was sure that as usual Peter was lying and without any of his old cunning.

"Peter, this story does not help you. You are about to die, and no one — can help you — I have tried in vain — nothing can save you. Why at a time so solemn as this do you lie to me? Why did you desert? and for stealing chickens? nonsense!"

"Well, then, it was about a woman. Josiah knows — he saw it all. I did n't desert — I was tied to a tree — he could clear me. They left me tied. I had to enlist; I had to!"

"A woman!" Rivers understood. "If he were to tell, it would only make your case worse. Oh, Peter, let me pray for you."

"Oh, pray if you want to. What's the good? If you won't telegraph the Squire, get me whisky; and if you won't do that, go away. Talk about God and praying when I'm to be murdered just because my father drank! I don't want any praying — I don't believe in it — you just go away and get me some whisky. The Squire might have saved me — I wanted to quit from drink and he just told me to get out — and I did. I hate him and — you."

Rivers stood up. "May God help and pity you," he said, and so left him.

He slept none, and rising early, prayed fervently for this wrecked soul. As he walked at six in the morning to the prison hut, he thought over the man who long ago had so defeated him. He had seemed to him more feeble in mind and less cunning in his statements than had been the case in former days. He concluded that he was in the state of a man used to drinking whisky and for a time deprived of it. When he met him moving under guard from the prison, he felt sure that his conclusion had been correct.

As Rivers came up, the officer in charge said, " If, sir, as a clergyman you desire to walk beside this man, there is no objection."

" Oh, let him come," said Peter, with a defiant air. Some one pitiful had indulged the fated man with the liquor he craved.

Rivers took his place beside Peter as the guards at his side fell back. Soldiers off duty, many blacks and other camp-followers, gathered in silence as the little procession moved over the snow, noiseless except for the tramp of many feet and the rumble of the cart in which was an empty coffin.

" Can I do anything for you? " said Rivers, turning toward the flushed face at his side.

" No — you can't." The man smelled horribly of whisky; the charitable aid must have been ample.

" Is there any message you want me to carry? "

" Message — who would I send messages to? " In fact, Rivers did not know. He was appalled at a man going half drunk to death. He moved on, for a little while at the end of his resources.

" Even yet," he whispered, " there is time to repent and ask God to pardon a wasted life." Peter made no reply and then they were in the open space on one side of a hollow square. On three sides the regiment stood intent as the group came near. " Even yet," murmured Rivers.

Of a sudden Peter's face became white. He said, " I want to tell you one thing — I want you to tell him. I shot the Squire at Gettysburg — I wish I had killed him — I thought I had. There! — I always did get even."

" Stand back, sir, please," said a captain. Rivers was dumb with the horror of it and stepped aside. The last words he would have said choked him in the attempt to speak.

Six soldiers took their places before the man who stood with his hands tied behind his back, his face white, the muscles twitching, while a bandage was tied over his eyes.

"He wants to speak to you, sir," said the captain.

Rivers stepped to his side. "I did not tell my name. Tell my mother I was shot — not how — not why."

Rivers fell back. The captain let fall a handkerchief. Six rifles rang out, and Peter Lamb had gone to his account.

The regiment marched away. The music of the band rang clear through the frosty air. The captain said, "Where is the surgeon?" Tom McGregor appeared, and as he had to certify to the death bent down over the quivering body.

"My God! Mr. Rivers," he said in a low voice, looking up, "it is Peter Lamb."

"Hush, Tom," whispered Rivers, "no one knows him except Josiah." They walked away together while Rivers told of Josiah's recognition of Lamb. "Keep silent about his name, Tom," and then went on to speak of the man's revengeful story about the Colonel, to Tom's horror. "I am sorry you told me," said the young surgeon.

"Yes, I was unwise — but —"

"Oh, let us drop it, Mr. Rivers. How is John? I have been three times to see him and he twice to see me, but always he was at the front, and as for me we have six thousand beds and too few surgeons, so that I could not often get away. Does he know of this man's fate?"

"No — and he had better not."

"I agree with you. Let us bury his name with him. So he shot our dear Colonel — how strange, how horrible!"

"He believed that he did shoot him, and as the ball came from the lines of the 71st when the fight was practically at an end, it may be true. He certainly meant to kill him."

"What an entirely, hopelessly complete scoundrel!" said McGregor.

"Except," said Rivers, "that he did not want his mother to know how he died."

"Human wickedness is very incomplete," said the surgeon. "I wonder whether the devil is as perfectly wicked as we are taught to believe. You think this fellow, my dear old schoolmaster, was not utterly bad. Now about wanting his mother not to know — I for my part —"

"Don't, Tom. Leave him this rag of charity to cover a multitude of sins. Now, I must leave you. See John soon — he is wasted by unending and dangerous work — with malaria too, and what not; see him soon. He is a splendid replica of the Colonel with a far better mind. I wish he were at home."

"And I that another fellow were at home. Good-bye."

McGregor called at John's tent, but learned that at six he had gone on duty to the trenches.

CHAPTER XXVIII

L ATE on Christmas morning of this year 1864, Penhallow with no duty on his hands saw with satisfaction the peace-making efforts of the winter weather. A thin drizzle of cold rain froze as it fell on the snow; the engineers' lines were quiet. There was no infantry drill and the raw recruits had rest from the never satisfied sergeants, while unmanageable accumulations of gifts from distant homes were being distributed to well-pleased men. Penhallow, lazily at ease, planned to spend Christmas day with Tom McGregor or Roland Blake. The orders of a too energetic Colonel of his own Corps summarily disposed of his anticipated leisure. The tired and disgusted Captain dismounted at evening, and limping gave his horse to Josiah.

"What you done to Hoodoo, Master John? He's lame — and you too."

Without answering John Penhallow turned to greet Tom McGregor. "Happy Christmas, Tom."

"You don't look very happy, John, nor that poor beast of yours. But I am glad to have caught you at last." The far-away thunder of the siege mortars was heard as he spoke. "Nice Christmas carol that! Have you been to-day in the graveyards you call trenches?"

"No, I was not on duty. I meant to ride over to your hospital to have a home-talk and exchange grumbles, but just as I mounted Colonel Swift stopped with a smartly dressed aide-de-camp. I saluted. He said, 'I was looking for an engineer off duty. Have the kindness to ride with me.'"

"By George! Tom, he was so polite that I felt sure we were

on some unpleasant errand. I was as civil, and said, ' With pleasure.' A nice Christmas celebration! Well, I have been in the saddle all day. It rained and froze to sleet on the snow, and the horses slipped and slid most unpleasantly. About noon we passed our pickets. I was half frozen. When we got a bit further, the old colonel pulled up on a hillside and began to ask me questions, how far was that bridge, and could I see their pickets, and where did that cross-road go to. The aide was apparently ornamental and did not do anything but guess. I answered with sublime confidence, as my mind got thawed a little and the colonel made notes."

" I know," laughed Tom. " Must never admit in the army that you don't know. You can always write ' respectfully referred ' on a document. When General Grant visits our hospital and asks questions ten to the minute, I fire back replies after quick consultation with my imagination. It works. He assured the surgeon-in-charge that I was a remarkably well-informed officer. So was he!' "

" Come in," said Penhallow. " I am cold and cross. I expect a brevet at least — nothing less; but if Comstock or Duane reads the colonel's notes, I may get something else."

" Have you had a fall, John? You are pretty dirty, and that horse with the queer name is dead lame. How did you come to grief? "

" I had an adventure."

" Really! What was it? "

" Tell you another time — it was a queer one. Here 's Mr. Rivers." He was followed by a contraband black with a basket.

" Happy Christmas, boys. I bring you a Christmas turkey and a plum-pudding from your aunt, John."

He was made heartily welcome and was in unusually good spirits, as Josiah took possession of these unexpected rations and John got into dry clothes.

They fell to familiar talk of Westways. "I fear," said Rivers, "that the colonel is worse. I am always sure of that when Mrs. Penhallow writes of him as cheerful."

"My father," said Tom, "tells me he has days of excessive unnatural gaiety, and then is irritable and cannot remember even the events of yesterday."

"Can you account for it, Tom?" asked John.

"No, but he ought to take dad's advice and see Professor Askew. It makes him furious. Oh! if we were all at home again, Mr. Rivers — and out of this row. You are limping, John — what's wrong? Let me see that leg."

"No, you don't," cried John merrily. "You promised to get even with me after our famous battle — I don't trust you. I bruised my knee — that's all."

"Well, I can wait."

They talked of home, of the village and its people, and at their meal of the way they proposed to conduct the spring campaign. Many bloodless battles were thus fought over mess-tables and around camp-fires.

"For my part," said John, "I want to get done with this mole business and do anything in the open — Oh, here comes Blake! You know our clergyman from home, the Rev. Mr. Rivers? No! Well, then I make you the Christmas gift of a pleasant acquaintance. Sit down, there is some turkey left and plum-pudding."

"Glad to see you, McGregor," said Blake. "I know Mr. Rivers by sight — oh, and well, too — he was back of the line in that horrid mix-up at the Bloody Angle — he was with the stretcher-bearers."

"Where," said McGregor, "he had no business to be."

Rivers laughed as he rarely did. "It may seem strange to you all, but I am never so happy"— he came near to saying so little unhappy —" as when I am among the dying and the wounded, even if the firing is heavy."

Blake looked at the large-featured face and the eyes that, as old McGregor said, were so kindly and so like mysterious jewels as they seemed to radiate the light that came from within. His moment of critical doubt passed, and he felt the strange attractiveness which Rivers had for men and the influential trust he surely won.

" I prefer," remarked McGregor, " to operate when bullets are not flying."

" But you do not think of them then," returned Rivers, " I am sure you do not."

" No, I do not, but they seem to be too attentive at times. I lost a little finger-tip back of Round Top. We had thirteen surgeons killed or wounded that day. The Rebs left eighty surgeons with their wounded. We sent them home after we got up enough help from the cities."

" It was not done always," said Penhallow. " More 's the pity."

" We had Grant at the hospital yesterday," said the doctor. " He comes often."

" Did you notice his face? " queried Rivers.

" The face? Not particularly — why? "

" He has two deep lines between the eyes, and crossing them two lateral furrows on the forehead. In Sicily they call it the ' cross of misfortune.' "

" Then it has yet to come," said Blake.

" Late or early," said Rivers, " they assure you it will come. Some men find their calamities when young, some when they are old, which is better."

" Let us be thankful that we have no choice," said Blake.

" May God spare you now and always," said Rivers. The habitual melancholy he dreaded took possession of his face as he rose, adding, " Come, Tom, we must go."

" And I," said Blake.

" Happy Christmas to you all — and a happier New Year

than 1864." They left John to the letters Josiah placed on the table.

The night was now clear and the stars brilliant, as Penhallow saw Blake mount his horse and Rivers and McGregor walk away to find the hospital ambulance. "There at least is peace," said John, as he watched the Pleiades and the North Star, symbol of unfailing duty. "Well, it is as good as a sermon, and as it belongs there on eternal guard so do I belong here for my little day; but I trust the spring will bring us peace, for — oh, my God! — I want it — and Westways." He went in to his hut and stirred the fire into roaring companionship.

Meanwhile Rivers, walking with McGregor, said, "Did the figure of that doomed wretch haunt you as we talked to John?"

"It did indeed! I had never before been ordered to certify to a death like that, and I hated it even before I bent down and knew who it was."

"How far was he accountable, Tom?"

"Don't ask me riddles like that, Mr. Rivers. It is a subject I have often thought about. It turns up in many forms — most terribly in the cases of the sins of the fathers being loaded on the sons. How far is a man accountable who inherits a family tendency to insanity? Should he marry? If he falls in love, what ought he to do or not do? It is a pretty grim proposition, Mr. Rivers."

"He should not marry," replied the clergyman, and both moved on in silent thought.

"Oh, here is our ambulance," said Tom. They got in, Rivers reflecting how war, parent of good and evil, had made of this rough country-bred lad a dutiful, thoughtful man.

Presently McGregor said, "When we were talking of our unpleasant duties, I meant to tell you that one of them is to tattoo a D — for deserter — on the breast of some poor home-sick fellow. After that his head is shaved; then the men laugh as he is drummed out of the lines — and it's disgusting."

" I agree with you," said Rivers.

John lighted a fresh pipe and sat down by the fire to get some Christmas pleasure from the home letter in Leila's large and clear script. His aunt had ceased to write to him, and had left to her niece this task, insisting that it should be punctually fulfilled. This time the letter was brief.

" Of course, my dear John, you know that I am under orders to write to you once a week."—" Is that explanatory? " thought the reader.— The letter dealt with the town and mills, the sad condition of Colonel Penhallow, his aunt's messages and her advice to John in regard to health. The horses came in for the largest share of a page. And why did he not write more about himself? She did not suppose that even winter war con-sisted only in drawing maps and waiting for Grant to flank Lee out of Petersburg and Richmond. " War," wrote the young woman, " must be rather a dull business. Have you no adven-tures? Tom McGregor wrote his father that you had a thrill-ing experience in the trenches lately. The doctor spoke of it to Aunt Ann, who was surprised I had never mentioned it. Don't dry up into an old regular like the inspecting major of ordnance at the mills.

" Expectantly yours,
" LEILA GREY.

" A Happy Christmas, Jack."

" Oh, Great Scott! " laughed John. He read it again. Not a word of herself, nor any of her rides, or of the incessant read-ing she liked to discuss with him. Some dim suspicion of the why of this impersonal letter gently flattered the winged hopefulness of love. "Well, I think I shall punish you, Miss Grey, for sending me a Christmas letter like that." Oh, the dear old playmate, the tease, the eyes full of tenderness when the child's shaft of satire hurt! He laughed gaily as he went through the historically famous test of courage in snuffing the flaring candle wicks with his fingers. The little cabin was warm, the night silent, not a sound came from the lines a mile away to disturb the peaceful memories of home within the thirty thousand pickets needed to guard our far-spread army. Men on both sides spoke this Christmas night, for they were often near and exchanged greetings as they called out, "Halloa, Johnny Reb, Merry Christmas!"

"Same to you, Yank," and during that sacred night there was the truce of God and overhead the silence of the solemn stars.

As the young Captain became altogether comfortable, his thoughts wandered far afield — always at last to Josiah's pansy, the many-masked Leila, and behind her pretty feminine disguises the serious-minded woman for whom, as he smilingly consulted his fancy, he found no flower emblem to suit him. The letter he read once more represented many Leilas. Could he answer all of them and abide too by the silence he meant to preserve until the war was over? The imp of mischief was at his side. There was no kind of personal word of herself in the letter, except that he was ordered to talk of John Penhallow and his adventures. He wrote far into the Christmas night:

"DEAR LEILA: To hear is to obey. I am to write of myself — of adventures. Nearness to death in the trenches is an every-second-day adventure enough — no one talks of it. Tom was ill-advised to report of me at home. I used to dream of the romance of war when I was a boy. There is very little romance in it, and much dirt, awful horrors of the dead and wounded, of battles lost or won, and waste beyond conception.

After a big fight or wearying march one could collect material for a rummage-sale such as would rout Aunt Ann's ideal of an amusing auction of useless things.

" My love to oné and all, and above all to the dear Colonel who is never long out of my mind.

" Yours truly,

" JOHN PENHALLOW."

" I put on this separate sheet for you alone the adventure you ask for. It is the only one worth telling, and came to me this Christmas morning. It was strange enough.

" An old Colonel caught me as I was about to visit Tom McGregor at the hospital. I was disgusted, but he wanted an engineer. He got me, alas! We rode far to our left over icy snow-crust. To cut my tale short, after we passed our outlying pickets and I had answered a dozen questions, he said, ' Can you see their pickets ? ' I said, ' No, they are half a mile away on the far side of a creek in the woods. That road leads to a bridge; they may be behind the creek.'

" ' Do you think it fordable ? '

" ' I do not know.' Like a fool, I said, ' I will ride down the road and get a nearer look.' He would be much obliged. I rode Hoodoo down an icy hill with a sharp lookout for their pickets. As I rode, I slipped my revolver out and let it hang at my wrist. I rode on cautiously. About a quarter of a mile from the creek I made up my mind that I had gone far enough. The creek was frozen, as I might have known, and the colonel too. As I checked Hoodoo a shot rang out from a clump of pines on my right and a horseman leaped into the road some twenty yards in front of me. I fired and missed him. He turned and rode pretty fast toward the bridge, turning to fire as he went. I like a fool rode after him. We exchanged shot after shot. He was on the farther end of the bridge when he pulled up his horse and stopped short. He held up a hand; I felt for my sword, having emptied my revolver. It was rather ridiculous. By George! the man was laughing. We were not fifty feet apart when I reined up Hoodoo. We had each fired six shots in vain — I had counted his.

"He called out, 'A rather pretty duel, sir. Don't ride over the bridge.' A picket shot from the left singing over my head rather emphasized his warning. 'It would not be fair — you would ride right into my pickets.' It was an unusual bit of chivalry.

"I called out, 'Thank you, I hope I have not hit you. May I ask your name?'

"'I am at your service. I am'— here Captain John wrote merrily —'Scheherazade who says —

"Being now sleepy, the Caliph will hear the amazing sequel to-morrow night or *later*.

"There you have my adventure all but the end. If I do not hear more of Miss Grey's personal adventures she will never — never, hear the name.

"JOHN PENHALLOW."

He laughed outright as he closed and directed the envelope. I suppose, he wrote in his diary, that as there are several Leilas, there are also several John Penhallows, and I am just now the mischievous lad who was so much younger than Miss Grey. Would she laugh over the lesson of his letter or be angry, or cry a little and feel ill-treated, or — and even that was possible — say it was of no moment who the man was. He felt the gaiety which in some men who have not the mere brute courage of the bull-dog is apt to follow for many hours the escape from a great danger. The boylike mischief of his letter was in part due to some return of the cheerful mood which possessed him after the morning's risks. He went out to question the night of the weather. As he looked over the snow and then up at the mighty clock-work of the stars, he responded slowly to the awe this silentness of immeasurable forces was apt to produce; a perfect engine at the mills in noiseless motion always had upon him the same effect. As he moved, his knee reminded him of the morning's escape. When he rode away from the bridge, with attentions from the enemy's pickets following and came near the waiting colonel, his horse came down and like his rider suffered for the fall on frozen ground.

There was just then for a time less work than usual for the engineers, and he had begun to feel troubled by the fact that two weeks had gone by since Leila wrote, without a home letter. Then it came and was brief:

" DEAR JOHN: I have truly no better and no worse news to send about dear Uncle Jim and this saddened home. To be quite frank with you, your letter made me realize what is hardly felt as here in our home we become used to war news. I thought less of your mischievous attempt to torment my curiosity than of your personal danger, and yet I know too well what are the constant risks in your engineer duties, for I have found among Uncle Jim's books accounts of the siege of Sevastopol. As to your naughty ending, I do not care who the man was — why should I? I doubt if you really know.

" I am,

" Your seriously indifferent

" LEILA GREY.

" P.S. I am ashamed to admit that I reopened my letter to tell you I fibbed large. *Please* not to tease me any more."

He replied at once:

" DEAR LEILA: I am off to the front as usual. The man was Henry Grey. An amazing encounter! I had never seen him, as you may know. I did not wait to reply to him because the Rebel pickets were not so considerate as their colonel. I recalled Uncle Jim's casual mention of Henry Grey as a rather light-minded, quixotic man. I am glad he is, but imagine what a tragedy failed to materialize because two men were awkward with the pistol. But what a strange meeting too! It is not the only case. A captain I know took his own brother prisoner last month; the Rebel would not shake hands with him. Do not tell Aunt Ann — or rather, do what seems best to you. I trust you, of course. The encounter made me want to know your uncle in some far-off happier day.

" In haste, Yours,

" JOHN PENHALLOW."

CHAPTER XXIX

WHEN late in March Grant about to move left the engineer brigade at City Point, the need to corduroy the rain-soaked roads called some of the corps to the front, and among them John Penhallow. As usual when unoccupied they were set free to volunteer for staff duty. It thus chanced that Penhallow found himself for a time an extra aide to General John Parke.

The guarded outer lines of the defences of Petersburg included forests with here and there open spaces and clumps of trees. More than a half mile away from the enemy, on rising ground, amid bushes and trees, lay the army corps of General Parke. It was far into the night. The men were comfortably asleep, for on this second of April, the air was no longer chilly and there were no tents up. In the mid-centre of the corps-line behind the ridge a huge fire marked the headquarters. As the great logs blazed high, they cast radiating shadows of tree trunks, which were and were not as the fire rose or fell. Horses tied to the trees moved uneasily when from far and near came the clamour of guns. Now and then a man sat up in the darkness and listened, but this was some new recruit. For the most of the sleepers the roar of guns was less disturbing than the surly mosquitoes and the sonorous trumpeting of a noisy neighbour. Aides dismounted near the one small tent in the wood shadows, and coming out mounted horses as tired as the riders and rode away into the night. Here and there apart black servants and orderlies slept the deep sleep of irresponsibility and among them Josiah. Beside the deserted fire John Penhallow sat smoking. A hand fell on his shoulder.

"Halloa, Blake!" he said, "where did you come from?"

"I am on Wright's staff. I am waiting for a note I am to carry. There will be no sleep for me to-night. We shall attack at dawn — a square frontal attack through slashes, chevaux-de-frises and parapets; but the men are keen for it, and we shall win."

"I think so — the game is nearly played out."

"I am sorry for them, Penhallow."

"And I. I was thinking when you came of the pleasant West Point friends who may be in those woods yonder, and of the coming agony of that wonderful crumbling host of brave men, and of my uncle's friend, Robert Lee. I shall be a happy man when I can take their hands again."

"How many will be left?" said Blake.

"God knows — we shall, I hope, live to be proud of them."

"My friend Francis sees always the humorous side of war — I cannot."

"It does have — oh, very rarely — its humorous side," returned Penhallow, "but not often for me. His mocking way of seeing things is doubly unpleasant because no man in the army is more in earnest. This orchestra of snoring men would amuse him."

As Blake sat down, he said, "I wonder if they are talking the language of that land — that nightly bourne from which we bring back so little. Listen to them!"

"That's so like you, Blake. I was reflecting too when you came on the good luck I had at the North Anna when you pulled me out. Mark Rivers once said that I was good at making acquaintances, but slow at making friendships."

"Thank you," said Blake, understanding him readily. "I am somewhat like you."

The solemnity of the night and of the fate-laden hours had opened for a minute the minds of two men as reserved and reticent as are most well-bred Americans, who as a rule lack the strange out-spoken frankness of our English kin.

"Oh! here is my summons," said Blake. "Good luck to you, Penhallow. I have about the closing of this war a kind of fear I have never had before."

"That is natural enough," returned Penhallow, "and I fancy it is not uncommon. Let us part with a more pleasant thought. You will come and shoot with me at Grey Pine in the fall? Bye-bye."

Blake rode away. His friend deep in thought and unable to sleep watched the dying fire. The night hours ran on. Obedient to habit he wound his watch. "Not asleep," said a pleasant voice. He rose to face the slight figure and gently smiling face of General Parke.

"What time is it, Penhallow?"

"Four o'clock, sir."

"I have sent back Captain Blake with a word to General Wright, but he will have too long a ride. I want you to carry this same request. By taking the short cut in front of our lines, you can get there in a third of the time. You will keep this side of our pickets to where our line turns, then go through them and down the slope a bit. For a short distance you will be near the clump of trees on the right. If it is picketed — there are no pickets nearer — you will have to ride hard. Once past the angle of their line you are safe. Am I clear?"

"Certainly, sir. There is some marshy ground — I climbed a tree and looked it over yesterday — it won't stop the men, but may slow a horse."

"I see. Here is my note."

Penhallow tucked it in his belt and roused Josiah. "See to the girth," he said. "Is Hoodoo in good order?"

"Yes, sir. Where you going, Master John?"

"A little errand. Make haste."

" I know those little errands," said the black. " The good Lord care for him," he murmured, as the man he loved best was lost in the darkness.

He was aware of the great danger of his errand and was at once in that state of intensity of attention which sharpens every sense. He rode for the fourth of a mile between the long lines of infantry now astir here and there, and then an officer saw him through their picket-line. " Good luck to you! " he said. " I think the Rebs have no outlying pickets, but the woods are full of them."

Penhallow rode down a slight incline, and remembering that the marsh lower down might be difficult turned aside and came on a deep gully. The night was still dark, but a faint glow to eastward made haste desirable. The gully, as he rode beside it, flattened out, but at once he felt that his horse was in trouble on marshy ground. He dismounted and led him, but always the better footing lay nearer to the clump of trees. He made up his mind to ride for it. While on foot he had been as yet hardly visible. A shot from the salient group of trees decided him. He mounted and touched Hoodoo with the spur. The horse bounded forwards too quickly to sink in the boggy ground. Then a dozen shots told the rider he had been seen. Something like the feeling of a blow from a stick was felt as his left arm fell with gripped reins, and the right arm also dropped. Hoodoo pitched forward, rose with a gallant effort, and sinking down rolled to left upon the rider's leg.

The horse lay still. Penhallow's first sensation was astonishment; then he began to make efforts to get free. His arms were of no use. He tried to stir his horse with the spur of the free foot. It had no effect. Something must be wrong with him. He had himself a feeling of weakness he could not comprehend, aware that he had no wound of the trunk. His useless arms made all effort vain, and the left foot under the weight of the horse began to feel numb. The position struck him as past help until our people charged. He thought of Francis's axiom that there was nothing so entirely tragic as to be without some marginalia of humour. The lad smiled at his use of the word. His own situation appealed to him as ridiculous — a man with a horse on him waiting for an army to lift it off.

The left elbow began to recover from the early insensibility of shock and to be painful. Then in the dim light, as he lifted his head, he was aware of a Rebel soldier in front covering him with a revolver. Penhallow cried out with promptness, " I surrender — and I am shot through both arms."

The soldier said, " You are not worth taking — guess you 'll keep till we lick the Yanks," and walking around the helpless officer he appropriated his revolver.

" Can you get my horse up? " said John.

" Horse up! I want your boots."

" Well, pull them off — I can't."

" Oh, don't you bother, I'll get them." With this he knelt down and began on the boot which belonged to the leg projecting beneath the horse. " Darn it! They 're just my size." As he tugged at it, Hoodoo dying and convulsed struck out with his fore legs and caught the unlucky soldier full in the belly. The man gave a wild cry and staggering back fell.

Penhallow craned over the horse's body and broke into laughter. It hurt his arm, but he gasped with fierce joy, " Francis would call him a freebooter." Then he fell back and quite helpless listened. Unable to turn his head, he heard behind him the wild rush of men. Leaping over horse and man they went by. He got a look to right and left. They tore through the slashes, dropping fast and facing a furious fusillade were lost to sight in the underbrush. " By George! they 've won," he exclaimed and fell back. " They must have carried the parapet." He waited. In about a half hour a party of men in grey went by. An officer in blue cried out, " Up the hill, you beggars!" More of the grey men followed — a battle-grimed mob of hundreds.

"Halloa!" called Penhallow. "Get this horse up. Put your hand in my pocket and you will find fifty dollars." They stopped short and a half dozen men lifted the dead animal. "Thank you, set me on my feet," said Penhallow. "Empty my pockets — I can't use my arms." They did it well, and taking also his watch went on their way well pleased.

John stood still, the blood tingling in his numb foot. "Halloa!" he cried, as the stretcher-bearers and surgeons came near. A headquarters surgeon said, "We thought you were killed. Can you walk?"

"No — hit in both arms — why the deuce can't I walk?"

"Shock, I suppose."

A half hour later he was in a hospital tent and a grim old army surgeon handling his arms. "Right arm flesh-wound — left elbow smashed. You will likely have to lose the arm."

"No, I won't," said Penhallow, "I'd as leave die."

"Don't talk nonsense. They all say that. See you again."

"You will get ten dollars," said John to a hospital orderly, "if you will find Captain Blake of General Wright's staff."

"I'll do it, sir."

Presently his arms having been dressed, he was made comfortable with morphia. At dusk next morning his friend Blake sat down beside his cot. "Are you badly hurt?" he said. A certain tenderness in the voice was like a revelation of some qualities unknown before.

"I do not know. For about the first time in my life I am suffering pain — I mean constant pain, with a devilish variety in it too. The same ball, I believe, went through some muscle in the right arm and smashed my left elbow. It's a queer experience. The surgeon-in-charge informed me that I would probably lose the arm. The younger surgeon says the ball will become what he calls encysted. They probed and could n't find it. Is n't that Josiah I hear?"

"Yes, I will bring him in."

In a moment they came back. "My God! Master John, I been looking for you all night and this morning I found Hoodoo dead. Did n't I say he 'd bring you bad luck. Oh, my! — are you hurt bad?"

"Less noise there," said an assistant surgeon, "or get out of this."

"He 'll be quiet," said Blake, "and you will have the decency to be less rough." The indignant doctor walked away.

"Poor Hoodoo — he did his best," murmured John. "Get me out of this, Blake. It 's a hell of suffering. Take me to Tom McGregor at City Point."

"I will, but now I must go. General Parke hopes you are doing well. You will be mentioned in his despatches."

"That is of no moment — get me to McGregor. Hang the flies — I can't fight them."

John never forgot the ambulance and the rough railway ride to City Point, nor his pleasure when at rest in the officers' pavilion he waited for his old playmate. As I write I see, as he saw, the long familiar ward, the neat cots, the busy orderlies. He waited with the impatience of increasing pain. "Well, Tom," he said, with an effort to appear gay, "here 's your chance at last to get even."

McGregor made brief reply as he uncovered the wounded joint. Then he said gravely, "A little ether — I will get out the ball."

"No ether, Tom, I can stand it. Now get to work."

"I shall hurt you horribly."

"No ether," he repeated. "Go on, Tom."

McGregor sat beside him with a finger on the bounding pulse and understood its meaning and the tale it told. "It will not be long, John," and then with attention so concentrated as not even to note the one stir of the tortured body or to hear the long-drawn groan of pain, he rose to his feet. "All right, John — it's only a slug — lucky it was not a musket ball." He laid a tender hand on the sweating brow, shot a dose of morphia into the right arm, and added, "You will get well with a stiff joint. Now go to sleep. The right arm is sound, a flesh-wound."

"Thanks," said John, "we are even now, Tom. Captain Blake telegraphed your father, Tom — but write, please."

"To whom, John?"

"To Leila — but do not alarm them."

"I will write. In a week or two you must go home. That is the medicine you need most. You will still have some pain, but you will not lose the arm."

"Thank you — but what of the army? I am a bit confused as to time. Parke attacked on the second of April, I think. What day is this?"

"Oh, they got out of Petersburg that night — out of Richmond too. Lee is done for — a day or two will end it."

"Thank God," murmured John, "but I am so sorry for Lee."

"Can't say I am."

"Oh, that blessed morphia!"

"Well, go to sleep — I will see you again shortly. I have other fellows to look after. In a few minutes you will be easy. Draw the fly-nets, orderly."

Of all that followed John Penhallow in later years remembered most distinctly the half hour of astonishing relief from pain. As his senses one by one went off guard, he seemed to himself to be watching with increase of ease the departure of some material tormentor. In after years he recalled with far less readiness the days of varied torment which required more and more morphia. Why I know not, the remembrance of pain as time goes by is far less permanent than that of relief or of an hour of radiant happiness. Long days of suffering followed as the tortured nerves recorded their far-spread effects in the waste of the body and that failure of emotional control which even the most courageous feel when long under the tyranny of continuous pain. McGregor watched him with anxiety and such help as was possible. On the tenth of April John awakened after a night of assisted sleep to find himself nearly free from pain. Tom came early into the ward.

"Good news, John," he said. "Lee has surrendered. You look better. Your resignation will be accepted, and I have a leave of absence. Economy is the rule. We are sending the wounded north in ship-loads. Home! Home! old fellow, in a week."

The man on the cot looked up. "You have a letter, I see," and as he spoke broke into childlike tears, for so did long suffering deal with the most self-controlled in those terrible years, which we do well to forgive, and to remember with pride not for ourselves alone. The child-man on the bed murmured, "Home was too much for me."

The surgeon who loved him well said, "Read your letter — you are not the only man in this ward whom pain has made a baby. Home will complete your cure — home!"

"Thank you, Tom." He turned to the letter and using the one half-useful hand opened it with difficulty. What he first felt was disappointment at the brevity of the letter. He was what Blake called home-hungry. With acute perception, being himself a homeless man, Blake made his diagnosis of that form of heart-ache which too often adds a perilously depressing agency to the more material disasters of war. Pain, fever, the inevitable ward odours, the easier neighbour in the next bed who was of a mind to be social, the flies — those Virginia flies more wily than Lee's troopers — and even trifling annoyances made Penhallow irritable. He became a burden to hospital

stewards and over-worked orderlies, and now the first look at
Leila's letter disturbed him, and as he read he became indignant:

" DEAR JOHN : Mr. Blake's telegram telling us of your
wound caused us some anxiety, which was made less by Dr.
McGregor's somewhat hastily written letter. Aunt Ann thought
it was excusable in so busy a man. Poor Uncle Jim on hearing
it said, ' Yes, yes — why did n't John write — can't be much
the matter.' This shows you his sad failure. He has not mentioned it since.

" It is a relief to us to know that you were not dangerously
hurt. It seems as if this sad war and its consequences were
near to end. Let us hear soon. Aunt Ann promises to write
to you at once.

" Yours truly,
" LEILA GREY."

He threw the letter down, and forgetting that he had asked
Blake and the doctor not to alarm his people, was overcome by
the coldness of Leila's letter. He lay still, and with eyes quite
too full felt that life had for him little of that which once
made it sweet with what all men hold most dear. He would
have been relieved if he could have seen Leila when alone she
read and read again McGregor's letter, and read with fear between the lines of carefully guarded words what he would not
say and for days much feared to say. She sat down and wrote
to John a letter of such tender anxiety as was she felt a confession she was of no mind to make. He was in no danger.
Had he been, she would have written even more frankly. But
her trouble about her uncle was fed from day to day by what
her aunt could not or would not see, and it was a nearer calamity and more and more distressing. Then she sat thinking
what was John like now. She saw the slight figure, so young

and still so thoughtful, as she had smiled in her larger experience of men when they had sat and played years ago with violets on the hillside of West Point. No, she was unprepared to commit herself for life, for would he too be of the same mind? For a moment she stood still indecisive, then she tore up her too tender letter and wrote the brief note which so troubled him. She sent it and then was sorry she had not obeyed the impulse of the kindlier hour.

The nobler woman instinct is apt to be armed by nature for defensive warfare. If she has imagination, she has in hours of doubt some sense of humiliation in the vast surrender of marriage. This accounts for certain of the cases of celibate women, who miss the complete life and have no ready traitor within the guarded fortress to open the way to love. Some such instinctive limitations beset Leila Grey. The sorrow of a great, a nearer and constant affection came to her aid. To think of anything like love, even if again it questioned her, was out of the question while before her eyes James Penhallow was fading in mind.

John Penhallow was shortly relieved by McGregor's order that he should get some exercise. It enabled him to escape the early surgical visit and the diverse odours of surgical dressings which lingered in the long ward while breakfast was being served. There were more uneasy sleepers than he in the ward and much pain, and crippled men with little to look forward to. The suffering he saw and could not lessen had been for John one of the depressing agencies of this hospital life. The ward was quiet when he awoke at dawn of April 13th. He quickly summoned an orderly and endured the daily humiliation of being dressed like a baby. He found Josiah waiting with the camp-chair at the door as he came out of the ward.

" How you feeling, Master John? "

" Rather better. What time is it? That Reb stole my watch." Even yet it was amusing. He laughed at the remembrance of having been relieved by the prisoners of purse and watch.

For Josiah to extract his own watch was as McGregor said something like a surgical operation. "It's not goin', Master John. It's been losing time — like it was n't accountable. What's it called watch for if it don't watch?"

This faintly amused John. He said no more, but sat enjoying the early morning quiet, the long hazy reaches of the James River, the awakening of life here and there, and the early stir among the gun-boats.

"Get me some coffee, Josiah," he said. "I am like your watch, losing time and everything else."

Josiah stood over him. His unnatural depression troubled a simple mind made sensitive by a limitless affection and doglike power to feel without comprehending the moods of the master.

"Captain John, you was sayin' to me yesterday you was most unfortunate. I just went away and kept a kind of thinkin' about it."

"Well, what conclusion did you come to?" He spoke wearily.

"Oh, I just wondered if you 'd like to change with me — guess you would n't for all the pain?"

Surprised at the man's reflection, John looked up at the black kindly face. "Get me some coffee."

"Yes, sir — what's that?" The morning gun rang out the sunrise hour. "What's that, sir?" The flag was being hoisted on the slope below them. "It's stopped at half-mast, sir! Who's dead now?"

"Go and ask, Josiah." McGregor came up as he spoke.

"The President was killed last night, John, by an assassin!"

"Lincoln killed!"

"Yes — I will tell you by and by — now this is all we know. I must make my rounds. We leave to-morrow for home."

John sat alone. This measureless calamity had at once on the thoughtful young soldier the effect of lessening the influences of his over-sensitive surrender to pain and its attendant power to weaken self-control. Like others, in the turmoil of war he had given too little thought to the Promethean torment of a great soul chained to the rock of duty — the man to whom like the Christ "the common people listened gladly." He looked back over his own physical suffering with sense of shame at his defeat, and sat up in his chair as if with a call on his worn frame to assert the power of a soul to hear and answer the summons of a great example.

"Thank you, Josiah," he said cheerfully. "No coffee is like yours to set a fellow up." A greater tonic was acting. "We go home to-morrow."

"That's good. Listen, sir — what's that?"

"Minute guns, Josiah. Have you heard the news?"

"Yes, sir — it's awful; but we are going home to Westways."

CHAPTER XXX

AS the trains went northward crowded with more or less damaged officers and men, John Penhallow in his faded engineer uniform showed signs of renewed vitality. He chatted in his old companionable way with the other home-bound volunteers, and as they went through Baltimore related to McGregor with some merriment his bloodless duel with Mrs. Penhallow's Rebel brother Henry. The doctor watched him with the most friendly satisfaction and with such pride as a florist may have in his prospering flowers. The colour of health was returning to the pale face and there was evidently relief from excessive pain. He heard, too, as they chatted, of John's regrets that his simple engineer dress was not as neat as he would have desired and of whether his aunt would dislike it. Nearing the station of Westways Crossing, John fell into a laughing account of his first arrival and of the meeting with Leila. The home-tonic was of use and he was glad with gay gladness that the war was over.

As the train stopped, he said as he got out, "There is no carriage — you telegraphed, McGregor?"

"Yes, I did, but the service is, I fancy, snowed under just now with messages. I will walk on and have them send for you."

"No," said John, "I am quite able to walk. Come along."

"Are you really able?"

"Yes — we'll take it easy."

"There isn't much left of you to carry what remains."

"My legs are all right, Tom." He led the way through the woods until they came out on the avenue. "Think of it, Tom,

— it is close to nine years since first I left Grey Pine for the Point."

In the afternoon of this sunny day late in April the Colonel sat on the porch with his wife. Below them on the step Rivers was reading aloud the detailed account of Lincoln's death. Leila coming out of the house was first to see the tall thin figure in dark undress uniform. She was thankful for an unwatched moment of ability to gain entire self-command. It was needed. She helped herself by her cry of joyous recognition.

"Aunt Ann! Aunt Ann!" she cried, "there is Dr. McGregor and — and John and Josiah." The aunt cast a look of anxiety at the expressionless face of James Penhallow, as he rose to his feet, saying, "Why was n't I told?"

"We did not know, sir," said Rivers, dropping the paper as he went down the steps to meet the new-comer.

Then the wasted figure with the left arm in a sling was in Ann Penhallow's embrace.

"My God!" he said, "but it's good to be at home." As he spoke he turned to the Colonel who had risen.

"Got hit, John? It runs in the family. Once had a Sioux arrow through my arm. Glad to see you. Want to be fed up a bit. Lord! but you 're lean." He said no more, but sat down again without appearance of interest.

Rivers made John welcome with a pleasant word, and Leila coming forward took his hand, saying quietly, "We hardly looked for you to-day, but it is none too soon." Then she turned to McGregor, "We have much to thank you for. You will stay to dine?"

John, still too sensitive, was troubled as he realized his uncle's condition, and felt that there was something in Leila's manner which was unlike that of the far-remembered Leila of other days. She had urged McGregor to stay and dine, and then added, "But, of course, that pleasure must wait — you will want to see your father. He is so proud of you — as we all are."

" That is a pleasant welcome, Miss Leila; and, dear Mrs. Penhallow, I do not want a carriage, I prefer to walk. I will see you, John, and that lame arm to-morrow. Good-bye, Colonel."

The master of Grey Pine said, " Nice young man! Ann ought to kill the fatted calf. Tell John not to be late for dinner."

" It is all right, James," said Mrs. Ann, " all right."

Rivers watched with pain the vacant face of the Colonel. This mental failure constantly recalled the days of anguish when with despair he had seen all who were dear to him one after another die mentally before their merciful exit from life.

" John must be tired," he said. Leila, who noted on the young soldier's face the effect of sudden realization of his useless state said, " Your room is ready, John."

" Yes," said John, " I should like to rest before dinner."

With a word as to the fatigue of his journey, Leila followed him into the well-remembered hall.

" Good heavens, Leila. It seems an age since I was here. Send up Josiah. I am like a baby and need him to help me."

She looked after him pitifully as he went up the stairs. " Surely," she thought, " we have paid dearly our debt to the country."

He came down at six o'clock, still in his undress uniform, but thinking that his aunt would not like it. In a day or two he would have the civilian clothes he had ordered in Philadelphia. He need have had no such anxiety; she was indifferent to all but her husband, who sat at table speechless, while Leila and John too consciously manufactured talk of the home and the mills — and the ending of the war. After the meal Ann began her patient efforts to interest the Colonel with a game of cards and then of backgammon. It seemed only to make him irritable, and he said at last, " I think I must go to bed."

" Certainly, dear." She went with him upstairs, saying, " Good-night, children."

" She will not return, John. This is what goes on day after day."

" It is very sad — I did not fully comprehend his condition."

" He is often far worse, and complains of his head or is resolutely — I should say obstinately — bent on some folly, such as walking to the mills and advising them. Aunt Ann never contradicts him — what he wants, she wants. Not the most reasonable opposition is of any use."

" Does he never ride, Leila ? "

" Never, and is vexed when Dr. McGregor calls to see him and advises a consultation. Once we had a distressing outbreak."

" And yet," said John, " there should have been other advice long ago. Somehow there must be."

" Mr. Rivers has urged it and made him angry; as for Aunt Ann, she sees only the bright side of his case and humours him as she would a sick child."

" She is greatly changed, Leila. I hardly know how to state it. She has a look of — well, of something spiritual in her face."

" Yes, that is true. Are you in pain, John ? " she added.

" Yes — not in great pain, but enough. For two weeks I did suffer horribly."

" John! Oh, my poor Jack! We never knew — is it so bad ? "

" Yes, imagine a toothache in your elbow with a variety of torments in the whole arm."

" I can't imagine. I never had a toothache — in fact, I hardly know the sensation of serious pain."

" Well, I broke down under it, Leila. I became depressed

and quite foolishly hopeless. Some day I will tell you what helped me out of a morass of melancholy."

" Tell me now."

" No, I must go to bed. I am getting better and will get off with a stiff elbow, so Tom says. At first they talked of amputation. That was awful. Good-night!"

It was none too soon. She was still unsure of herself, and although no word of tender approach had disturbed her as he talked, and she was glad of that, the tense look of pain, the reserve of his hospital confession of suffering nearly broke down her guarded attitude. As he passed out of view at the turn of the stairs, she murmured, " Oh, if only Uncle Jim were well."

Josiah came at the call of the bell. She detained him. She asked, " How was the Captain wounded? No one wrote of how it happened."

" Well, missy, he would ride a horse called Hoodoo — it was just the bad luck of that brute done it." Josiah's account was graphic and clear enough. John Penhallow's character lost nothing as interpreted by Josiah.

" It was a dangerous errand, I suppose."

" Yes, Miss Leila. You see, when they know about a man that he somehow don't mind bullets and will go straight to where he's sent, they're very apt to get him killed. At the first shot he ought to have tumbled off and played possum till it was dark."

" But then," said Leila, " he would have been too late with General Parke's message."

" Of course, Master John could n't sham dead like I would. — I don't despise bullets like he does. Once before he had orders to go somewhere, and could n't get across a river. He was as mad as a wet hen."

" A wet hen — delightful! Did he do it?"

" Guess you don't know him! When Master John wants anything, well, he's a terrible wanter — always was that way even when he was a boy — when he wants anything, he gets it."

"Indeed! does he? I think he is waiting for you, Josiah."

The black's conclusive summary hardened the young woman's heart. She sat a while smiling, then took up a book and failed to become interested.

As John became familiar with the altered life of a household once happy and in pleasant relation to the outer world, he felt as Leila had done the depressing influence of a home in which the caprices of an invalid life were constantly to be considered. Meanwhile his own spare figure gained flesh, and on one sunny morning — he long remembered it — he was rather suddenly free from pain, and with only the stiff elbow was, as McGregor described it, " discharged cured."

For some time he had been feeling that in bodily vigour and sense of being his normal self he had been rapidly gaining ground. The relief from the thraldom of pain brought a sudden uplift of spirits and a feeling of having been born anew into an inheritance of renewed strength and of senses sharpened beyond what he had ever known. A certain activity of happiness like a bodily springtime comes with such a convalescence. Ceasing to feel the despotism of self-attention, he began to recover his natural good sense and to watch with more care his uncle's state, his aunt's want of consideration for any one but James Penhallow, and the effect upon Leila of this abnormal existence. He began to understand that to surely win this sad girl-heart there must be a patient siege, and above all something done for the master of Grey Pine. He recognized with love's impatience the beauty of this young life amid the difficulties of the Colonel's moods and Ann Penhallow's ill-concealed jealousy. A great passion may be a very selfish thing, or in the nobler natures rise so high on the wings of love that it casts like the singing lark no shadow on the earth. He could wait and respect with patient affection the sense of duty which perhaps — ah! that perhaps — made love a thing which must wait

— yes, and wait too with helpful service where she too had nobly served.

When the day came for his first venture on a horse and he rode through the young leafage of June, no enterprise seemed impossible. How could he be of use to her and these dear people to whom he owed so much? War had been costly, but it had taught him that devotion to the duty of the hour which is one of the best lessons of that terrible schoolmaster. There was, as he saw every day, no overruling common sense in the household of Grey Pine, and no apparent possibility of reasonable control. Just now it was worse than ever, and he meant to talk it over with the two McGregors. With Josiah riding behind him, he left a message here and there in the village, laughing and jesting, with a word of sympathy where the war had left its cruel memories. He had been in the little town very often since his return, but never before when free from pain or with the pleasant consciousness that he had it in his power to be to these friends of his childhood what the Colonel had been. He talked to Joe Grace, left a message for Pole's son, and then rode on to his appointment.

He sat down with father and son in the unchanged surroundings of the untidy office; even the flies were busy as before on the old man's tempting bald head.

"Well, John," said the doctor, "what's up now? The Squire won't see me at all." Tom sat still and listened.

"There are two things to consider, and I want your advice; but, first, I want to say that there is no head to that family. I wonder how Leila stands it. I mean that your advice shall be taken about a consultation with Prof. Askew."

"You want my advice? Do you, indeed! Mrs. Penhallow will ask the Colonel's opinion, he will swear, and the matter is at an end."

"I mean to have that consultation," said John. Tom laughed and nodded approval.

"It's no use, John, none," said the older man.

"We shall see about that. Do you approve? — that is my question."

"If that's the form of advice you want, why, of course — yes — but count me out."

"Count me in, John," said the younger surgeon. "I know what Askew will say and what should have been done long ago."

"An operation?" asked his father.

"Yes, sir, an operation."

"Too late!"

"Well," said John, "he gets no worse; a week or two will make no difference, I presume."

"None," said Dr. McGregor.

"It may," said Tom.

"Well, it may have to wait. Just now there is a very serious question. Aunt Ann made last night the wild suggestion that the Colonel might be amused if we had one of those rummage-sales with which she used to delight the village. Uncle Jim at once declared it to be the thing he would like best. Aunt Ann said we must see about it at once. Her satisfaction in finding an amusement which the Colonel fancied was really childlike. Leila said nothing, nor did I. In fact, the proposal came about when I happened unluckily to say what a fine chance Uncle Sam had for a rummage-sale after a forced march or a fight. I recall having said much the same thing long ago in a letter to Leila."

"Then there's nothing to be done just now, John," remarked Tom McGregor, "but I cannot conceive of anything more likely to affect badly a disordered brain."

The older man was silent until John asked, "Is it worth while to talk to Aunt Ann about it — advise against it?"

"Quite useless, John. I advise you and Leila quietly to assist your aunt, and like as not the Colonel may forget all about it in a day or two."

" No, Doctor. To-day he had Billy up with him in the attic bringing down whatever he can find, useful or useless."

With little satisfaction from this talk, John rode homeward. Sitting in the saddle at the post-office door, he called for the mail. Mrs. Crocker, of undiminished bulk and rosiness, came out.

" How's your arm, Captain? I bet it's more use than mine. The rheumatism have took to permanent boarding in my right shoulder — and no glory like you got to show for it."

" I could do without the glory."

" No, you could n't. If I was a man, I'd be glad to swap; you've got to make believe a bit, but the town's proud of you. I guess some one will soon have to look after them Penhallow mills." Mrs. Crocker put a detaining hand on his bridle reins.

" Yes, yes," said John absently, glancing well pleased over a kind letter of inquiry from General Parke. " Well, what else, Mrs. Crocker? "

" The Colonel quite give me a shock this morning. He's not been here — no, not once — since he came home. Well, he walked in quite spry and told me there was to be a rummage-sale in a week, and I was to put up a notice and tell everybody. Why, Mr. John, he was that natural. He went away laughing because I offered to sell my old man — twenty-five cents a pound. I did notice he don't walk right."

" Yes, I have noticed that; but this notion of a rummage-sale has seemed to make him better. Now, suppose you let my reins go."

" Oh, Mr. John, don't be in such a hurry. It's surely a responsible place, this post-office; I don't ever get time for a quiet talk."

" Well, Mrs. Crocker, now is your chance."

" That's real good of you. I was wanting to ask if you ever heard anything of Peter Lamb. He wrote to his mother he was in the army, and then that was the end of it. She keeps

on writing once a week, and the letters come back stamped
'not found.' I guess he's wandering somewhere."

"Like enough. I went to see her last week, but I could
not give her any comfort. She couldn't have a worse thing
happen than for Peter to come home."

"Well, Captain John, when you come to have babies of your
own, you'll find mothers are a curious kind of animal."

"Mothers!" laughed John. "I hope there won't be more
than one. Now, I really must go."

"Oh, just one more real bit of news. Lawyer Swallow's
wife was here yesterday with another man to settle up her husband's business."

"Is he dead?"

"They say so, but you can't believe everything you hear.
Now, don't hurry. What most killed Swallow was just this:
He hated Pole like poison, and when he got a five hundred
dollar mortgage-grip on Pole's pasture meadow, he kept that
butcher-man real uneasy. When you were all away, Swallow
began to squeeze — what those lawyers call 'foreclose.' It's
just some lawyer word for robbery."

"It's pretty bad, Mrs. Crocker, but two people are waiting for
you and this isn't exactly Government business."

"Got to hear the end, Captain."

"I suppose so — what next?" Dixy wondered why the spur
touched him even lightly.

"Pole, he told Mrs. Penhallow all about it, and she wasn't as
glad to help her meat-man as she was to bother Swallow, so she
took over the mortgage. When the Squire first came home from
Washington and wasn't like he was later, she told him, of
course. Now everybody knows Pole's ways, and so the Squire
he says to me — he was awful amused —' Mrs. Crocker, I asked
Mrs. Penhallow how Pole was going to pay her.' She said she
did put that at Pole, and he said it wouldn't take long to eat
up that debt at Grey Pine. He wouldn't have dared to speak

like that to your aunt if she had n't got to be so meek-like, what with war and bother." By this time Dixy was with reason displeased and so restless that Mrs. Crocker let the reins drop, but as John Penhallow rode away she cried, "The price of meats at Grey Pine has been going up ever since, until Miss Leila —" The rest was lost to the Captain. He rode away laughing as he reflected on what share of Pole's debt he was to devour.

CHAPTER XXXI

THE bustle and folly of a rummage-sale was once in every two or three years a frolic altogether pleasant to quiet Westways. It enabled Ann Penhallow and other wise women to get rid of worn-out garments and other trash dear to the male mind. When Leila complained of the disturbing antecedents of a rummage-sale, Mrs. Crocker, contributive of unasked wisdom, remarked, "Men have habits, and women don't; women have blind instincts. You'll find that out when you're married. You see marriage is a kind of voyage of discovery. You just remember that and begin early to keep your young man from storing away useless clothes and the like. That's where a rummage-sale comes in handy."

Leila laughed. "Why not sell the unsatisfactory young man, Mrs. Crocker?"

"Well, that ain't a bad idea," said the post-mistress slyly, "if he's a damaged article — a rummage-sale of husbands not up to sample."

"A very useful idea," said the young woman. "Good-bye."

In the afternoon a day later, Leila, making her escape from her aunt's busy collections, slipped away into the woods alone. The solitude of the early woodland days of summer were what she needed, and the chance they gave for such tranquil reflection as the disturbance and restless state of her home just now made it rarely possible to secure. She tried to put aside her increasing anxiety about her uncle and had more difficulty in dealing with John Penhallow and his over-quiet friendliness. She thought too of her own coldly-worded letters and of the suffering of which she had been kept so long ig-

norant. He had loved her once; did he now? She was annoyed to hear the voice of Mark Rivers.

"So, Leila, you have run away, and I do not wonder. This
turmoil is most distressing."

"Yes, yes — and everything — those years of war and what
it has brought us — and my dear Uncle Jim — and how is it to
end? Let us talk of something else. I came here to be —well,
to see if I could find peace of soul and what these silent forests
have often given me, strength to take up again the cares and
troubles of life." He did not excuse his intrusion nor seem to
notice the obvious suggestions, but fell upon their personal application to himself.

"They have never done that for me," he said sadly. "There
is some defect in my nature — some want. I have no such
relation to nature; it is speechless to me — mute, and I never
needed more what I fail to find in myself. The war and its
duties gave me the only entire happiness I have had for years."
Then he added, in a curiously contemplative manner, "It does
seem as if a man had a right to some undisturbed happiness in
life. I must go. I leave you to the quiet of the woods."

"I am sorry," she said, "I am sorry that you are able to
imply that you have never known happiness. Surely you cannot
mean that." It was all she could say. His look of profound
melancholy hurt her, for like all who knew Mark Rivers well,
she loved, respected and admired him.

He made no explanatory reply, but after a brief silence said,
"I must go, Leila, where there are both duties and dangers —
not — no, not in cities."

"I trust you do not mean to leave us — surely not!"

"No, not yet — not while I can be of use to these dear
friends."

As she moved on at his side or before him, he saw too well
the easy grace of her strong young virgin form, the great blue
eyes, the expressive tenderness of features which told of dumb

sympathy with what she had no knowledge to understand. He longed to say, "I love you and am condemned by my conscience to ask no return." It would only add to his unhappiness and disturb a relation which even in its incompleteness was dear to him. The human yearning to confess, to win even the sad luxury of pity beset the man. In his constant habit of introspection, he had become unobservant and had no least idea that the two young people he loved so well were nearing what was to him forever impossible.

"Let me sit down," he said unwilling to leave her; "I am tired." He was terribly afraid of himself and shaken by a storm of passion, which left his sensitive body feeble.

She sat down with him on a great trunk wrecked a century ago. "Are you not well?" she asked, observing the paleness of his face.

"No, it is nothing. I am not very well, but it is nothing of moment. Don't let it trouble you — I am much as usual. I want, Leila, what I cannot get — what I ought not to get." Even this approach to fuller confession relieved him.

"What is there, my dear Mr. Rivers, you cannot get? Oh! you are a man to envy with your hold on men, your power to charm, your eloquence. I have heard Dr. McGregor talk of what you were among the wounded and the dying on the firing-line. Don't you know that you are one of God's helpful messengers, an interpreter into terms of human thought and words of what men need to-day, when —"

"No, no," he broke in, lifting a hand of dissenting protest. The flushed young face as she spoke, his sense of being nobly considered by this earnest young woman had again made him feel how just the little more would have set free in ardent words what he was honestly striving to control.

"Thank you, my dear Leila, I could wish I were all you think I am; but were it all true, there would remain things that sweeten life and which must always be forbidden to me."

He rose to his feet once again master of his troubled soul. " I leave you," he said, " and your tireless youth to your walk. We cannot have everything, I must be contented in some moment of self-delusion to half believe the half of what you credit me with."

" Then," cried Leila, laughing, " you would have only a fourth."

" Ah! I taught you arithmetic too well." He too laughed as he turned away. Laughter was rare with him and to smile frequent. He walked slowly away to the rectory and for two days was not seen at Grey Pine.

Leila, more at ease and relieved by the final gay banter, strolled into the solemn quiet of the pines the Squire had so successfully freed from underbrush and left in royal solitude. At the door of the old log-cabin she lay down on the dry floor of pine-needles. The quick interchange of talk had given her no chance to consider, as now she reviewed in thoughtful illumination, what had seemed to her strange. She tried to recall exactly what he had said. Of a sudden she knew, and was startled to know. She had come into possession of the power of a woman innocent of intention to inflict pain on a strong and high-minded man. A lower nature might have felt some sense of triumph. It left her with no feeling but the utmost distress and pitiful thinking of what had gone wrong in this man's life. Once before she had been thus puzzled. The relief of her walk was gone. She gathered some imperfect comfort in the thought that she might not have been justified in her conclusions regarding a man who was in so many ways an unexplained personality.

During the next few days the village was in a state of anticipative pleasure and of effort to find for the rummage-sale articles which were damaged or useless. At Grey Pine John and Leila Grey were the only unexcited persons. She was too troubled in divers ways to enjoy the amusement to be had out of what delighted every one else except John Penhallow. To please his aunt he made some small and peculiar offerings, and daily went away to the mills to meet and consult with the Colonel's former partners. He was out of humour with his world, saw trouble ahead if he did as he meant to do, and as there was an east wind howling through the pines, his wounded arm was recording the storm in dull aches or sharp twinges. He smoked, I fear, too much during these days of preparation for the rummage-sale, and rode hard; while Leila within the dismantled house was all day long like the quiet steadying flywheel in some noisy machinery. What with Billy as the over-excited Colonel's aide and her aunt aggrieved by a word of critical comment on her husband's actions, Leila had need of all the qualities required in a household where, as it seemed to her, it was hard to keep tongue or temper quiet.

Mr. Rivers towards the end of the week came in often, and would, of course, see that the Sunday school hall was made ready for the sale. He would make some contributions and help to arrange the articles for the sale. The Colonel's continuity of childlike interest deceived him into sharing the belief of Ann Penhallow, who was, Leila thought, unreasonably elated. Meanwhile Leila felt as a kind of desertion John's successive days of absence. Where was he? What was he doing? Once she would have asked frankly why he left to her the burden of cares he ought to have been eager to share, while Mark Rivers was so steadily helpful. When Ann Penhallow asked him to act as salesman, he said that he was at her disposal. The Colonel declared that was just the thing, and John must uncover and announce the articles to be sold. He said, "How long ago was the last sale? Was n't it last year?"

"No, dear, not so lately."

"I must have forgotten. Perhaps, Rivers, we might sell a few useless people. What would Leila fetch in the marriage market?" Ann somewhat annoyed said nothing; nor did

Rivers like it. The Colonel continued, "Might sell John — badly damaged."

"I must go," said Rivers. "I have my sermon to think over. I mean to use the text you gave me, Leila, some two weeks ago."

Sunday went by, and Tuesday, the day of the sale, came with a return of the east wind and a cold downpour of rain. The Colonel and Billy were busy late in the day; Mrs. Ann was tired; while John in some pain was silent at dinner. The carriage took the Colonel and his wife to the hall. He was now quiet and answered curtly the too frequent questions about how he felt.

"We will send back for you, Leila," said her aunt.

"No, I want to walk there with John."

The Captain looked up surprised, "Why, yes, with pleasure."

She came down in her rain-cloak. "Take a large umbrella, John. How it blows!"

As they set off in the face of a rain-whipped wind, he said, "Take my arm, Leila — the other side — the sound arm."

"You were in pain at dinner, John."

"It is my familiar devil, the east wind, but don't talk of it."

She understood him, and returned, "I will not if you don't wish me to talk of it. Where have you been all these uneasy days?"

"Oh, at the mills. Uncle refuses to speak of business and I am trying to understand the situation — some one must."

"I see — you must explain it all to me later."

"I will. One of the mill men of my Corps needed help. I have asked Tom to see him. How depressed Mr. Rivers seems. Gracious, how it rains!"

"Yes, he is at his worst. I am sorry you missed his sermon on Sunday — it was great. He talked about Lincoln, and used a text I gave him some time ago."

"What was it?"

"It is in Exodus: 'Ye have seen what I did unto the Egyptians and how I bare you on eagles' wings, and brought you unto myself.'"

John's ready imagination began for a silent moment to play with the words. "How did he use it, Leila?"

"Oh, he told the preceding story briefly, and then his great seeking eyes wandered a little and he said, 'Think how the uplift of God's eagles' wings enlarged their horizon!' Then he seemed to me to have the idea that they might not comprehend, so he made one of those eloquent pauses and went on to say, 'You can all, like Lincoln, rise as he rose from the lesser things of a hard life to see more widely and more surely the duties of life. The eagle-wings of God's uplifting power are for you, for me, for all of us.' He made them understand."

"I am sorry I missed it. I spent the Sunday morning with my engineer."

"Are n't you getting wet, John?"

"No. How did he end?"

"What I did not like was the dwelling on Lincoln's melancholy, and the effort it must have cost him — at times. It seemed to me, John, as if he was preaching to himself. I wonder if clergymen often preach to themselves. Some of us have to. The sketch of Lincoln's life was to me a wonder of terse biography. At the close he did not dwell on the murder, but just said —' Then — and then, my friends, God took him to himself.'"

"Thank you, Leila. What a lot of wagons — we must have half the county — and in this rain too."

"Now, John, you hate this affair, and so do I; but the Westways people think it great fun, and in the last few years they have had very little."

"*Ni moi non plus, Mademoiselle Grey.*"

"Yes, yes," she said, "I know, John, but make it go — make it gay, John. It will soon be over."

"I will try." They left their wet garments in an empty outer room and entering by a side door stood beside the raised platform at the end of the crowded hall.

Quite a hundred villagers or farming people, young and old, filled the room, and the air was oppressively heavy. At one end on a raised platform the Colonel was seated, and near by his wife well pleased to see him smiling as he recognized here and there some of the farmers who had been the playmates of his youth. John stood by the long table on which, covered by sheets, lay the articles for sale. Rivers came forward to the front of the platform, leaving Leila, who declined to sit down, at one side with Mr. Grace and the two McGregors.

The murmur of voices ceased; there was an appearance of expectant attention. Rivers raised a hand, and said, "You are all, I am sure, most glad to welcome the friend who like others among you has paid so dearly for keeping unbroken the union of the States." Loud applause followed, as he paused. "An occasion like this brings together young and old for good-humoured fun, and may remind you of a similar meeting years ago. This is to be a rummage-auction of useful things out of use, and of useless things. If you will explain why anybody wants useless things I shall know why some of you come to hear me preach or "— with a slight pause —" my friend, Grace." Every one laughed, and John and Leila alike felt that Rivers had struck the right note.

"Captain John Penhallow "— loud plaudits —" Captain John Penhallow will mention the articles for sale. Now, as you see, they are all hidden — some of them I have never seen. Whoever makes the highest bid of the sale for the most useless article will collect the whole product — the whole proceeds of the sale, and "— he laughed —" will pay it over to the girl about to be married."

This was really great fun, and even John felt some relief as the hall rang with merry laughter. Only Tom McGregor was grave while he watched the Colonel. As Rivers spoke, Colonel Penhallow stood up, swayed a little, straightened his tall figure, and waving Rivers aside said, "I shall now conduct this sale." This was only a pleasant surprise to the audience, and was welcomed with noisy hands.

The two McGregors exchanged looks of anxious alarm as the Colonel said, "Now, John!" Mrs. Penhallow smiled approval.

John uncovered a corner of the nearest sheet and brought out a clock without hands. "First article! Who'll bid? I think the hands have all struck like the mill-hands down East. Five cents — do I hear ten? Going — gone," cried the Colonel.

A rag doll came next and brought a penny. There was high bidding over a heavy band-box. When it went for half a dollar to Mrs. Crocker and was found to contain a shrivelled pumpkin of last year's crop, the audience wildly congratulated the post-mistress.

John, who was now thoroughly in the spirit of their fun, produced two large apples. "Now what daughter of Eve will bid," said the elated Colonel. Leila laughing bid fifty cents. "Going — gone."

"Look out for the serpent, Miss Grey," said Grace.

Leila handed the apples to a small girl, who losing no time followed Eve's remote example. "Oh, mother!" she cried, it's got a five-dollar piece in it — most broke my new tooth."

"The root of all evil," said Grace.

There were pots that were cracked or bottomless, old novels, and to the evident dismay of John a favourite smoking jacket. Ann clapped her hands with delight as John shook at her a finger of reproach. Then came tied up in paper, which John unrolled, the long-forgotten cane of his youth, and how it got there the Squire or Billy may have known. John bid, but at a warning signal from Leila gave up, as she recaptured her property. There were other apples, with and without money; and so with fun and merriment the sale went on to Westways' satisfaction.

"What's this," said John, with an unpleasant shock of annoyance as he uncovered the Colonel's war-worn uniform. He hesitated, looking towards his uncle who seemed bewildered. "That's that rascal, Billy — it's a mistake," exclaimed the Colonel.

"No, sir," shouted Billy, "Squire told me to take 'em. There's a sword too. Squire said it wasn't any use now."

No one laughed; it was obviously one of Billy's blunders. John put the worn uniform and the sword aside and threw a cover over them. It was an unpleasant reminder of the Colonel's state of mind and disturbed the little group at one side of the stage. John made haste to get away from it.

"Last article for sale — it's large and must be bought covered up. Who will bid?" Amid laughter the bids rose. At a dollar and ten cents it fell to Mrs. Pole, and proved when uncovered to be another band-box. Mrs. Pole came forward, and Ann Penhallow pleased to have been able to amuse her husband said, "We are curious, Mrs. Pole, open it." Mrs. Pole obeyed, and as she held up the rolled package it dropped into the unmistakable form of a man's breeches.

Westways exploded into wild applause, understanding joyously this freak of fortune. Mrs. Pole joined in their merriment, and the carpenter punched the butcher in the ribs for emphasis, as he said, "How's that, Pole?" The butcher made use of unpleasant language, as John relieved said, "The sale is over. You can settle with Mr. Grace." As he spoke he moved over to where Leila stood beside the two McGregors.

The people rose and put on their cloaks preparing to leave. Then John heard Tom McGregor say, "Look out, father! Something is going to happen."

The Colonel moved forward unsteadily. His face flushed,

grew pale, and something like a grimace distorted his features, as he said, "The sale is not over, sit down."

People took their places again wondering what was to come. Then with the clear ringing voice the cavalry lines knew in far-away Indian wars, he cried, "We will now sell the most useless article in Westways. Who'll buy silly Billy?"

"Can't sell me," piped out Billy's thin voice as he fled in alarm, amid laughter.

"The sale is over, uncle," said John.

"No, sir — don't interrupt. I'd like to sell Swallow."

This was much to their taste. "Guess he's sold a many of us," cried an old farmer.

"Why, he's dead," said Mrs. Crocker.

The Colonel's gaze wandered. The little group of friends became hopelessly uneasy; even Mrs. Ann ceased to smile. "You stand up, Polly Somers — you are the handsomest girl in the county," which was quite true.

The girl, who was near by, sat still embarrassed. "Get up," said Penhallow sharply.

"She's withdrawed these three months," cried a ready-witted young farmer.

"Oh, is she? Well, then, we will go on." Tom McGregor went quietly up the two steps to the platform. All those who were near to the much-loved master of Grey Pine stood still aware of something wrong and unable to interfere. Rivers alone moved towards him and was put aside by an authoritative gesture. The moment of silence was oppressive, and Leila was hardly conscious of the movement which carried her up beside Dr. McGregor to the level of the platform.

"Oh, do something," she whispered; "please do something."

"It is useless — this can't last."

"Uncle Jim," she exclaimed in her despair, and what more she would have urged was unheard or unsaid as the Colonel turned towards her and cried, "One more for sale!"

No one spoke. At last these various people who loved the man well saw more or less clearly that he was no longer their James Penhallow of other days. He went on at once with raised voice: "Last sale — Leila Grey — likely young woman — warranted sound — single or double harness. Fetch her up." His confusion of mind was painfuly apparent. "Who 'll bid?" A suppressed titter rose from the younger people.

"She is withdrawn, uncle," said John Penhallow distinctly.

"Ah! who did you say — Like Polly, owner withdraws her — Can't you speak out?"

"I said, withdrawn, sir," John repeated. As he spoke he saw the Colonel stagger backwards and sink into his chair; his face became white and twitched; his head fell to one side; he breathed stertorously, flushed slightly, and was instantly as one asleep.

Ann Penhallow and the two doctors were at his side. Rivers called out, "Leave the room, all of you, please. Open the windows, Grace!"

"Is he dead?" asked Ann of McGregor.

"No, no — it is a slight fit — there is no danger."

A moment later Penhallow opened his eyes, sat up, and said, "Where am I? What 's all this about?"

John said, "A bit faint, uncle. The carriage is waiting." He staggered to his feet, and seizing Rivers's arm followed Ann and John in silence. With Rivers they were driven back to Grey Pine. Of all Ann Penhallow's schemes to amuse or interest her husband this had been the most utter failure.

Every one had gone from the hall when John missing Leila returned to the outer room to put on his cloak. The boy-cap Leila liked to wear in bad weather, her rain-cloak, his umbrella, were as they had been left. He stood still in the first moment available for thought and knew that here was a new trouble. She must have been so shocked and ashamed as to have fled in the rain eager to get away.

Neither he nor any man could have realized what she felt as her uncle talked wildly — and she had been put up for sale. She used none of the resources of reason. All her body was hot with the same flush of shame which burned in her face. In her passion of disgust and anger, she hurried out into the storm. The chill of the east wind was friendly. She gave no other thought to the wind-driven rain, but ran through the woods like a wild thing, all virginal woman, unreasonable, insulted, angry as a child is angry — even her uncle was forgotten. She ran upstairs, the glory of her rain-soaked hair in tumbled disorder, and in her room broke into the open speech which passion confides to the priest solitude.

"Oh, John Penhallow, how could you! That ends it — a man who could — and oh, John Penhallow!" She cried a little, wailing in a childish way, and then with some returning sense of anxiety put herself in condition to go downstairs, where she learned that her uncle was in bed. She went back to her room.

CHAPTER XXXII

A HALF hour later John sat alone in the library. He had much to disturb a young man trained to obey and at need command, and was feeling the responsibility of an unusual position. At last he wrote a note to his aunt and sent it up to her by a maid. In a few minutes Ann Penhallow appeared.

"What is it, John? I cannot leave James alone long." She sat down. "Now don't keep me."

"I need not detain you long, but I feel that you ought to know, Aunt Ann, that I have had a talk with Tom McGregor and have sent a telegram to Dr. Askew desiring him to come at once and see my uncle. I ought to hear to-morrow."

She rose to her feet. "You did this, John, without a word to me and knowing that your uncle has over and over said he would not listen to anything of the kind. You have taken a great liberty — I shall telegraph for your doctor not to come. James is always better after these attacks."

Much surprised, he said, "These attacks — has he had them before?"

"Oh, twice — very slight."

"But, aunt, do you not understand how serious this one was?"

"He is better already — much better. There should not be any need to remind you that you are not the head of this house. I shall telegraph at once, in the morning, and stop him."

"It will be too late, aunt."

"Then your doctor may go back. I will not see this doctor if in spite of my telegram he should come. You will understand, John, that this ends it. I certainly will not have James constantly irritated. I shall telegraph now — at once."

476

"You will do, aunt, as it seems best to you." He saw the telegram written and heard her order to send it to the Westways office.

His aunt, having settled the matter, went upstairs, an angry and indignant woman, leaving in the library a man resolute not to accept defeat.

He wrote a second message: "Disregard Mrs. Penhallow's telegram. Come at once. Fee at discretion. Will meet you at Westways Crossing."

He roused up Josiah and gave his order. "Ride to the mills and get this despatch sent to-night or early to-morrow — oh, to-night, somehow. It is important. Pay some one — only get it sent. Here are five dollars."

He was of no mind to meet either Leila or his aunt, and to escape them breakfasted early next morning, and riding to the mills was pleased to avoid another painful interview. On his return at evening the dinner at Grey Pine was made rather less uncomfortable by the presence of Rivers who talked to Ann Penhallow while the Colonel dozed in his armchair. Accustomed to have her decisions obeyed in her home, Ann Penhallow had now dismissed the question of a consultation as settled, and had quite lightly mentioned to Leila that John had revived the subject and that she had once for all put an end to it.

She was sorry to have had to be so positive, but was pleased to be done with the matter in dispute. She little knew the young soldier. When he was certain that the consultant would come, he began to consider what he would do if his aunt did simply refuse to see Dr. Askew. She might, in fact, be as resolute as her nephew.

In her trouble about her husband's mishap, Ann Penhallow hardly regarded her niece's unpleasant share in the sad ending of the rummage-sale — it was relatively of no moment. Nor would the girl herself have been willing to discuss it. John Penhallow should have held his tongue, and now all Westways must be laughing — and she would never — never — forgive him. Evidently her aunt had scolded him about that consultation. She had a little curiosity to know how he had taken it and how he looked when he came to match the will of his young manhood against the unreasonable obstinacy of the woman he had been taught to obey. She observed next day at breakfast that John was more than usually gay, as he asked if there were any errands. There were none. He loitered about waiting and at last went out to the back porch where he stood a minute looking over the box hedge which bounded the garden. Leila was busy taking tribute from the first roses of the summer days. As she bent over, she let them fall one by one into the basket at her feet. Now and then she drew up her tall figure, and seemed to John as she paused to be deep in thought. When she became aware of his approach, she fell again to harvesting roses.

He said, "Leila, before I go to the mills, I want to talk with you about what is troubling me. In fact —"

Without looking up she broke into his attempt to explain himself, "I am in no mood to discuss anything, John Penhallow."

He was frankly puzzled. Of the many Leilas, this was a new acquaintance, but he said quietly, "It is necessary to make a statement — I want first to explain."

She refreshed her rising anger with words. "I do not want any explanation — there are things no woman can pardon. I was insulted."

"My dear Leila, upon my honour I do not know what you mean."

She was near to saying, "I am not yours, or dear." Something in the look of the attentive face and the calmness of his manner put her on guard, and she said only, "That is, I presume, because you are not a woman."

He said, "I do not regret that, but you clearly are thinking of one thing and I of another. It must be the rummage-sale.

I have no desire to discuss that sorrowful business, Miss Grey. You have quite misapprehended me. It is of Uncle Jim I want to talk — in fact, to ask advice."

"I did not understand," she said, flushing a little. His formal manner was very unpleasant, and to be called Miss Grey was ridiculous. If he had shown anger or even annoyance it would have eased the situation. He went on to explain himself, rather aware of her embarrassment and not altogether sorry for her mishap.

"I said I want help — advice. I have sent for Prof. Askew. Aunt Ann has telegraphed him not to come. I wired him to disregard her message. He has answered me that he will be here at the house, if the train is on time, about six to-day. It is our last hope, but it is a hope. Aunt Ann must see this gentleman — I say she must. Now, how can it be managed?"

Leila let fall a handful of roses into the basket and faced him. "Take time," he said. "I do really need help — how can I make Aunt Ann see this famous surgeon? Take time," he repeated.

Here was for Leila a rather astonishing revelation of resolute aggressive manhood — a new John Penhallow. Relieved to have been taken out of her angry mood, she stood still a moment while he waited on her counsel. "There is but one way," she said, "it is the only way. I do not like it — whether you will be willing to accept it, I do not know."

"And still you advise it?"

"I do not."

"Well, what is it?"

"At about six every afternoon, when Uncle Jim is asleep, Aunt Ann is almost certain to be in her little library-room. Take Dr. Askew in, present him, and walk out. She will hate it, but she is sure to be what she is always to a guest. He will have his chance."

"Thank you, Miss Grey." — How she hated that! — "You

have helped me." He touched his army cap in salute and left her alone. At the garden gate he looked back — Miss Grey was also looking back, and vexed at being thus caught bent down again and cut buds and roses with sharp nips of the scissors.

It was not in the nature or breeding of John Penhallow to like Leila's plan for securing to the surgeon a chance to impose on a reluctant woman a clearly stated opinion which otherwise she might have the courage to disregard. But what else could he do? A little after six he met the carriage far down the avenue and walked slowly to the house with the younger McGregor and the surgeon.

"You are most welcome," said John. "Dr. McGregor has, I trust, told you of our difficulties with my aunt?"

Askew smiled. "Yes; it is no uncommon case. I may add that Dr. McGregor's letters have satisfied me that an immediate operation offers the only and too long delayed chance of success. I must, of course, see Mrs. Penhallow — the sooner the better."

"Yes — pray follow me." He led the way across the hall, opened the library door, and said to the astonished lady, "Prof. Askew, Aunt Ann." Then he went out.

Well aware of being trapped, Mrs. Penhallow stood up and apparently at perfect ease said, "You must have had a very tiresome journey."

"Not very," he returned, as he accepted a seat.

Then the little lady sat up and said, "You must pardon me if I say that this consultation has been brought about by my nephew against my husband's wishes."

"And your own?"

"Yes, my own."

"I so understand it. May I say in my defence that I missed your telegram and only saw it when it was sent after me on the train, but now I am here." She had not the courage to say what she would have liked to say, and he went on. "General

Hancock saw me a day or two back. What he said of your husband gave me at once a personal interest in him. Is n't it odd how one is brought to realize what a small place our world is? I was at Fort Delaware before the war ended and saw there — I was on inspection duty — a Confederate Colonel, Henry Grey — a prisoner. Is he not a relation of the handsome Miss Grey we met on the avenue?"

"My niece. He is my brother."

"Indeed! I gave some advice about his wound — it was not serious. May I talk to you a little about your husband?"

She felt herself cornered, and could not escape without discourtesy, of which she was quite incapable; "Or," he added, "may I not rather talk first to Colonel Penhallow, and later to you? It is, I take it, his view of this very grave matter which naturally influences you."

For the briefest of moments she made no reply. Then she stood up and felt the force conveyed in the personality of George Askew, as he towered over her, a man of unusual height. She looked up at the large kind face the long sad wards knew so well. The lines of thought were deeply graven below a broad forehead thinly crowned with yellow hair now fast greying. He showed no sign of impatience. "Yes, she said, "that will be better — you must see Mr. Penhallow before you talk to me. If he consents to do what you want to do — I — Well, Dr. Askew, I am just now too angry to reason. Have the kindness to follow me."

She was unwilling to give her husband any more choice than John Penhallow had given her. If the Colonel became irritable and declined to accept the visit of this impressive personage as a surgeon, well, that must of course end the matter. But as he went upstairs behind her, there arose in her mind a storm-battered hope.

The surgeon was smiling and so far pleased. He was greatly interested in the case he was about to see. It had excited some discussion as unusual, and the unusual in surgery or medicine has many times been the guide to broad highways of usefulness where the daring of the one has made easy the way for the many. Now he meant to win the confidence of the man, if he proved sane enough to reason. He might also have to make more complete his conquest of this coldly civil hostess. It was for him an old game, and he played it with tact and skill.

She paused at the door. "Pray wait a moment, Doctor. No — he has wakened, I hear him." He stopped her.

"Before we see the Colonel — before I see him — I want you to be heartily in accord with any decision we may reach. There are but two courses which seem to me possible, and I do want you to feel sure that either you will have to watch a mind crumble hopelessly or, if we succeed, see one of those amazing recoveries which are like the dawning of day. I say this most earnestly, because your hearty help may be wanted. If he says *no* to our decision, his fate may really rest with your will to stand by me."

This was pretty hard, and no time was given for discussion. She looked up at the kind pleading face, and while feeling that she must yield, hesitated — so distinctly hesitated that the surgeon's brow became severely grave as the furrows between the eyes deepened in growing wonder. He took her hand as if to get into some personal touch with a woman whose opposition he could not understand. "You will help me? In this man's condition a word may win or lose a game in which the stake is a life — oh, that is little — or the restoration of a noble, useful mind. I know you will help me."

She looked down, and said faintly, "Yes."

"Thank you." He smiled —"Bless me! what a little hand," he said, as he let it fall.

She opened the door and as he followed her, stepped aside, saying bravely, "Here is a friend, James. You will like to see Dr. Askew."

He took the chair she set at the bedside, while the Colonel regarded him suspiciously, saying, " I think I heard of you after Gettysburg."

"Yes, I took care of General Hancock. A lot of us went down to help. Curious case his — a ball hit the pommel of his saddle and drove a nail into his leg."

"Yes, I heard of it. It was thought they were firing nails — queer that! "

Askew seized on the moment of illumined intelligence, wondering what dull surgeon had set in this man's mind an obsession which forbade all other opinion. " Hancock will suffer long — but now, about you — did no one think you could be relieved by an operation? Take your time to answer me."

Penhallow, groping in the confusion of remote memories, returned, " I seem to recall — yes — it was talked of —"

"But not done? Some one is responsible for these years of pain. You do suffer? "

"Oh, my God! yes. I try to bear it." His eyes filled. " Is it too late? "

"No," said Askew, " it is not." What doubt he had he put aside.

"Then we will see to-morrow."

"An operation! " said Ann, alarmed. A look conquered her. " You will do, James, whatever Dr. Askew wishes? "

"I will — but don't make me talk any more, Ann — my head aches."

Askew rose. " Please to send up the Drs. McGregor. May I make use of another room? "

"Yes, of course."

Ann Penhallow found Dr. Tom and his father on the porch with Leila and John. She said, " Take the doctors up to my own room, Leila, and I want to talk with John — there are some arrangements to make."

Leila, guiltily conscious of her share in securing the sur-

geon's interview with her aunt, was glad to accept the hint
and the chance to escape.

Ann sat down beside John, and said, " John, why did you trick
me into a talk with Dr. Askew? "

" Because, aunt, you said you would not see him — and it
was necessary."

" You took me too literally."

" I took you at your word — something had to be done. If
it fails, we are no worse off."

" But it may fail — oh! what if it does, John."

" Aunt Ann, I am in despair. Listen to me; no, I must talk
it out. The agreement with uncle's old partners ended with the
war. Things at the mills are in confusion — what is to be
done? I asked Uncle Jim to give me a power of attorney to
act for him. He refused. You supported him. Delay is
ruinous, and yet we can do nothing. You are vexed with me —
Yes — you have not given me my morning kiss for days.
Leila is unreasonably angry with me because that dreadful
night I did the only thing possible in my power to stop my
uncle. I am most unhappy. I sometimes think I had better
go away and look for work as an engineer, and — you did love
me once." He rose and walked up and down the porch silent;
he had emptied mind and heart. Then he paused before her.
She was crying, as she said, " Don't reproach me, John — I can't
bear it — I have had to bear too much to-day — and you were
so naughty." He leaned over and kissed her forehead.
" John," she said, " there is to be an operation to-morrow. It
is terrible. May the good God be kind to him and us. Now go
away — I want to be alone. See that Dr. Askew is well cared
for."

" Certainly, Aunt Ann." He had won his battle.

At dinner the doctor was at pains to dispel the gloom which,
as he well knew, falls on those who love when one of the critical
hours of life approaches. When they left the table he went into

the library with the doctors and John, where they smoked many pipes and talked war.

At breakfast next day Askew's account of his early morning drew a smile even from Ann Penhallow. "Sleep! Yes, I suppose I slept. There was a blank of some hours. I am apt to waken early. At dawn there was a bright red-eyed sky, then it clouded as if the eyes had shut. A little later Miss Grey rode away on a chestnut horse. I walked through your garden and an unseen lady gave me this rose-bud. I had a joyful swim. As I came back I saw Captain Penhallow ride away — and why not with you, Miss Grey? You may perceive that I am a dangerous man to entertain. If you do not prefer better society, may I ask to ride with you to-morrow?"

"What better society?" asked Leila.

"Oh, Miss Grey, alone — by herself."

The two young people understood the charitable gaiety of his talk, but although one of them at least was feeling a sudden access of relief the quick jesting chat and laughter became distressing to Ann Penhallow. At last she rose and excused herself, saying, "Another cup? My niece will give it to you."

"One moment," he returned — his face became grave. "I shall operate early this morning. You must go out-of-doors — the porch — I suggest the porch. I shall send down Dr. McGregor to tell you frankly the result of my operation. I want Captain Penhallow, and with him and the two McGregors we shall care for my patient. I hope the doctors will let you see the Colonel in a week. I shall trespass on your hospitality for two days more."

"I could wish it were a week. I shall do precisely what you desire."

John Penhallow caught some signal of amused surprise in Leila's looks. He checked his own smile of partnership in mirth at Ann Penhallow's sudden subjugation, feeling that with Leila the intimacies of mirth were at an end.

Ann took her knitting and went out upon the back porch. "How many rows can I knit until I hear? No, Leila — I want to be alone. Here is a note from Mr. Rivers. The Bishop met him at Harrisburg and carried him off to Philadelphia. I hope there is no scheme to take him away. Now go, dear." She heard the voices of the McGregors as they went upstairs. She sat alone and waited.

Among the friends who know me only through my summer-born books, there must be many who can recall such hours of suspense as Ann Penhallow endured. The clock in the hall struck ten. A little later her keen sense made her aware of the faint odour of ether from the open windows on the second floor. She let fall her work, went down the garden path, and walked with quick steps among the firstlings of June. Then came Tom McGregor swiftly, and in his smiling face she read good news.

"It is all right," he said; "it is over. There was a fracture of the fragile inner layer of the bone — a piece was pressing on the brain — it was easily removed. The doctor is very much pleased. Oh, my dear Mrs. Penhallow, there are better days ahead for you and him. Now, I must go back."

"Thank God!" she said, "and — and you — and — John. God forgive me, I have been a fool!"

The next two days went by without incident. Askew rode, walked, and had no news for her except, "He is doing well." He would say no more. What hours of doubt, of watchful fear, he had, she never knew. On the morning of the third day, while the carriage waited to carry him away, Mrs. Penhallow led him into her library.

"Now," she said, with her cheque-book open before her, "we owe you a debt none can pay, but let me offer you my most humble apologies for my behaviour when you came."

"Please, don't," he returned.

"But I had to. And now, let me know what is our lesser and more material debt?"

He rose, smiling. " It has been my happy, unbroken rule to take nothing from any soldier who served in this sad war — oh! on either side. I have made, I hope, some friends. The Colonel asked to-day about a horse Dixy — I think — and when could he ride. You may imagine my pleasure. He will get well, but you must be patient. I leave him in competent hands, and in the fall I mean to come back and shoot your woodcocks. Good-bye." He was gone.

CHAPTER XXXIII

A WEEK later Ann Penhallow was told that she might see her husband. She entered his bedroom with timidity. "Oh, Ann, my most dear Ann!" he cried, as she kissed him. His expression of recovered intelligence overcame her for a moment.

She faltered, "How are you feeling, James — any better?"

"Better — I am well."

"Hardly, dear — do be careful." She was unable to accept as a wholesome reality this amazing resurrection of a mind.

He understood her need for some reassurance, and said, "Don't worry about me, Ann. It is like a vague dream, all these many months — but a dream you know fades fast. My own memories get clearer — some things are quite lost — some are as distinct as if they happened yesterday. The war is a puzzle to me — and — if I try to remember, it confuses me. But I must not talk war to you — I do remember that. I won't do it again, dear."

There was something so childlike in this that it almost overcame the woman's steadily guarded calm. She had been warned to be careful that there should be no excitement to agitate a mind which was slowly groping its way out of the shadows of half-illumined memories.

"Oh, my dear James," she said quietly, "talk of war or anything; it is over." Despite her cautious command of her voice it trembled with emotion as she said, "Nothing is of any moment but you — you. What do I care for the war or — or anything but to have you as you were? Oh, my God! I am thankful."

It disturbed him, as she saw. He felt and looked puzzled as he said, " I see — I am not quite clear-headed yet, Ann."

" No, but you will be. Don't try too hard, James. We must be patient and wait."

" I will — I will — and it is such a relief to have no pain and to see you."

Then as he asked about Leila and the mill work, the younger doctor came in and said, " Time is up, Mrs. Penhallow."

" What — already, Tom ? "

" But I want to know more," said the Colonel. " Wasn't there a rummage-sale —"

" Yes; but now you must let Mrs. Penhallow go. You are mending daily. To-morrow Mrs. Penhallow may come again, and there will be to-morrow, and many happy to-morrows." She went out and downstairs singing in a low sweet voice — a long lost habit.

If to watch with an aching heart the hopeless decay of a mind be the most distressing of all human trials, surely there can be few greater joys than to see a disordered intellect emerge day by day into possession of its long lost capacities. James Penhallow was soon able to sign a power of attorney enabling John to reconstruct the old partnership with his own name added to the firm.

Very soon town and county shared in the growth of prosperity which followed the war. Rivers was the only one who was not what his friends desired, and never was his melancholy mood more noticeable.

The master of Grey Pine was, of course, many months in recovering his normal state of mind. The man's bodily strength had not been seriously impaired, and the return of his natural gaiety and his eager resumption one by one of his old habits filled his home with that cheerfulness which is the relieving and precious gift of convalescence. Penhallow's remembrances of the war were rapidly recovered as he talked to John, but much of his recent life was buried in the strange graveyard of memory, which gave up no reminding ghosts of what all who loved the man feared might haunt him.

When satisfied of the certainty of his uncle's recovery John Penhallow hurt by Leila's continual coldness and seeing for it no reasonable explanation gave more and more time to the mills in which the family fortunes were so seriously concerned. On the first of September he was glad to go away on business which carried him to several of the large cities, and resulted in orders which would keep the works busy for many months. He no longer wrote to Leila, nor did he expect letters from her. He considered any nearer relation than friendship to be at an end, but to lose that also seemed to him a quite too needlessly cruel loss, and now for the first time on returning he approached Grey Pine without pleasure. He had telegraphed to have a horse sent to meet him at Westways Crossing, that he might ride on to the mills after seeing his uncle.

Having taken the night train, it was about noon when Leila saw him coming up the avenue. She went forward to the roadside and as he sat in the saddle shook his hand, saying, "I am sorry you were delayed, John. You will be disappointed to know that Uncle Jim and Aunt Ann left home yesterday." She wished that he had not quite so clearly shown the limits of his regret, as he said quietly, "Well, I shall miss them, of course."

"A letter from aunt's brother, Henry Grey, asked them to visit him at the old Maryland home. I think it both pleased and surprised Aunt Ann. I am to join them later. Josiah is to matronize me — or, if you like, patronize me. Uncle Jim was delighted to be asked and hopes to reconcile the brothers. Henry's letter was very kind, but he is still suffering from his wound. Of course, Aunt Ann was happy."

He looked down at the upturned face as he sat in the saddle. She had given him no warm word of personal welcome. "Well, it can't be helped. I had much to talk over with uncle." Then he laughed.

"What amuses you, John?"

"Oh, I should like to see the interview. Both Uncle Jim and I had queer encounters with Henry Grey."

"Uncle Jim! — what — when?"

"Ask him. I should have liked to add George Grey to the party. As for your Uncle Henry "— John smiled —" a serious wound is rather productive of the unexpected, as I know. I will see you at dinner — now I must go on to the mills." He rode away thinking without pleasure of being alone with Leila.

The presence of the maids who waited at dinner kept their conversation on the Colonel's rapid gain in health, village incidents, and the mill life — mere loitering disconnected talk of no interest except to fill the hour of two people who would have preferred to be silent.

John said, as he rose from the table, "I have a letter to write, Leila, and so I must leave you to the better company of your book." Once — but a little while ago — he would have asked what book was now on hand. "Any messages for aunt or uncle?"

"None — I wrote this morning."

He sat down in the library at his old desk and wrote: "Dear Leila "— Then he stood up — the easy freedom of the letter was denied to him. He was in the mood when outspoken speech, always for him the more natural way of expressing himself, became imperative. He went back to the hall.

The book lay face down on her lap. "What is it, John?" she asked.

"I want to talk to you — not here. Come into the library; those maids hear everything."

"Certainly," she said, "if you want me."

She sat down, and John leaning against the mantel and looking down at her, said, " I came in here to write to you what is not easy to write or say — I prefer to put it into speech."

" Indeed! I am quite ready to listen."

" After your recent treatment of me, I have no inclination to make myself needlessly unpleasant. You have made it plain to me that what my heart longs for is to be put aside forever. There is something due to a man's self-respect. But if you were a man, Leila, I could say more easily something else. Are we — am I to lose also your friendship — or is even that at an end?"

The blue eyes became less adventurous as she said, " I don't understand you, John."

" I think you do. Long as I have known you, I cannot have known you fully. Blake used to say that everybody is several people, and just now — here has come into my life some one I don't know — and don't want to know."

" Indeed! It must be rather confusing to be several people. Your friend, Mr. Blake, as your letters showed, was rather given to enigmatical statements. I should like to know him. Would you please, John, to bring me my fan — I left it in that delightful book you interrupted."

" Certainly," he said, now a trifle more at ease. For Leila to ask of any one such a service was so unlike her that he felt it to be a betrayal of embarrassment, and was humorously pleased as he went and came again.

She took the fan and played with that expressive piece of a woman's outfit while John brought the talk back to its starting-point.

" Cannot you be the Leila I used to know — a frank girl; or are you to use one of your many disguises and just leave things as they have been of late?"

" If you will say plainly just what you mean, John "— the fan was in active use —" I will be as frank as possible."

" But you may not like it, Leila."

" Oh, go on. I know you are going to be unpleasant."

He looked at her with surprise. " We are fencing — and I hate it. Once at West Point I was fencing with a man, my friend; the button broke off my foil and I hurt him seriously. He fell dead beside me in the trenches at Vicksburg — dead ! "

" Oh, John ! "— the fan ceased moving.

" What I mean is that one may chance, you or I, to say something that will leave in memory that which no years will blot out. Don't be vexed with me. I have had a cruel summer. What with Uncle Jim and Aunt Ann — and now with you, I — well — you told me after that dreadful night when Uncle Jim was so wild that I had insulted you —"

" Don't talk of it," she cried. " I was put to shame before all those grinning people. You ought to have said nothing — or something better than that farmer boy said —"

" Well — perhaps, Leila; but the point is not *what* I said in my desire to help you and stop a man for the time insane. The point is that I did not insult you; for an insult to be really that it must be intentional."

" Then you think I was unreasonably angry? "

" Yes, I do; and ever since then you have been coldly civil. I cannot stand it. I shall never again ask you for what you cannot give, but if you are to continue to resent what I said, then Grey Pine is no home for me."

She stood up, the fan falling to the floor. " What do you want me to say, John Penhallow? "

" Wait a little — just a word more. It was what poor Uncle Jim said that hurt you. You could not turn on him; in your quite natural dismay or disgust you turned on me, who meant only to help in a dreadful situation. You know I am right "— his voice rose as he went on —" it is I, not you, who am insulted. If you were a man, I should ask for an apology; as you are the woman I have hopelessly loved for years, I will not ask you to say you were wrong — I do not want you to say that. I want you to say you are sorry you hurt me."

"I am sorry I hurt you, John. Will that do?"— her eyes were filling.

"Yes — but —"

"But what?"

"Oh, I want you to feel sorry."

"Don't say any more," she returned. "Let us be friends again." She put out her hand, he took it, picked up her fan, laid it on the table, and saying "Thank you!" opened the door towards which she moved and closed it after her.

"And so "— she kept saying to herself —" we are to be no more than friends." She sat still staring across the hall, trying to read. She was fast losing control of the woman who was fenced in by social rule and custom, trained to suppress emotion and to be the steady mistress of insurgent passion. "My God," she murmured, "I should never have been angry when he bought me, if I had not loved him — and now it is all over — perhaps!"

Some readjustment there may have been, for when he re-entered the hall an hour later, she was reading. He said, as she looked up, "I mean to have a long tramp to-morrow. I shall start early and walk to the mills and on to the ore-beds. Then I shall return over the hills back of Westways, and bring you, I hope, a few wood-pigeons. I may be a little late for dinner."

"But, John, it is quite twelve miles, and you will have to carry a gun — and your arm —"

John laughed happy laughter. "That was so like Aunt Ann!"

"Was it? — and now you will say 'yes, yes, you are quite right,' and walk away and do just as you meant to do, like Uncle Jim."

"I may, but I will not walk further than Grey Pine." The air had cleared — he had done some good!

"Good-night," he said, "it is late."

"Don't go too far, John. I shall read a while. This book is really so interesting. We will talk about it."

"Good-night, once more."

The woman he left in the hall laid her book aside. Her unreasonable vexation had gone, defeated by the quiet statement of his simply confessed unhappiness. She looked about the hall and recalled their youth and the love of which she still felt sure. The manliness of his ways appealed to her sense of the value of character. Why she had been so coldly difficult of approach she did not know. What woman can define that defensive instinct? "He shall ask me again, and I — ah, Heaven! — I love him." A wild passionate longing shook her as she rose to her feet.

At early morning John wandered away through the woods feeling the joyful relief from the hot air of cities. After his visit to the mills and the iron-mines, he struck across a somewhat unfamiliar country, found few birds, and the blackened ravage of an old forest fire. He returned to the well-known river-bank below the garden and the pines, and instead of going to Grey Pine as he had meant to do went on as far as the cabin, failing to get any more birds. He had walked some fourteen miles, and was reminded by a distinct sense of fatigue that the body had not yet regained its former vigour.

It was about five of the warm September day when he came to the old log-house. Smiling as he recalled the memories of his childhood, he went into the cabin and found its shelter pleasant and the cooling air of evening grateful. He took off his game bag, laid it on the floor, set his gun against the wall, and glad of a rest sat down. Having enjoyed his first smoke of the day, he let his head drop on the floor, and by no means intending it fell asleep.

Leila too was in a happier mood, and sure of not meeting John set out to walk through the forest. After a pleasant loitering stroll she stopped at the cabin door, and as she glanced in saw John Penhallow asleep. She leaned against the door post and considered the motionless sleeper in the shadows of the closing day. She was alone with him — alone as never before. He would neither question nor make answer. Strange thoughts came into her mind, disturbing, novel. How could he sleep without a pillow? It must be an army habit after tentless nights of exhaustion in the deadly trenches. People — men — had tried to kill this living silent thing before her; and he too — he too had wanted to kill. She wondered at that as with the motion of a will-less automaton she drew nearer step by step. Her feet unwatched struck the half-filled game-bag. She stumbled, caught her breath, and had a moment of fear as she hung the bag on the wooden hook upon which as a child she used to hang her sun-bonnet.

Then again some natural yearning moved her, and unresisting as in a dream she drew still nearer — merely a woman in an unguarded moment once again under the control of a great passion which knew no social rule of conduct nor the maiden modesties of a serenely dutiful life. At each approach, she stood still, unashamed, innocent of guile, thrilling with emotion which before in quiet hours had been felt as no more disturbing than the wandering little breezes which scarcely stir the leafage of the young spring. She stood still until she won bodily mastery of this stormy influence with its faintly conveyed sense of maiden terror. Her thoughts wandered as she looked down on the sleeper. In voiceless self-whispered speech she said, " Ah me! he used to be so vexed when I said he was too young to ask me — a woman — to marry him. How young he looks now!" The wounded arm forever crip-

pled lay across his breast. She caught her breath. " I
wonder," she thought, " if we get younger in sleep — and then
age in the daytime. Good Heavens! he is smiling like a baby.
Oh! but I should like to know what he is thinking of." There
was unresisted fascination in the little drama of passionate
love so long repressed.

She knelt beside him, saw the one great beauty of the
hardy bronzed face, the mouth now relaxed, with the perfect lip lines of a young Antinous. She bent over him
intent, reading his face as a child reads some forbidden
book, reading it feature by feature as a woman reads for
the first time with understanding a passionate love-poem. Ah,
if he would but open his eyes and then sleep again and
never know. He moved, and she drew back ready for flight,
shy and startled. And now he was quiet. " I must — I must,"
she murmured. " His lips? Ah! would they forgive? — and
— if, if he wakens, I shall die of shame. Oh, naughty love of
mine that was so cruel yesterday, I forgive you! " What would
he do — must he do — if he wakened? The risk, the urgent
passion of appealing love, gave her approach the quality of a
sacred ceremonial. She bent lower, not breathing, fearful,
helpless, and dropt on his forehead a kiss, light as the touch a
honey-seeking butterfly leaves on an unstirred flower. He
moved a little; she rose in alarm and backed to the door. " Oh!
why did I ? " she said to herself, reproachful for a moment's
delicious weakness. She looked back at the motionless sleeper,
as she stood in the doorway. " Why did I ? — but then he does
look so young — and innocent."

Once more in the world of custom, she fled through the forest
shadows, and far away sank down panting. She caught up the
tumbled downfall of hair, and suddenly another Leila, laughed
as she remembered that he would miss the game-bag he had set
at his side. How puzzled he would be when he missed it.
Amused delight in his wondering search captured her. She

saw again the beauty of his mouth and the face above it as
she recalled what her Aunt Margaret Grey had mischievously
said to her, a girl, of James Penhallow. "He has the one
Penhallow beauty — the mouth, but then he has that monu-
mental Penhallow nose — it might be in the way." She had
not understood, but now she did, and again laughing went away
homeward, not at all unhappy or repentant, for who would ever
know, and love is a priest who gives absolution easily.

CHAPTER XXXIV

IN her room she went straight to the long cheval glass and looked at Leila Grey. "So, he will never ask me again?" The mirror reported a quite other answer. "Mark Rivers once said conscience runs down at times like a watch. I must have forgotten to wind up mine. How could I have done it!" She blushed a little at the remembrance. "Well, he will never know." She dressed in white summer garb with unusual care and went down the stairs smiling.

"The Captain is not in yet," said the maid.

She waited long for John Penhallow, who had gone up the back stairs, and now at last came down to dinner.

"Excuse me, Leila. I was so very tired that I fell asleep in the old cabin, but I had a noble tramp, and there are some birds, not many; I shot badly." He said no word of the displaced game-bag, which made her uneasy, but talked of the mills and of some trouble at the mines about wages. She pretended to be interested.

After dinner, she said, "You will want to smoke — come into Uncle Jim's library. I like the pipe smell. How Aunt Ann detests it!"

"Has Uncle Jim gone back to his pipe?" he inquired, as she sat down.

"Yes, and Aunt Ann declares that she likes it now."

"How pleasantly you women can fib," remarked John.

She made no reply except, "Well, sometimes." He did not fill his pipe although he lighted in succession two matches and let them burn out.

"Why don't you smoke, John?" This was a vague effort

at the self-defence which she felt might be needed, the mood of the hour not being at all like the mood of two hours ago.

"No," he replied, "not yet. Where did you walk — or did you walk?"

"Oh, I took a little stroll through the woods."

"Did you chance to go by the old cabin?" This was very dreadful.

"Oh, one hardly remembers if one passes places seen every day. Why do you ask, John?"— and then knew she was fatally blundering.

"Why? Oh, I fell asleep, and when I woke up my game-bag had mysteriously hung itself on the wall."

"You might have put it there and forgotten it."

"No, some one must have been in the cabin."

"Oh, John, how stupid of us! Why, of course, it was Josiah."

John was in a state of mind to enjoy the game, and shaking his head in negation said, "No, Josiah passed me long before. He had a lot of frogs he caught in Lonesome Man's Swamp."

Miss Leila having exhausted all the possible explanations, said with sweet simplicity, "Did you ever find out the origin of that name? Who was the *lonesome man?* You see, John, lonesome seems to stand for lonely and sad, as Mr. Rivers said." This was rather too clever, but the young woman was so near detection as not to think wisely.

John repeated her words, "Lonely and sad." He had been humorously sure of his prey, but the words she used had the effect of bringing into direct speech the appeal she had been trying to evade and knew was near at hand.

He stood leaning against the mantel, his crippled arm caught in his waistcoat. Repeating her word "lonesome" "more than merely alone "— he put aside his pipe, the companion of many camp-fires. His moment of after-silence caused the blue eyes to question timidly with upward glance as their owner sat below him. He was very grave as he said, " I have come, Leila, to a critical time in my life. I loved you in a boy's unmeaning way; I loved you as a lad and a man. I have said so often in one way or another. You told me at West Point pretty plainly that — oh, you made it clear — that I was a boy asking a woman for her heart. It was years ago."

" John, I — want to —"

" Well — later — now I mean to have my say. You were not altogether wrong. I told you that I should ask again when I had more to offer than a boy cadet. Since then I have held my tongue, or said enough to be sure that your reply made clear that my time had not yet come.

" You cannot know how much you have been a part of my life. I went gladly into the war because it was a righteous cause. No man thinks as he goes into action, this is for my country, but — well, Leila, many times when men were falling around me, you have been with me. If a fatal ball had found me, I should have carried with me to another world a thought of you. This is not mere lover's talk. I believe in you — you are a noble-minded woman, worthy of any man's love, but "— and he smiled —" as Josiah put it, you are rather numerous."

" Am I? — I am much obliged by Josiah's study of my character."

" Don't, please, Leila! It is true. I have been as good as my word. I have been through all that can tempt in camps and cities. I was only a young officer, but I have won praise from men whose praise is history. Did you ever think that an honest love may be to a man like a second — an angelic — conscience? By Heaven! Leila, it should make a woman careful."

The woman's eyes had long since been lost to the man's, as with bent head she listened intently, for the first time amazed at what she had been to a man whose ideals were of the highest and his ways beyond reproach. A coy upward lift of the proudly carried head — a mere glance of transient reply — too brief for the man to read — might have meant, "Have not I too been careful of my life!"

He went on slowly. "You and I have not been spared the discipline of responsibility. Action, danger — helps a man. You at home have had the worst of it — you dear, sweet, beautiful thing. It would have made some women peevish or rebellious. You have grown under it in mind and heart, and I think the soul has fed the dear body. To have set you free from Aunt Ann's morbid unreason and the sorrow of Uncle Jim's condition would have been enough to repay my taking over responsibilities which Aunt Ann should have borne."

"John — I —"

"No, dear, let me say a word more. I have at last talked myself out — or almost. It is vain to put me aside again. You do not dare to say you do not love me —"

"You have not asked me," she murmured.

"No, I said I would not yesterday. A tender word would have brought me to your feet — and I was very sore."

"If you were a woman, you would have understood and —"

"Oh, wait a little," he said. "You are going to ask me to marry you, Leila Grey —" She was on her feet. "Take care," he cried, and a smile on the strong battle-tried face arrested her angry outburst.

She said only, "Why? — I ask — you — why indeed?"

"Because, Leila, you owe it to my self-respect — because you have given that which implies love, and all I ask —"

She looked up at him with eyes that implored pity, but all she found herself able to say was, "I don't understand."

"You kissed me in the cabin this afternoon — I was not asleep — I had half risen when I heard you, and I fell back in wondering quiet to see what you would do or say when you should wake me up."

She was silent.

"And then you kissed me —"

"Oh, John! how wicked of you — why did you keep so still?"

"I waited — longing."

"For what?"

"Hoping you would kiss me again."

"What! twice?" she cried. "How could you think I would kiss you twice — I was so ashamed —"

"Well, Leila?"

She began to feel that she was perilously close to tears, as he said softly, "Leila Grey!"

"John Penhallow, will you take me — oh, John! I love you."

He caught her hand and touched it with his lips reverently.

"If," she cried, "if you do not give me back my kiss, I shall die of shame."

He bent over her and kissed her forehead lightly, as though he were in fear of too familiar approach to a thing too sacred for a rude caress. A great surf-like rush of comprehension swept over the woman. "Was I so loved as this — so honoured?" Then she said suddenly, "You are pale — are you in pain?" for she saw him grasp the wounded arm and set his teeth.

"Yes, yes — sometimes — when things happen — it wakes up and reminds me. I shall be better in a moment. Take care" — for her arms were around him —"I think, dear, I am not yet as strong as I shall be — but love is a great tonic, and — I can bear no more to-night. I am in pain. I fear this has been too much for me."

Then he kissed her on lips that took it as a great draft from the fountain of youth and love. "To-morrow, dear, we will ride together — in the morning. Ah, together!"

"Where — Jack?"

"Oh, into fairyland! God bless you! Great Heavens, how beautiful you are! Good-night!"

She fell into a seat as he went out, and heard his feet on the stair — then he stood beside her again.

"Leila, forgive me — I was hard — uncourteous — to make you say —"

"Hush!" she cried, between tears and laughter, as she put her hand over his mouth, "no one shall abuse my Jack — not even Captain Penhallow. There, sir! I deserved it." She ran by him, and was gone.

I have not the pass-words into fairyland, and where they rode that morning in September is not within my knowledge; nor can I say what adventures they may have met with. The by-ways of this enchanted land here and there by ill-luck come near to the haunts of men, who may catch glimpses of such as ride through fairyland unsuspicious of other eyes. Billy neglectful of mails this morning, was on the river bobbing for eels. To be long attentive to anything was for him impossible, wherefore his wandering gaze caught sight for a moment through the fringe of willows of two people riding slowly. He saw with amazement that on horseback in fairyland the feat of kissing is possible.

Some hours later, my lovers, feeling as John wickedly quoted, that "the world is too much with us," rode into Westways to get Billy's neglected mail.

Mr. Crocker, lean and deaf, at ease in charge of the grocery counter, sat unoccupied in his shirt sleeves, while Mrs. Crocker bent over the mail she had sorted. There were letters for the little group of village folk, who read them at once as they sat on the step or as they moved away stumbling along the sidewalk.

Mrs. Crocker sallied out with a batch of letters. "Quite a lot, Captain. Good-morning, Leila."

"Mail these, Mrs. Crocker," said the travellers fresh from fairyland.

"I saw some was from the Squire and some from Mrs. Penhallow — Squire's writing better."

"You wicked Mrs. Crocker," said John, "how much you pick up of folk's secrets, I should like to know —"

"Secrets!" laughed Leila. "They can't be read on the outside of letters."

Then Mrs. Crocker on the sidewalk to them on horseback began to talk. John seeing that Leila was interested and amused sat still and listened.

"Secrets," exclaimed the post-mistress, "ain't all inside of letters. They're on the envelopes sometimes. Oh! I've seen 'em in war time, letters that looked like they'd been out in the rain — sort of blistered; and people here in those days just tore open their letters and laughed or cried." Mrs. Crocker caught her breath and paused.

"I know, John," said Leila in a low aside.

"And there used to come back from the front letters marked 'missing' or 'can't be found.' Folks used to come in gay and go away with a letter just crumpled up in a hand. And now it's all over — and up you come right gallant and happy. Here comes old Granny Lamb tottering along. I'd invent a letter from that brute if I could. I tell you, Leila, mother-hope dies hard."

"It is sad — dreadful. Come, John."

"One minute, please," said Mrs. Crocker, "I'm not half done. I tell you, Captain John, there's a heap of human nature comin' and goin' through a post-office. Well, good-bye."

They rode away to Grey Pine exchanging bits from their letters. Their uncle and aunt would be home in a week. "Sooner — if they get the letter I mailed last night," laughed Leila.

"I should like to have seen it."

"No doubt."

At the open avenue gate Josiah was waiting. He saluted in soldier fashion, Penhallow acknowledging the greeting in like manner.

Josiah said, " Would n't you just let me have a minute with the Captain ? "

Leila laughed. " Certainly." She rode away wondering what Josiah had to report alone to the man who for him was and always would be Captain despite the old custom of the regular army.

" Well, Josiah — nothing wrong, I trust."

" No, sir — everything just entirely right — but first I got to ask your advice. I 've had a letter from the Colonel — he just says some things ought to make a man kind of blush."

John had the odd thought that a blush must be the securely private property of a fellow as black as this grey-headed old friend. " What does he say, Josiah ? "

" He wants to give me a farm."

" Well, why not — you have earned a dozen."

" I 'd like it — but — if you 're goin' to marry Miss Leila, I 'd rather live with you."

" Good Heavens ! " said the traveller out of fairyland, " what put that in your head ? "

Josiah smiled. " You 'll please to excuse me, Captain — but I thought I ought to tell you about that fool Billy. He was bobbin' for eels — and — he saw you go by —"

" Well, what else ? "

" He met me and he said, ' Saw Mr. John kissin' Miss Leila ! ' He was off like a shot singin' out ' Goin' to get married, sure.' It will be all over Westways by noon, sir."

John laughed. " Well, it 's true, Josiah — Confound Billy ! Well, what more ? "

" Oh, I would rather live with you. The Colonel wants to give me a farm — don't want any farm."

" Well, well — we 'll see about it later."

" The trouble would be, sir, who 's to shave the Colonel ? "

" That 's serious," said John, as he rode away to rejoin Leila, who had meant to keep their secret from the village until their aunt's return. Three days went by before Ann Penhallow's letter of reply came to hand.

"Well, any more news, Leila?" said John.

"Yes, but not altogether pleasant — I am to leave early tomorrow. Uncle Jim will meet me in Philadelphia — and, oh! I know Aunt Ann well — there will be no end of shopping."

"I should feel worse about it, Leila, but I see by one of my letters that there is some row in Pittsburgh over our last rails. I am not responsible, but I must go to-night and see about it. Isn't it dreadful, Leila?"

The two having come of late into a great inheritance in fairyland demanding close personal attention were at one as regarded absence.

After dinner Leila said, "My order to report to headquarters from heart-quarters was in the second post-script. I have saved the rest of the letter for you."

"Read it, please."

"MY DEAR CHILDREN: You are a pair of young ostriches — you know what they do. Did you suppose a middle-aged ostrich could not use her eyes? I did think it took a quite needless length of time."

"Isn't that absurd, John, as if —"

"Well, what more?" She read on — "I dislike long engagements —"

"Now, that is better, Leila."

"Your uncle says you must live at Grey Pine. I said, no — young married people had better be alone. He must build you a house on the river nearer the mills. I am making a list of what furniture you will require —"

"There is more of that — much more, John, and a list of

things to be done before her return. Is n't that like what aunt was before the war?"

John laughed. "Well, she will have her way."

"More or less," said Leila. "Oh, there's another postscript!"

"Well?"

"I think you should be married about Christmas week. Of course, Mark Rivers will marry you, and I shall ask the Bishop to assist, when I see him on our way home. Don't fail to write to both your uncles."

"It is certainly complete," said John. He left for Pittsburgh that night.

I have little to add to this long story. The days went by swiftly, and after a week all of the family, except John, were once more together at Grey Pine. Mark Rivers had also returned. He was too evidently in one of his moods of sombre silentness, but his congratulations were warm and as he sat at dinner he made unusual efforts to be at his agreeable best.

When they left the table, he said, "No, Colonel, I shall not smoke to-night. May I have a few minutes of your time, Mrs. Penhallow?"

"Certainly, Mark — I want to talk to you about the Bible Class — I mean to take it up again." She led the way into her own little library. "Sit down — there is so much to talk over. Of course, you will marry these dear children somewhere about Christmas time."

"No," he said, "I shall be far away."

"Away! Oh, Mark! surely you do not mean to leave us."

"Yes, I am going to live as a missionary among the Indians."

"You cannot — you really cannot — where could you be more useful than here?"

"No, I must go. My life on the whole has been most happy here — and how to thank you I fail to be able to say."

"But why," she urged, "why do you go?"

"Oh — I want — I must have an active life, open air, even risks. The war gave me what I need for entire competence of body and mind to use in my Master's service. But now, the war is at an end —"

"Thank God! But all you ask — and more — Mark, except danger, are here — and oh, but we shall miss you, and more than ever when we miss too these children. Think of it — don't make up your mind until James talks to you —"

"No, I go to-morrow."

"But it does seem to me, Mark, that you are making a serious change without sufficient consideration of what you lose and we lose."

"Yes, yes," he returned, "I know — but to remain is for me impossible."

"But why?"

He was silent a moment, looking at this dear friend with the over-filled eyes of a troubled and yet resolute manhood. Then he said, "I did not mean to tell you why in my weakness flight alone will save me from what has been to me unbearable here and ever will be."

"Can I in any way help you?"

"No."

"But what is it — trust me a little — what is it?"

He hesitated, and then said, "It is Leila Grey! God pity my weakness, and you will say good-bye and give the Squire this note and them my love." He was gone.

The woman sat still for an hour, pitiful, and understanding the flight of a too sensitive man. Then she gave her husband the note, with her good-night, and no other word. Of why her friend had gone she said later nothing, except to defend him for his obedience to the call of duty. Late that evening John returned.

When after breakfast next day he and Leila were riding through the wood-roads of the forest, John said, " I cannot or I could not see why Mr. Rivers went away so abruptly."

" Nor I," said Leila. Then there was one of those long silences dear to lovers.

" What are you thinking of, Jack? "

" Uncle Jim told me last night the story of the early life of Mark Rivers."

" Tell it to me."

He told it —" But," he continued, " that was not all of him. I have heard Mr. Rivers hold at the closest attention a great crowd of soldiers with that far-carrying voice; and then to hear as he led them singing the old familiar hymns — perhaps a thousand men — oh, it was a thing to remember! And they loved him, Leila, because behind the battle line he was coolly, serviceably brave; and in the hospital wards — well, as tender as — well, as you would have been. I wondered, Leila, why he did not marry again. The first was a mistake, but I suppose he knew that for him to marry would have been wrong, with that sad family history. Probably life never offered him the temptation."

" Perhaps not," said Leila, and they rode out of the woods and over the meadows. " Let us talk of something less sad."

" Well, Leila, a pleasant thing to discuss is Tom McGregor. I suspect him of a fortunate love affair with the daughter of the General at Fortress Monroe."

" Indeed — but what else? Oh, our own great debt to him! "

" Uncle Jim is considering that. We may trust him to be more than generous. Yes, surely. Now for a run over this grass. Can you take that fence? "

" Can I, indeed! Follow me, Jack."

" Anywhere. Everywhere, Leila! "

THE END